The Cornish Hideaway

First published in Great Britain by Simon & Schuster UK Ltd, 2022
This paperback edition first published 2023

1 3 5 7 9 10 8 6 4 2

Simon & Schuster UK Ltd
1st Floor
222 Gray's Inn Road
London WC1X 8HB

Simon & Schuster Australia, Sydney
Simon & Schuster India, New Delhi

www.simonandschuster.co.uk
www.simonandschuster.com.au
www.simonandschuster.co.in

A CIP catalogue record for this book
is available from the British Library

Paperback ISBN: 978-1-3985-1781-3
eBook ISBN: 978-1-3985-0816-3

Typeset in Bembo by M Rules
Printed and Bound in the UK using 100% Renewable
Electricity at CPI Group (UK) Ltd

MIX
Paper | Supporting
responsible forestry
FSC® C171272

The Cornish Hideaway

JENNIFER BIBBY

**SIMON &
SCHUSTER**

London · New York · Sydney · Toronto · New Delhi

To the Bibberts family with all my love – my parents John and Diana, Chris, Kristina, Amelia and last, but certainly not least, Luna xx

Chapter One

Freya closed her eyes and sank back against the stark college walls, head in hands. Taking a deep, shaky breath, she wished she could rewind the clock fifteen minutes. *Don't cry*, she urged herself. *Whatever you do, don't cry.* There had to be some sort of mistake. But when she opened her eyes, a four-letter word was still staring back at her in bold black ink, and not the one she'd been expecting.

At the bottom of her Master of Arts results slip was the word 'FAIL'.

Freya didn't understand. How could she have failed? For the past four months, she'd sacrificed everything in her life to focus on her final project. She'd quit the three jobs she'd been working in an assortment of bars and cafés, rarely seen her friends, plus she and her boyfriend Matt had become ships that passed in the night. She had believed the sacrifice would be worth it but now she had no money, no job and no degree. She didn't know what stung most: wasting her money on the tuition fees, or having some faceless examiner think she was lacking in artistic merit. She winced at the thought.

Freya paced up and down the corridor, not knowing what

to do next. From inside the studio, she could hear the pop-ping of Prosecco corks and jubilant exchanges between her peers. Should she try to sneak out from a different exit, or should she fake it? She tried to muster up a bright smile but her lips wouldn't stop wobbling. It was no use. There was no way she could pretend it was all fine, not when her stomach was churning with disbelief and her brain was struggling to process her result. You're in shock, she told herself as she attempted a deep breath.

The office door swung open, and Freya glanced up to see Audrey Harper, her final project supervisor, coming towards her, arms open.

'Freya, darling! I did all I could to try and get you a pass, honestly I did,' she cooed sympathetically as she bundled Freya into a hug. 'But the examiners were a tough bunch to please this year.' She lowered her voice and shared, 'Actually, no one got what they deserved, despite all the celebrating.' She indicated towards the studio as a cheer sounded.

Freya wiped her eyes. 'But no one else failed, did they?'

Audrey looked sheepish and considered her answer for a lot longer than necessary. 'No. Oh, Freya, don't look so glum, I fought tooth and nail for a better mark, honestly, but there was no budging them. You can appeal the decision, you know? I could try and track down some more sympathetic external examiners?'

'What's the point?' Freya shrugged, accepting the tissue Audrey handed her and dabbing at her eyes. 'This has all been a huge mistake. It wasn't my best work. If only—'

'Stop! Don't beat yourself up. You tried so much harder than anyone else. The examiners didn't really understand the concept, but we can work on that – tidying it all up, fixing it so that it passes and you can resubmit next year. If you wish,' she added. 'No pressure.'

Freya's stomach dropped. She didn't think she could ever face picking up a pencil again, let alone resubmitting her failed final project. She was artistically burned out. 'Thanks, but I haven't got the money for a retake. I've put everything I had into this . . . for what?' Freya started to sob and tried to catch the tears with the now-soggy tissue. She dreaded having to break the news to her friends and family, having to face their sympathetic looks and the inevitable suspicions that she just didn't have any talent. Surely her first-class undergraduate degree hadn't lied?

Audrey bundled her into another hug. 'There, there, get it out. Art is a cruel business because it comes from the heart of us. Please, don't take it personally. This is not about you or your talent, Freya. You are a good artist – your eye for detail is astounding. You have quite a bit more talent than most other people on your course. Natural talent too, not just talent bought with Daddy's money.'

Freya had to smile at that. 'But in this case talent doesn't mean anything, does it?' Audrey opened her mouth to speak, then closed it. Freya sighed bitterly. 'I should've done fine art, not contemporary art.'

'Maybe, but hindsight is a wonderful thing.' Audrey stepped back. 'Here's what I suggest you do. Touch up your

make-up, make the most of all that free fizz and go on holiday – take a break, read a book, go cycling, I don't know,
just do something different. But don't try to make art. It'll
come back when you least expect it. And I'm here anytime
you want to chat. I know this has been a huge shock for you
and it's probably not sunk in yet. If you want to come back
and resubmit, or appeal the decision, let me know and I'll see
what magic I can work.' She waggled her bejewelled fingers
in a witchy way and dropped her voice. 'You deserve success,
Freya. You're one of the best pupils I've had in a long time,
and all your hard work will pay off, I'm sure.'

Freya filed away Audrey's words for contemplation later.
'Thanks, I don't feel any of that, but thank you. You've been
such a support.'

Audrey smiled and winked. 'Now, go off and enjoy yourself. And keep in touch! Toodle-pip.'

Freya sighed as she watched her bustle back into the office.
Being Audrey's favourite was not going to help pay the
rent. She checked her phone – nothing from Matt, which
irked her. He knew it was results day. Although she wasn't
relishing telling him she'd failed. She wondered if she could
pretend she'd passed, but when she ducked into the toilets,
her smudged mascara told a different story. Freya stood back
and studied herself, all dressed up like a winner: the white
dress covered with rainbow stars, which she'd found in a
vintage shop; her long dark hair waved and curled as if she
was going to a premiere; expertly applied make-up all faded.

She did her best to patch it up, reapplied her lipstick and

headed back into the studio, head held as high as she could manage. Her peers had gone, leaving a half-drunk bottle of fizz next to a note telling her which pub they'd be in. Freya picked up the bottle and took a swig – the bubbles went up her nose, making her sneeze – and then crumpled up the note and tossed it in the bin. One silver lining of finishing her master's was never having to see her smug, overindulged, entitled colleagues ever again.

Freya left the college building and headed out onto the busy Central London streets, into the crowds of commuters surging aggressively around her. She swigged again from the bottle of fizz and wandered slowly, aimlessly, naturally weaving through the tourists taking selfies. She allowed her eyes to stray up over the tall, imposing buildings, but that only made her feel even smaller than she already did.

When she reached the pub her colleagues were in, she paused and tried to compose herself into a picture of success. But she could barely muster a smile. *Stuff it*, she thought, *I'm not going. I really don't care and neither do they.* She fished her phone out of her bag and took a selfie, posing with the bottle of champagne and pulling a smile that didn't quite reach her eyes. *Ugh.* She thrust the phone away, ignoring all the message notifications. How could she post on social media that she was a verified failure?

Her feet took her towards Trafalgar Square, a path Freya had regularly wandered when she needed a break from the claustrophobic creativity of the studio. Nelson's Column stretched into the evening sky, and the open space gave Freya some peace. Everyone was small against this backdrop. On her breaks, she had loved to meander around the National or the Portrait galleries, daydreaming about her own future successes hanging on similar hallowed walls. As she perched on the steps now, those dreams dissipated. Freya was embarrassed that she'd ever thought herself anything like Turner, Constable or Van Gogh. Head in hands, she sat there for a few minutes, allowing London to flow around her.

Her phone beeped, and she checked it; still not Matt. Something unpleasant settled in her stomach. He couldn't have forgotten it was results day; she'd written it on their shared kitchen calendar in pink sparkly ink.

Freya lifted the bottle and realized the fizz was finished. Enjoying the decadent way it blurred her edges, she hoisted herself up, stuck the empty bottle in a bin and went in search of more. Nothing fancy – Tesco would do. As evening started to close in, Freya knew she would have to head home. Briefly, she wondered if Matt would even notice if she didn't turn up. Probably not.

She hopped onto the tube towards Angel where she would swap it for the bus that would take her to the flat she shared with Matt. Her stomach rumbled, and she realized she'd not eaten all day, so before jumping on the bus, Freya nipped into a kebab shop and bought some chips. It seemed faintly ridiculous to be eating a greasy end-of-the-night snack at barely seven o'clock, but she greedily polished them off before heading home.

Home was a little ground-floor flat near Newington

Green into which Freya and Matt had moved soon after graduating from university. Freya recalled that hopeful day: their scant possessions, the smug feeling of being proper grown-ups, the Chinese takeaway they'd eaten among the debris of half-constructed IKEA furniture. The memory still brought a smile to Freya's face. However, there hadn't been much to smile about recently. The flat had become a battleground for their opposing personalities – Matt's neat lines born of years of graphic design, and Freya's boho creativity, or 'mess' as Matt had started to not-so-affectionately call it. Matt was keenly saving for a soulless city flat, and Freya's guilt that she couldn't provide more towards their living costs, other than paying a few bills and buying food, nibbled away at her.

Freya lingered outside the door for a few moments and tried to formulate the words she'd been failing to think of since leaving the college. *Maybe he's not in?* she thought hopefully. After all, the past few weeks had been full of business meetings and late nights. He was after a promotion, but that was as much as Freya remembered.

In the past, Matt had always been the one to make things better, had always been her biggest fan, and she clutched at this in the desperate hope that he would tell her it would all be fine. Like he had so many times before.

Freya turned her key in the door and pushed it open. Gently closing it behind her, she paused and listened. From the living room came the electric sounds of guns being fired and a flicker of blue light. So, Matt was home, playing computer games. Freya took a deep breath to still her sudden flash of anger and counted to ten before pushing open the door.

'Hey,' she said, trying for nonchalant, but Matt didn't even glance up, just grabbed his bottle of beer for another swig. She stared at him, still in his work clothes minus the tie and jacket, not one strand of his neatly cropped blonde hair out of place, a half-eaten Chinese on the coffee table in front of him. Freya stared in disbelief as the man she'd spent seven years of her life with continued to kill cartoon zombies without even a glance in her direction. Not giving it a second thought, she marched over to the TV and pulled out the plug.

Matt leapt up with a wail. 'Hey! I was playing that! It's taken me weeks to reach that level.' The controller dangled helplessly from his hand as he looked from the TV to Freya and back again.

Anger rose inside her. 'Do you know what day it is?'

'Tuesday?' Matt shrugged, then, seeing her clouded face, asked, 'What?'

'Results day,' she supplied. 'My master's results day. Only the most important day of the year.'

Matt at least had the decency to look slightly guilty as he sunk back onto the sofa. 'Oh. That. How did it go?'

Freya perched on the edge of the armchair. She probably could've got away with not telling him. Could have pre-tended everything was fine. The urge to lie was strong. She could already feel his judgement seeping into the room. Freya placed the bottle of fizz on the floor, knowing she wasn't going to get any sympathy. 'It was awful,' she began, 'a really tough year apparently. They marked everyone down.' She risked a glance at Matt, who was staring at her, impatient for her to get on with it. Freya ripped the plaster off. 'I failed, Matt. They failed me.' She choked on sobs; saying it out loud made it horribly real.

Freya watched Matt's reaction. Instead of leaping off the sofa to comfort her, he rubbed his face and swore under his breath.

'Jesus Christ, Freya, what a waste. You've literally spent thousands on that stupid degree.'

Stunned, Freya stared at him in disbelief. 'I know. You don't need to make me feel any worse,' she snapped. 'Audrey said I can resubmit or appeal the decision.'

Matt shook his head. 'I can't do this anymore, Freya. I'm sorry, we need to talk.'

Those dreaded words settled on her like lead. They never preceded anything pleasant. Freya remained silent and watched Matt's face churn as he tried to find the right words.

'Freya, before I start, I want you to understand how hard this is for me. I've come close to saying all this several times, but I always bit my tongue.' Matt glanced down at his feet before looking back at her, face twisted with guilt. 'Freya, I think it's time you grew up and stopped hoping you'll win the Turner prize, or whatever it is you're after. I know art is important to you, but you're trying to make a life out of a silly hobby. We're twenty-seven now – adults, not children. Yes, it was cute when we met at university, but honestly, I

---

thought by now you'd have grown up and got some sense of responsibility. Instead, you're wafting around like you're on some higher mission, throwing paint around, or bending coat hangers or whatever it is you do. I just don't care about it. You need to stop all this pissing about and get a proper job.'

Freya opened her mouth to protest, to try to defend herself, but then she thought again about those four black letters on her results slip. Maybe he had a point.

'You've never sold anything,' he continued. 'Dreams aren't going to pay the rent, are they? And I'm sick and tired of working all these hours to support you. When you're not painting you're working in some seedy pub or coffee shop and you think that's okay! You think that's contributing! Buying food or paying the water bill isn't enough, Freya. I can't carry us both anymore, especially not now. I'm being lined up for promotion. What are you going to do? I am working my arse off to become a partner in the firm and I need someone who is supportive, who I can take along to corporate events, who has the same drive as me. I'm sorry, Freya – it was great when we were students, but you just don't fit anymore.' He signalled to her floaty dress.

Stunned into silence, Freya stared at him. Matt's words spun as her brain tried to process them. She opened her mouth to tell him she'd do better, that she'd go on that teacher training course her parents kept dropping hints about, but she stopped and looked at him – really looked at him. Sitting across from her was not the sweet boy she'd met in the student union bar, who'd carried her home after one too many tropical VKs. This was not the man who'd slid cartoons under her dorm room door in a bid to woo her. Or who had taken her up the Eiffel Tower and drunk champagne they couldn't afford on her twenty-first birthday. The man sitting across from her was a Matt-shaped stranger. It was like Freya was seeing him properly for the first time in years. There was no denying it: since Freya had started her master's a year and a half ago, they had grown apart.

'I'm sorry, Matt. I had no idea you felt like that. Why didn't you say something before? We could've tried, I don't know, to fix things?' Freya sniffed, determined not to cry. 'I thought you were okay with this arrangement until I got my MA.'

Matt glanced down at his clasped hands. 'But you haven't got it, have you?' He sat back and sighed. 'I thought I was okay with it too, but recently I've realized I'm not.'

'How long have you felt like this?'

'Since Christmas. There was all that pressure for us to get engaged – all those little hints – and it just made me realize it was the last thing I wanted.' He pulled a face.

'Oh, Matt, it was hardly that bad,' she shot back venomously.

'I couldn't understand how no one else could see it wasn't working. Did you have no idea?'

Freya shook her head slowly and admitted, 'I guess I was too wrapped up in other things. You talk about what you've done, what you've given – I've given you seven years of my life too, you know. This isn't all about you.'

They lapsed into a final, spent silence. Neither of them needed to voice that this was clearly the end. Matt stood up and stretched. 'I'll get some of my things and go and stay at Sudhir's for a couple of nights, give you a couple of days to move out.'

'But where am I meant to go?'

Matt shrugged. 'I don't know. Start taking some responsibility. Stand on your own two feet. I'll get my stuff.'

Freya slumped back into the chair, exhausted. What the hell was she going to do now? She glanced around the living room until her eyes fell on the bottle of Prosecco next to her bag. Well, there was nothing else for it. She popped the cork and took a long swig. Oblivion would work for now.

Chapter Two

For a few blissful moments before opening her eyes, Freya forgot everything that had happened the previous day. Rolling over, she snuggled into the duvet, enjoying the morning light streaming through the window, having forgotten to close the curtains. Then, thanks to the pressure in her bladder and the banging in her head, the sheer awfulness of the previous day made an unwelcome return. Freya struggled out of bed and made her way to the bathroom, dizzy and disorientated. Catching sight of herself in the mirror – tangled hair and panda eyes – results day came back to her in all its horrific life-changing glory. The fail. Being dumped by Matt. *Oh God.* The two bottles of fizz. Her stomach heaved, but nothing came up. Freya sat back against the bath until the nausea passed. There was no way she could face this mess without tea and toast.

The flat was quiet, which wasn't abnormal since Matt was an early riser and usually hit the gym before heading to the office, but something about this silence felt final. It was a silence that was waiting for her to move out.

Freya filled the kettle. Where on earth would she go? Her

stomach heaved again when she realized she would have to call her parents and tell them everything. They had texted her the previous night but had assumed she was out celebrating and Freya had seen no reason to disabuse them of that notion. Going back home was the last thing Freya wanted, but she doubted she'd be able to earn enough money to rent a room in London.

The kettle boiled and Freya made her tea. The kitchen clock told her it was just after eight. Was that all? Far too early to be making rash life decisions. She bought herself some time by sticking a couple of slices of bread in the toaster, and while waiting for it, she pushed open the window. Outside, the day was bright with early-summer promise.

Mechanically, Freya drank her tea and munched her toast while flicking through everyone else's social media drivel. And there, staring back at her, was the photo Freya had posted in her results day dress. There were over a hundred likes and loads of comments wishing her luck and asking how it had gone. Her thumb hovered as she prepared to type a response, but she couldn't find a way to sugar-coat the fail into something digestible for social media. Freya closed the app and pushed her phone away, tears spilling over again. More tears? She hadn't thought she had any left. She frantically tried to wipe them away.

Needing crisis talks, Freya fired off a quick text to her best friends, Lily and Fiona, asking them to meet that evening. They quickly texted back with a time and the name of their usual bar. The familiarity of the suggestion warmed Freya. Usually, they met to discuss one of Fiona's disastrous dates, so it was weird to think it would be Freya's broken heart they'd be trying to patch up this time. Having never been dumped before, Freya had no idea what she was supposed to do next. Guzzle a tub of ice cream? Cut all her hair off? Burn Matt's stuff? Hmm ... the latter was very tempting, but she didn't have the cash to replace anything, and he'd one hundred per cent expect her to foot the bill for new suits. When on earth had he morphed into such a corporate git, she wondered. Probably around the time he realized he was forking out for a girlfriend who was completely away with the fairies on some hare-brained artistic mission. Freya hid her face in her hands, embarrassed that she'd allowed him to cover all of the rent. It wasn't very twenty-first century of her, she thought with a mix of guilt and mortification.

After a bout of ugly, snotty crying, Freya couldn't believe that it was still only nine a.m. The practical part of her brain kicked in, reminding her that she needed to pack up and make a plan. With her emergency meeting set up for that evening, Freya tapped back into social media and unfriended Matt, which was slightly less satisfying than she expected it to be. She took one last look at his smug face posing outside his office building and closed his profile. She then clicked on her own status box and sat staring at it for a few moments. As she typed, she told herself it wasn't a lie, that she was just being economical with the truth.

> MA over and done! Exhausted! I need
> a holiday!

Satisfied that would keep questions at bay for a while, Freya went and scrubbed away the emotional dirt from the previous night under a long, hot shower.

Refreshed and dressed, Freya surveyed the mess that was the bedroom. She had only one suitcase ... and no idea where to start. The idea of picking through their accumulated lives and packing up her bits felt overwhelming, and she sank down onto the bed. If she rang her parents, she knew her dad would load up the car with bags and boxes and drive down the very same day. Everything would be packed up and she'd be spirited away to Bedford. It was a comforting thought, but Freya wasn't ready to admit that sort of defeat. Needing some space, she slipped on her Converse and grabbed her bag. A walk usually helped clear her head. It was an absolutely beautiful day, the sort of day that filled people with hopeful thoughts of picnics, beer gardens and summer dresses. But Freya hardly took it in, her mind too wrapped up in what had happened with Matt – which at least distracted her from dwelling on her failed degree.

How had she been so blind to the situation? How had she managed to convince herself that Matt's non-committal grunts at her art were him being supportive? What she failed to comprehend was, if he believed her artistic ambitions to be so childish, why hadn't he said anything earlier? Freya winced as she recalled everything he'd thrown at her the previous night. But maybe he had tried to talk to her and she'd just buried her head into pots of paint? Freya wracked her brain, going over the past couple of years, and was ashamed at what she turned up. She had been so engrossed in the idea of herself as this great artist that she had pretty much neglected everything else. Freya chewed on her bottom lip as the realization dawned that she was responsible for the mess she was in. The blame couldn't all be heaped at Matt's feet.

The past was too big to contemplate, and what she really needed to do now was figure out the immediate future. There would be plenty of time to chew over what had happened once she was more settled. Freya pushed open the door to a café and, while waiting in the queue, realized she had hardly enough skills to cover the back of a receipt let alone a CV. The hopelessness of her situation engulfed her as she waited to place an order she probably couldn't afford. The cappuccino and millionaire's shortbread were a guilty luxury, but didn't she deserve something nice after the shitty day she'd had?

'One cappuccino, please, and a slice of millionaire's shortbread?' she asked the barista, a young man with floppy dark curls. Then on a whim, enquired, 'Do you have any jobs here?'

He pushed her coffee over to her and shook his head. 'Sorry, no, but if you want to leave a CV we can keep it on file?'

Freya smiled and shook her head. 'Thanks.' She had no CV to leave anyway, so she picked up her coffee and over-priced treat and headed to the armchair in the corner. She sprinkled sugar over the coffee's foamy top and watched it sink in. Then she placed her phone on the table next to it and allowed herself a moment of silence.

The temptation to break down – to just lie on the floor until someone came and scooped her up – was overwhelming. But she had too much to do. She needed to pack, which she would start as soon as she got in. Then she'd print off her CV and hand it out everywhere. Maybe Lily or Fiona would let her camp out for a few nights? Or she could just go home. Right now, the thought of being looked after by her parents was comforting. It would be a breather. Maybe her sister, Olivia, a museum curator, could help fix her up with something? At least at home she would be loved, even if going there would be the cherry on top of her epic failure.

No, packing and CV first, Freya told herself as she sipped her drink, which was a little stronger than she liked. Her phone started to ring, and Freya froze. If it was her parents, she would have to bite the bullet and tell them. Putting down her cup, Freya lifted her phone, relief washing over her when 'Lola' flashed across the screen. Bar the odd text and social media update, Freya hadn't heard from Lola since her friend had announced she was buying a café down in Cornwall earlier in the year.

'Hello!' Freya said brightly. 'How are you? It's been ages!'

'I know! I'm fine. More importantly, how are you, my darling?' Lola's voice was tinged with concern.

Freya swallowed. She'd forgotten that her friend was blessed with 'second sight' and had regularly made ends meet fortune-telling. 'Erm, not so good,' Freya said. There was no point in lying.

'So, tell your Auntie Lola what's happened. How did your results go?'

'Lola, I failed,' Freya told her in a small voice. 'An outright fail. Audrey said she tried to get them to pass me but they wouldn't.'

'Oh, hon, I'm so sorry! You put so much into it. What are you going to do now?'

'No idea. I can appeal the decision or resubmit next year. Audrey said she'd find some more sympathetic external examiners, but I have no money. I left my jobs to concentrate on this.' Freya sniffed and took some deep breaths to stop herself from crying. 'This was everything for me, Lola, I put everything into it. It was supposed to be my biggest moment.'

'Don't cry, it'll all be okay. You're talented, you don't need a degree to tell anyone that,' Lola pointed out. 'What did Matt say?'

Freya took another shaky breath, aware that the barista was watching her. 'He dumped me. Apparently my artistic ambitions are childish, and he's going for a big promotion so needs a partner who fits the corporate image better.'

'No! What a toerag! Oh, Freya, I think you're better off without him. What a git! Corporate my arse!' Lola scoffed.

'It gets better, Lola: I have to move out. I have nowhere to go and no job. I'm just putting off calling my parents and admitting defeat. It's all gone completely to shit.' While the situation did seem hopeless, Freya had to admit that she felt less alone having shared her misfortune with Lola.

'You clearly weren't on the right path,' Lola said mystically.

'The universe has a habit of shoving you off the wrong path quite violently if you're not reading the signs properly. Come and stay with me. Come for a holiday – stay as long as you like! That's why I'm ringing, I saw your Facebook post about needing a break.'

'I can't do that,' Freya protested, even though the thought of a holiday was more than tempting. 'Wouldn't everyone just say I ran away?'

'Nonsense. You can come and work in my café over the summer. With all this talk of a heatwave, I think we'll be busy. I know you have coffee-making skills – it's all you've done other than paint for the past God knows how many years. Think about it. It'll give you some space and perspective to think about what you really want. When does Matt want you out?'

'Soon as possible. He's sleeping on a friend's sofa.'

'Perfect!'

'No, Lola, I can't. I can't impose on you.'

'Oh, Freya, stop being a martyr to your misery. I'm inviting you down – you won't be imposing, you'll be helping. You can stay with me and help in the café. Nope, stop it, I won't hear any more protests. Just book your train and let me know your arrival time. That is, of course, unless you'd like to go back to your parents'?' Lola dangled the alternative.

Freya closed her eyes and took a deep breath. It had been years since she'd had a holiday, and Cornwall was a lot more tempting than her childhood bedroom in Bedford. It was hardly a choice, really. 'Okay, Lola, you've twisted my arm. I'll go home, pack up and book my train ticket.'

Lola let out a whoop of joy. 'I can't wait! You'll love it. Oh, that's the bell, I'd better go. I have a cake to bake and a customer's just come in. Love you, see you soon!' She hung up before Freya could return the sentiment.

Freya sat back and stared at her phone, fresh excitement fizzing in her belly. If she had to run away, then the seaside was the perfect destination. She sipped her now tepid coffee, opened the train app on her phone and searched for the cheapest tickets, booking them without a second thought.

Freya was running late as always, but at least this time she actually had an excuse, she reasoned as she jumped off the bus and ran to the pub. Her chat with Lola had lifted her spirits greatly, and once back at the flat, she'd grabbed a few black bin liners and crammed them full of anything she didn't think she'd need in her new life, ready for the charity shop. She doubted she'd need dangly earrings or slightly tacky going-out handbags in Cornwall. By the time she should have been leaving to meet her friends, three fat bags were sitting by the door ready for collection. She'd quickly changed out of her holey leggings, slapped on a bit of make-up and made her way to the pub.

Pausing to catch her breath and straighten out her hair, Freya looked through the window at her two best friends sitting on a high table, a bottle of fizz on ice between them. Shit, she'd have to tell them. Freya's stomach turned and she took a fortifying breath. She knew Lily and Fiona would understand; they'd bonded over tea and Hobnobs on their first night in student accommodation, and despite studying an array of different subjects, they had been inseparable since. Well, maybe not so much since Freya started her master's and her friends started chasing promotions, but still, they were a very welcome and comforting sight for sore eyes.

She pushed open the door and stepped inside. The bar was modern with pale grey walls and ferns dotted about the place. Fiona spotted Freya first and, leaping off her stool, grabbed the bottle of fizz and popped it while whooping and screaming 'Congratulations!' Lily held out a hand to stop her spraying them all in the style of Formula One drivers. The overenthusiastic display drew everyone's attention.

Freya's face flushed as she bundled them into a hug. 'Seriously, ladies, calm down.'

Fiona poured out three glasses and passed them around. 'Cheers! To Freya Harris – the next big thing in the art world!'

'Ah, about that ...' Freya winced as she took a seat and waited for her friends to calm down. Once she had their attention, she took a deep breath and, proud that her voice shook only slightly, announced, 'I ... erm ... failed. They failed me.' Lily and Fiona stared at her in disbelief. 'They said it was a really tough year; the examiners marked everyone down and I got a fail.' Freya gave them a sad smile; it was getting slightly easier to say each time.

'Oh my God!' Fiona gasped. 'That's awful. But your project was so good! I loved it.'

'But not good enough, apparently.' Freya took a sip of her bubbles and then put her glass down; it was a bit too soon for fizz after that morning's hangover.

'What are you going to do now?' Lily, ever the practical one, asked.

Freya outlined her options: resubmit or appeal, already knowing she'd do neither. Watching the bubbles in her glass, she made her next announcement. 'Ladies, that's not all of it. When I got home, Matt was in. He thinks my artistic ambitions are childish and so he dumped me.' She watched as both her friends' mouths dropped open; somehow telling them both and seeing the outrage on their faces took the edge off her pain.

'What a dick,' Lily spat as Fiona jumped off her stool and gave Freya a reassuring squeeze.

'He has seemed quite full of himself lately,' Fiona said. 'What happened?'

Between sips of fizz and sniffles, Freya recounted the whole sorry story. 'The thing I'm most embarrassed about is how I thought everything was okay. He's right, to an extent – I did just swan around doing arty things while he worked hard. But I just thought we were going through a rough patch, that once I'd graduated it would all go back to how it was. I'd start earning money with my art and it'd be more equal. Apparently, his ambitions mean he needs a more "corporate" partner.'

'Oh my God, Freya, sounds like you're better off without him.' Fiona pulled a face. 'What an idiot.'

Lily topped up their glasses. 'Seriously, Freya, I agree he's a prize moron, but did you really not see any of this coming? We've not seen you out together for months, not since Matt's birthday back in January, and you were hardly acting like love's young dream then.'

'What? We've been together seven years; we aren't love's young dream, Lils.' Freya stared at her friends. 'Hang on, you're both saying you could see this coming?'

Fiona cast a guilty look at Lily. 'Sort of. You didn't seem happy. Either of you.'

'I was concentrating on my master's,' Freya said, but it was starting to feel less like an excuse and more like the sole cause of all her problems. 'Oh my gosh, I've really messed everything up, haven't I? This is all my fault for doing that stupid degree. Now I have no job, no home, no degree and no boyfriend.'

Fiona gasped and clapped her hands together. 'You're like a blank slate!'

Lily silenced her with a look. 'What do you mean by no home?'

'He's . . . thrown me out too,' Freya admitted with a wince.

'Jesus Christ, Freya! What a bastard. How can he do that? He made your failure all about him, which is pretty low in itself, but then to kick you out?' Lily shook her head in disbelief. 'Where will you go? You can stay with me for a few days – my housemate is away.'

'Thanks, Lily. I was thinking about going home, but it turns out I have a fairy godmother.' Freya did a little shimmy.

'Lola has said I can go and stay with her, work in her café if needs be. You know she opened one in Cornwall.'

Fiona almost spat out her drink and shot a glance at Lily, who was staring at Freya like she was mad. Freya's smile wavered.

'Are you sure that's wise? You know she doesn't stay anywhere for long,' Lily cautioned. She'd never approved of Lola's bohemian lifestyle.

Freya counted to ten before replying. Lily was known for being the practical one, always planning and organizing, and Freya suspected she was slightly envious of the easy, spontaneous friendship she had with Lola. 'I have to leave London,' Freya said. 'I can't afford to stay here with no job and, come on, what skills do I have? If I go to Cornwall, I get a bit of a holiday and some space to think. There are too many memories here. Please, don't judge me. You both have your five-year plans and your nice office jobs and I don't even know what I'm doing in five minutes.'

'It's because we care about you,' Lily said. 'We don't want to see you wasting your life making coffee.'

'Not that there's anything wrong with coffee,' Fiona piped up. 'And you make a really good cup, Frey.'

Freya shot her a grateful smile, determined not to let Lily burst her bubble. 'Thanks, Fi. The alternative is that I move home, live with my parents and train to be a teacher, so excuse me if I pick a holiday.'

Lily mumbled something about running away, but Freya chose to ignore it. Fiona lifted her glass and excitedly pointed out, 'There'll be loads of fit surfer dudes down there. All long hair, buff, walking around in their board shorts.' She fluttered her eyelashes and pulled a dreamy face.

Freya laughed. 'I've just been dumped! I think surfer dudes might be off the menu.'

'Best way to get over Matt is a rebound fling,' Lily said.

Freya grimaced; she couldn't think of anything she wanted less. 'Right now, I need to discover me. I'm going to Cornwall to find myself, not love. I don't think I can be trusted with love.' She watched Fiona's face fall. 'But I'll let you know if I see any fit surfer dudes.' She glanced at both of her friends anxiously. 'I still have to tell my parents, so it'd be nice if I at least had my friends' blessing.'

Lily reached across and squeezed her hand. 'Of course, you do. I'm just worried you're stuck in a rut of working in bars and cafés. You have so much more to offer the world, and I don't want you to still be in the same place come September.'

Freya squeezed her hand back. 'Thank you.'

Fiona raised her glass and toasted, 'To surfer dudes!'

Freya clinked her glass against her friends'. They might not fully agree with her scant life choices, but it was reassuring to know they were going to cheer from the sidelines.

Despite her, again, slightly fuzzy head the following morning, Freya set about getting the flat sorted, buoyed up by her new plans. She heaved the bin bags to the local charity shop and then went back to get rid of the accumulated, useless stuff; boxes of old make-up, tubes of dried -out paint and stiff brushes she no longer needed. Hoisting the bulging sacks into the communal bins was, to an extent, therapeutic. She packed all her wearable, non-paint-stained clothes into her suitcase, ready to leave for Cornwall the following morning.

Slowly, the surfaces began to empty of her stuff, her presence gradually wiped from the flat, leaving behind the clean lines Matt liked. Matt owned nothing in excess. Everything had a purpose: work suits, weekend jeans, gym wear. All of his books were on a Kindle and he'd long got rid of the DVD collection from their student days. Once Freya was gone, the transformation into a stark, masculine pad would be complete. Effectively, he was putting her out with the trash. The thought did not help Freya's general low mood.

Freya's phone had been beeping continually all day. Lily and Fiona had sent detailed plans for how they were going to do away with Matt. Lola had sent tempting photos of cupcakes and sea views. Freya swooned with anticipation, and glee flickered in her heart at the thought of being by the sea when Matt would be stuck in this poxy little flat all summer. When she put it like that, Freya started to feel like she might be getting the better end of the deal.

Less cheering were the four texts from her older sister, Olivia, asking how she was with increasing degrees of worry and nosiness. Freya sent a stalling replying to say she was busy and that she'd call when she had the chance. She didn't want to go through the whole spiel – again – about how her life had collapsed. At least not yet. She was tired from a day of packing and needed an early night, not another lecture or smothering reassurance. Olivia replied with a reminder that she was having dinner at their parents' the following night, which Freya knew was a massive hint to get in touch. She'd call her family when she was safely in Cornwall; that way they wouldn't be able to stage a rescue mission quite as easily.

Freya's alarm was set for the ungodly hour of half past five. The half-seven train had been the cheapest – probably, she reasoned, because no one else wanted to travel so early. She woke to a muted early-June morning, the sun struggling through the thin dawn clouds. Freya opened her eyes and listened to the birds singing outside her window; the knowledge that this was the final time she'd lie in this bed was overwhelming, and she had to stop herself mentally travelling back through all the mornings she and Matt had spent in bed drinking coffee and planning their joint future. As melancholy threatened to seep in, Freya threw back the covers and headed into the bathroom where the citrusy scent of her shower gel momentarily lifted her spirits. *This is a new beginning; I am a clean slate*, she told herself. *It's an adventure and adventures are meant to be exciting.*

Freya dressed comfortably for the long journey: Converse, and her favourite pair of blue and white tie-dye trousers, which Matt had loathed. Pulling them on, she smiled smugly; from now on she wouldn't have to worry about what Matt thought. She teamed it with a white vest top, a long caramel cardigan and a bright shawl Olivia had brought back from Marrakesh. Even if she didn't quite feel it inside, the reflection in the mirror beamed back a care-free bohemian.

In the hall, her suitcase was waiting almost impatiently for their departure. Freya checked that all of her essentials were in her handbag, double-checked that all the drawers were empty and triple-checked that nothing she needed was hiding under the bed. One last whizz around the flat showed Freya that she'd successfully cleaned away any trace of her existence. How would Matt feel when he came home? Relieved or regretful? She supposed it no longer mattered.

Freya unlocked the front door, heaved her backpack on and hoisted the case over the threshold. The air still had its early-morning freshness which would burn off into an unbearable stickiness by lunchtime. Freya locked the door and posted the keys through the letter box, listening as they hit the mat. She stood there for a moment, expecting to feel something monumental, but instead she just felt a bit empty. It was surreal to know she would never return to the flat, but whatever strength she'd mustered to make herself pack up and physically move out prevented the expected tears from falling. Steeling herself, she grabbed her suitcase handle and, without a backward glance, marched towards the bus stop, head held high. Her only regret was that she didn't have enough money for a taxi to Paddington.

Chapter Three

In her current mental state, Freya wasn't sure whether a five-hour train journey, with no book, was a good thing. The subdued silence on the train was suffocating. Freya glanced around at the other passengers, clearly all on much happier journeys than her own. She ate her picnic earlier than she'd planned as a distraction, and then scrolled through her phone, which only reminded her of a happier past.

When she closed her eyes, she was unable to drift off, so Freya texted Matt to let him know she'd posted the keys through the letter box, but he only sent a frustrating 'ok' back. Their relationship reduced to two letters that were up to more interpretation than any other letters coupled together. Was that really all he had to say to her? Freya seethed, but it at least allowed her to spend the next twenty minutes composing, in her head, a suitable reply telling him where he could stick his 'ok'.

With a cup of tea from the buffet cart and a plastic-wrapped blueberry muffin to nibble on, Freya gazed out of the window as the train pulled in and out of Bath and then continued down along the coast. There was nothing else for it: she would have to confront all of the things she'd been desperately pushing to the back of her mind. Maybe a pity party on the train would actually help her get it out of her system? She wasn't quite ready to face her artistic dreams going down the drain, but she knew that 'FAIL' had cut deeper than the split with Matt, and that spoke volumes.

Matt, Matt, Matt ... where on earth had it all gone wrong? At what point had he turned from her geeky graphic designer into a cut-throat corporate cliché who watched too many episodes of *The Apprentice* and hungered for more money? That wasn't the Matt she'd met in the student union bar, who had wooed her with his quirky charms and by posting cartoons under her dorm door. Those little cartoons were now stashed in a box full of uni memories in her parents' attic. She doubted she'd want to look at them for a long time.

Freya sighed and tried to conjure up the devastation she knew she should feel, but it didn't come; there was just anger and resignation. Failing her degree had rather stolen the thunder from Matt dumping her.

She sank lower in her seat and bundled her shawl around her like a blanket, struggling to keep the tears back. Was her art really that bad? So bad she'd get dumped over it? Surely there was no way she'd deceived herself for this long about her ability, and anyway, she'd graduated from her undergraduate with first-class honours, which proved something. She'd had the pick of master's degrees, but had she just chosen badly and basically thrown her savings down the drain?

Postgraduate study had been more daunting than

undergraduate. She'd turned up early on her first day, brimming with excitement, a new sketchbook tucked under her arm, and had been met with stern faces and serious, non-artistic airs. She'd soon realized that her peers were desperate to outdo one another, one even going as far as taking a hammer to a sculpture in an act of brutal sabotage.

The one saviour from this artistic hell had been Lola, a woman more likely to be an artist's muse than the artist. Their friendship had been formed over dirty martinis and a summer working at a shambolic cocktail bar in Islington. Lola had always provided sweet relief for Freya, and the momentary respite of those gossipy drinks had given her the boost she needed to continue her own work, in her own vein, and not care what anyone else thought.

Much good that had done her. She sighed inwardly as the train trundled through Devon. But at least Lola was an excellent provider of safe harbours.

'Sorry, hon, caught up with something, I'm sending a taxi to meet you. Look out for a red Astra! Kettle is on! Xxx' Freya's phone tinkled as the message from Lola dropped in. Tucking it back in her pocket, she hoisted up her bag and trundled her case out of the tiny station. The pavement was damp from an earlier rain shower, and a red Astra was parked outside. The driver, flat cap pulled low over his bushy eyebrows, nodded at her and with his cigarette still in his mouth shoved her case into the boot. Freya climbed in the back and waited for him to finish his cigarette. The car smelled of musty wet dog and she wondered if it was an official taxi or just a local farmer Lola had bribed into doing her bidding.

'Been to Cornwall before?' he inquired, casting a glance in the rear-view mirror as he pulled out into the local roads.

'No. No, I haven't.' Her voice was rusty after hours sitting in silence on the train. 'I'm here to visit a friend.'

He nodded in a slightly disapproving way. 'It's always the same down here – people moving for the dream, squeezing all us natives out. Still,' he justified, almost begrudgingly, 'that Lola makes a pretty good scone, I'll give her that.'

Not quite knowing the right way to respond, Freya nodded, then lapsed into silence as she watched Cornwall unfold around her. The narrow roads totally and utterly disorientated her. After about twenty minutes, by which time Freya had completely lost her bearings, they began to slowly wind down a long, steep road, past little whitewashed cottages perched on the hillside. Freya spied the sea through the windscreen and a rush of childlike excitement flashed through her. Olivia had always beaten her at the 'who can spot the sea first' game, so this felt like winning.

The driver expertly steered the car through the narrow streets and Freya was struck by how small the hamlet was.

'Once, this was all just fishermen,' the driver told her. 'Now, well, it's mainly just tourists, if they come. It's a shame to see, but what can you do? The young ones don't want to fish no more. All second homes and the like.'

This man had clearly never known the crush of the Tube at rush hour, or the angry elbows of the coffee queue first thing on a harried Monday. He was, Freya decided, probably all the better for it. Weariness washed over her and she wiped the memories of London from her mind. The city had always demanded more than Freya was ever able to give.

They pulled up by the harbour wall. Freya fumbled for her purse, but he stopped her. 'Lola already paid, plus she gave me half a Victoria sponge for the trouble.' He smiled for the first time, and Freya returned the smile gratefully. Lola winning over the locals with a bit of baking amused her; the woman had a knack for making people love her.

Freya pushed open the door and stepped out, dragging her bag behind her. The clean sea air and the silence, broken only by the whoosh of the waves and the caw of the gulls, settled around her. She stepped over to the harbour wall and took a deep breath. She'd forgotten the joy of quiet, it was slightly strange but welcome. Her suitcase landed with a thud on the pavement and, with a doff of his cap, the driver climbed back in the car and sped off the way they'd come, leaving Freya alone with a view with which she fell instantly in love.

The tide was out, leaving a small curved beach, clutched by headland on either side, scattered with a few small boats. Along the jetty to her right stood a slightly ramshackle pub, and behind her, the other side of the road was lined with tiny cottages painted in an array of ice cream shades. Pale green, baby pink, yellow and blue. Lola's was the blue one, her pink Mini a bright contrast outside.

To Freya's left were a few shops: a newsagent, which had a display of neon plastic buckets and spades stacked up outside;

a fish and chip shop, currently closed; and then at the end, just before the road bent up towards the headland, was Lola's little café, its new paint job fresh and hopeful for the summer ahead. The village was the smallest place Freya had ever been to, and as she stood there, allowing the sea breeze to ruffle her hair, she fancied she could feel dozens of pairs of eyes on her, wondering exactly what she would do next. Freya herself wished she knew.

'Freya!' She spun around to see Lola hurrying over, her red vintage curls perfectly in place despite the wind. 'I'm so glad you're here!' Lola bundled Freya into a hug, pulling her close and squeezing her. Freya inhaled the sweet sugary scents of baking, but remained speechless, overcome with emotion. Lola stepped back and held Freya at arm's length. 'Oh, hon, don't cry! He's not worth crying about. Come and have some tea.' True to her vintage vision, Lola believed a cup of tea fixed all evils – well, at least until it was socially acceptable to crack open the gin.

Lola seized Freya's case and trundled it across the road towards her little cottage. The door was on the latch, so Freya followed her in and plonked her bag on the floor, rubbing her shoulders with relief.

'Looks like you're moving in!' Lola remarked.

'Oh, no, I didn't know what to bring. Well, I sort of had to bring everything now I'm homeless.' Was that the right word? It felt strange. After all, she had places she could go. Maybe *displaced* was more suitable.

Lola flicked away her answer. 'You are welcome to stay as

long as you like. I'm looking forward to having an extra pair of hands in the café, especially with summer coming. There's a heatwave predicted.' She rolled her eyes. 'They predict a heatwave every year and it lasts, what? Three days? Come on, I'll show you your room.'

Freya followed Lola up the narrow stairs and, wide-eyed, took in how Lola had transformed the basic cottage into her own little cosy hideaway. Fairy lights were twisted through the banisters and vintage travel prints hung on the wall. There was a small landing that led to two bedrooms and a tiny bathroom. Lola pushed open the door to the smaller bedroom at the back with a flourish. 'Home sweet home! Go on, I'm not sure we'd both fit!'

'Wow, it's amazing!' The walls were painted a pale cream and a shelf ready to be filled with books and trinkets ran along the wall above the bed. There was a glass jar of shells already on it, accompanied by several faded paperbacks and two sturdy cookbooks. The room was cosy; a handmade crochet throw was draped over the edge of the bed and fairy lights had been entwined through the metal bedhead. Freya flopped down onto the bed and sighed. 'This is bliss after five hours on a train.' She sat up and ran her hands over the patchwork bedspread, taking in the pile of pillows and cushions. 'Matt would've hated all those. Said you only needed one cushion or pillow per person.'

Lola made a disparaging sound. 'Well, thank God he's not here to judge. I'll go and make the tea.'

Tiredness washed over Freya and, knowing she'd drift

off to sleep if she didn't get up and move soon, she hauled herself off the bed and pushed open the window. The view looked towards the headland. Below her there was a small garden, less carefully tended than the house; an overgrown patch of grass and a few flowerpots. After years squashed into a London flat, any sort of outdoor space, no matter how scrubby, was a luxury. How lucky Lola was to have all this. Freya went to the bathroom, splashed water on her tired face and pulled her long dark hair up into a ponytail. It was wavy and she'd long given up straightening it, which she suspected was a good thing, what with the sea air. Satisfied she'd done all she could to refresh herself, she headed downstairs.

Lola was in the kitchen singing as the kettle boiled and gazing wistfully out the window. Freya's friend was nothing short of immaculate. Always decked out in vintage attire, never a strand of pillar-box red hair out of place. Freya felt a rush of affection for her saviour. 'Is there anything I can do?' she asked.

Slightly startled, Lola whipped round and laughed. 'I've lived alone way too long! Just take the cake into the front room and I'll bring the tea.'

Freya almost drooled at the sight of the plump Victoria sponge oozing jam and cream. She carried it through to the front room, which, like the rest of the house, was bedecked in vintage glamour. A dark green wingback chair was positioned by the window, in perfect place to keep an eye on village comings and goings and stock up on gossip, which Lola loved. The television was hidden in a polished walnut cupboard, and the alcove next to the fire was full of books. Freya ran her eyes over the spines; they turned out to be autobiographies of the stars of the golden age of Hollywood. She placed the cake on the coffee table and collapsed onto the sofa, stretching out her legs and wiggling her toes. A half-finished crochet throw was stuffed into a basket in the corner, further proving there was no end to Lola's talents.

'So, tell me everything!' Lola demanded as she entered with a heavily laden tea tray. 'What on earth happened?'

Freya watched as Lola sliced generous portions of the cake and passed her a plate, complete with tiny cake fork.

'I don't know. It all came out of nowhere.' She sat back. 'I knew I'd struggled with my final piece, but I didn't think it was that bad. I'm not even going to collect the work; they can burn it for all I care. All that money, and for what? Nothing. It makes me feel like Mum was right about art being a waste of time.' Freya took a mouthful of cake. 'Oh God, this is amazing. Are you winning Cornwall over one bake at a time?'

'Hmm, something like that, but this isn't about me!' Lola got up from the chair and poured the tea. 'I never felt like you really fitted in, Freya. I'm amazed you stuck it out to the end. Can you get a refund?'

'Nope, but I can appeal or resubmit. But I've decided to do neither, wash my hands of them.'

'I don't blame you. You're talented and talent, in my opinion, doesn't need a certificate. You know that.' Lola paused and fixed her gaze on Freya as she considered her next gambit. 'I must confess, I never liked Matt. He was always a bit smug and self-righteous.'

'Oh, now you tell me!' Freya spluttered. 'Actually, Lily and Fi said the same thing. How long have you all felt like this?'

Not one to mince her words, Lola said, 'Since I first met him. Look, hon, it's rubbish what's happened, but did you really, really love him? Could you really see a life together? Marriage? Babies? Arguing about car insurance? Would you have wanted to be hanging off his arm while he schmoozed clients? You met at university,' she surmised. 'You've both changed. It's just rubbish because you didn't get in first.'

Freya digested this, shuddering slightly at the thought of a long-term future with Matt. 'I thought we were happy. I thought it was just a rough patch. I feel like such an idiot.'

'Don't. You've been busy – you've been concentrating on your art – and he's been focusing on his career. These things happen. You're both at that age when it's time to either commit or break free completely. You're only twenty-seven – far too young to be saddled with someone like him.'

'But I have no idea what I'll do next!' Freya pushed her lips together; she would not cry.

'You just need to take it slowly. Baby steps. It will all be fine. You're here and that's all that matters. The key is to not think, to just be and see what comes along, trust the universe.' Lola shrugged. 'I never know what I'm going to do next, and look, here I am!'

Freya glanced around the room, brow furrowed. 'What

made you buy a café? I never got a chance to ask on the phone. I never thought I'd see you settled in one place.'

'I had an inheritance from Grandmother Ruby. It just felt the right thing to do. I was getting tired of life on the road. Don't get me wrong, I'm thankful for all the amazing opportunities it gave me, the people I met, but it was all a bit samey. Even a showgirl has to hang up her feathers at some point.' Freya suspected she wasn't getting the full story but Lola quickly deflected back to her. 'But this is all about you. It doesn't matter if you don't know exactly what happens next – something will turn up. It's always a blessing in disguise when relationships end. Trust me.'

Sensing that Lola would not be drawn out if she asked questions, Freya pocketed this revelation for later. There had to be more behind her itinerant friend's decision to settle down in a postcard-perfect seaside village miles from anywhere. 'Okay,' she said. 'I trust you, Lola, but I'm struggling to see the positives in this.'

'You're by the sea? Everyone wants to live by the sea!' Lola said. 'If you hadn't come here where would you be?'

'At my parents', having teaching degrees shoved at me. Oh gosh, I've still not told them any of it!' Freya covered her face with her hands and groaned.

'Well, no time like the present. Give them a call. You have the safety of distance.'

Imbued with the calming effects of tea and cake, Freya took herself off to the privacy of her new bedroom, and practically hanging out the window to get some signal, video-called Olivia.

'Hang on, Freya,' her sister said. 'I'll just get Mum and Dad.'

Freya watched Olivia as she made her way from the living room into the kitchen, where their mum was busy stirring a pot. Once they'd located her dad and three expectant faces were looking back at her, Freya swallowed, steeling herself to begin. Her family, who had supported her through everything, gazed back at her expectantly, and while she was figuring out how to break the news to them, a seagull squawked as it flew past the window.

'Are you by the sea?' Olivia asked, eyes narrowing with suspicion.

'Yes, I'm in Cornwall–Polcarrow. With Lola.' Freya threw it all out there and waited while her family voiced their surprise, flinging how and why questions at her. Once they'd managed to calm down a bit, Freya smiled and filled them in. 'Matt and I have split up. He asked me to leave and Lola needed someone to help her with the café over the summer, so that's why I'm here. I guess we're sort of helping each other out.'

'Lucky you!' her dad said, rubbing the beard he had started to grow since retiring from his financial job. Olivia had taken to calling him the oldest hipster in Bedford.

'Lola has a café?' was her mum's shocked input.

Olivia just gave Freya a long look, which told her she knew there was more to the story. 'What about your degree?'

Freya's face fell. Her heart raced and, taking a deep breath to steady her tears, she confessed, 'I failed.' Telling her family was far harder than telling Lily, Fiona and Lola. As Freya sniffled through the whole story, part of her wished she was with them so they could give her a big hug. But the other part was glad she was far away so that she didn't have to defend her artistic ability.

'Oh, Freya, I wish we could give you a hug,' her dad echoed her thoughts.

'But is running away really the right thing to do? You should've come home. I bet there's still some places on that teaching course . . .' Her mum was cut short by Olivia nudging her in the arm.

Freya summoned up a weak smile. 'I know you're all worried, but I have to do this. Everything has been a hundred miles an hour lately and I need some time to just pause and figure out what I want.' A sudden pang of loneliness hit her; she was missing her family, having not seen them since Easter. 'Anyway, I'm fed up talking about me, what have you all been up to?'

With the whoosh of the waves providing a soothing backdrop, Freya sat back and listened to her family talk about the new takeaway they'd discovered, the cocktail bar Olivia declared was 'divine', the neighbour's cat Mum was waging a war with. Freya smiled at the simple domesticity of their lives, reassured that somewhere life was carrying on as normal.

Two hours later, having been lulled to sleep by the distant sound of the waves and then treated herself to a steamy shower, Freya emerged feeling much revived. Making her way downstairs, she allowed the homeliness of Lola's cottage to envelop her: the sound of her friend singing along to the radio, the sizzle of something in the pan and the delicious aroma of home cooking. Freya's stomach gurgled happily.

'God, that smells good,' Freya remarked as she entered the kitchen. 'I can't remember when I last ate something homemade.'

'Good thing you have me to look after you now.' Lola smiled smugly. 'Sorry, it's nothing fancy, but I've never had any complaints about my risotto before. There's a bottle of wine in the fridge.'

Freya located the glasses – mismatched like all of Lola's crockery, picked up from an array of vintage fairs – and poured two glasses of crisp white wine. She passed one to Lola and they chinked their glasses as Freya perched on the kitchen stool.

'Lola settled by the sea,' Freya mused and hoped she didn't sound as if she was prying. 'Didn't think I'd see the day.'

Lola chuckled. 'Well, the desire to settle comes to us all,' she said cryptically. 'But who knows? I may stay here for a year, two years, or I might wake up in August and decide to move on again.'

Freya smiled affectionately and left it at that. Lola was clearly not yet quite ready to spill the beans on her rapid descent into domesticity.

*

After living off convenience food and a lot of sandwiches while finishing off her degree show, Lola's risotto was the equivalent of Michelin-starred fare as far as Freya was concerned. Upon finishing her bowl, she leant back and groaned with pleasure. 'That's the best thing I've eaten in a long time.' She patted her stomach for effect.

Freya had never been one to cook, which Matt had found endearing to begin with and then, as time progressed, increasingly infuriating. Freya had always had bigger things on her mind, but now, effectively back at the starting line, she wondered if her artistic tunnel vision had been her greatest failure. Her life was like Snakes & Ladders, and now, just before reaching the final square and claiming victory, she'd slid all the way down the big snake, right back to the start. She topped up their glasses. At least there was wine.

'What on earth am I going to do?' she asked Lola. 'Honestly, none of this "it'll all be fine; the universe has your back" stuff. What am I going to do with my life?'

A mischievous glint shone in Lola's eyes as she rummaged around in her sewing basket and produced a stack of well-worn, gilded cards. Freya groaned. Over the years, Lola had made a bit of money on the side reading fortunes for lovesick girls and worried women, but Freya generally tried to avoid getting involved in Lola's mystical side. 'I meant practical advice, Lola,' she said.

'Humour me,' Lola instructed. 'I'm thinking of plying this trade from the back door of the kitchen. People always want their fortunes read.'

Freya put down her wine glass and took the cards; they were heavy in her hands, the gold edging worn away with use. Awkwardly, she began to shuffle them and, as instructed, tried to think about what she wanted from the future. She'd always eschewed Lola's attempts at fortune-telling in the past. It made her feel uneasy; what if her friend saw something she didn't like? Although, in hindsight, maybe that would've helped her avoid the mess she was now in.

'Okay, when you're done, divide them into three piles and choose the pile you feel most drawn to.'

Freya did as she was told and studied the three, slightly messy piles. Firmly, she chose the one in the middle. Lola spirited the other piles away, seized the selected one and began to set the cards out on the coffee table, making little noises of encouragement and surprise as she went along. It was Lola's raised eyebrow that made Freya sit forward and ask, 'What have you seen?'

Lola didn't respond; instead she tapped the cards and shivered. 'You need to step into your power, there is something in your life you have lost all faith in, but the cards are telling me that you need to avoid the doubt and carry on. It won't be easy though and you will have to set aside your pride and accept help.'

Freya nodded and watched as Lola pushed all the cards together and handed them back. 'We'll do three rounds. Shuffle, divide and select, please.' After slightly less shuffling, Freya chose the middle pile again.

'Big decisions to be made.' Even Lola had the grace to

laugh. 'Tell me about it! Decisions about location, about work and even your love life. But it says when the right decision presents itself, you will be in no doubt that that is the path to take.'

There was a third and final deal and Freya found herself swayed towards the left. Lola held the cards momentarily and slowly began to lay them out. As she did so, something in the air began to cool. Lola sat and stared at the cards for so long Freya leant forward, unnerved, and asked, 'What's the matter?'

'Nothing, nothing!' Lola said with clearly fake brightness, 'but they are extremely interesting. There is a dark figure approaching, a man. He is troubled. It will be a true soul connection, which comes with its own challenges . . . and . . . Yes . . . Oh, you need to trust him. It will be difficult, but if you can learn to trust him, there is a chance of love and happiness. If you don't . . . Well, actually, I wouldn't worry too much about it,' she hurried on. 'But it says not trusting him will lead to a different, less fulfilled path in life.' Lola sat back and smiled bravely, even though Freya could tell she was troubled. Lola sloshed wine into the two glasses and offered a toast: 'To new love, Freya!'

'What? No! I've only just split up from Matt,' she protested. 'I'm not at all ready to start looking for new love. This needs to be about me!'

Lola raised her eyebrow again. 'Nonsense! Everyone wants love. The cards don't lie.' She tapped a finger on the middle card with a sense of finality before gathering them all up and tucking them safely back in her sewing basket.

Chapter Four

Lola's café may have been small, but it was perfectly formed and just as perfectly located. After her first night in Polcarrow Freya was keen to see what the café was like. Tacked on the end of the small parade of shops on Harbour Row, it was painted a pale cream with dove grey accents, and had space outside for a couple of tables and chairs ready for the summer.

'Painted it myself,' Lola said, smiling proudly as she looked up at her new empire. 'Aggie and Dave were retiring and, after years of being one grade up from a greasy spoon, I felt it needed a bit of a lift and lots of love.' She unlocked the front door and Freya followed her inside. 'Trade has been slow, but I'm confident it will pick up with the summer coming. Plus, I have plans for social media, events – you name it, I'm already thinking of it. The village is so charming and I have everything crossed this will work. It has to work, Freya.'

The blinds were drawn, but Freya could see what Lola had done to the place and felt her passion for the project. The interior walls were pale yellow and the tables and chairs were light grey, with a variety of handmade cushions placed on them. A jolly assortment of vintage teapots sat on a shelf by the counter and bunting hung from the walls, giving the place a homely, welcoming feel. Freya imagined how cosy it would be once the coffee aroma started to circulate and mingle with the sweet scent of freshly baked cakes.

'Stripped and painted all these as well,' she told Freya, giving one of the chairs a pat. 'God, it was hard work, but I enjoyed it – being outside, the sea air, the seagulls. Caused a bit of a stir. Everyone had to come and take a look. Good for business, though. Right.' She turned to Freya. 'If you're going to be my assistant, you can start by showing me your coffee-making skills.'

'I can guarantee they are better than my baking skills,' Freya quipped as she darted behind the counter. The coffee machine was easy enough to use and Freya was proud of the two cappuccinos she placed on the counter. She stared at them, wondering if coffee -making would be the sum of her existence.

'Hmmm.' Lola pretended to study them. 'Not bad, not bad. Now, there should be a Victoria sponge under the counter that needs polishing off – do fish it out and we can have a decadent second breakfast.' She swept the coffees off the counter and sashayed over to the window seat.

Smiling to herself, Freya rummaged around and located the cake, some dainty plates, a knife and some cake forks. If there was one thing Lola could be relied upon for, it was to do everything with decadence. Freya studied her friend, sitting in the window seat. Red hair coiled up on top of her head, make-up perfectly applied, a pair of blue dungarees hugging her figure; she looked like a glamourous Rosie the Riveter. Plus, a seaside café and a house to add to that. Lola really was full of tightly kept surprises. Freya was so proud of what her friend had created, and she vowed to help Lola make the success she deserved of her new venture.

Freya sat the second breakfast down on the table and watched as Lola lifted the glass dome and chopped the remaining cake in half. Freya's eyes nearly popped out of her head.

'Lola! If I keep eating cake like that I'll be huge.'

'Nonsense. You need the sugar to keep yourself going. Everyone will be in this morning to check you out. Anyway, there's nothing of you. A bit of cake will do you good.' Lola pushed the plate closer.

Still, Freya silently vowed to take up running, just in case. She didn't have the money to replace her wardrobe on top of everything else. Then again, she'd been promising to take up running for years without ever having even started. 'So, what is it like here?' Freya asked, sneaking a glance out the window towards the sea.

'Small. Everyone has their nose in everyone else's business. But once they've got the measure of you, it's all very welcoming. I won them over with cakes, scones, half-price coffees. It helped that Aggie and Dave gave me their blessing. And the vicar, but he's new here too, so we've sort of ... erm ... clubbed together.' Colour rose in Lola's cheeks.

Freya clocked how the mention of the vicar made Lola

bashful and almost split her coffee in shock. 'Lola! You and a vicar? I never would have thought it.' Freya put her coffee down.'I'm guessing he's not got tufty hair, a stained cardigan and wonky teeth, then?'

'Behave! It's nothing like that,' Lola said quickly. A bit too quickly, Freya thought. 'He's young, late thirties. He arrived in January. He'd been working in Birmingham, and he needed a break, some sea air and respite. It's nothing like that. Honest. But we've been a huge support to each other. He usually comes in with his paper first thing, has a cup of tea, some toast, and we chat about the village goings-on – also, the parishioners know to find him here. Apparently it's a lot less stuffy than the vicarage.'

Freya nodded; it was a good excuse, but she wasn't convinced. The little gleam in Lola's eye gave away everything she wasn't saying. But, knowing not to push, Freya changed the subject. 'What will I be helping with, other than making coffee and serving?'

Lola glanced out the window and back before replying. 'It's my first summer so I suspect it'll get busy and I can't serve and bake, so it'll all be a bit of trial and error. I come in first thing, bake the cakes and scones and get the soup on. Over lunchtime, I'll make sandwiches, so I'll need help serving, taking orders, making coffees. The usual really.'

'Nothing I haven't done before,' Freya reassured her with a grin. 'Sounds like it could be fun. I'm so excited for you, Lola – your own little café!'

'I know. I love it, but sometimes I do wonder if I've done

the right thing.' She gestured to the sea view. 'That is gorgeous and I love seeing how different it is every morning, from stormy winter dawns to beautiful sunrises, but will I wake up one day and think I've had enough? I've never been in one place for longer than a few months, but this place feels right. I think.' She smiled sadly at Freya. 'I may have an ulterior motive for inviting you down, though. I could really do with an ally while I get all this working. It's been hard to give up on the nomadic life, even if it was the right thing to do.' Lola took a deep breath and smiled reassuringly at Freya. 'I don't want to get all carried away with the future. Right now, this feels good. It feels good and right and we'll have a fantastic summer. I promise you that, Freya.' She picked up her coffee cup and bumped it against Freya's. 'Cheers!'

'To a fantastic summer!' Freya echoed, Lola's optimism wrapping itself like bubble wrap around her bruised heart. 'Whatever it is, Lola, I'm here for you. I promise we'll make this work.'

Freya helped Lola whip up a lemon drizzle cake and a slightly wonky Victoria sponge, although, with her limited baking skills, Freya felt she was more hindrance than help. A batch of scones and some sticky blocks of flapjack followed and Freya marvelled at how calm and methodical her friend was in the kitchen.

'I feel like I'm seeing a whole new Lola,' Freya said as she picked up the cakes to take out to the counter.

Lola laughed. 'I just have hidden depths that I'm slowly

revealing. All those years as a showgirl, tour guide and cocktail maker, but this is the real me. I forget all my troubles when I'm cooking. I loved catering college – I loved cooking – but my first stint in a kitchen scared me so much that I backed off. I'll never forgive that grumpy chef.' Lola bustled about refilling bowls of sugar packets and tweaking the vases on the tables, full of fake sweet peas. 'Last summer I helped out in a café in Scotland and I loved it, you know. It really gave me a buzz and I started to think, I could do this. And then the idea just didn't go away and I realized I couldn't resist the call. Believe me, I've resisted the call for a lot of things. Don't you resist the call when it comes, Freya,' Lola warned. 'It will only hound you until you listen.'

Freya, stacking some flapjacks, furrowed her brow. 'Honestly, Lola, I'm all about survival right now, but thanks. I'm trying not to think about the next step – it's too frightening. I mainly feel a fool for wasting all that money on a degree. Think of what else I could have done with it – actually, don't, I don't want to know. God, this is deep for first thing in the morning!' She laughed, trying to lighten the mood, but Lola looked as if she was dying to get her hands on her and stick her back together. Freya wasn't ready to be patched up yet; she still had a lot to make sense of. 'I appreciate all your help, Lola, throwing me this lifeline, and I know you want to help me, but I need to do this myself. I haven't yet got my head around everything that has happened.'

After placing the cakes on the countertop, she opened the blinds and, feeling optimistic about the sunny morning, set up the chairs outside and flipped the sign to open. While waiting for customers, Freya explored the nooks and crannies behind the counter, discovering a box of adorable knitted tea cosies, supplies of sugar, salt and pepper, a *Take a Break* magazine and a pile of aprons. Freya shook her head in awe; the Lola she had known had never seemed organized enough to run a business, especially not one that ran as smoothly as the café seemed to.

Lola had been right about one thing: her customers were creatures of habit. Just after nine a.m., the door swung open and a tall man in his late thirties came in. His blonde hair flopped over his tanned forehead and his blue eyes glittered with kindness. Freya clocked the dog collar, and her mouth dropped open; she instantly understood why Lola had squirmed under questioning. He was rather easy on the eye.

'Ah, good morning! You must be Lola's little helper.' His voice had a slight accent to it, northern perhaps. Freya couldn't quite place it. 'I'm Tristan.' He held out his hand and Freya shook it.

'Freya.' She smiled, relieved that he was as friendly as Lola had implied.

'Lovely to meet you, Freya.' He leant in conspiratorially. 'We non-locals have to stick together. I hope you're prepared for a busy morning – everyone will be in to eyeball you. Honestly, it's ridiculous. The first Sunday service I took, the church was rammed full, everyone curious, and as they walked out you could hear them muttering and discussing me. Church has never been as busy since!' He laughed. 'I think I passed muster. They've not chased me out of town with their pitchforks . . . yet!'

His jovial manner was infectious and Freya laughed. She'd worked in bars and coffee shops over the years, but in the city you barely got more than a grunt from a customer, or, at most, a demand for whipped cream or less froth. To have an actual conversation was a blessing. 'They can't be worse than grumpy businessmen in a hurry on a rainy Monday morning. What can I get you?'

'Oh, the usual.' Tristan dropped his voice to explain what that was. 'Which is a pot of Earl Grey tea, lemon, no milk, two slices of toast and marmalade. The cakes are good but I need to watch my waistline.' He patted his rather trim body.

Freya rung everything through the till. He paid and headed over to the window seat, ready to pay court to any parishioners who cared to pay a visit. She took his tea over to him, having enjoyed choosing which teapot and cosy to use; she'd settled on a rather jaunty-looking knitted chicken. Tristan chuckled at it. Lola came out with the toast, looking unusually flushed, Freya thought.

'Morning, vicar,' Lola said with a flirtatious wink. Freya watched as Lola shifted from foot to foot and laughed at something Tristan had said. His eyes never left hers.

As Lola made her way back to the kitchen, Freya mockingly shook her head. 'Oh dear, Lola, flirting with a vicar. That's a new one for you.'

Lola's face flushed and she gave Freya a playful whack on the arm. 'Sssh, you! Behave, and not so loud.'

'Not denying it, I see,' Freya teased as Lola vanished into the kitchen, treating them to a blast of vintage radio as the door swung open and shut.

The café had a calm air and Freya found she was enjoying being back behind a counter. It was a huge improvement on some of the chains she'd worked in.

She watched as an older man shuffled into view outside, a fluffy sheepdog bounding along beside him. He calmed the dog down, getting it to sit at the third attempt, and then pulled a treat from his pocket, which the dog snaffled with delight. The man said a few words to the dog before they came into the café.

'Morning, vicar,' he called out, his accent as thick as clotted cream. He spotted Freya and doffed his cap. 'Good morning, missy. You must be Lola's new helper. My name's Alf.' He made his way over to the counter and held out his hand. Freya shook it. She noticed his hands were sun-worn and calloused, his face weather-beaten and craggy, but his blue eyes sparkled merrily.

'I'm Freya,' she supplied. 'What's your gorgeous dog called?'

'Oh, that's Scruff. Don't let him hear you call him gorgeous; it'll go to his head. Lola said I can bring him in if that's all right with you? I'd be happy for him to sit in the sunshine and get five minutes' peace, but he just whines, don't you, boy? Ever had a dog? No? Well, they're delightful, but they need all your attention. Still,' he surmised, 'I wouldn't be without him. Now, can I have a cup of tea and a piece of flapjack? Has Lola got any of the caramel ones left? I shouldn't really, but what the doctor doesn't know . . .' He trailed off with a mischievous wink.

Lola stuck her head out the kitchen door. 'Morning, Alf! Freya, I saved him a flapjack – it's wrapped up next to the sugar.'

Freya rummaged around and pulled it out, proudly presenting it to Alf. 'Here you go.'

'Excellent! Lola looks after us. Never had cakes like hers!'

'Take a seat and I'll bring it over to you.' Freya watched as Alf made his way over to Tristan, who put away his paper and cleared the decks, ready to chat to the old man. Freya put the teapot, flapjack, cup and saucer on a tray and carried it over, neatly setting it down in front of Alf.

Alf chuckled at the rainbow-striped tea cosy. 'My mum used to knit these. Didn't know they still existed until Lola showed up with them.'

'Well, Lola does live in a sort of time warp,' Freya reminded him.

'I know. It's delightful, though – takes me back,' he said with a sigh and appeared to momentarily drift off to another time.

Freya dropped to her knees to give Scruff a fuss, rubbing him behind the ears and watching his eyes close in doggy bliss. He lay on the floor behind Alf's chair in a shaft of sunlight and Freya envied him his sunbathing. The idea of languishing on a beach was very tempting, even if it wasn't quite what she was here for. Maybe on her day off; it'd been ages since she'd had a holiday, or since her legs had seen any sun.

'Is there anything I should be doing?' Freya asked Lola

when she popped into the kitchen. Lola was poring over some paperwork and making a list on the back of an envelope.

'Huh? No. It's a bit quiet, but I'm confident it'll pick up once holiday season begins. I've only been open a couple of months, so it's early days. Anyway, there's usually a mid-morning flurry.'

Freya left the kitchen and hoisted herself up on the stool behind the counter. She needed something to busy herself with; if not, she'd start to think, and thinking would make her maudlin. Mulling over problems had been a pastime with Lily and Fiona, but those problems had always been trivial. Whether or not to text a guy back; should Fiona buy a new pair of shoes; Lily getting into arguments with her housemate and suchlike. None of them had ever experienced anything as life-changing as Freya's last few days, and Freya felt woefully unprepared to deal with the fallout. Not knowing how to get her head around it, let alone verbalise it, she started to doodle on the order pad and then stopped. What was the point? It wasn't like she was any good at art. It had always been her solace but now even doodling reminded her of her failure.

She fished out the the magazine and completed an ancient crossword. Just as she was trying to figure out thirteen down, the door banged open and a gaggle of giggling women bustled in.

'Careful, Jan, don't knock the new paintwork, not with it looking so lovely.'

'It slipped! It slipped!' Jan protested, pulling off her cardigan. 'Hope she's got some of that Victoria sponge.'

The three women encircled the counter and peered over at Freya, inspecting her. They reminded Freya of vultures. They clearly weren't here just for the cake. Trying not to be intimidated, Freya tucked a loose strand of hair behind her ear and asked, 'What can I get you? The cakes are fresh this morning.'

'Ooh in that case, it's got to be the Victoria sponge, hasn't it?' The woman named Jan, her blonde curls bobbing around her head, almost drooled over the uncut cake.

'Three slices please, two teas, and what are you having, Cathy?' This was the woman who was clearly in charge, and who, Freya noted, looked the most friendly.

Cathy, steely grey bob, glasses hanging from a cord around her neck, paused and gave it a bit of thought. Then, 'Latte, please, two shots. Those blasted seagulls kept me awake all night.'

The one who seemed to be in charge pulled out her purse and turned to Freya. 'Hello, you must be new here. I'm Sue and this is Cathy and Jan.' Jan waved but Cathy didn't even acknowledge the introduction; she was too busy trying to find the perfect place to sit. 'I'm president of Polcarrow WI. We've almost convinced Lola to join us.' She pulled a flyer from her bag and passed it to Freya. 'Just in case you fancy meeting some locals.'

Freya turned it over and skimmed the list of activities. Line dancing, learning to tie ship knots, scrapbooking, litter collecting. It sounded interesting and a world away from spending evenings trawling snazzy London bars or flopped in front of the telly. Freya folded the flyer and slipped it into her jeans pocket.

'We meet every other Wednesday in the church hall,' Sue continued. 'Come along next week! We're doing bottle decorating. We've done all sorts in the past. Yoga, flower arranging, stargazing, even yodelling, but the less said about that, the better.'

Freya was warming to her; Sue clearly wanted to make her feel welcome and included. 'Sounds fun; I'll think about it.' It wasn't as if Polcarrow had a throbbing social scene to tempt her elsewhere. 'Oh, I'm Freya by the way. I'll bring your cakes over.'

'Perfect!' Sue gave her a sunny smile and waved at Tristan as he said his farewells and made his way out, citing 'urgent church business'.

Freya took their orders over to them and then relaxed. What a pleasant morning it had been; a gentle introduction to village life as the locals sussed her out. Alf and Tristan seemed to have accepted her, and the WI ladies seemed to want to test her, but all in all, Freya realized running away had been the best decision she could have made.

'Well, you survived your first day, so I think that calls for a trip to the pub!' Lola announced as she flipped the open sign to closed and held the door open for them to leave. 'How did today go?' she asked as they made their way along the seafront.

'I really enjoyed it,' Freya enthused. 'Alf and his dog are so adorable. It made such a change from the grumpiness I got in

London. Although, in London, I never had to worry about figuring out anyone's hidden agenda. They just wanted their coffee and wanted it quick.'

'I love Alf; he's a total gem. I forgot people like him existed until I came here. Don't be fooled by Scruff, though – that dog has a wily habit of getting titbits off everyone. Lord knows what a vet would say.' Lola shuddered.

'I wasn't sure about the WI ladies, though,' Freya ventured.

'Oh, they definitely came to suss you out,' Lola confirmed. 'I was surprised they weren't waiting outside the door when we opened. Don't worry about them, though. They mean well, see themselves as the caretakers of the village. I think I'm winning them over with my baking, but Cathy used to be their star baker, so I have to tread carefully.'

'Tristan seems ... nice,' Freya probed pathetically.

'Hmm, that he is, that he is.' Lola linked her arm through Freya's and they made their way along the harbour, but she said no more. The air was thick with the scent of the sea, the evening sun glimmering temptingly on the damp sand. Freya marvelled at how quiet the village was: just the call of the seagulls and the gentle lapping of the waves. Not a plane, traffic jam or siren to be heard. She hadn't realized how polluted her brain had become with the cacophony of the city, and she couldn't remember a time when she'd last been in such perfect peace.

They came to a stop outside a pub and Lola pushed the door open. The low ceiling was beamed, the walls wonky, and there were horse brasses hung around the bar area and a hearth that would be cosy in the colder months. Freya fancied that, without all the modern accoutrements, they could quite easily have been transported back to an eighteenth-century smugglers' paradise.

'All right, Steve?' Lola called as a bald man sporting an eye patch came into view.

Lola gave Freya a whack on the arm when she saw her gaping at his eye. 'There's nothing wrong with his eye. Don't indulge him. He never got to drama school and likes to ham it up now. He's our resident pirate, Father Christmas and Easter bunny.'

'Yep, can't waste all my talents behind a bar,' he said, eyes twinkling and adding a piratical 'yaarrrr' for effect. 'What can I get you ladies?'

'Two glasses of white wine, please,' Lola ordered, and then turned to Freya. 'It's thanks to me that he now serves a passable Sauvignon Blanc. Before that it was whatever white wine had fallen off the back of a lorry.'

Steve cackled with laughter as he poured two generous glasses without measuring them. 'On the house,' he said. 'Got to welcome your new friend into the fold.'

Lola insisted on paying and, after a bit of haggling, which resulted in Steve throwing in a couple of free bags of peanuts, they went outside into the fantastically located beer garden; full of pots of bright flowers, it had an enviable view of the sea and the headland that Freya thought she'd never get bored of. 'It's so beautiful here,' she said as they sat down. 'I'm so glad I came, Lola.'

'Me too,' Lola said. Lifting her glass, she proposed a toast. 'To new beginnings.'

'I will certainly drink to that.' Chinking her glass against Lola's, Freya took a sip and sighed blissfully. 'I have so missed this, Lola – us in a pub garden, drinking wine and putting the world to rights. Graham's cocktail bar might have been a disaster but it brought me my fairy godmother.'

Lola laughed. 'Gosh, that bar was a complete dive. I think it's the only place that's failed before I got the chance to leave. Still, it was all good fun, even if the cocktails were a little on the pre-made side.'

Freya smiled as she recalled the summer after graduation when she'd rocked up to work at a new bar in Angel and among the other bar staff had found Lola, who had instantly taken her under her wing. Lola had wrangled the rota so they were on the same shifts, and they'd enjoyed a summer full of strawberry daiquiris, city workers with too much cash to spend, and evenings that ended with chips and Diet Coke in the kebab shop as they rested their sore feet and cast out their dreams for the future.

'Matt didn't approve of me enjoying myself back then. Thought I should've been trying to find a sensible job.'

Lola made a face. 'But who will have better memories of that time? Him with his overtime, or us in charge of the playlist and sneaking secret drinks?'

Freya beamed at her friend. 'Us, of course, and I'm hoping this summer will be just as much fun.'

'Well, just leave that to your fairy godmother,' Lola said with a wink.

Warmth flooded through Freya; the feeling of coming home.

The rhythm of life in Polcarrow was set to the beat of the waves on the sand, and Freya quickly settled into it. The sea brought Freya peace the likes of which she had never known existed. The gentle crash of the waves surrounded her, making her feel safe. She loved lying in bed at night, window open, the crash of the sea on the shore sending her off to sleep; it soothed her, lulled her into a deeper slumber than she'd enjoyed for years. Even if it was strange to have a bed to herself after so many years of sharing with Matt. Slowly, she began to inch out, taking up the space he'd always pushed her out of. That must mean something metaphorically, Freya mused. It had taken the split for her to realise she had outgrown him and the boundaries he'd tried to draw for their lives.

Every morning, upon waking, Freya found herself refreshed in a way she'd never been in London. Back there, her life had been lived on a treadmill; there had always been somewhere she needed to hurry to, or if she was not in a rush, someone else was. Elbows and tuts as they squeezed past her on the way to the Tube, the impatient honking of traffic, the buildings that stretched greedily towards the sky. Everything in London was demanding, and it had slowly sucked the life out of Freya. She hadn't realized how exhausted she was until she'd rocked up on Lola's doorstep, looking for something to fix her broken heart and displaced life.

She was, she knew, a bit broken. Her heart rattled like pieces of broken glass in her chest. Yet when she thought of Matt, it was not with sadness; it was with anger, and the tears that pricked her eyes were hot with rage. This feeling was layered like a onion: anger at Matt for dumping her; a burst of shame that she'd let him string her along; disbelief that he'd picked the moment when she'd been most vulnerable to give her that extra kick. The betrayal hollowed her out, and she generally tried not to confront it, seeking to fill that space with the good things that came with seaside life.

Mostly, she discovered, she was angry with herself: a blinding rage that she'd not had the sense to see that their relationship had been dying for a very long time. The naïve assumption that it had all been okay, that Matt was fine with her swanning around in an artistic daze. But what she couldn't understand was why he hadn't tried to talk to her about it all. Surely that made him just as complicit in their relationship's demise?

Still, Freya blamed herself for her insistence on pursuing her artistic career, on indulging a creativity that should have stayed in an undergraduate classroom. She had never, ever had cause to doubt her talent, but postgraduate study had been just one more thing in the city that had grabbed at her and demanded things from her that she didn't have to give. What was so wrong with painting landscapes? With washing over a canvas with a half-constructed dream? Why did art always have to mean so many things? Art was more than a portfolio submitted at the end of the year; it was Freya's lifeblood, her reason for living, and to have it deemed not worthy stung.

Her artistic failure and the questions it raised were harder to deal with than having been dumped, so down in Cornwall her art materials were banished under her bed. Sometimes she opened the box, looked at them, lifted the lid on the palette of watercolours and gazed down at their bright, condensed shades, thinking briefly of how she'd use them to interpret the stunning sunrises that crept over the bay, the reds and pinks pushing through the night, a bleed on the horizon. She had always been fascinated by the beauty of nature, and the charming landscapes of Polcarrow was starting to rekindle that love. How could that love be wrong or without merit? However, her paints were always put back under the bed without being used.

Being by the sea had turned Freya into an early riser. She'd slip out of the cottage as the first rays of sun filtered through her window. It was liberating not to have to explain her new habits to anyone, nor seek approval. She marvelled at how different each dawn was. Some, soft with promise; others, dark as if the world was grumpy to have been woken so early. In the absence of painting, she began to take photographs, inundating her social media with comforting photos of nature. Freya was pleased to see that living by the sea garnered her more followers than when she'd been posting photos of overpriced cocktails in pretentious London bars.

Each dawn, she stood by the harbour wall watching the boats go out, the seagulls waiting for the catch, and while Polcarrow stretched itself awake, Freya smothered the urge to grab her paints and pencils and commit the scene to paper. The desire to create crept down her arms, into her fingers, which she clenched in defiance, trying to ignore the urge. She was all washed up and painted out, and she needed a break; that's what she told herself. The call and the desire were in her, butting up against her depleted confidence, but the most she ever gave into was doodles, simple scratches of pen on the soft paper of the order pad.

Lola had been instrumental in keeping Freya busy, which she was thankful for. Without Lola bustling her in and out of her schemes and activities, the evenings would have felt long and would have provided far too much time to dwell.

Above the café was a small studio flat that Lola had renovated with the hope of turning it into a holiday let. With little money to spruce it up, they had spent a couple of evenings painting the walls a pale cream, scrubbing the bathroom and kitchen cabinets and adding a few homely touches. It was basic, but Lola hoped that it would attract travellers on a budget lured by the sea views and tempted by the scents of baking. It amused Freya no end to see just how many pies Lola had her fingers in, although the more crafty ones, such as crocheting bespoke blankets that she sold on the internet, didn't suit Freya. She always ended up in knots.

'Maybe you could paint some pictures and sell them?' Lola had suggested in a practised, casual manner one morning as she set about making a new batch of scones. 'We could display them in the café. People would love them! A unique painting of the seaside – you could make a small fortune.'

Freya shook her head as the fear gripped her, running hot and cold over her skin. 'I'm not ready. And I'm not sure the world needs another person painting watercolours of fishing boats, to be honest. It's a bit overdone.' As soon as the words were out of her mouth Freya hated herself for saying them. She had never been one for artistic derision before.

Lola replied with a long look, but it spoke volumes about how much she disagreed with her friend just giving up. Freya was grateful that Lola did not push, though; her brain really did need a break. It had been a welcome relief to be taught how to bake, even if the results had been pretty shocking. Lola, Tristan and Alf had enjoyed tucking into a rather wonky, but perfectly baked Victoria Sponge Freya had made but she resigned herself to the fact her talents lay elsewhere. Freya had listened as they exchanged village gossip as if it was the juiciest scandal. Tristan, she'd learned, was very keen to sample everything Lola lovingly baked and Lola had grown used to using him as her official taster.

All of Lola's efforts and the surprising welcome from the villagers made Freya feel accepted in a way she never had in her previous life. She settled into this vanilla-scented, sugar-dusted sense of security and thought she'd be very happy to never leave.

Chapter Five

He arrived with the storm.

A low rumble on the horizon drew closer as the village battened down the hatches in the wake of its arrival. The atmosphere had been wired all day, on edge with expectation. Customers had flittered in and out of the café, distracted as they placed and then changed their minds about orders. Lola buzzed around, agitated, unable to settle, and having exhausted all her cleaning chores, had claimed she had an errand to do and nipped off in her Mini, leaving Freya effectively trapped behind the counter.

She didn't mind, and she wasn't usually bored having only been in Polcarrow two weeks, but today the clock felt as if it was ticking backwards. Once the breakfast regulars had trickled out, the morning had turned into a blank, empty afternoon. The weather kept the few visitors to Polcarrow off the beaches and coastal paths. For the first time since arriving, Freya didn't know what to do with herself. She straightened out the chairs, and ate two pieces of millionaire's shortbread, which she instantly regretted. A rifle through all the cupboards turned up nothing more exciting than a spare pack of tarot cards and some faded laminated menus from the café's past. Freya picked the cards up but they were new and shiny and several scattered over the floor. Scooping them up, she shuddered to see Death, the Dark Man and the Lovers. Unnerved and knowing she shouldn't be snooping, she pushed them back in the pack and slammed the cupboard door on them.

Deciding it was safer to stay in the café, she took up position behind the counter once again, her fingers fidgeting to be active. Usually when she felt like this Freya would draw. Back in London she'd never been without pencil and sketchbook, even doodling away in wine bars while waiting for her friends to arrive. Outside, the clouds were shifting; a spectral light filled the sky, an unusual, bruised brightness that fascinated her. She took a few photos on her phone but the reproduction was flat, lifeless. She knew she could paint it better but she squashed that feeling down and buried it.

Sensing rain in the air, she decided to bring the outside chairs in. It was four o'clock and she doubted they'd be getting any customers, so she began the packing-up and cleaning-down process, wrapping up the cakes to keep them fresh, wiping down the coffee machine. A low thrum began to grow along the harbour, and Freya, never having heard a storm make such an unusual sound, stopped wiping tables and hurried back to the window.

Peering through the blinds, she watched as a large black and chrome motorbike pulled up in front of the café, the engine nosily announcing its arrival. What on earth? The rider dismounted, pulled off his helmet and ran his hands through long, thick, tangled dark hair. Freya's heart juddered as she watched him march over to the harbour wall, place his hands upon it and survey the deserted beach. Then he spun round and took in the village as if sizing it up. Freya flinched and let the blind drop in case he saw her spying. Quickly scooting behind the counter Freya tried to look as if she was busy working and not spying.

The door swung open, the bell jingling a warning, and the rider stepped inside. Tall and broad and dressed head to toe in bikers' leathers, he was a black mark on their otherwise pristine café. Freya's eyes widened, intrigued. He was not their usual clientele; something about him looked unnerved, as if he wasn't quite sure what he was doing in such a quaint place. He took a few steps inside, taking in the chintzy chair coverings, the small vases of flowers, the shelf of floral teapots. He was attractive, in a dishevelled Jesus kind of way, if that was your thing. Freya realized with a jolt that, actually, it might be her thing.

He rubbed his face and said, in a voice that was almost a growl, 'Where am I?'

Their eyes met and it was as if all the air had been sucked out of the room.

Freya stared at him, blinking in disbelief, and said, 'Sorry, what? Lola's café.'

'No, where am I? What is this place?' He swung his arm towards the window to indicate the village.

Freya continued to stare at him, confused. Who on earth

70

didn't know where they had driven to? 'You don't know where you are?'

'Yep,' he said, adding with a nervous laugh, 'something like that.' At least he had the decency to look embarrassed.

Having never heard anything quite so ridiculous, Freya told him, 'Polcarrow Bay. You're in Cornwall.'

The man tried the name out several times, and, seemingly deciding he liked it, nodded to himself and made his way over to the counter. Freya got a not-too-unpleasant waft of leather and wild man. Despite his jumpy manner, his dark eyes glittered with barely concealed amusement as he looked at her. 'Does it get busy here?'

Freya thought about lying, or laying on her best local tourist board act, but something about him made her think he'd not come for the scenery. 'Actually,' she admitted, 'I don't know. I've not been here long myself. I'm helping my friend in the café for the summer.' She watched as he digested this, carefully considering her words. He loomed over her like a shadow; long dark hair, dark eyes and skin that looked as if it should be tanned, but was rather tainted with a sleepless pallor. The dark man, a voice echoed, which she instantly dismissed. Lola was not going to be right about this. But could it be? No, Freya was done with love. Plus, this man clearly had no idea where he'd travelled to; he didn't exactly seem the most reliable sort to throw her heart at, even if he was wolfishly attractive.

'Can I get you anything?' Freya asked.

'A double espresso, please. It's been a long day.' He smiled, visibly relaxing, and studied the menu chalked on the board behind Freya. 'And a toastie. Ham and cheese would be fine. If it's not too much trouble – if you're packing up, don't worry.'

Freya flashed him her best customer-service smile. 'Don't worry – no trouble at all.' Their eyes met; something flickered between them, and they both stepped back.

Freya tore her eyes away from his and keyed the order into the till before making his coffee, strong and black like fuel. She was pleased to have the distraction of the hiss and gurgle of the machine, not to mention the delicious aroma, to give her something else than this stranger to concentrate on. With a flurry and a smile, she passed it to him. The man picked up the cup and inhaled, relief washing over his face. 'Bliss,' was all he said.

'Take a seat,' Freya said. 'I'll go and make your sandwich.'

She ducked into the kitchen, flicked on the toastie machine and waited for what felt like forever for it to heat up. While she waited for the cheese to ooze out of the corners of the bread, she gave herself a stern talking-to. There had been plenty of good-looking men popping in and out of the London cafés she'd worked in; she shouldn't be this flustered by an attractive man. Then again, she mused as she checked how the toastie was coming along, none of them had ever made her feel like she was all thumbs like this one did. Lola would've parped something about love at first sight, but Freya flushed at the ridiculousness of this notion. Better, she decided, to concentrate on what she was good at: feeding customers.

The sandwich was done, the smell savoury and tempting, and Freya wished she hadn't filled up on caramel shortbread earlier. She carried it out to him and was taken aback to see he'd taken a seat at the table closest to the counter, facing her, when there was a whole stormy sea view to feast his eyes on. He was looking at her, almost studying her, and she found she couldn't take her eyes off him either. Her brain forgot how to engage someone in conversation, so she just placed the plate in front of him and stood there awkwardly with a smile on her face.

'Thanks, that smells divine.' He gave her a wolfish smile and tore into the toastie. Realizing it would be weird to watch him eat, Freya placed herself safely back behind the counter and pretended to be busy sorting out the condiments.

Silence descended, and as it grew around them, the café felt full of questions. Freya slipped looks at the man; his phone was on the table and he was swiping things on the screen in a rapid, dismissive manner. Then he turned the phone off and put it in his pocket. Why would you turn your phone off, Freya wondered, unless you didn't want anyone to contact you? There was something almost jumpy about the man, an alert energy as if he was almost waiting to be caught. Half of her wanted to tell him to calm down; he was putting her on edge.

Unable to stand the silence much longer, Freya asked, in what she hoped was a conversational way, 'So, what brings you here?'

Sandwich paused halfway to his mouth, he seemed to

consider the question for a few seconds. Perhaps he was figuring out an alibi, Freya thought. The man was just about to answer when the door was thrown open and a rather damp Lola swept in. She threw her umbrella in the corner and let out a puff of air.

'Christ almighty, it's blowing a gale out there! Whose bike is that . . .' She trailed off as her eyes fell on the man's broad, leather-clad back. Lola raised an expertly plucked eyebrow and mouthed to Freya, 'The dark man!'

Freya rolled her eyes. Lola sauntered over to the man and gave him a smile that was much sunnier than the weather outside. 'Hello. Is that your bike?'

'Yes,' he said, throwing a glance at Freya for reassurance, seemingly confused by the intrusion. 'I can move it if it's a problem.'

Lola shook her head. 'Oh no, leave it, you'll get soaked going back out there. Honestly, I've never seen a storm like it.' She clocked the coffee cup and now empty plate. 'Glad to see Freya has been looking after you, erm . . .'

'Angelo,' he supplied, annoyance flashing in his eyes. Freya shook her head in disbelief at Lola's skills; she was a masterclass in getting people to reveal their secrets.

Lola, her lemon gingham dress splattered with rain, pulled out the chair opposite him and sat down, picking up where Freya had left off. 'What brings you down here? We don't get many bikers in these parts – mostly ramblers and kids wanting to build sandcastles.'

Angelo scratched the back of his head nervously. 'Well, I

just needed to get away for a . . . bit,' he explained lamely, in a way that did nothing to douse their intrigue.

'Well, you can't get more away than down here!' Lola said cheerily.

Freya folded her arms and gave her friend a pointed look, trying to tell her she'd had this under control and didn't appreciate the intrusion. There was no chance of her getting a word in edgeways once Lola was in full investigation mode. In disbelief, she watched as Lola reached for the man's hand and peered at his palm.

'Hmmm . . . interesting, interesting,' she mused to herself.

Angelo snatched his hand away angrily. 'I'm sorry, but I don't go in for fortune-telling.'

Taken aback, Lola stood up and joined forces with Freya behind the counter. 'Is there anything else we can get you?' she asked rather stiffly.

Angelo gave a nervous smile. 'Actually, there is, I was wondering if you know of anywhere I can stay? Nothing fancy – a hotel, caravan, bed and breakfast. I think it's too much to go back out again today.'

Lola turned to Freya, eyes like saucers, and Freya felt all control over her own life vanish. She gave Lola a warning look but she was in full, mad matchmaking mode.

'Well, actually, funny you should ask,' she said. 'There's a flat above this café that I was hoping to use as a holiday let. It's a bit basic – I haven't had a chance to add the finishing touches – but there's a bed and a kitchen and small bathroom. You are more than welcome to stay for as long as you wish.'

Lola quoted a price so low he was unable to refuse, and Angelo looked from Freya to Lola and back again, almost as if seeking her approval. The way he looked at her made her feel off-kilter yet grounded at the same time. There was something familiar about him, something she couldn't quite place. She gave a tiny encouraging nod to show she was happy for him to stay.

'Okay, well, that sounds grand, looks like today is my lucky day!' He laughed, but it was with false mirth, as if the day had been anything but lucky. 'I'll just get my things.'

When he was safely out of the café, Freya turned to Lola and hissed, 'What on earth are you doing? I had that under control before you came in!'

'The dark man!' Lola whispered back, grabbing Freya and giving her a little shake. 'My God, the way he looked at you!'

Freya rolled her eyes. 'We've been through this. No matchmaking. No men. He didn't even know where he was when he rocked up, so he's hardly a good candidate.' Although part of her was dying to hear exactly what Lola meant about the way he'd looked at her.

Freya's protests only seemed to make Lola more interested. 'I love a man with a hidden story.'

Freya shook her head, resigned, and before she could argue further, Angelo came back in, carrying a small bag, his hair wet from the rain.

'Travelling light?' Lola quipped.

'You could say that,' he sparred back.

Freya, pleased to see that he would not be so easily pulled into any games, gave Lola a satisfied smile.

But Lola was not easily discouraged. 'Okay, follow me, I'll take you up.' She grabbed the keys from her bag.

Angelo did as he was bid, with Freya following behind. They made their way up the small narrow staircase that led directly from the café to the flat above. Lola unlocked and pushed the door open, standing aside for Angelo to enter. From her vantage point, Freya thought the flat looked depressingly like student accommodation; magnolia walls in much need of brightening, a dated kitchen and a basic dark red curtain hanging a bit pathetically across the window. At least it would have a sea view, she reasoned.

Plonking his bag on the kitchen table, Angelo made his way over to the living area, peering through the window at the squally sea view.

'It's perfect,' he announced, pulling a wodge of cash from his pocket and peeling off enough twenty-pound notes to cover a month's rent.

Lola took them, slipped them into her dress pocket and held out her hand. 'A pleasure doing business with you, Angelo . . .'

'Borelli.' He froze, realizing his misstep. His handshake was firm but swift as he drew away.

Angelo Borelli, Freya repeated to herself as he turned away, indicating their presence was no longer welcome. That name rang a bell.

*

Lola hurriedly listed all of the local amenities to Angelo before they left him to settle in. Freya locked up the café, casting a glance at his bike; it looked like Angelo had just swerved onto the pavement rather than making any attempt to park properly. They made their way towards the cottage, the wind battering them. The sky scowled, the clouds gathered low, muscling in for a fight. It amazed Freya. She loved watching nature unfold, and although a sunrise was easy on the eye, a storm was much more thrilling; there was more to be awed by. Her parents had always had to stop her standing in the middle of the lawn when it thundered. A low rumble on the horizon sent a familiar excited buzz through her.

'Coming?' Lola called, holding the cottage door open.

Freya shook her head and said, 'I want to watch the clouds for a moment. I love a storm.' Actually, what she needed was five minutes to get her thoughts together before Lola started on about Angelo.

'Suit yourself.' Lola shrugged and hurried into the safety of the cottage. Freya, finally alone, felt her shoulders drop and her breath begin to slow. She thought about Angelo's sudden arrival and how Lola had swooped in and taken over, and irritation flashed through Freya like the lighting breaking on the horizon. How dare Lola decide that Angelo was Freya's fate just because of some stupid card reading? Freya wasn't even sure she believed in all that hocus-pocus stuff, and inviting Angelo into their fold was definitely taking the joke a step too far. Freya wasn't blind: he was attractive in a smouldering bad-boy way, but surely, straight from a break-up, a smouldering bad boy was the last thing she needed. You need to heal, she told herself as her imagination threatened to run away from her. She needed to decide how she was going to live her life, not start mooning over dark-haired strangers. No matter how sexy. Or how they looked at her.

Freya closed her eyes and leant into the cold wind; it smelled of salt spray and change, fresh against her skin, slipping under her collar and whipping her hair all sorts of ways. It was cleansing, blowing out her mental cobwebs. Raindrops splashed on her bare arms, one, two like a gentle warning, insistent that she seek shelter, even though she'd never minded being out in the rain, never fussed about getting her hair ruined. As the rain grew more aggressive, Freya dug out her phone and took some photos of the gathering storm, the choppy sea, to keep them for later, still pretending she didn't want to grab some charcoal and furiously render the scene on paper. Slipping her phone into her pocket, she dashed across the street, splashing through the puddles.

By the time she'd reached the cottage, the storm had set in, thunder cracking out over the bay and the heavens releasing a torrent of rain. Freya let herself in and grabbed a towel; she'd have a nice warming bath later. She peered around the door to the living room, where Lola was curled up on the sofa, her laptop balanced on an embroidered cushion, and a mischievous glint in her eyes.

'I don't want to know!' Freya held out a hand in protest as she rubbed her hair dry.

'But . . . surely you're curious?' Lola's eyes were wide and greedy. 'A gorgeous man washes up on our shores, looking a bit shifty, and pays rent for a month? Surely you want to know why!'

Freya shook her head. 'Of course I do, but . . .' She trailed off, wondering how to explain. 'Think about it, if he's trying to get away from something, then he probably wants some privacy.'

'Nonsense. I'm his landlady – it's my prerogative to find out about who's renting my flat.'

Freya flopped onto the other end of the sofa and closed her eyes. 'What would you do if you found out he was wanted for murder? Or something like that.'

'Well, call the police. I'm not totally daft, and I wouldn't try and set you up with a criminal.' Lola pretended to be offended.

They sat in silence listening to the storm raging outside, the wind whistling spookily down the chimney. Angelo Borelli; the name was still irritating her. Her mind kept catching on it. Whatever Lola had discovered settled tantalizingly between them. Lola made a big show of tapping some buttons, peering at the screen and making surprised little noises.

'Okay . . . I give up! One thing,' Freya groaned.

Lola's eyes shone. She leant over her laptop and, making the words sound like a lure, uttered, 'He's an artist.' Then with a dramatic flourish slammed the laptop shut.

Freya shot up. An artist; that was it! That was why she recognized his name. Angelo Borelli had been the wild child of the art world, taking it by storm in his early twenties with an exhibition that had sold out and garnered demands for his work. He had been mooted as the next big thing but had vanished into obscurity soon after. His story was used as a moral, a warning rather than something to aspire to.

'No way,' Freya whispered, feeling like she had stumbled upon artistic gold. 'No way.' The desire to try to unearth what had gone wrong and to solve the modern art world's biggest mystery battled with the knowledge that coming to a tiny fishing hamlet on the wild coast of Cornwall were the actions of a man who wished to be left alone.

Freya turned to her friend. 'Lola, we have to leave him alone, okay? He was sort of a big deal about ten, twelve years ago, and then he vanished from the art world,' she explained. 'I imagine whatever reason brought him here, it's not one he wants us sticking our noses into. I don't care if you think he's my soulmate or whatever – he's probably trying to sort some issues out, and there's something a bit shifty about him, like he's on the run.' Freya shrugged, indicating it was some inexplicable feeling she had.

Lola slid the laptop back onto the bookshelf. 'Okay,' she replied slowly, 'we'll wait for him to tell us.' She closed her eyes and rubbed her temples, making a show of pretending to channel something. 'He's clearly come away to be fixed. I'll pull some cards for him, get some guidance.'

'No.' Freya firmly placed her hand on Lola's as she reached for her cards. 'I think we should just leave him be. Not everyone needs fixing – some of us just need to figure things out.'

Lola considered this while staring out at the changing light, the sky like a purple shroud shot through with silver fronds. She nodded and squeezed Freya's hand. 'Okay, if it's that important to you, I'll leave him to come to us.'

Chapter Six

A group of schoolboys were gathered around Angelo's bike when Freya arrived to unlock the café the following morning. The less bold of the bunch took a step back, but their leader carried on, proclaiming all sorts of probably made-up knowledge about the bike and how fast he'd gone when he'd ridden one. Considering he was about twelve, Freya thought this highly unlikely, but his enthusiasm made her smile as she unlocked the café. Their boisterous boasting was soon carried away by the school bus and Freya was left to the washed-clean peace of the morning. A few wispy clouds covered the blue sky and the early-morning sun shone in the puddles. She offered up a silent thank you that she had been so lucky as to end up somewhere as beautiful and inspiring as Polcarrow. *Inspiring* – she hadn't used that word for a long time. The Cornish coast was certainly working its charm. She busied herself with the start of the day chores, giving the tables a wipe, turning on the radio and setting up the till.

'Good morning,' a voice said. 'Glad to see you survived the storm! Did it wash that bike up?'

Freya looked up from where she was fitting a new till

roll. 'Oh hi, Tristan. Yes, we survived. And Lola's taken in another waif and stray – he's upstairs.'

Tristan smiled fondly. 'Lola the good Samaritan, always doing a good deed.'

Freya studied him; there was definitely something going on there. 'Your usual, vicar?' she asked.

'Yes, please. Tea and toast. Lola not about?'

'No, not yet, she's gone to pick up some eggs from the farm.'

Tristan nodded, clearly disappointed, his blonde hair flopping onto his forehead. He was, Freya had to admit, a very pleasantly attractive man. 'Well, I hope she won't leave you too long on your own; I reckon you'll be busy today.' He indicated the bike. 'The villagers do like to sniff out the gossip.'

Tristan was right. The same welcome party that had turned up to inspect her arrived to sniff out Angelo later that morning, although Freya liked to think that Alf was just after his usual flapjack, which he crumbled up, feeding bits to Scruff.

'Imagine having a go on that!' His eyes sparkled with youthful excitement as he jerked a thumb towards the bike. 'Imagine the speeds it gets up to.'

Freya shuddered. 'I'm not sure it's for me, Alf, but maybe if you speak nicely to the owner, he'll give you a go.'

Alf spluttered with laughter. 'I'm eighty-nine, love. Wouldn't even be able to get on it! You're young, what have you got to be afraid of?'

'Falling off, doing myself an injury, death?' she suggested with a shrug.

Alf shook his head. 'Youngsters these days,' he said sadly and ruffled Scruff's ears. 'You're too scared of living, that's it. In my youth, we were off in those fishing boats, rain or shine, waves as high as the church tower – it was just what we did. Now, love, can I have another piece of that flapjack? I think Scruff stole most of it.' He winked.

Freya didn't mind Alf giving her a bit of a poke, even if she suspected he might be right and that made her a little uncomfortable. She wasn't scared, she reminded herself; surely running away to the seaside was a bit off the sensible scale? But she didn't have time to further contemplate Alf's words because the café was soon heaving. Thankfully, by the time all of the tables were occupied, Lola had made it back with her boxes of eggs, a wheel of cheese and some ham, and proceeded to knock out a cherry and almond tray bake, which flew off the shelves.

'Bloody nosey lot,' Lola muttered from the kitchen door. 'What are they expecting? A grand unveiling?'

Whatever they were expecting, Angelo did not oblige. Freya was amused to see the villagers lingering over their coffees, or coming in for lunch when they usually grabbed something to take away. In the middle of the rush, Cathy came bustling in and plonked her handbag on the counter, her stare as steely as her bob.

'Who does that monstrosity outside belong to?' she demanded shrilly. The café instantly hushed to listen in.

'We have a guest. He arrived yesterday evening after a long journey,' Freya explained patiently.

'I don't care! He can't just leave his bike blocking the pavement like that. It's an eyesore!'

Several pairs of eyes turned towards the window as if trying to see it from Cathy's perspective.

'Can you ask him to move it? Now, please?'

'I'm sorry, but he's had a long journey and he's not up yet. I don't think it's fair to go banging on his door,' Freya said, trying for a friendly, apologetic tone.

Cathy tutted. 'Sounds like a lazy good-for-nothing. We don't want those sorts of Hells Angels in our village, disrupting our quiet way of life. Can you go and ask him to move it? If not, I will.' She stepped towards the door that separated the café from the flat, but Lola, having heard the commotion, swiftly blocked her way.

'You will do no such thing. As Freya said, he had a long journey, and you will not be waking him. The bike is doing no harm out there, but I will ask him to move it when he is up and about. Now, can I get you anything?' Lola added sweetly.

Flustered, Cathy blustered, 'No.' Defeated, she snatched her bag off the counter and stormed out. Not wishing to incur the wrath of Lola, everyone else quickly turned back to their plates or companions, suddenly engrossed.

The villagers soon grew tired of waiting for Angelo to make an appearance and decided it was better to just get on with their day. By three o'clock, the café was empty, except for a group of ramblers tucking into steaming bowls of tomato soup and thick cheese toasties while trying to outdo each other over whose feet were more tired.

Lola had an appointment to provide some crystal healing for a client over in the next bay, so skipped out, chasing off the schoolboys who couldn't believe their luck that the bike was still there. Freya was left to close up, which she didn't mind. It was satisfying to set the café straight at the end of the day, tucking the chairs under, wiping down the tables and mopping the floor; making order of everything helped calm her mind. She made herself focus on each task, which meant she didn't think about Matt, or failing her degree. Freya's nights had been disturbed with worry, which she hadn't shared with Lola. Her friend had a habit of either blowing troubles aside, as if they were nothing more than dandelion seeds, wishes to be cast into the air, or launching into a full forensic investigation of the issue. Freya needed some space to solve her own problems.

Freya took her time pulling down the blinds and flipping the sign to closed. The café was quiet, almost too quiet. She strained to listen for movement upstairs but there was nothing. Who on earth spent all day stuck in some tiny flat? Surely all the commotion in the café would have woken Angelo.

Freya picked up her bag. It was none of her business; she was getting as bad as the rest of the villagers. But at the door she paused, trying to pinpoint why she was so worried. It was undeniably odd for him not to surface. What if he was dead?

No – Freya shook her head – that was overdramatic. But in the light of such thoughts, she decided that a little check-up wouldn't hurt.

Leaving her bag on the counter, she tentatively made her way up the stairs, concerned, not curious, she repeated to herself. Freya paused on the landing and listened. She couldn't hear any sounds so tentatively knocked on the door. Three slightly apologetic raps echoed in the space, but there was no response. She tried again, harder this time, but still nothing. Where was he? Reaching out, she tried the handle, and to her surprise, the door opened. What sort of person left their door unlocked? A complete idiot or – she gasped – someone who wanted to be found?

Freya pushed the door open and quickly stepped inside. The air was thick with the stale scent of unwashed man and the lingering grease of fish and chips; the remnants were strewn across the kitchen table as if eating had been an after-thought. So, he had braved the storm after all. She almost tripped over his boots, kicked off in the doorway, one keeled over, the other standing above it like a victor.

'Hello?' Freya called, her voice slicing through the neglected stillness of the apartment. His keys were tossed carelessly on the side, his bag in the doorway to the living area. The detritus of Angelo's small life littered every surface as if to mark his territory.

No answer. Fear prickled at the back of her throat. Freya's foot caught on something, and when she stooped down to pick it up, her hands folded around his T-shirt, black but greyed from too many washes. Before she even knew what she was doing, Freya lifted it to her nose and inhaled; the sharp tang of sweat, the residual warmth of his skin, smoky and tanned. She breathed deeper and inhaled the scent of summer days, of fear, of adventure. She smelled his secrets woven into that fabric, the faded remnants of the life he had led. His shirt reeked of mystery and misery and Freya kept hold of it as she gingerly tiptoed into the living room.

The curtains were drawn against the evening light and the room was thick with the fug of second-hand alcohol. There was a single glass on the coffee table and on the floor an empty bottle of whisky. Freya picked it up and winced. It was not a quality brand; clearly chosen for oblivion. She placed it down on the table before glancing towards the sofa, where Angelo was lying, face down but thankfully still breathing.

Freya stepped forward, reached out to wake him, and then stopped. On his bare back was the most magnificent tattoo she had ever seen. Jesus on the cross ran up his spine flanked by the two Marys on his lower back and two weeping angels on his shoulder blades. Why on earth would someone have a crucifixion tattooed for all eternity on their back? Freya leant closer, holding her breath, not ready to disturb him and not wanting to be caught. Through the half-light, she studied the faces, beautifully executed with painstaking detail. How long had it taken? What agony had he endured for it? She stopped herself from touching him. Wanting a better look, she pulled back the curtain and the daylight flooded into the room. As it dawned over Angelo, he winced and groaned. Freya flinched back, caught out.

With nothing else for it, Freya pulled back the other curtain and stood in the light, arms crossed, his T-shirt still balled in her hand, and watched as he squirmed back into life.

'What day is it?' he croaked, his voice ravaged by whisky. He rolled onto his back and threw his arm across his eyes.

'Thursday.' She angrily threw the T-shirt at him, and he looked at her in surprise. He didn't seem bothered that she was in his flat. 'Everyone has been fussing around the café all day wanting to have a look at you, or wanting you to move your bike, or both.'

Angelo shrugged and grunted, clearly not caring if his bike had been an inconvenience.

Exasperated, Freya shook her head, gaze flashing around the room as she composed herself. 'Anyway,' she retorted, 'what were you doing drinking all that whisky?' She seized the bottle and shook it at him. 'You could have choked on your vomit or something.'

'What do you care?' he snapped, but his heart clearly wasn't in it.

'And you left your door unlocked. Anyone could have come in. They could have stolen your keys or wallet or . . .' She threw her hands up, exasperated by this man who seemed to care so little.

'But then how would you have found me if I'd died choking on my vomit? You would have had to bash the door down.' Despite the state he was in, his dark eyes glinted with humour, leaving her speechless.

With a thump Freya set the bottle back down and went into the kitchen. She ran the tap, filled a glass and carried it back to him. 'That's going to be one hell of a hangover when you properly wake up,' she warned him. 'I have some paracetamol downstairs. Join me when you're ready and I'll get you something to eat,' was her parting peace offering.

Think, Freya, think, she urged herself as she entered the kitchen and started pacing. Running her hands desperately through her hair, she breathed deeply to calm herself. She flung open various cupboards, searching for inspiration, and then pulled open the fridge. Bacon sandwich! That'd do it; the classic, perfect hangover cure. She whacked the bacon on the counter and switched the grill on, then cut two slices of bread and popped them in the toaster.

'Ugh,' a voice groaned and Angelo staggered into the kitchen. 'I've not been this hungover in years!' He pulled up a stool and collapsed onto it, head in hands, dishevelled hair all over the place. He peered through it. 'Is that bacon?' His stomach rumbled loudly.

'Do you want a coffee? Or is that a silly question?'

Angelo smirked. 'Double espresso, please.'

Freya nipped into the café and quickly made his coffee, dark and strong enough to wake the dead. She placed it and a selection of sugar packets in front of him. Angelo stirred in one sugar, waited a few agonizingly long seconds for the coffee to cool, and then gulped it back. This time he groaned with happiness. Freya checked the bacon; it was sizzling nicely and making her own stomach grumble.

'Thank you,' he said. 'I must clarify this isn't normally what I do – rock up at a place, dump my bike on the pavement, get completely wasted. It's been ... well ... a tough couple of months.' He sighed and glanced away, clearly not wanting to elaborate.

Freya shrugged, trying to play it cool. 'It just seemed a bit odd not seeing you all day. I did wonder if you might be dead or something. Or, clearly, just hiding.'

Angelo laughed. 'You really thought that I might be dead?' He looked intrigued.

'Honestly? I had no idea. I thought we'd see you at some point today, and when you didn't appear, something just didn't feel right,' she explained with a shrug, not quite ready to acknowledge quite how relieved she felt that he was fine. 'Don't worry, I won't tell anyone about the whisky, even though I can't believe you drank a whole bottle!' She grimaced and shuddered.

'Funnily enough, neither can I. My God, I can feel it now. I think I'm just going to eat this and go back to bed.' Angelo groaned again, his head in his hands.

'I'd suggest a walk along the seafront to clear your head, but I suspect the braying crowd is still out there.' She checked the bacon; nicely crisp without being burned. Her stomach grumbled again, and she wondered why she'd not whipped one up for herself.

'Did they honestly come in today just to gawk at me?' He glanced around twitchily, as if expecting the villagers to be hiding in the kitchen cabinets. 'I came here to get away from things like that, find some peace.'

Although curious, Freya ignored the theatrics and placed the sandwich in front of him. 'Sauce?'

'Yes, brown, please.'

She passed him the bottle and tried to reassure him. 'They mean well. They're interested, that's all. Lola, Tristan and I all got the same treatment, but we are a bit less Hells Angels than you are … so …' She shrugged, but Angelo wasn't really listening anyway; having swigged his coffee he was now concentrating on the sandwich.

Angelo took a bite and sighed with pleasure. 'Oh God, that's good. Can you look after me like this all the time?'

As she wasn't known for her culinary skills, Freya put the compliment down to his famished state. 'No, you're a grown man; you can look after yourself,' she quipped as she began to tidy up the kitchen. She concentrated on wiping down the grill and putting the bacon away, trying to give him a bit of privacy. But the silence grew and Freya couldn't resist testing the water. 'What brings you here?' she asked in what she hoped was a casual voice.

The atmosphere suddenly grew tense and taut; it crept up Freya's arms. She risked a glance at him. He was staring at his half-eaten sandwich, deep in thought, as if wrestling with something. Angelo looked up and caught her eye; the playful light from moments ago had gone out.

'If it's all very well with you, I'd rather not talk about it. I'm still figuring some things out,' he replied gruffly, and picking up his sandwich, counter-attacked with the same question. 'Why are you here? You said you were here for the summer.'

'Well remembered.' Freya paused. What should she tell him? All of it? No; she couldn't face telling anyone about the degree. 'I split up with my boyfriend and had nowhere else to go,' she said with false brightness. 'And what's better than a summer by the sea?'

Angelo studied her, clearly suspecting that she was telling him a severely edited version of her story. 'I'm sorry to hear that,' was all he said. Polite, not wanting to venture into more personal waters. There was a long silence and then he asked, 'Freya, do you mind if we keep this our secret? I'm a bit embarrassed by it, to be honest.'

'The drinking? No problem! And don't be, we've all been there.' She offered him a reassuring smile.

Angelo laughed. 'Somehow I don't see you as the downing a bottle of whisky sort.'

Freya grimaced. 'When I was sixteen, my best friend at the time managed to get hold of a bottle of tequila and three of us hid in the local woods and downed it. Just after completing our final GCSEs. I've never been that ill in my life, and I've never touched tequila since.' Freya shuddered at the memory; she'd felt rotten for days. Not to mention how mad her mum had been when she'd finally managed to stagger home, minus one of her shoes. 'It was fun at the time.'

Angelo smiled fondly at the confession. 'Let's not go into my hidden wild youth, before you ask.'

'Oh! So there is one,' she teased, realizing he had no idea that she knew who he was. That sort of wild youth made hers seem amateur. Booze, women and probably drugs.

'Yes, and that is all I'm saying.' He stood up to signal the finality of his statement and brought the plate over to Freya at the sink. He passed it to her. 'Thank you.' He gave her a long look that made her insides squirm. 'What on earth would I have done without you?' His voice was soft, ponderous, and the words spoken almost to himself. He stepped back. 'Well, I'd better go and move my bike before the villagers chase me out with pitchforks. See you tomorrow,' he called from the door, 'and thank you!'

Freya squeezed washing-up liquid onto a sponge and finished cleaning, telling herself that she was just flushed from the hot water, not from the rather hot man who'd landed at her feet.

Chapter Seven

The following day dawned like a bright promise of summer.
Blue skies without a single wisp of cloud. Freya could smell
the sun lotion and taste the ice cream already, and excitement rushed through her when she set up the tables outside.
Angelo had kept his word and moved his bike, much to the
disappointment of the schoolboys. Freya imagined Cathy's
smug face when she noticed it had gone and part of her
wished he'd left it on the pavement a little longer.

'Looks like our visitor's been up and about,' Lola
commented.

Freya merely nodded. Lola hadn't asked why she'd been
late back last night, too busy trying out a new recipe for a
chocolate cherry cake, which had gone down well with a
glass of pink fizz. She'd also been figuring out some summer
plans for the café. Freya had been all too happy to pitch
in, although she wasn't as enthusiastic about Lola's suggestion to offer frappés; they'd always been her least favourite
thing to make.

Lola now bustled into the kitchen, leaving the leftover
chocolate cherry cake on the counter.

'Give some to Tristan and Alf; see what they think,' she instructed as she pulled her apron on.

'Okay!' Freya trimmed a bit off for her own breakfast. She really was going to have to take up running; she was naturally lean, but being surrounded by cake all day surely wasn't going to do her any good. She went through the usual routine of making coffees, pulling up the blinds, setting up for the day.

Tristan turned up, local paper tucked under his arm. 'The usual?' Freya called from the counter as he sat at his favourite table.

'Of course! I see the bike has gone. That'll please some quarters.' Tristan peered out of the window before sitting down. 'Glorious morning out – maybe the forecasters will be right about the heatwave?'

'It'd be lovely if they were, but every year they predict the hottest summer ever. At least it'll be nicer than being in a London flat.' Freya brought his tea over, a slice of chocolate cherry cake on the side. 'It's a new recipe Lola is trying out. Apparently you're her designated guinea pig.'

Tristan looked at it curiously and took a bite, chewing thoughtfully. 'Whenever Lola does this I like to pretend I'm a judge on the Great British Bake Off, not that I know an awful lot about cakes. It's very nice – I'd certainly order it if it was on the menu. It's got a good . . . erm . . . crumb, is that what they say? Nice cake to icing ratio. Bit early for cake for me, though.' But that didn't stop him polishing it off.

Freya passed the feedback on to Lola when she collected the vicar's toast. 'Cake has passed religious muster.'

Lola sighed with relief. It seemed strange that her heathen soul would crave holy approval for her bakes. 'Try Alf, but make sure he doesn't feed it all to Scruff. I don't think dogs are meant to have chocolate and I won't be held responsible.'

Alf was delighted to be used to test Lola's cake. 'Oh, come on, love, a bigger bit than that. How can I tell you what it's like from a morsel?' Freya laughed as he mimed peering through a magnifying glass and swapped it for what Alf called 'a proper slice'.

'That's mighty good. Scruff approves.' The dog greedily licked the crumbs off his fingers. They were laughing at Scruff begging for more when the door from the flat opened. Angelo stepped in and silence descended.

Freya straightened up; he looked a lot better than he had last night. The shadows under his eyes had been slept away and his hair was damp from the shower. She smiled reassuringly at him, trying to indicate that none of them would bite. Not even Scruff, who was the soppiest thing. 'Morning,' Freya said gently. 'How are you?'

'Much better, thank you.' His eyes flittered around the café; he seemed relieved that there was only a small welcome party.

'Well, don't just stand there, boy, come over here and say hello.' Alf pushed the third chair away from the table and patted it. 'Scruff doesn't bite!'

'Can I get you anything?' Freya asked with her best waitress smile in place.

'Yes, double espresso, please.'

Angelo sat down with the other two men, and seemingly trying to take the focus off himself, he bent down and gave Scruff a scratch behind the ears. The old sheepdog closed his eyes in doggy bliss. Freya smiled to herself to see that once Angelo was relaxed and his attention elsewhere, Alf chose his moment.

'I'm Alf, I've lived here all my life. What I don't know about Polcarrow isn't worth knowing. I'm eighty-nine. I remember when we used to fish from this harbour – oh, those were happy days. Now, it's just me and old Scruff here. You've caused quite a stir here, young man.' Alf sat back and studied Angelo for a long time. 'No worries, though, I'm sure you'll reveal yourself when the time is right. Don't listen to those busybodies; they're just nosey. I told Freya the same. Don't pay them any mind. You here for long?'

Freya set the coffee down on the table and, as an after-thought, a slice of the chocolate cherry cake, accidently cutting Angelo off as he vaguely told Alf he was trying to get a different perspective on life.

'But I don't . . .' Angelo stared at the gooey cake.

'It's a new recipe. Lola's trialling it. Anyway, who doesn't eat cake?' Admittedly, Angelo didn't look the sort to tuck into a slice of Victoria sponge but Freya just smiled and held out a fork.

'It's very good. If you don't eat it quickly, Scruff will be after it,' Alf warned.

Angelo took a bite and the others tried very hard not to study him as he ate. 'I don't know much about cake,' he

confessed, clearly out of his comfort zone. 'It's good, very . . .
light. Thought it would be a lot sweeter, being . . . chocolate.'

'I'll pass all your feedback on to the chef. I'll leave you to
get acquainted.' Freya figured that it couldn't hurt for Angelo
to have a couple more allies in the village. She ducked into
the kitchen to watch from the window. Alf was clearly telling
Angelo some long-winded story, but she was surprised to see
that Angelo looked engrossed in it. Tristan nodded along and
they both laughed at the funny bits.

'What's happening?' Lola squeezed in next to Freya. 'Ah,
good. The initiation ceremony. They seem to be getting on
well.' She turned to Freya and announced, 'I'm giving you
the morning off.'

'Why?' she asked suspiciously.

Lola raised an eyebrow. 'You'll see.' With that, she sashayed through the café, Freya trailing in her wake. Tristan's
eye's nearly popped out of his head when he saw her.

'Good morning, Angelo. I trust the apartment is all up to
scratch?' Lola enquired.

'Yes, yes, it's fine.' He shifted in his chair, rightly suspi-
cious that something was going on.

'And it's such a glorious day outside, it would be a shame
to waste it. I'm giving Freya the morning off to show
you around. She's new here, so I'm sure you'll have lots
in common.'

Freya and Angelo stared at each other agog. Both aware
of Lola's unsubtle intentions, yet feeling like two children
forced together at a family party.

'But, won't you need me here? If it's going to be a nice day, surely it'll be busy,' Freya protested.

'Nonsense, I can cope, and if you're not back in time for lunch, people will just have to be patient. Don't you find everyone is so demanding these days?' she asked the table.

The three men stared back at her, baffled. Then Alf nodded his head in agreement. 'People need to slow down.' He slurped his tea. 'Back in my day, there was never this need for the latest gadget or to go rushing about.'

'Right, that settles it, off you go.' Lola reached behind Freya and tugged at her apron tie. Resigned, Freya fought her off and did it herself, passing the apron back to Lola with narrowed eyes.

Without further ado, Angelo finished his coffee and followed Freya outside into the bright June sunshine. Tristan had been right: it was a glorious morning, one for sunbathing on the beach, and Freya was secretly pleased to have this small break from the café. Angelo followed her over to the harbour wall. Freya was at a loss as to how she, a newcomer herself, would tell Angelo anything useful about a village she was still sussing out. Alf would've been better suited to this job. Then again, Lola wasn't trying to matchmake Alf and Angelo.

She glanced up at Angelo. His head was back, eyes closed, soaking up the sun. Was this supposed to be some sort of first date? Freya had never been on a proper, grown-up date, so she had no idea what the etiquette was. Having met Matt at university, all that wining and dining, asking questions and assessing each other's life goals had passed her by. If Lily and Fiona's dreadful and comedic experiences were anything to go by, Freya didn't think dating sounded all that fun. But now, well, she could have a go with Angelo.

'We're being watched,' Freya told him in a low voice, even though they were too far away to be overheard.

Startled, Angelo glanced back and saw Lola, Tristan and Alf at the window, pretending not to watch them. 'Oh. Are they always like this?'

'Lola is. Not sure about the rest. Come on, the longer we stand here the longer they'll look. Warning – Lola is very nosey and if she gets an idea in her head then God help everyone!' Freya told him as they started to amble along the harbour wall to the sound of seagulls circling above.

'Oh, like what sorts of ideas?' Angelo stopped walking, worry flashing across his face, like he was mentally checking he'd closed all the doors on his secrets.

'Us,' was on the tip of her tongue, but looking up at his worried face she didn't dare say it. The panic in his eyes told Freya she'd been right not to pry into his past. Deciding to change the subject, she pointed to the blue fisherman's cottage. 'That's where we live. Well, it's Lola's; I just live with her.'

Angelo nodded. 'How do you know each other?'

'We worked together the summer after I graduated at some really naff cocktail bar that didn't last the season. It might not have been a dream job, but it was fun. Lola's always been a bit of a nomad. I only used to see her whenever she was passing through from one mad adventure to another. She's older than me, so had none of the hang-ups my other friends had. It was a blast. Cocktail drinking, dancing until dawn.' Freya smiled at the memories; life with Lola had been like a continuous festival. 'Needless to say, my ex-boyfriend and friends didn't really like her. Thought she had too much influence, but in my hour of need she was the only one with a proper solution.'

'People tend to be full of advice but never solutions,' he said wryly, glancing around. Angelo took in the wide sweep of beach, the cottages poking up from the hills like wonky teeth, the wild headland. 'What a perfect place to come.'

They reached the end of the harbour wall and stopped next to the pub. Freya smiled fondly at the little village, its brightly painted cottages, the languid pace of life. 'Yes, it is. I'd forgotten how quiet and gentle life can be.' She paused before asking, 'Are you feeling better after your night on the whisky?'

'Yes, thank you.' He cringed. 'I feel like such a fool. You should never have had to find me like that. I'm a grown man who should know better. I promise not to do a repeat performance.'

'I'll hold you to that.' Freya paused and looked up at him. 'You know, I'm not like Lola. If you ever want to talk about anything, just let me know.' She shrugged to indicate it was no big deal. 'I'm good at keeping secrets.'

'Oh, are you?' He looked amused. 'But how do I know I can trust you?'

Freya opened and closed her mouth. 'I guess you'll just

have to figure out if you can. I'm not a gossip.' She couldn't tell him she'd stopped Lola digging up his past on the internet, and if she let slip she knew who he was then she was sure Angelo would make a hasty retreat from their slowly forming bond.

Angelo took her hand and squeezed it. The touch transferred a warm fuzzy energy between them. 'Thanks, Freya. I believe you. I'm okay at the moment, though,' he said gently, and let go of her hand. 'What else is there to see?'

Still buzzing from the hand squeeze, Freya admitted, 'I'm probably not the best person for this tour. That would be Alf. It's a sort of sleepy place. There's some really old cottages, a few local shops, but none of the glitz or glamour of the bigger towns. No restaurants or galleries. Alf said it used to be a little fishing village, but no one wants to fish anymore. Too much like hard work!'

Angelo laughed at her spot-on impression of the old fisherman and they started to wend their way through the little streets. 'He's fantastic. I want to hear everything he has to say about living here. I had forgotten people like him existed.'

'I know. It's easy to get all wrapped up in that hectic London bubble. You forget life is simple in some places.' Freya glanced at him but he didn't take the London bait. They ambled their way up the street by the pub; it was steep, the cobbles worn away by centuries of feet rushing to and from the sea, and the incline set their pace to slow. They passed a jumble of holiday homes and local residences painted in jolly pastel shades, each with their own personalized items outside; hanging baskets, benches, flowerpots. It was picture-postcard quaint. Freya took a few photos.

'Anywhere else all these colours would look a bit silly.' Angelo ran his fingers over a lilac painted wall. 'Are you thinking of staying here?'

Freya stopped to take a photo of a beautiful pink and purple hanging basket, the colours rich like jewels. 'No idea. It's summer, and I'm helping Lola. I'm trying not to think about the future too much. My parents want me to train as a teacher, but I just can't face it. Too much work, I hope that doesn't make me sound lazy, but I always thought teaching was a calling, not a last-minute choice.'

'Not at all! Teaching is hard. I think you need some drive and ambition in that area to do it.' Angelo paused and gave the flowers in the basket a sniff. 'I think I'll join you in the not thinking too much about the future.' They reached the top edge of the village and turned around. The houses gently fell away towards the harbour. 'Wow, this is a small place. I bet everyone really does know everyone.' Angelo's voice jiggled with nerves.

'If you sneezed at breakfast everyone would know about it by lunchtime,' Freya quipped. 'I guess it's nice to be part of a community, though.' Hands on hips, she stared out to sea where the sun was glittering on the waves. 'I don't think anyone means any harm,' she reassured him, watching as he scanned the village.

'What's that building up there?' Angelo was pointing to a wide, art deco style house that sat at the top of the hill, presiding over the village.

Freya followed where he was pointing. 'Bayview House? I don't know much about it. Alf is the one to ask. I think it was built as a holiday home, but it's hardly been used. It's been for sale for ages, apparently, but it needs a lot of repairs so no one's prepared to take it on. It's a shame – imagine waking up to that view.' She sighed.

Angelo nodded, still looking at the house with curiosity.

'Come on, we've seen everything other than the church.' Freya started to make her way back down the hill towards the harbour; Angelo trailed behind her, casting backwards glances at the abandoned house. 'The local kids think it's haunted,' she added, since he seemed so interested in the house.

'And is it?' he asked, surprised.

Freya shrugged. 'It's always been empty; they're kids; maybe their parents told them that to stop them trespassing. Who knows?'

Angelo thought about this. 'Do you believe in ghosts?'

Freya laughed and considered her answer. 'I'm not sure. I don't think I'd like to see one. What about you?'

Angelo stuffed his hands in his pockets and gave the house one last lingering look. 'Yes, I think I do,' he said as if it had just occurred to him that he did.

'Fair enough. I'm sure Alf could tell you if it really is haunted.' Freya paused outside the church, hand on the door. 'But I reckon he'd think ghosts are a bit rubbish. Shall we go in?'

Angelo swallowed and looked up nervously at the building. 'Sure,' he said, clearly trying, and failing, to sound casual.

Freya paused. Why would a man with a crucifix tattoo on his back be anxious to go into a church? She almost asked but stopped herself. She'd made good progress – Angelo had opened up a bit – and she didn't want to cause the shutters to slam back down. 'Actually, I've not been in here myself. We can explore together.'

Angelo looked grateful at this suggestion. Freya held the door open and together they stepped through it. It creaked closed behind them, as it must have done behind generations of local families.

The church was simple, the walls painted white, the furnishings dark, polished wood, similar to every other small parish church she'd visited. Light flooded in through the windows on each side, but the thing that took her breath away was the window behind the altar: glass stained in all shades of blue, from deepest midnight to the frothiest sea foam, arched above the simple altar and flooded the church with a shimmering blue light, giving it the effect of being under the sea.

'I've never seen anything like it,' Angelo whispered. 'And I've been in so many beautiful Italian churches.'

'Neither have I. It's beautiful,' Freya said, too stunned to ask about the Italian churches Angelo had seen.

They moved down the aisle together, Freya's fingers drifting over the tops of the pews, nicked and scratched by praying hands. How many frantic prayers had been uttered in this building? Men lost at sea, sick children, money woes. It was beyond comprehension. Angelo drifted off, studying the plain walls. Church had never featured in Freya's life, other than the obligatory Christingle service when she was at school, and being inside one made her feel like she was trespassing. Like God would know she didn't believe. To believe must be a huge comfort, she thought.

Angelo was speaking almost to himself, running his hands over the smooth walls. 'It seems such a waste to have all this space and not have anything on them. If this was Italy it'd be covered in angels and saints ... and ...' He trailed off when he saw Freya watching him, and backed away as if he'd said too much.

She couldn't tell him she felt the same, that such an expanse of unadorned white wall made her fingers itch to fill it. She sat on the front pew, dazzled by the blue light, wondering whose idea it had been. Angelo wandered up to the altar, held his arms out into the light, and watched as it shimmered over his skin. Despite its simplicity, the church clearly captivated and fascinated him. For a man who had been reluctant to enter the church, he certainly seemed at peace now. His reaction was beautiful and Freya's resolve to protect him from the village gossip strengthened.

Their silent reverence was broken by the side door opening and banging shut. 'Oh, I didn't think we'd have visitors so early!' Tristan said.

Angelo jumped back as if caught.

'It's my fault; I brought us in here. The door was open,' Freya explained.

Tristan smiled and opened his arms. 'The door is always

open, although that seems to be the most clichéd thing a vicar can say.' He laughed and ran his hand through his floppy blonde hair.

Angelo seemed to have been struck down with silence, so Freya took over. 'I hadn't been in here before – I had no idea it was so beautiful.'

'You mean the light? I've never seen anything like it either. It's proof that the village lives and breathes the sea. I was split between two churches in my last parish – one a broken, dirty Victorian building that would've been right at home in a Dickens novel, the other an equally ugly new build with no soul. I had no idea somewhere so heavenly could exist.' He paused and shook his head. 'Did you see the seashells pressed into the wall around the main door? Apparently they were pressed in as an act of gratitude for everyone returning safe after a storm.'

Freya shook her head. What a comforting idea. 'I'll look on my way out.' Freya headed towards the door then waited to see if Angelo was going to follow, but he was lingering, as if he had something to confess.

Freya watched Angelo wrestle with something internally, twisting his hands together in agitation. What on earth was his secret? What had brought him here? She'd believed Lola to be prying with her desire to snoop, to be sticking her nose where it didn't belong, but maybe Lola had really been picking up on something about this troubled man who'd arrived with the storm. A man with a religious tattoo, who seemed ill at ease in a church, yet fascinated by it at the same time. Freya found herself suddenly wanting to pull back those layers, delve right into the heart of him and try to uncover whatever was clearly troubling him.

But he is not yours to fix, a voice reminded her. And who was she to fix anyone when she was just as bashed about and cracked herself? Freya sighed inwardly; she knew she should be getting back to the café. Angelo and Tristan looked at her as if they had forgotten she was even there.

'I think I'd better get back. The lunchtime rush will be starting,' she explained.

Tristan nodded and Angelo gave her a smile; a true warm, grateful smile that made her heart sing. Freya made her way up the aisle and pulled open the door. She turned to wave at them, but the two men were closer together, Tristan listening as Angelo spoke in a low agitated voice, nodding at whatever he was saying. All Freya could make out was, 'Can I come and talk to you sometime?'

Tristan put his hand on Angelo's shoulder. 'My door is always open.'

Intrigued, but knowing delaying her departure would be no better than snooping, Freya slipped out, pulling the door closed behind her. She studied the wall and, sure enough, alongside the wooden door frame were ancient seashells pressed into the wall, kept together in their fragility by mortar and faith.

Chapter Eight

'Can I leave these here, please?' Sue asked, plonking a pile of aqua-blue leaflets on the counter by the till, giving them a little pat to keep the pile neat.

Freya picked one up and read the white lettering. 'Fisherman's Fair? What's this?'

Sue's face lit up. 'Well, we've not held one for years – these sorts of things dwindled away in the Nineties and early Noughties – but this year the Polcarrow Committee has decided to bring it back. I'm sure Alf could tell you a lot more about its heyday than I can, but it's a celebration of our fishing heritage. There used to be all sorts: best-presented boat, musicians, dancing, it was a chance for everyone to let their hair down and not worry about the catch for a day.' Sue looked down at the flyer. 'This year we're having a barbeque, face painting, a sandcastle competition. We want to bring it into the modern day but still retain some of the original charm. Is Lola about? We're trying to sign people up to help and since she's such a wonderful baker . . .'

As if on cue, Lola stuck her head round the door. 'What

was that, Sue? Did I hear my name being uttered by your dulcet tones?'

'We were wondering if you can bake some cakes for the Fisherman's Fair. It's mid-August.' Sue was poised with her pen and notebook.

Lola picked up a leaflet and read the words, nodding thoughtfully. 'What about a huge batch of scones and everyone can tuck into a cream tea? Everyone loves a cream tea and it's a Cornish tradition.'

Sue beamed at the suggestion. 'That would be perfect! What a wonderful idea. I'll pop you down for scones.' She scribbled in her notebook and, glancing up at Lola and Freya, confided, 'I'm hoping the fair will draw in tourism; we really need people to start visiting.'

'Of course! I'm sure they will come and keep returning once they see what we offer. If there's anything else I can help with, do ask,' Lola offered. 'I really want my café to be a success, but more importantly this village has so much warmth and potential . . . so anything other than some scones, let me know and I'll work my magic.'

Sue smiled at Lola. 'Thank you. It's wonderful to have a new business open and I'm sure we can find a way to work together to get Polcarrow on the map. Your cakes are divine; I'd hate it if you had to shut up shop.' Sue gathered up her bags and bustled out, stooping momentarily to give Scruff a scratch behind the ears before going out to join Cathy to distribute more flyers. Cathy refused to come into the café when Scruff was in residence; she claimed it breached health and safety. Even Sue rolled her eyes at that.

'Oh, I do love the Fisherman's Fair,' Alf began, his eyes hazy with happy memories. 'The highlight of the year. So glad they're bringing it back. Shame there's not many of us left. My old Betsey Jane has seen better days, though. You know what, I think I might do her up and give her one last hurrah.'

'Who's Betsey Jane?' Freya asked.

'The loveliest little fishing boat you'll ever see, that's who. Won best-presented boat three years in a row in the Seventies. Seen better days though, like me.' He chuckled. 'Ah, Angelo, come and join me!'

Angelo had emerged from his upstairs hideaway. He'd been a bit distracted since Freya had left him in the church yesterday and had returned to the café so deep in thought no one had dared disturb him. Atoning for his sins, Lola had suggested naughtily, but to her frustration, Freya had refused to be cajoled into revealing anything she might have discovered about him. Even that tattoo, which still baffled her, remained a secret. She had no idea how to bring it up anyway.

But there was no denying that something was troubling Angelo; that was clear from his distracted manner this morning. Freya took him his coffee, with a couple of freshly baked biscotti tucked on the side of the saucer. She tried to catch his eye, but he was too busy looking everywhere except at her. Freya slunk back behind the counter, safe behind its barrier.

'Have your coffee, son, and I'll take you to meet old Betsey. You too, Freya.' When Angelo looked confused, Alf rolled his eyes and clarified. 'My boat! Jesus. The way you lot are carrying on you'd think I had a secret wife tucked away in my shed!' He chortled to himself.

Alf heaved the door to the boat shed open, sending a flurry of peeling emerald-green paint onto the cobbles. He batted away Angelo's offer of help. 'I might be old, lad, but I'm not incapable. Been pulling open this door for longer than you've been alive!'

Angelo and Freya exchanged indulgent glances. Scruff whimpered and hunkered down obediently at their feet, having been witness to the old man's tenacity for many years. Alf fiddled with securing the door before pushing open the second one a lot more easily. As sunlight flooded the shed, the shape of an old, slightly dilapidated fishing boat emerged through the gloom.

Alf shuffled in and gave the old boat an affectionate pat. 'Meet Betsey Jane. We've had some good times, haven't we, girl?' There was a glint in his eye that Freya imagined had never been bestowed on a woman. Alf plonked himself down on an upturned bucket and summoned Freya and Angelo in. 'Come on, don't be afraid. Just mind the ropes and whatever else is lying on the floor. I can't seem to tidy up like I used to.'

Freya stepped into the boat shed, inhaling a heady scent of old varnish and briny sea salt ingrained in the wood. A few gnarled lobster pots were discarded in one corner and a rickety shelf contained tins of paint that had rusted shut. She wondered how long it had been since anyone other than Alf had set foot in the shed.

Angelo had gone straight over to the boat. He was tall enough to peer over the side into the tiny, fogged-up cabin, and Freya noticed that he was running his hands over the smooth wood as lovingly as Alf had.

'You want to show her at the fair?' Freya asked.

'That I do, lass. You can't have a fisherman's fair without a few boats. Mind, she needs a lick of paint, but I've got plenty of time if I do a bit each day, hey, Scruff?' The old sheepdog had wobbled over to his master and closed his eyes as Alf scratched him behind the ears. 'Got everything in here you could need to restore a boat.'

Angelo glanced at Freya, and she could tell what he was thinking. Yes, he did have everything, if you had been planning on refurbishing a boat thirty years ago. Angelo hoisted a tin of varnish off the shelf. 'Alf, I think you might need to get some more stuff.' He held it out to the old man.

'Well, I never!' Alf wheezed with mirth. 'Look at that. I think you might be right. I'll have to draw up a list. And go and get the stuff.' The smile on his face faded and Alf seemed to sink into himself. 'Maybe it's too much for an old sailor like me, hey, Scruff?' As if sensing his master's deflation, Scruff sunk down at his feet, head on his paws.

Freya watched Angelo; she didn't know anything about restoring a boat, but she hated to see Alf so disheartened. Angelo was studying the boat, his hands still caressing

115

the old wood; she could almost see the cogs turning over in his mind.

'Alf, I have a bit of experience with wood. If you'd let me, I could help you.' Angelo's voice was brittle with nerves, as though he was putting himself out there in a way he wasn't fully comfortable with.

'What, lad? You'd give up your holiday to help me and my boat? I couldn't ask that of you.'

Angelo came round to Alf's side of the boat and leant against the wood. 'I'm not on holiday as such. I'm here to sort my head out. A few things back home didn't go well. I like ... well ... I need to be busy. I used to make things from wood a long, long time ago. It would be an honour to help you, and learn boat skills from you.'

Alf looked at him long and hard, his eyes shining with tears. He reached out and squeezed Angelo's hand. 'Bless you, son. That's the kindest thing I've heard in a long time. Now, pull up a stool. There should be some paper lying around; we'll make a list. You'll have to go shopping!'

Being in Cornwall, surrounded by so much natural beauty and shifting light tugged at Freya's heart. She tried to ignore the tugging, but somehow it managed to work its way through her body; a nagging voice in her brain and an itch tingling in her fingers. She knew what it wanted – it was a call to pick up her paintbrush and start to paint – but her fingers remained empty, stilled by echoes of doubt. Witnessing Alf and Angelo's joy in restoring the *Betsey Jane* stirred her own creative desires. This, coupled with Lola's very carefully dropped hints that she should have a go, didn't help.

She tried to pour all of her attention into making coffee, or walking along the headland, or talking to Alf. It partially worked but these activities only blotted out the urge like a cloud momentarily skidding across the sun. When not helping Alf, Angelo had spent the weekend hanging around the café and as her attraction towards him grew so did her need for distraction. Eventually, on a quiet Sunday evening, when the world was nestled down waiting for the new week to start, Freya took a deep breath and tugged the box that contained her art materials out from under her bed. Sitting back, she lifted the lid and surveyed the treasures inside.

Compared to the stash she'd crammed into her London flat, her supplies here were paltry. Just a few rescued items she'd managed to stuff into her case alongside her clothes. At the time, she'd not regretted leaving her art tools to Matt's whims, and the thought of them filling the bin had caused her no heartache. Now, she wondered if she'd been a bit rash. Both her heart and pride had felt wounded and beyond repair. But over the past few weeks, as Polcarrow had opened its arms to her, Freya had learned that nothing was ever beyond repair; all you needed was support, love and lots of cake. Lola and the kindness she'd received from the villagers, especially Tristan and Alf, had plastered over the battered parts of her and Freya found herself bruise-free and ready to dip a tentative toe back into the waters of life.

Freya lifted out the sketchbooks; slim, small, easily slipped into a bag or pocket. They were blank, the first few pages torn out years ago in an artistic rage no doubt. Tucked underneath them was an array of pencils, sharpened and worn down, nestled together with a handful of well-kept brushes, their tips clean compared to their scarred handles. Freya flicked the tips against her palm reflectively. At the bottom of the box was a tin of watercolours. She scooped the pencils and brushes out and lifted the tin, prizing the lid open. The blocks of colour nestled inside were dry, slightly cracked, waiting for a drop of water to bring them to life. They were dipped in the middle from use, but Freya had not dared awaken their magic for years, watercolour having been practically banned on her postgraduate degree in favour of experimentation that had ultimately led to the crushing of her artistic dreams.

You can paint, though, she reminded herself, don't ever forget that. At school she had achieved minor celebrity status for her artistic talents, and her peers had gathered around to watch her paint during her GCSEs. She may have been rubbish at physics but she'd certainly earned that art A★.

But what if twisting coat hangers, experimenting with textures and pushing her boundaries had meant she'd forgotten how to paint? Freya gazed up at the window, the evening light twisting through the sky. Well, there was only one way to find out.

Without allowing herself time for second thoughts, Freya pushed her feet into her trainers, grabbed one of the sketchbooks, a pot to put water in, and a couple of brushes. Her heart raced as she darted down the stairs, across the road and plonked herself on the harbour wall. The light was stunning, sultry as a siren, bruised and blushing in equal measure. Freya opened the tin, tipped some water from her bottle into the pot and opened the first page of her sketchbook, heart racing, whether from hurrying across the street or nerves, she wasn't sure.

Brush poised, she took in the scene, trying to smother the self-destructive thoughts that were fighting her desire to paint. With trembling fingers, Freya started with a wash of pale blue, the base of the sky and the sea. She held it out and studied it critically.

Okay, so it wasn't too bad. Freya let out a sigh of relief and rolled her tense shoulders; she could do this. Deep breath, slowly does it, she reminded herself. It doesn't matter what it looks like. Gradually she began to build up the colours, adding in the harbour arm, dark puffs of cloud on the horizon. She was a bit too keen and the colours bled together slightly, but she was surprised how quickly the joy of creating returned to her and she lost herself in her miniature creation. Slowly, with each brushstroke, her confidence began to grow and Freya became oblivious to the light fading around her, settling over the village like a blanket, lulling them to sleep. Painting put peace in her heart, a peace that had been missing when she had been in London.

Chapter Nine

Once she had opened the Pandora's box of paints, Freya found it increasingly difficult to put the lid back on. With that first brushstroke, she realized that the only way to heal herself was to confront the one thing that had broken her. After that first illicit painting, which upon inspection turned out to be not half bad, she continued to doodle in the café, and she quickly found herself yearning for some decent colouring pencils with which to bring her ink sketches to life.

Freya began to look forward to dusk and dawn and the possibilities they splashed across the sky. After years of having to peg her art into other people's holes, it was a relief to just create what she wanted without having to wait anxiously for a grade, or to be expected to share her work; the latter still made her shiver with anxiety. Freya briefly toyed with using seawater in her painting, but that was as experimental as she dared be, and even then it remained just another idea nestled in the back of her mind.

One of the joys of painting at dawn was that she was undisturbed. In the peace and quiet, she was reminded that none of her postgraduate colleagues was likely to win the

Turner Prize. They would all probably move on, submit to galleries, maybe illustrate greetings cards or work as teachers. Freya had expected to be surrounded by artistic greatness in London, but had found it sadly lacking. Yes, they'd all had fun and she had sometimes thrived in the creative, free-spirited atmosphere, but mostly it had been a tiring slog of early mornings in the studio and late nights doing the rounds at various galleries, pretending to be fascinated when really she was just tired. No one in her year group had been creating anything that showed huge potential.

Twee seaside artists had been scorned by her peers, and Freya now revelled in the thought that she was one of them. Except there was nothing quaint about what she was doing. The sea was all-powerful, the dawn raw, bursting through the clouds. She loved the light, the colours it turned the sand and the sea, reflecting off the houses with their window-like eyes. This morning, the sky was dark, petulant and unable to rouse itself, yet on the horizon was a slit of pale yellow, like hope pushing its determined way through. Freya snapped a few photos so she could finish her painting later and quickly uploaded one to social media; the moody light didn't need a filter. She was steadily growing a following that made her hopeful of one day having a ready-made audience for her work. Not that she was thinking of selling or sharing anything yet. She knew the scorn of her peers held some truth: seaside scenes were two a penny.

Hair pulled on top of her head, wrapped in a fluffy dressing gown that was grey with pale pink hearts dotted over it, Freya perched on the harbour wall, determined to find an angle on the seaside that no one else had. She firmly believed art stirred people's emotions, and so did the sea – it was certainly managing to stir hers – so why not couple them together? She was so engrossed in mixing grey and purple together, one eye on the palette, one on the slowly shifting sky, that she didn't hear the footsteps behind her.

'Painting by dawn, how romantic.' Angelo's voice was amused, triumphant to have caught her, but his smile faded as she cast him a look, a look that told him he was trespassing.

Freya was almost clutching her work to her; there was no way she wanted someone of his calibre to see and judge it. 'What are you doing here?'

'I see you every morning coming out here, setting up, and I was curious.' Angelo shrugged, hands in pockets. 'I wanted to see what you were doing, but if I asked, you'd never have told me.'

Freya knew he was right. 'What if I don't want to show you?'

Angelo shrugged. 'I saw the drawings in your notebook in the café,' he confessed. 'They're good . . . I don't know why you're hiding them.'

Heart racing, she stared at him. 'You've been snooping?' Her outrage was almost matched by her pathetic desire to know what he, Angelo Borelli, thought of her work. 'I haven't gone snooping through your life, have I? I know perfectly well who you are,' she threw back at him in defence.

Freya watched as Angelo stepped back, visibly stung by

her words. Panic flickered across his face as he weighed them up. They regarded each other, and more than artistic desire was stirred by the dawn breeze. Slowly, Freya lowered her sketchbook and laid her painting, a half-formed swirl of grey and purple, between them, an attempt at a truce. Angelo flicked through the pages, studied the few paintings she'd made. Arms folded, Freya watched him run his fingers over the pages, almost as if he was afraid to touch them. Angelo glanced at Freya, then down at the paper before looking back at her in a way no one had ever looked at her before, a mixture of despair and longing swirling in his dark eyes. An understanding flickered between them. Freya leant forward, but as she moved, Angelo slammed the book shut and shoved it towards her.

'Just another seaside watercolourist, is that all you want to be?' he snarled.

It stung her like a slap. Freya stared in disbelief from the sketchbook to Angelo. Rage bubbled up inside her. 'How dare you!' She leapt off the harbour wall. 'I'm sick of people like you giving me their opinion. What is so wrong with painting? We revere people like Leonardo, Rembrandt and Turner, but when I want to paint it's seen as not enough. Well, it is enough for me.' She waved the sketchbook at him. 'Anyway, what are you doing? At least I'm making some art, not moping about.'

Angelo said nothing, just sagged in on himself with resignation, no fight left in him. Freya watched him spin around and retreat back to the apartment and wondered if she'd imagined the understanding that had briefly passed between them.

'Why the glum face, Freya?' Lola asked as she locked up the café and gave Freya a long look. 'You've been moping about all day. What's up?'

'Ugh, it's nothing,' Freya mumbled. 'Must've just got out of bed on the wrong side this morning.'

Lola smiled knowingly. 'Umm, or maybe it's getting up early to go and paint. What? Don't look so shocked. The back gate bangs in the wind and I sleep at the front, remember.'

Freya wondered how much to reveal as they made their way slowly along the seafront towards home. The day had remained as overcast as Freya's mood. 'What did you see?' Freya asked.

'Everything,' Lola said, clearly proud of her big scoop.

Freya considered this as Lola unlocked her front door. It was either the truth or Lola was fishing.

'I saw Angelo storming off,' her friend added as she pushed open the door.

Freya's resolve gave way. The exchange had been gnawing at her all day and it would be a relief to get it off her chest. She followed Lola into the homey little cottage, stopping to pick up the post Lola had stepped over. A few circulars, a postcard from Italy and a bill. 'Ooh, you have a postcard from someone called Jared.' Freya waved it in the air. Lola snatched it from her, her face blanching. Intrigued, Freya pocketed her reaction for later.

'Come on, Freya, put me out of my misery. Is it just painting or are you meeting Angelo for secret dawn trysts?' Lola went to flick the kettle on, then thought better of it and grabbed a bottle of white wine from the fridge. She had a quick look out of the window. 'Get two glasses. We can sit outside – I don't think it's going to rain.'

Freya selected the glasses and followed Lola out. 'I am not meeting Angelo for secret trysts. Can you please stop going on about me and him? He's an egotistical moody bastard, nothing more.'

'Ooh, that hit a nerve!' Lola poured the wine. 'The cards never lie, Freya. They never lie. Why did he storm off?'

Freya took a sip of wine, cool and crisp, then another before leaning back, closing her eyes and groaning. 'Okay, I give in. Yes, I have been painting. I've been getting up every morning and going out. I love the way the light comes over the bay, but I'm still not sure my work is any good. You're asking why he stormed off? Well, because he upset me. Told me I should paint more than just seaside watercolours and I snapped back. Lola, he looked down on me; he sneered at me with all his dried-up artistic has-been glory and put my painting down. At least I'm painting something! I don't think he's made art in years,' Freya scoffed. 'I don't know why you want me to be friends with him. He's as prickly as a bloody cactus.'

Lola snorted with laugher. 'Come on! He's not that bad; he's just a fish out of water. Think about it – we're all cute and happy and pastel-coloured, and he's landed like a big black grumpy crow. But I don't think he's all bad. He's paid me up until the end of the summer, you know, so he's planning on sticking around. Personally, I think you have a lot to do with that – no, don't shake your head, he can't take his eyes off you.'

'Mean and moody,' Freya reiterated, although the idea that he might have been looking at her in that way made her stomach flip.

'I disagree. He's helping Alf with his boat; Tristan likes him. You were with Matt for so long you have no idea what dating in the adult world is like. It's all awkward and complicated.' Lola mock-shuddered.

'Lola, please, how many times do I have to say I'm not ready for love? It's been what, a month?'

Lola made a face. 'Honestly, Freya, stop using Matt as an excuse. You only ever mention him when this sort of conversation crops up. Honestly, I thought we'd be spending the evenings drinking gin while you cried over young love. But you've hardly even mentioned him, so don't use him as an excuse not to get to know Angelo better. You fell out of love with that boring stuffed shirt years ago and you're just using him as a barrier.'

Freya went to counter-attack, but stopped herself. Maybe Lola was right. Freya sipped her wine and studied the bright pink flowers that were flourishing in pots dotted around the little back garden. 'But I don't think I should throw myself at Angelo,' she said. 'He's volatile, moody and didn't like my art.'

'What if he's actually impressed with your skills but

doesn't know how to articulate it? Or thinks you have more talent than painting seaside scenes, hmm?' Lola suggested with a shrug. 'Yes, he may be moody, but I'm not sure about volatile. Here's what I see, other than dark and sexy: I see someone who's clearly hurting about something. You need to find out what. I see the way he looks at you, like he can't believe you exist, or you're a puzzle he didn't expect having to solve. He's probably afraid to do something because you keep dismissing him as moody. What do you know about him other than he was a successful artist who suddenly vanished from the art world?'

'Nothing,' Freya responded begrudgingly.

'Then find out. Make up your mind based on him, what he tells you. If he's an axe murderer, we'll call the police. If he's hurting over something, just be gentle with him. I'm not trying to push you both together, honestly, Freya, I'm not, but we both know there's a connection there and I'd hate to see you waste it.'

Freya reached across and squeezed Lola's hand. 'All right, fine, I'll give him a proper chance. When did you get so wise?'

'I've always been wise, darling,' she said with a wink. 'Plus, the cards never lie. Remember that – they never lie.' Lola glanced at the hem of her skirt and fiddled with a loose strand.

Freya watched her, sensing something was up, that the warning about the cards came from experience, but she couldn't quite figure out how to ask without probing. She sat back and listened to the birds twittering in the neighbour's tree, the distant rush of the waves and the seagulls circling above them. Would it be so hard to give Angelo a chance? No, it wouldn't. After all, she had to admit she was intrigued by him, attracted to him even. She glanced back at Lola and, seeing her friend's face shadowed with sadness, asked, 'What really made you come here? I never thought I'd see you settle in one place.'

Lola topped up their glasses and sighed. 'I was bored, Freya. I'm going to be forty at the end of the year and I've had enough of being everywhere. I've seen everything now. I loved being on the road,' she said wistfully, 'but honestly, it was tiring. When I came here, I knew ... I just knew I needed to stay. I think I know why now. You, Angelo, Tristan.'

'Tristan?' Freya wiggled her eyebrows.

'Ssh, yes, Tristan, but I don't know what to do about him,' Lola said sadly. 'We're too different.'

'Well, I never. Lola not knowing what to do! Have you consulted the cards?'

She shook her head. 'Somehow it doesn't feel right. He's a vicar, Freya, we're polar opposites. I don't know if it could work. Plus, you're not the only one who's had their fill of love.'

'What happened?' Freya asked gently.

Lola smiled sadly at Freya. 'Let's just say I ignored the cards. Never ignore the cards, Freya, they never lie.' She took another sip of wine and before Freya could press any further, Lola was up and struggling back into her usual bright persona. 'So, fancy fish and chips for tea? My treat.'

'Sure, haddock for me and mushy peas, please.' Freya knew when not to press, but she couldn't help but wonder if that postcard had something to do with Lola's maudlin mood.

One bottle of wine had swiftly turned into two, the alcohol not quite soaked up by the deliciously greasy fish and chips as Freya woke with a dull head the following day.

The weather was overcast again and people were grumbling about the summer already being over. Freya optimistically tugged the chairs and tables outside, but didn't flip the sign over to 'open' just yet as the start-of-the-day chores still needed doing. Plus, she desperately needed a big cup of tea and a few moments of peace and quiet. It hadn't just been the wine that had kept her awake, but Lola's advice to extend the friendship branch to Angelo. Had she really been putting up a barrier? Surely Angelo was just as guilty, with his hot and cold behaviour.

Freya made herself a large mug of tea and a bowl of porridge, sprinkling berries over the top and watching them sink in. Coming out from the kitchen, she noticed a large package propped up on the other side of the glass door to the hallway that lead up to Angelo's apartment. Curious, Freya unlocked the door and the package fell with a thud onto her feet. There was a note stuck on the front, her name written on it in bold black letters, as dark and firm as the man himself. Angelo. She scooped up the package and carried it over to the table.

Pulling out the contents, she gasped; Lola was right.

Inside were two large sketchbooks, the paper thick and better quality than anything she had ever been able to afford. Freya ran her fingers over it before closing it up and setting it aside to explore the rest of the bag. She pulled out a tin of pencils, a packet of pastels. She hadn't used pastels in years, but had always loved the way the colours rubbed together and stained her skin. There was also a new box of watercolours; she prized the lid open and inhaled the fresh scent, the colours laid out waiting hopefully to be awoken. Freya upended the bag and new paintbrushes cascaded down onto the table along with some fat tubes of blue and white oils. No one had bought her art stuff for years. Matt had always fallen into the safety of perfume and jewellery gifts that she never wore.

Shocked into silence, Freya sat down, pulled the note off the front of the bag and unfolded it. Angelo had written in bold, thick marker; **I'm sorry, I was a fool to say such things. I hope this will encourage you to not listen to me but still forgive me. A.** Freya held the note to her lips. It smelled of him, of that wild abandonment he carried on his person, a hint of danger and the need for salvation. Freya tucked the note in her pocket and ate her breakfast while surveying the gift, happiness bubbling away in her belly. Maybe, a little voice whispered, he's not all bad, after all.

Chapter Ten

Freya hid the gift under the counter; she wasn't yet ready for either Lola's scrutiny or to admit that her friend had been right. Instead, Freya got carried away thinking about what she would draw or paint, trying to ignore the little voice that was telling her she needed to forgive his snappiness.

Angelo didn't come down for his morning coffee and Freya realized she was disappointed not to see him. She cringed inwardly when she thought about her outburst. Maybe he was embarrassed or thought she'd throw the gift back in his face?

Lola ducked out early to go and administer some crystal healing therapy to a client, which gave Freya the perfect opportunity to sneak her parcel out and try the contents until it was time to close up. The last hour of the day passed quickly as she tried out the pencils, making quick sketches on the corner of the first page of the book. Almost losing track of time she caught sight of the clock ticking towards five and hurriedly packed up the café.

Freya was just pulling down the blinds when the adjoining door opened, and standing there, dark as a shadow, was

Angelo looking sheepish. His bronzed forearms were lightly covered with sawdust and there was a scent of warm wood about him. They studied each other, neither wanting to be the first to speak.

'I got your gift,' Freya said, at the same time as Angelo said, 'Would you like to go for a drink?'

Their peace offerings clashed together, but the awkward icebreaker did the trick and they both laughed. Freya studied him; was that Angelo looking shy? Emboldened by this, Freya grabbed her bag and joined him, leaving the heavy art supplies behind.

'Come on, let's go.' She gave him a nudge out of the door. Outside, the summer sun was still bright. 'Gorgeous day again,' she commented as she locked up the café. 'It's like a perpetual summer holiday. Except I have to work.' She made a face. 'Not that Lola is a bad boss or anything.' She pulled her dark hair out of its messy bun and in lieu of a comb dragged her fingers through the tresses, loosening any knots. 'How's the boat?' she asked in an attempt to ease the tension.

'All going fine but coming along slowly. We've been sanding off all the old cracked paint today. I'm going to feel it tomorrow!' Angelo stretched his arms out and winced. 'It's been a long time since I did some honest hard work, but it feels good deep in my soul, you know what I mean, to be using my hands?' Angelo flexed them in front of him.

Freya forced herself not to stare at his large, strong hands. 'I've never done that sort of hard physical graft, but yes, it's a nice notion, good for the soul. Sort of healing.'

'Exactly. The type of work where you have to focus on the task at hand.' Angelo smiled at her gratefully as she pushed open the gate to the pub garden. 'What would you like?'

'Ooh, I'll have a bitter shandy, please. Too early to start on the wine. I'll grab us a table.'

Angelo made his way into the old pub while Freya headed to a table tucked in one of the far corners of the pub garden. Whatever it was that was starting here, whatever things they needed to talk about, she knew they needed some privacy.

Freya took out her phone and nervously flicked through some of the apps, liking a few of her London friends' posts and snapping a quick photo of the sunny beer garden with its sea view for her Instagram story. Then she put her phone away, tucked it at the bottom of the bag and waited. The butterflies in her stomach were somersaulting but she told herself off for feeling nervous. She fiddled with her hair, plaiting and unplaiting it, before flipping it back, wild over her shoulders. She settled down, her heart jumping every time the pub door opened, until Angelo finally emerged, two pints in his hand, a couple of bags of crisps balanced on their tops. Freya watched him make his way over to her, a premonition shivering down her spine. This could be her future, by the sea with this man. She quickly shook the notion away.

Angelo placed the two drinks on the picnic bench. 'I don't know if there's a picnic bench in the world that isn't wonky,' he said as he dropped the bags of crisps and slipped in. 'Cheers!' They chinked glasses and Freya experienced a moment of pure bliss. He pushed the crisps towards Freya. 'I took a wild guess.'

'You chose well!' She grinned at him as she reached for the salt and vinegar. 'My favourite.' She turned over the other bag; sea salt and cracked black pepper. 'No cheese and onion, phew.'

Angelo opened the sea salt bag. 'Not a fan?'

Freya pulled a face. 'I can always taste them in my mouth hours later. Not nice. What about you?'

'Personally, I have nothing against cheese and onion, but I have made a note of the offence a bag would cause.' Angelo tapped his head. 'Prawn cocktail is the big no-no for me, I mean, come on, it's nothing like the actual thing.'

Freya tore into the bags so they could share them easily. 'I think being around cake all day has started to make me immune to the allure of sweet treats,' she told him. 'All I ever dream of now is savoury things. I never used to be without a KitKat, but I've not had one in weeks.' Angelo helped himself to a few crisps and they lapsed into a silence that was potent with so many unsaid things.

Freya took a fortifying sip of her drink. 'Thank you for the present.' It sounded weak so she added, 'You didn't have to. I was just as horrible to you.'

Angelo shook his head. 'Don't. It's an apology. I realized that I was out of line talking to you like that, basically telling you your painting was rubbish. It was unprofessional and uncalled for. Of course everyone should be allowed to paint whatever the hell they like.' He sighed with a soul-weary exhaustion.

'You snooped through my stuff, though.'

Angelo looked at her long and hard. 'Yes, yes I did and I apologise. But what I want to know is why you're sneaking out at dawn and hiding your painting and your drawings. Looking in your notepad I can see you have a good eye and no small talent.'

'Do you really mean that?' She realized his response mattered. Despite all her self-assurance that she could paint whatever she liked, she still craved artistic validation. Freya crossed her fingers and prayed Angelo Borelli would not find her wanting.

He shrugged. 'I was curious about what you were doing. You were always bent over your order pad and no one is that engrossed in a coffee order, but you hid it every time someone came near.' He mimed someone scribbling away and hiding it behind their arm. 'Tell me, what were you studying in London?'

Freya sighed; there was no way around the truth. 'Art. But it didn't go quite as I expected.'

'How come?' he asked gently.

To buy herself some time to compose her story, Freya picked at the crisps, licking the salt off her fingertips. 'I aced my undergrad, got an easy First and I had the best time. I loved uni. It allowed me to embrace being every sort of art student cliché going. Charity shop clothes, hanging out in the studios. I loved the freedom.' She smiled wistfully. 'I felt like I belonged. That's where I met my ex-boyfriend. We were one of those annoying couples who met during fresher's week and were inseparable.' Freya smiled at the memory. 'I made some great friends but they all studied subjects that projected them into graduate schemes and full-time work. I just wafted on behind. In hindsight, I should've got a proper job, but I worked in bars, galleries, cafés, museums and saved so that I could do a postgraduate degree.

'I stupidly chose Modern Art. By the time I realized it wasn't right for me, it was too late to withdraw or change course. Plus, I'd paid the fees and they would've been non-refundable. Thousands of pounds that would've been better off spent elsewhere. I have only ever loved to paint. I love seeing how the light falls on things and trying to capture or replicate it.

'But on my course, painting was basically banned. They wanted us to do all sorts of things I just wasn't comfortable with. Then . . .' Freya paused took a deep breath and admitted, 'I failed. I worked so, so hard, threw everything I had at it but still they failed me. Apparently the examiners were hard to please, but honestly, a fail? I still don't understand it. Oh, and to top it all off, I went home and my boyfriend dumped me and told me my art was stupid. So, there you go. You can probably see why I'm hiding away.' She added a shrug as if to indicate it was all no big deal, but it felt therapeutic to get it all off her chest to someone who she suspected understood.

Angelo was silent for a long time, processing what he'd

been told. 'Wow. I had no idea. I can see why you were so ready to slap me the other morning. For what it's worth, I don't think your art is crap. I think you have talent – more talent than a lot of students I've seen – and I can see your confidence has been dented. But after all that, it takes an awful lot of courage to pick up the paints again. You should be proud.'

'Thanks.' Freya paused. 'Students? You've had students?'

Angelo sighed and ran his hands through his mane of dark hair. 'Ugh. I guess if you've told me your tragic past, it's only fair that I share mine, but, Freya, please keep this to yourself.' He glanced around the pub garden nervously. 'I'll tell you what I'm ready to and only because you're the only person who knows who I am. Angelo Borelli.' He gestured to himself. 'Who'd have ever thought this was where I'd end up?' He let out a bitter laugh and took a long draught of his beer. 'I guess you spent all your years at art school imagining how wonderful it would be when you made it big, when you sold something and had enough money to secure a studio, when your name was listed as someone to watch. Don't shake your head – for as much as we all harp on about how noble it is to create, what we really want deep down is some recognition, or fame, but certainly money. It is great for a while; it really is. You get feted. People flatter you. And then suddenly it dawns on you that it was all for their gain only.' Angelo took a sip of his drink. 'Anyway, sorry, I'm digressing. I graduated from university, was nominated for the Turner Prize – it was a fluke really, but everyone wanted a piece of me. Money was thrown at me to see what I'd do next. I did a couple of things, painting mostly, but it wasn't what I enjoyed.'

'What did you enjoy?'

'Sculpture. I loved making things with my hands. I fancied myself as a bit of a classic Renaissance artist like Michelangelo.' He laughed, apparently slightly embarrassed by this admission.

Freya sighed. 'When I was twenty-one, I would've thrown myself at you to learn how to sculpt! It was the one thing I never did and I was hungry for everything. So that's how you know how to help Alf with his boat?'

'Yep. I love working with wood – sanding it, revealing the texture and patterns in the grain, how it warms to your touch, even the smell. There's something primal about it.' Angelo inhaled deeply. 'I keep smelling it on myself after days in Alf's shed. Anyway, I decided I wanted to give back, to help people, so I started to teach at various art schools, though I guess I never made it to yours, and slowly everything I was started to vanish and I lost myself. It's been a hell of a couple of years, Freya. It's been awful. I've doubted everything I am and it turns out the people who I thought would support me in my darkest hour only kicked me when I was down. They used me. So, believe me, I know how you feel. I needed a break, to clear my head. That's why I'm here. Well, I didn't plan to be here exactly, but I needed space and freedom. No one knows where I am,' he admitted.

Shocked, Freya paused with her glass halfway to her mouth. 'What? No one? No friends or family?'

Angelo shook his head, lips pushed together as if keeping the rest of the story firmly shut in. 'They only know that I am safe and need time. The trouble is, the longer I'm here, the less I want to ever go back.' His eyes made a circle of the harbour and rested with intent on Freya. Their stares lingered for long enough that whatever this was that was growing between them bloomed a little more.

Freya broke the moment. 'I agree. I don't know what I'd be going back for anymore. Or where I'd go. I don't think I could do London again and going back to my parents' in Bedford doesn't sit well either. I don't know how to make others understand this – that I need some time. But I'm not sure I could convince everyone that staying here and making coffees is a viable life.'

'Don't forget painting,' he reminded her. 'Painting is a valid reason.'

Freya smiled at him. 'Only if I'm making some money.'

'Could you not try to sell them? It's not such a crazy idea. Give it a go. I'm sure the tourists would love a souvenir. Sorry, I didn't mean to make it sound banal. Try going to a local gallery or something, see what they say. I think you're good enough.'

She regarded him with disbelief; he thought her work was good enough to try to sell. 'Angelo Borelli's seal of approval.' Freya shook her head with disbelief.

'What do you have to lose?'

'Nothing,' she admitted before asking, 'I was wondering how you got all those art supplies back on your motorbike.'

'I didn't,' he confessed, 'I used the bus.'

'The bus?' Freya exploded with mirth imagining Angelo dressed like a dark demon shuffling onto the bus with a group of old ladies. 'This place really is softening you.'

Angelo gently touched her fingers. 'Not just this place.' He paused, glanced down at their hands, and seemed to carefully consider the next thing he was going to say. 'I need to confess something. This has been eating away at me. Part of the reason I lashed out at you was that I was envious of you sitting out there just painting. I've not painted or drawn in months.' Angelo held out his hands, palms up, staring at them forlornly like they'd let him down. 'Every morning I see these hands, hands that brought me so much, got me where I am whether I like it or not, and they do nothing much now.' He sighed, exasperated, sad and defeated.

Freya regarded him; despair seemed to emanate from him, and she wondered how long he'd been angry with himself. She reached out, pushed his hands together hiding their emptiness, and gave them a squeeze with her own. 'Start small,' she advised with a reassuring smile, 'just doodle. You're helping Alf with his boat – that's enough for now, don't forget that.'

Angelo squeezed her hands back but the sadness in his eyes reminded her what she too felt: that filling a few moments of the day with a quickly dashed off doodle would never be enough for someone who'd lost their soul to art, only to have it engulf them.

*

The mood was saved by the arrival of Tristan and Lola bursting into the garden, clutching drinks and quiz night score sheets. They looked momentarily taken aback to be caught out but Lola covered it well and bustled over.

'You two can join our team!' she chivvied, motioning for Freya to shift up the bench and instantly diving in to hoover up the last few crisps. 'We were supposed to be discussing the fair but apparently Tristan can't say no to a pub quiz, so here we are!'

Angelo raised an eyebrow at Freya, while Lola jabbed Freya in the ribs and gave her a suggestive wink. Tristan remained oblivious, having been cornered by one of the villagers who'd seen this as the perfect opportunity to voice a concern, despite the vicar clearly being off duty.

'It never ends!' He sighed as he joined them. 'Even if I take the dog collar off, they still get me. Cheers!' He held up his pint. Angelo, noticing that his was empty, went inside to replenish his drink and Freya's.

'So?' Lola asked as she sipped her gin.

'So what?' Freya shrugged nonchalantly. 'So? to you too.'

Lola smiled indulgently but didn't press the subject. Freya knew that although Lola liked meddling in other people's affairs, her own were strictly off limits.

Angelo re-emerged followed by Steve and his loud hailer; they'd decided to do the quiz outside. Anyone who hadn't been planning on taking part was quickly roped in, and fresh quiz sheets and an assortment of pencils were passed around. Lola, Freya, Tristan and Angelo hunkered around the score pad. As he had the best writing, Tristan was del-egated as scribe. The questions were ridiculously hard for a local pub quiz, but the entire garden gave it their best shot as the evening light dimmed and the drinks were topped up. The quiz was won by a group of tourists who were stay-ing in one of the rented cottages on the outskirts of town, Freya's table coming in a respectable third place, but voicing their annoyance that there were no questions about baking, religion or art.

They wandered back into the village in semi-triumphant state, Freya a little wobbly after three shandies and no dinner. Tristan said his goodnights first, with a long lingering look at Lola before heading off to the vicarage. When they reached Lola's cottage Angelo paused, not quite sure what to do. Lola lingered at the door, giving them space but still making sure she didn't miss out on any of the action.

Freya shivered, her bare arms chilled by the sea air. 'Thanks,' she said to Angelo. 'I had a lovely evening.'

Angelo, hands thrust in pockets, nodded. 'Me too, although I'm shocked at how bad my general knowledge is!'

He leant in slightly but Freya gave a nod in Lola's direc-tion. 'We have an audience.'

Angelo glanced at Lola too and pulled back. 'I'll see you in the morning. Sleep well.'

Freya nodded and watched him make his way along the seafront before she joined Lola. Had that been an almost kiss? Or a prelude to an almost kiss? Or was she just tipsy? One thing Freya knew for certain was that she didn't have a clue when it came to men and dating. 'I need toast and bed,' she announced, 'and I'm saying nothing more than I took your advice and decided to be nice to him.'

'Good,' Lola said slightly smugly. 'I'm always right. I can wait, though, for you to tell me the rest.' Her eyes twinkled and not for the first time did Freya wonder if her friend really was magic.

Chapter Eleven

Despite having guzzled a pint of water and snaffled up three slices of toast before bed, Freya woke with a groggy head the following morning and a pervading desire to do something nice to pay Angelo back. She hauled herself into the shower, the hot steamy water reviving her slightly, and replenished her alcohol-addled body with some strawberries. Lola was already up and out, no doubt in the café preparing for the start of the weekend trading.

It was only quarter to eight and Freya decided a burst of fresh air would help her recover. Pulling her hoodie on, she stepped outside, the salt in the air instantly clearing her head. Seagulls squawked and the early-morning sun glittered on the waves; the scene put Freya instantly at peace. She didn't think she'd ever be able to leave here. The thought of returning to a landlocked town or city constricted her heart. But where did that leave her? Serving coffees forever? Was Angelo right? Could she make money out of her painting? The idea began to grow into a thrilling possibility.

Freya meandered up to the headland and looked over the little village that had given her more contentment than anywhere else she'd ever been. If someone had told her six months ago that she'd soon be here and not missing the twenty-four-hour city life, she would have thought them mad. But here she was, happier than ever.

She took a few photos and sent some texts to friends and family, feeling guilty that she hadn't been in touch as much as she'd intended. If she had to be honest, Olivia's gentle probing about her post-summer plans didn't help. Freya wondered why there always had to be a next plan. Wasn't that what had pushed her into this position? Always fretting about what came next: the degree, the exhibition, waiting with bated breath for the engagement that had never come. Freya closed her eyes and allowed herself to just be. The only 'next' she wanted to figure out right now was what she could do for Angelo.

He'd looked so forlorn at the sight of his bare hands, unmarked by paint, the creases not filled with shadows of charcoal. Her hands were the same; the cleanest they'd ever been. At university, no matter how much she had washed them, something from the studio had always lingered, under a nail or caught in a knuckle, a reminder of the dream. However, where Freya saw her hands as clean, fresh, ready for a new beginning, it was clear Angelo regarded his as barren, useless. She wanted to tell him that was not true; barren, useless hands did not help bring a fishing boat back to its former glory.

Freya headed back to the café knowing what she wanted to do. She needed to do something immediate, and unable to get into town, she knew the only option was to share Angelo's gift back with him. She let herself into the café and rummaged around under the counter, pulling out one of the sketchbooks and one of the pencils, and scrawled a quick note. Unlocking the adjoining door, she darted up the stairs and propped the book outside his flat. She thought briefly of knocking but, unsure of how her gesture would be received, she decided to just leave it for him to find. She headed back downstairs, and as if nothing had happened, made a pot of tea and carried it through to the kitchen where Lola was taking a carrot cake out of the oven.

'I thought I heard you on the stairs,' Lola said. 'What are you up to?'

Freya broke off a piece of flapjack and popped it in her mouth, feigning innocence. 'Nothing.'

Lola smirked knowingly. 'Well, in that case you can give me a hand with the washing up.'

Angelo almost tripped over Freya's gift. Without think-ing, he swooped down to pick it up, and then froze before retreating back inside his apartment. As he opened the book, a small folded piece of cheap lined paper fell out, her encour-agement scrawled in haste; Please, just have a go! 😊 He ran his hands over the paper, remembering the way he'd browsed the shop, tracking down the best quality, imagin-ing what he would buy if he was stocking up for himself. It had been longer than he cared to admit since he'd drawn in, let alone owned, something as simple as a sketchbook. It was the tool of a student, pages blank and hopeful, waiting for a future to be smudged and scribbled upon them. He swallowed, choked by the simple beauty of her gesture. It had been a long time since anyone had wanted to help him, especially with his art.

In the beginning, there had been encouragement, praise that he was now ashamed to admit had inflated his ego. It had all been too much, he too young. When he wasn't forthcoming with any large exhibitions, critics had held their breath and speculated: he'd either dried up or was storing up something so impressive that it would rock the art world. Even simply thinking back to these whispers made panic rise in his chest.

When that groundbreaking, earth-shattering work hadn't materialized, all he'd been met with was disappointment. Those who had invested in him were disappointed that he wanted to teach. Over and over he had tried, but failed, to get them to understand that he craved simplicity, that he enjoyed using his talents to inspire others. However, teaching masked his lack of production, although art schools loved having his name attached to them. When he did manage to paint, or sculpt for his own enjoyment, he found whatever he'd created didn't fit the specifications of those who sponsored him, so much that it remained locked in his studio where, until recently, it had still been languishing.

He was surprised that his path had never crossed Freya's before; he was sure he would have remembered her if it had. Then again, he had been so wrapped up in his own misery that he realized he'd stopped paying attention to those around him a very long time ago. In fact, if his girlfriend – well, he guessed ex-girlfriend now – Vanessa was to be believed, he'd even stopped paying attention to her, and yet, they seemed unable to let each other go. Until now. He winced to remember the bright lights, the bidding war, Vanessa's face smug with ownership, all ruined by the white-hot rage that had flashed through him.

Angelo stared at his hands, hands that were born to create but that in a fit of betrayed passion had destroyed so much. All that love – if it had ever been love, he mused bitterly – turned to sour hate. Too much to fix.

No, he would not think of that, he smothered the anger that snaked its way through his chest as he remembered how his relationship with Vanessa had changed with his lack of work. Now there was Freya and her infectious goodness to contend with. He had no idea what he would say to her. 'Thank you' would stick in his throat, words too pathetic for a gesture that, albeit apparently trivial, was rather substantial in the larger scheme of his life. She had given him hope, where there had not been any for a long time.

Angelo put the sketchbook to one side, reverently laid the pencils on top of it. He glanced around the apartment. It was sparse. He had picked up a few new clothes when he'd gone into town, but it was clear he was just borrowing this space. He leant back against the wall. Could he live here? Well, not in this exact apartment, but in Polcarrow itself? With the sea, the beautiful light that flooded the place, the clean, salty air that stuck to his skin. His mind strayed to the dilapidated art deco house on the edge of the village. Maybe that's what he needed; a different challenge, a reason to use his hands to make good. He was loving working on Alf's boat: the smoothness of the wood he sanded beneath his palms, the way the old man chattered about his time at sea, and how Angelo, who had once had no time for anything, found he had all the time in the world to stop and listen. The simple life was calling and it was seductive, shocking him.

Into this dream Freya often wandered, and although sometimes he'd let her linger, most of the time he quickly pushed her out. When he did his midnight flit from London, Angelo had not bargained on having his heart so quickly won by someone. Freya was the first woman he had met in a long time who was open and kind, who didn't care who he had once been, who wasn't after anything. What on earth could he provide her with? He basically had the clothes on his back and a bag full of secrets. He rubbed his face. He could start with being better; he could even give her the truth, despite knowing it would change how she saw him.

Outside, the church bells chimed nine a.m. Alf would be expecting him. Angelo ran his hands through his hair in lieu of a comb. He couldn't remember the last time he'd brushed it properly. Vanessa used to take a comb to it in an aggressive manner. He now wondered if that was indicative of how she'd really felt about him. He had no qualms banishing her from his mind as he made his way down the stairs and through the adjoining door. Freya was behind the counter, long dark hair piled messily on top of her head, looking as if a single tug would cause it to tumble down disobediently. She had her apron on and was laughing at something the postman was saying as he added sugar to his takeaway tea. She waved him off and turned to see Angelo, her smile faltering only slightly.

'One double espresso coming right up!' she chirruped, rubbing her hands nervously on her apron.

Angelo leant against the counter and watched her. When she placed the coffee in front of him, he thought, Yes, I could get used to this.

His eyes never left hers as he tipped in two sugars and gave it a quick stir. 'I found the book. I don't know how to thank you. It's the kindest thing anyone has done for me in a long time.' He saw the question in her eyes but rather than answer it, he knocked back his coffee, gave her a wink, and, heart racing, he headed for the safety of Alf's boat shed.

Angelo's reaction to her small gift stunned Freya. The kindest thing anyone had done for him in a long time? This got her brain ticking overtime. What on earth had been going on in his life that the simple gesture of a sketchbook and pencils was the nicest thing that had happened to him? His eyes had been sincere and that long, lingering look had given her hope rather than doubt. But what was this thing in his past that he kept skirting around so clumsily?

Freya grabbed her phone and opened her browser, typing in his name. Her thumb lingered over the search button, knowing his whole life would be available to her with that one click. She chewed on her bottom lip, discomfort creeping up her neck. Searching for him like this would be a betrayal. She couldn't tell Lola not to look him up and then indulge in the same activity. Plus, she'd scolded him for snooping through her notebook. Putting the phone down she watched him move away from the harbour wall and head towards Alf's.

Instead of delving into Angelo's past, Freya, emboldened by his praise, took to painting, happily filling all her spare time perched in various locations in Polcarrow, frantically splashing paint all over herself as she cobbled together scenes of a seaside life. She hung them out to dry on little pegs suspended on a piece of string across her bedroom where they fluttered like bunting. As her confidence slowly seeped back in, Freya started to think about the next step. Polcarrow didn't have its own gallery, so, once the paintings had dried, Freya trimmed the edges, tucked them into an old portfolio and decided it was time to see if anyone would like to display them. *Could you sell them?* Angelo's suggestion came back to her, *I think you're good enough to try.*

Butterflies in her stomach, Freya took the bus into the next town along the coast. It was only about twenty minutes away, but she realized it was the furthest she had travelled since arriving in Polcarrow. Sitting by the window, watching the coast drift past, she amused herself by thinking of Angelo taking the same journey when he'd gone to buy her supplies.

The town was larger, with more bustle and more polish

than the slightly ramshackle collection of houses and businesses she'd come to call home. Freya strolled along the seafront, taking in the souvenir shops selling everything from postcards to hand-crafted jewellery, and the cafés with their tables spilling out onto the quayside. There was an ice cream and fudge shop, its smell enticing, and next door to it was a small gallery. Freya took a fortifying breath, pushed open the door and went inside.

The gallery wasn't the usual neat style she was used to. The walls were covered with all sorts of paintings, most focusing on a seaside theme, all jumbled together in a bright cacophony. The eclectic mix made Freya smile as she browsed the wares, imagining her own work nestled between them. She had expected to be intimidated but was pleased to find the displays inspiring. Some of the paintings were stunning and Freya found herself humbled by the skill and imagination. There were boxes of photographic prints, postcards and greetings cards.

The gentleman behind the till peered over the edge of his glasses. 'Can I help you?' he asked, almost as if she was interrupting his reading of the paper.

Freya, knowing this would be her only chance, pulled her portfolio out of her bag and headed over to the counter. 'Hi, I'm Freya,' she introduced herself. 'I'm a local artist based in Polcarrow and I'm hoping you would like to display and sell some of my work. I've studied at the London School of Arts.' Her words trailed off as he gave her a long, unimpressed look. With a smile she pushed the portfolio over to him. 'It's the light I love the most,' she explained as he opened the first page. 'The way it falls on the sea, how it shifts and changes with dusk and dawn.'

The man flicked through the pages, his eyes hardly taking in her offerings. Freya's skin prickled with nerves, her mouth suddenly dry as she saw her paintings through his eyes. Her work was at best experimental and expressive; she'd been trying to capture the unique way the light fell on the bay, but she knew it was good. Her wispy and ethereal work was different from the paintings that glared down at her from the surrounding walls. Neat, bright, ready to be hung in people's living rooms, an accessible, easily understood memory. Not doing her research beforehand had been a huge mistake. When on earth would she learn not to just jump in feet first and hope for the best? Her heart sank as he closed the folder and looked up at her.

'You have good technique,' he began, 'but I'm sorry, I cannot sell these. They're not to my clientele's taste. The whole of Cornwall is full of seaside paintings, so it's a tough market to crack.' Without saying anything else, he turned back to his paper, dismissing her.

Freya reached across and grabbed her portfolio back, her heart heavy in her chest. How on earth could he know that no one would buy them? Did this mean Angelo was just being nice and her paintings actually were rubbish? She trundled around the rest of the town hoping that there would be another gallery, but her heart wasn't in it and all she found were quaint whitewashed cottages and cobbled streets. She headed back to the seafront and bought herself some fudge to try to lift her spirits. It worked momentarily until she boarded the bus and the twisty roads back to Polcarrow made her stomach churn.

Freya measured her breathing; sweets and travel had never mixed for her. Tears prickled her eyes and she tried her best to wipe them away. When she finally got off the bus she stopped at the harbourside and took some deep breaths until she felt less queasy. Just the sight of the tiny bay comforted her. The sunlight dancing on the waves lifted her spirits and even the seagulls were behaving, just nestling on the harbour wall rather than trying to steal any food out of the bins. Inhaling the sea air to compose herself, she headed back into the café. It was mid-afternoon and quiet. Lola was sitting in the window with Tristan, and in front of them was a mocked-up poster for the Fisherman's Fair.

'What's up?' Lola cried when she saw Freya's glum face. 'How did it go?'

Freya sank down onto the spare seat and put the rest of the fudge on the table for them, followed by her now redundant portfolio. 'I was told he couldn't sell them and to try something different. The whole of Cornwall is full of seaside paintings. I was stupid to think it'd work.' She sighed and rubbed her face. 'Ugh. I'm starting to wonder if the universe is actually trying to tell me to give up painting. I clearly can't paint anything anyone wants to buy.'

Tristan flicked through the portfolio. 'But these are lovely! They're all dreamy, especially this one.' He pointed to a candyfloss sunset she'd been particularly proud of. 'I'm sure another gallery would be happy to have them. Maybe he doesn't make any money with what he does have?' he suggested, a bit too wickedly for a vicar.

Freya smiled at his kind words. 'Thanks. Maybe. There certainly weren't any customers in there. I was stupid not to do my research first.'

'Well, some people don't know what they're missing. And since Polcarrow doesn't have a gallery, and I have plenty of space on my walls, I'm going to display them in here!' Lola bustled over to the counter and rummaged around underneath until she triumphantly unearthed a slightly dusty ball of Blu-Tack. Before Freya could protest, Lola was sticking little blue dots on the back of the paintings and attaching them to the café walls. When finished, Lola stepped back and surveyed her haphazard display with pride. Tristan applauded before getting up and gently straightening a wonky one.

'I'm not sure about this,' Freya protested weakly, but their kindness had touched her. Actually, the paintings didn't look too bad, apart from the one where the perspective was off, and the other where the colours had leaked together. Ugh, stop, she told herself.

'Nonsense!' Lola protested. 'No point in painting them, and then hiding them away. Maybe someone will see them and want to buy them.'

Freya smiled at her friend's hopeful suggestion, but now the paintings just looked hopelessly naïve. Instead of questioning anything, Freya slipped her apron on and headed behind the counter, leaving Lola and Tristan to their discussion about the poster. Clearly there were some things they weren't happy about.

'I don't like the heading,' Lola was saying, 'and it's all a bit crammed in. How can we convince them to change it without making it look like us townies think we know better?' Lola held the poster up. 'I was thinking something a bit more, well, vintage, you know like those classy railway posters? Or at least to have a fishing boat on it!'

Tristan regarded it thoughtfully. 'Not everything has to be vintage, Lola,' he reminded her. 'I think we could tell them it needs a boat, but we might need to just leave the rest of it just in case they think we're stepping on their toes.'

Freya watched as Lola struggled with this idea. 'Oh, okay, I guess you're right,' she eventually said with a sigh. 'I can see why you're so in demand with your gentle negotiation skills, vicar.' She said it so suggestively Freya was surprised Tristan didn't choke on his tea.

Freya was busy sweeping up the aftermath of a toddlers' food fight when Angelo returned. Lola was tucked away in the kitchen doing a stock check. The blinds were down, dimming the bright late-afternoon sunlight, and the café was a bit on the too-warm side.

Angelo was dishevelled but there was something about him that looked happy. He smelled musty, of sweat and wood and the sea, and the sheer manliness of his scent triggered her desire. She noticed the sketchbook was tucked under his arm and wondered if there was anything drawn inside it.

'Been decorating?' he asked, signalling to the array of paintings adorning the walls.

Freya stopped and leant against the broom. 'Lola's idea.' Freya paused before admitting, 'I took them into town to see if any galleries would want to buy them.' Angelo's face lit up hopefully and Freya shook her head. 'It didn't go well. I was told Cornwall is full of seaside paintings. He didn't even really look at them.'

Angelo winced in sympathy. 'Sorry to hear that, Freya. Put it down to experience. There's plenty more galleries out there. And there's the internet. Don't give up. You really do have something unique, even if you don't believe it yet.' Angelo was studying the paintings on the wall. 'Is that Blu-Tack? You need to sign them and frame them – that will make them look more special. Are you going to sell them from here? There's no reason not to.'

'Lola only put them on the wall to stop me putting them in the bin. Now I have to stare at them all day every day.' Freya rubbed her forehead. 'Honestly, I should just give up.'

'No!' Angelo was quick and firm. 'Don't. It's better when you work at it. If it all comes too easily, then you end up doubting yourself even more. I know that's hard to believe, but please don't give up. Leave these here for a week, see what happens. Art shouldn't just be about sales and moneymaking. Have faith. Have passion, that's the main thing.' He gave her shoulder a quick squeeze as he walked past and a backward glance as he went up the stairs.

Freya watched him go. A little voice in her head was reminding her that passion didn't pay the bills. Sweeping did, so she carried on with her chores, trying not to look at her paintings in case she found them wanting.

Chapter Twelve

It was a perfect summer's day, the sky only dotted with the odd wisp of cloud and the air fresh enough to lessen the heat of the sun. Never one to miss a business opportunity, Lola had rented a freezer and stocked up on ice creams from the local dairy. She and Freya had spent an evening sampling all the flavours until Freya had queasily announced that she never wanted to eat another ice cream again. They had decided, due to lack of space, that rather than scooping the ice cream onto cones, they'd stock up on individual tubs.

Alf hobbled in with Scruff. 'Is your young man still about?'

'He's not my young man,' Freya reminded him, 'but he's just talking a walk along the harbour before coming to yours.'

'I'm giving us both the day off. Far too nice to be cooped up in that shed. Reckon I better sit outside and catch him.'

'The usual?' Freya called after him.

Alf shook his head. 'I think I'll start the day with a scone. At my age there's no excuse not to have a cream tea for breakfast. Lola's scones are some of the best I've ever tasted, and believe me, I've had a fair few cream teas in my day.'

By the time Freya had assembled Alf's unorthodox breakfast, she noticed he'd managed to catch Angelo, so she quickly made his usual double espresso, added it to the tray and carried it out into the bright morning sunshine. Her eyes were drawn to a familiar black book that dominated the tiny table, its corners now scuffed and well used. A whittled pencil was threatening to roll off the table. Freya's heart soared with excitement; Angelo had clearly been at work. Alf's face lit up at the sight of the scone, Freya having selected the biggest one. He quickly went about loading it up with jam and cream, Scruff whimpering for his share.

Freya hesitated about where to place Angelo's coffee until he gestured to put it on top of the sketchbook. She went to ask what he'd been drawing but Alf got in first.

'You been busy, lad?' he asked, wiping stray cream off his chin.

Angelo stirred sugar into his coffee and shifted in his seat. 'Erm, not much, just some doodles.' His eyes met Freya's and she smiled encouragingly.

'Are you going to show us?' she asked. 'You've all seen my paintings, so I think it's only fair.'

Angelo moved his coffee cup and opened the sketchbook slowly. On the front page was a detailed pencil drawing of the harbour, intricate and well composed. He ran a hand over it and Freya saw the pride in his gesture.

'Wow, that's amazing,' she gushed, leaning over, almost pulling the book away for a better look. He had captured all the little details, and the perspective was perfect. A mix of envy and desire to learn how he'd made it so real flashed through Freya.

'You've got a good eye, lad. I'm impressed,' was Alf's seal of approval.

'Thank you.' Angelo's voice was humble. 'It's been a very long time since I've done any drawing like this. It was Freya's suggestion. It's been therapeutic to go back to basics. I think I got so wrapped up in the shock and awe of the art world that I forgot that true beauty is just this.' He gestured at the page.

'Were you in the art world too, son?' Alf asked.

Freya watched Angelo tense up, eyes flickering with panic. She smiled at him, reassuring him that it was safe to tell Alf the truth.

'Yes, a long time ago though.' He glanced down at his sketch. 'It's not . . . something I've done much of lately.'

Alf squinted up at them both. 'Two artists in a town that hadn't seen one for years. They always used to come down to the coast but rarely strayed to Polcarrow. It's good to see. And with this café, we're on the up, I'm telling you.'

Angelo studied the old man. 'Can I draw your portrait?' he asked. 'I've always been fascinated by faces, especially pencil-drawn ones like Michelangelo and Leonardo used to do.'

'Of course you can!' Alf bristled with pride and straightened up. 'Never had my portrait done before. It'll be a treat!'

Although she wanted to stay and watch, the other outside table had just become occupied, so Freya made her excuses and went to serve the newcomers. By the time she'd rung their order through the till and made Lola an Earl Grey tea, the café was filling up. 'Give Alf and Angelo one of those ice creams, see what they think,' Lola said as she slid two paninis across the counter to Freya and wiped her brow. 'If they're going to occupy one of my tables they might as well be useful. Jesus, if it gets any hotter in here I'll need to come to work in my bikini!'

'I'm sure Tristan would love that.' Freya ducked as Lola threw a tea towel at her in response.

By the time Freya had delivered the two paninis to eager customers inside and managed to make it back outside the vicar had joined them.

'Morning, Freya. Beautiful day,' he remarked. 'Sorry I'm a bit late for my tea and toast this morning. I had something I needed to sort out before coming down, so I had my breakfast at home – it was substandard to say the least.' He nodded towards Angelo who was deep in concentration. 'Have you seen what he's doing?' Tristan looked from the page to Freya and back in awe.

Freya scurried around and leant over his shoulder to have a look. Angelo tensed slightly but carried on drawing. Freya took half a step back; she'd never liked people peering nosily over her shoulder herself. Alf's craggy weather-beaten face was coming to life on the page. Angelo had even managed to capture the cheeky glint in the fisherman's eyes. Freya gave his shoulder a quick squeeze of encouragement.

'Absolutely stunning!' Tristan carried on.

'Thank you,' quipped Alf. 'I'm a well-preserved specimen,

should've seen me in my youth, breaking hearts all over the place.'

'Yet you never married?' Tristan remarked.

'No. I saw how tough it was for those girls waiting for us all to come back. I've seen whole crews of men washed to the bottom of the sea. That fate was not fair on any lass. How would I have left her and a babe at home knowing that I might never see them again? Don't give me those sad eyes, you lot. I've had a good, full life and wouldn't change it for anything.'

They all continued to watch Angelo, transfixed, until Freya piped up. 'Oh, I almost forgot! Lola is trialling ice creams. Since you're taking up one of her precious tables, she wants you to give her some feedback. We have chocolate, clotted cream and raspberry, strawberry, coffee, vanilla and mint choc chip.'

'I've had enough clotted cream for one morning, lass! I think I'll pass.' Alf patted his stomach happily.

Tristan gave the flavours thorough consideration. 'What a choice! I think chocolate wins, though. Even a vicar needs a weakness. I can never turn chocolate ice cream down.'

Freya laughed at Tristan's choice of vice. 'Angelo?' But he was too engrossed in finishing his portrait, so Freya guessed that he'd pick coffee.

Freya was so busy with orders inside the café that by the time she made it back out with the ice creams the portrait was complete. Alf was staring at it in amazement. 'It's like looking into a mirror!' he exclaimed, reaching across and squeezing Angelo's hand, his eyes shining with tears.

Angelo looked uncomfortable with the praise. 'Oh, it's nothing,' he said as he prized the lid off his ice cream, but Freya knew that he was secretly pleased with their approval.

Tristan was studying the portrait thoughtfully. 'Angelo, I have a proposition for you.' When Angelo nodded the vicar continued, 'As you saw, we have space for a mural in the church, and we've been looking for a long time for someone suitable to fill it, someone who can really capture the essence of the village and you, in that one drawing, have proven that you can. Would you like to paint the mural?'

Freya bristled that Tristan hadn't asked her first, but forced an encouraging smile onto her face as she turned to Angelo.

Freya watched as he turned the proposition over in his head. She understood exactly what concerned him. What if his vision didn't match with Tristan's? What if this sketch was just a fluke? Freya crossed her fingers, hoping Angelo would say yes and she'd be able to find a way to help. Angelo glanced from Alf and Tristan to Freya, as if seeking her approval. She nodded encouragingly at him.

'I'll do it, but on one condition.' He looked from Tristan to Freya. 'That Freya and I do it together.'

That evening, after an unexpectedly busy day in the café, Freya found herself in the church standing in front of a bare white wall, Angelo beside her, while Tristan stumbled over explanations of what he wanted.

'I have to warn you, I'm not sure how the parishioners will react to me commissioning a mural,' Tristan confessed.

'So you haven't asked them?' Angelo enquired tensely.

'Erm, no, but I will express the idea during service this Sunday.' Exasperated, Tristan signalled at the walls. 'Look at them, this church needs something, and they can't stay stuck in their ways for ever. The only specification is that it is religiously themed. This is the church of St Peter, the patron saint of fishermen, and I think it's only right that we honour that. Just because we're a local parish doesn't mean we can't have something impressive. I mean, look at the window.'

Angelo stepped over to the wall and ran his hands reverently over its surface. 'Nice and smooth,' he commented, 'perfect for a mural, but I can't promise you anything on the scale of the Sistine Chapel. When do you want it finished by?'

'I was thinking the Fisherman's Fair, if that's not too much trouble? I know it's tight, but I think it'd be a nice touch. It will add something a little extra to the day and hopefully bring in a bit of recognition to the village. Do you think you could do it?' Tristan held his hands in prayer position, a hopeful look on his kind face.

Freya watched Angelo sizing up the wall, covering the surface in his mind with pictures. 'It will be a lot of work, weekends, late nights and first I need to come up with a design. If Freya helps, then yes, it should be achievable.' He turned to Freya. 'Are you up for it?'

'I've never done mural work before but I've always loved a challenge. Plus, Tristan is right, the Fisherman's Fair needs to have something extra special.' She grinned. This was what she had always wanted. To be commissioned for a piece of work. Well, technically Angelo was the one with the commission, but she knew she'd be a fool to turn down the opportunity to work beside such a prestigious artist. She looked up to find him looking down at her as if he needed her, as if the whole project rested on her acceptance. 'Of course I'll help. I'd be mad to turn this down. Working with the infamous Angelo Borelli.'

'Of course, although I'm not planning on trading on the name.' Tristan smiled and gave Freya a wink to signify that he'd heard all about Angelo's former life from a pastoral perspective. 'When can you start?'

'I'll need access to the space because I'll need to scale up my drawings,' Angelo said. 'I'll need a few days to knock together a few ideas. There is one stipulation though.'

'Go on.'

'I don't want my name attached to the project. At the moment, as you know, I'm figuring some stuff out, so I request anonymity.'

'Of course, of course, I fully understand.' Tristan held his hands up in a placatory gesture before changing the subject. 'I have a small budget, anything you need I can order in.'

The two men locked eyes in understanding, leaving Freya in no doubt that whatever burden Angelo was carrying, he had shed some of its load onto the vicar's shoulders.

'So,' Freya ventured as they stood by the harbour wall watching the sun lower in the sky, the twilight lazy and dream-filled, 'do you know what you're going to do?'

Angelo's eyes were closed, his face turned to bask in the golden light. 'Not a clue,' he confessed. 'I'm starting to regret saying yes. I know what this place is like – everyone gossips; they can't help it. I've never been anywhere where so many people think it's okay to stick their noses into everyone else's business.' He turned to Freya. 'I'm enjoying being here, being anonymous without all those demands from my life. It's the most freedom I've ever had. I'm thirty-seven and I've never had a moment's peace until now. I've grown used to it so quickly.' Angelo sighed. 'Yet I can't turn Tristan's request down.'

Freya watched him. 'I know how you feel. It's so lovely down here; it's the first time I've heard myself think since I went off to uni. The first time I've allowed myself time to stop. Although my family do keep ringing and texting and asking what I'm going to do after this summer. Is it okay that I don't know?' Freya pulled a face and then looked up at Angelo for his answer.

Angelo considered this. 'Confession time. I don't know what I'm going to do after this summer, either. I can't hide forever, yet I don't want to go anywhere else.' Angelo paused and studied Freya in the golden light. 'It seems we are so alike.' The words were simple but laced heavily with meaning.

Eyes locked, they continued to gaze at each other, the magnetic pull between them growing stronger. Angelo was looking at her mouth and, suddenly conscious of the fact she'd very much like to kiss him, Freya broke her eyes away and returned to studying the harbour, closing her eyes against both the sun and a man she was starting to want very much.

'I guess when September comes we could just jump on your bike and ride away into the sunset,' she joked. In her heart it wasn't a joke, but a strange sort of yearning she wasn't ready for.

Angelo exhaled and stared out to sea for a long time before speaking as if thinking aloud. 'Maybe I'll draw Alf as St Peter and pop in other people's faces. Who knows?' He shrugged. 'My problem is that my imagination is already bounding ahead of me. Rather than thinking what is achievable in that small space, I'm thinking of the Sistine Chapel. I tried to manage Tristan's expectations, but it's my own I need to rein in. That was always my failure, Freya, thinking too big. It worked when I was young and everything was a gamble with little to lose but now the pressure to get it right ...' Angelo turned to her, 'I'm sure it'll be fine. Tell me it'll be fine, Freya.'

He was looking at her as if she had all the answers when in fact she had none. Freya patted him on the arm and flashed him what she hoped was a reassuring smile. 'Sure. It'll all be fine.'

Angelo roared with laughter. 'I'll need you to be a bit more convincing than that!'

'You, the great Angelo Borelli, are asking me, Freya Harris, a failed art student, for reassurance.' She shook her head in amusement. 'How my life has changed.'

Angelo stepped forward, closing the gap between them,

grabbing her hands in his. 'You are not a failed art student,' he growled. 'I don't ever want to hear you talking like that again, okay?'

Freya, her insides suddenly liquid, barely managed a nod. God, he was hot. 'Okay, so what am I?' she asked.

'My apprentice!' Angelo grinned wolfishly. 'I hope you like hard work.'

'What was all that about?' Lola peered over the top of her crochet when Freya breezed into the garden, a bottle of prosecco held triumphantly aloft.

Freya poured two glasses, excitement bubbling away in her. 'I am to be Angelo's new apprentice!' she announced. 'Cheers!'

Lola threw her crochet onto the patio table and leapt at Freya, bundling her into a hug. 'That's amazing, hon. I wondered where Tristan scooted you away to. You must tell me everything!'

Freya dropped into the chair opposite and stretched out her legs. The Cornish sun was turning them a lovely golden colour. She slipped off her flip-flops and wiggled her toes, her multicoloured nail polish slightly chipped but still passable. 'Before I tell you anything, you have to swear to keep it a secret.'

Lola rolled her eyes. 'Why does everything to do with Angelo have to be classified? And why do you think I'm the resident blabbermouth, hmm?' She raised an eyebrow at Freya, but then said, 'Actually, don't answer that.'

'It's not just you, and this doesn't come from me. Tristan

saw Angelo's portrait of Alf and asked him to paint a mural in the church, which he wants unveiled at the Fisherman's Fair. Angelo agreed but on the conditions that his involvement remains anonymous and that I help him.'

'Yes!' Lola fist pumped the air. 'I knew he fancied you.'

'Oi! What about my artistic talents that he wishes to use?' Freya pointed out with mock outrage, while the notion of Angelo fancying her was secretly thrilling. Freya pressed her lips together to hide the smile trying to sneak across her face, and countered with, 'I am the only other local artist.'

Lola shook her head laughing 'This bloke rocks up on a motorbike, claps eyes on you and decides to stay the summer. He buys you art stuff – don't think I didn't notice; I saw what you brought with you and you don't have very many hiding places in that café – and the first opportunity he has, he gets you involved in something artistic. What I'm most put out about is that you haven't told me anything about him and I know you know stuff!' She sat back and took a triumphant sip of her drink.

'It's not that easy,' Freya protested. 'Look, you need to keep this to yourself. He was big in the art world once upon a time, a proper quick rise to fame, but I don't think it made him happy. Something obviously happened that made him run away. I don't know what, but he seems troubled by it.' With a sigh she sat back. 'I'm just trying to get to know him. I know you mean well, but I can't push him. He's too spikey. Lola, I honestly don't know anything more than that. I think he trusts me, but I can't push that trust.'

Lola nodded, for once seeming to take Freya's point. 'Okay, so how do you feel about being involved?'

'I've never painted a mural before and the way Angelo was talking I don't think it's going to be your bog-standard mural. I think his mind has wandered straight back to the Renaissance,' Freya gushed, thinking back to Angelo's tattoo. She'd not seen him without his top on again and it didn't feel right bringing it up randomly. 'He's been in the church a lot. Tristan seems to know what's going on with him.'

Lola considered this for a long time. 'Damn it, he'll never spill. He's the first man I've met with real integrity. Tristan, that is,' she clarified.

'Is that why you like him?' Freya seized the opportunity both to steer the questions away from herself and find out more about Lola's feelings for the vicar.

Lola held Freya's gaze for a long time, sorting out the correct answer in her head. Exasperated, Freya pushed, 'You're always so interested in finding out about everyone else's life, Lola, always pushing and speculating about Angelo, but you remain tight-lipped about your own life. Why are you here after all these years on the road?' She topped up their glasses. 'I am legitimately curious. I never thought this would happen.' She gestured to the quaint little garden where courgettes and carrots were growing in a raised bed. 'It's all very homely.'

Lola fiddled with the hem of her sundress. 'I suppose you're right. The truth is I was fed up.' She sighed. 'I suddenly realized everyone was settling down, stopping, permanently pitching up their lives. All the people I'd started out with had bought houses, or had babies, or gotten married, or all three. And I realized that they were so much more contented than I was and it kicked me right here.' She indicated her heart. 'I felt like I hadn't achieved a single thing.

'Do you remember Jared?' Lola continued. 'Lovely, lovely Jared. No? Oh, maybe I wasn't with him when I met you, but he was beautiful.' She smiled off into the distance. 'I loved him, well, at least I thought I loved him. We were always together. He was a musician and magician and I was his assistant. There was never a show we didn't sell out. I really believed we were together for the long haul, but when I rejoined him on the road last summer he announced he'd met someone and they were having a baby. Oh, Freya, he brought out this delightful blonde ingénue, Dalia. She was gorgeous, I'll give her that, and she was pregnant, months along, in-your-face pregnant. They were so happy,' Lola said sadly. 'So overbearingly happy and it made me so miserable. I'd always believed Jared and I would end up together, even though the cards said otherwise. All that misery I brought on myself could've been avoided if I'd just listened to my own flipping cards. They were married, and I'd been replaced, and suddenly I saw it. Everyone else had managed to settle down, tick off the boxes and I knew I no longer fitted in. The cards had been pushing me away from that life for ages and I'd ignored them. I could've saved myself a whole load of heartbreak if I'd just listened.'

Lola ran her hands through her hair, loosening the tight curls at the nape of her neck. 'So after a lot of meditation – and consulting the cards, of course, which were pointing to a life by the sea – I came down here. We used to holiday in Cornwall when I was a kid, and I fell in love with this little place, so far away from everything I had known; it felt right for a new start. It's got such a gentle, soothing atmosphere, perfect for the healing business I hope to start one day. The cottage was for sale, and I had some inheritance from my Grandmother Ruby. It needed a lot of work, but I did it all myself. And Dave and Aggie wanted to retire so leased me the café. I really want this to work, Freya. I don't want to feel like a failure anymore, but also, Polcarrow has come to mean so much to me. I can't imagine living anywhere else now, which is something I never thought I'd say.'

Freya glanced around the room; Lola had turned it into a haven but she wasn't interested in hearing about the café. 'What about Tristan? All this flirting and circling each other is driving me mad.' Freya groaned for dramatic effect.

Lola laughed. 'Tristan and I became friendly because we arrived at basically the same time – two total outsiders pushing our way into this closed-off world. He's a vicar, though, a vicar! And I'm, well, what am I? Ex-showgirl, cocktail waitress, nude model and cake baker. As a vicar, he'd need to get married – he couldn't exactly live in sin – and that scares me, putting down proper roots. I'm not quite ready to take the next step. I need to concentrate on the business first.' Lola dropped her voice. 'You might not realize it but everyone is gossiping about us, so the interest in you and Angelo has actually given us some space! One thing I will set you straight on is that nothing has happened between us. He's a vicar for God's sake, so we both need to play it carefully. If something were to happen it would have to be serious, and even I'm a little worried that's a step too far for me.'

Freya regarded her friend as she digested all this. The light had lowered mercifully on her confession and the mood had dropped. 'I had no idea.'

'You weren't supposed to. I was always fun Lola.' She did a little shimmy. 'My life was always meant to be a great party and I loved it – I've had a great life – but suddenly it wasn't enough.'

'I know. Actually, I've been thinking the same about London. I don't think it was enough for me anymore, which is strange to say about a city.' Freya mused, 'I think it was probably a blessing that Matt dumped me. I'm finding it hard to imagine what my life would have been like had I stayed there.'

'Have you heard from him?'

'No. And I don't know how I feel about that. Relieved, I think. But, Lola, I'm scared because I don't know what happens next, and so much has happened already. I feel like I'm still catching up with myself. As for Angelo . . .' Freya trailed off and blew out a breath in exasperation.

Lola reached out and squeezed her hand. 'Trust what's going on. The cards never lie. He didn't have to ask you to help with the mural; that's a good sign.'

'True.' Freya smiled at her friend and squeezed her hand back. 'But what happens next?'

'Honestly? I haven't a clue. But we're all here for a reason;

we just need to see what that reason is. The universe will provide,' Lola said sagely and pointed to the sky.

'Do you really believe that?' Freya yawned; it was getting late and the excitement about the mural had died down.

Lola gazed up at the stars smattered across the sky, a crystalline undecipherable map, and smiled to herself. 'Yes, I think I do.'

Angelo did not sleep that night. Every time he closed his eyes he saw that blank wall in the church and he was unable to stop himself from mentally filling it. Midnight came and went and sleep still evaded him. He got up, switched on the bedside lamp and seized the sketchbook. He couldn't remember the last time he had been filled with such desire to just draw. Picking up the pencil, Angelo paused over the blank page, fear and excitement tingling in his fingertips as he slowly began to draw. He lost track of the passing of the dead hours of the night, filling page after page with sketches, ideas, rough line drawings and small details.

As a student, he had always drawn or sculpted in his room as and when the mood took him, sometimes not sleeping for days. His ex-girlfriend Vanessa had loved the idea of being seen on the arm of the latest bright young thing, but she was less pleased with his penchant for midnight flits to the studio and days of being out of contact. His mobile would frequently drain of battery and he'd forget to eat, but no matter how good the work he created was, her tantrums always won. As Angelo had learnt to his detriment, what

Vanessa wanted, Vanessa got. Her father had been Angelo's first patron; he'd wanted the work, his daughter had wanted the man, and between them they had assimilated him into their own nine-to-five version of an artist, not caring one jot that they were slowly killing him. They'd squeezed him into their boxes until he suffocated.

Now, he was living for himself. The desire to create was flaring in his blood, stirred in the most unusual way by a defiant young woman who stared down the sunset and painted even though everyone else was trying to stop her. Freya had a talent that she was unaware of. She had been squashed and pushed, like he had, into other people's artistic boxes. He wanted to tell her that, now that she was finally free from institutional art, she could pick up her brushes and create in whichever way she most desired. His mind wandered over her image, those large hazel eyes, the tumble of dark hair, the way she held herself back. Angelo yearned to drag her out of herself, to ignite the embers he saw in her, but his own insecurities stopped him. He didn't know if he could truly offer her what she wanted, what she deserved, and as much as he wanted to awaken everything in her, he was afraid that he wouldn't be good enough.

Angelo drew, his mind swirling all over the place, until the pale light of dawn cracked through the horizon. His eyes were red, his head ached, but he had never felt as alive as he did when he looked back at what he'd drawn. The faces staring back at him, one in particular rendered over and over. He closed the book and fell into a deep sleep.

Chapter Thirteen

Between helping Alf with his boat and drafting sketches for the church mural, Angelo's presence around the café became a bit of a blur. He'd emerge, quickly knock back an espresso and throw Freya a quick meaningful look on his way out. Stuck behind the counter serving, Freya wished she was also off on artistic adventures.

The sunny weather continued. Freya found frames for her paintings; she wasn't quite ready to attach a price to them, but now they were properly hung, they added a bit of jollity to the café walls. She continued to paint while awaiting instructions from Angelo about the mural. Each morning she was up, happy and contented to be sitting on the harbour wall with her paints, her artistic rhythm matching that of the tide. As Freya's work improved so did her confidence and the slight from the little gallery she'd visited no longer hurt as much.

'What do you think of these?' Angelo asked one morning, thumping the sketchbook down on the counter and flicking through the pages. Freya noticed that some had been carefully removed and wondered what had happened to them.

She glanced up at him and seeing his confidence falter, gave him a reassuring smile.

Freya pulled the book towards her and slowly pored over the pencil drawings. Angelo had an astounding eye for detail, his drawings reminiscent of a Renaissance master. Freya studied the things he'd drawn: hands and faces of locals, details from the village buildings; Alf from various different positions; even one done quickly from memory of her and Lola. 'Wow, they're amazing! So much detail. I'm rather envious. Portrait drawing has never been my forte.'

Freya was touched to see that, even after years of being feted by various art world dignitaries, her praise made Angelo smile shyly, as if he was still doubting his talent, which in turn melted her heart a little more. It was comforting to learn that, despite success, the artistic mind was in a state of constant progression.

'Thanks. Honestly, that means a lot. It's been a long time since I did some simple drawings.' He flicked reflectively through the pages. 'I'm thinking of doing something with St Peter for the mural, something to do with fishing and calling the faithful, but putting a modern spin on it. Like mermaids or something.' He shrugged. 'I'm not sure how it'll go down though. I don't know if Tristan has really thought about it either. I need to get the final scene together, get it approved and then I can scale it up. Have you ever scaled things up?'

Freya shook her head. Angelo looked surprised. Clearly working with him would be a further education.

'It's something I studied on my gap year in Florence, the

way the Renaissance masters worked. We have all this talk about modern art, new techniques, but if you don't know the basics . . .' He tapped the sketchbook and shrugged.

'You spent your gap year in Florence? I'd love to go there,' Freya drooled.

'Yes, plus the Italian side of my family is based in Tuscany. You've never been?' He sounded surprised.

Freya shook her head. 'The furthest I've been is Paris. Matt took me for my twenty-first. We were students and had no money. It was fun, but I don't think we really experienced it, just ticked off all the tourist sights. We even committed the sacrilege of eating in McDonald's. You make me feel like I've done nothing.'

Angelo made a face. 'I can only forgive that because you were students. There's plenty of time,' he reassured her. 'If you do everything when you're young then what do you have left?' He shrugged. 'Florence has been there for centuries and it'll be there for centuries to come. I needed some time out. I was losing sight of what I wanted to achieve artistically and needed to feel immersed somewhere that would make me reflect. It's impossible not to be awed by Florence, by all that grand art. It certainly put me in my place!'

'So you just swanned around for a year?' Freya teased, making some flouncing movements. 'Being all artistic.'

Angelo laughed. 'No, I worked, in a couple of cafés and bars, and in my downtime I sketched. I love drawing people, their unique expressions, the different combinations of features. In Florence it was so easy to sit there drawing a well-dressed woman, or a dusty workman, and to think they are the same faces that Leonardo would have encountered. Only our clothes really change.'

'Why did you stop portrait drawing?' Freya asked, taking advantage of the lull in custom to make them both a second coffee.

Angelo shrugged and stirred in some sugar. 'I wanted to push myself.' He held her gaze for a long time, his voice low. 'We're more similar than you think. The art world loves to admire the past, loves to revel in it, but always wants to be moving forward. You need confidence to stay in it. So I moved with the times. I produced what I knew would shock and awe, and it got me . . . well, it's brought me here.' Angelo signalled around him. 'Which I'm starting to think isn't as bad as it seems.'

'Lots of people would kill for a summer by the sea,' Freya reminded him with a smile. 'I secretly think all my friends and family are jealous.'

Angelo laughed. 'Yes, and so they should be. It's like a different world down here . . .' He trailed off, then brought the conversation back to artistic matters. 'Anyway, I'm planning on doing a sort of Renaissance-style modern fresco. I've figured if I combine the classic with the new, no one will complain. I don't think the people of Polcarrow are ready to interpret a pile of bricks.'

Freya laughed. 'The worst thing I did was bend a load of coat hangers and twist them together to symbolise the confusion of life. I still cringe to think of it today, but it was more warmly received than my paintings.'

Angelo glanced over at the wall. 'They're looking good. Framed and ready to sell.'

'No one's asked to buy them.' Freya pulled a sad face. 'They're the first ones I did and it always take a while to get into the artistic stride. I keep looking at them and seeing what I'd change.'

'Stop criticizing and see this as learning. You need to be able to recognize your own value as an artist. Trust me,' he added when Freya made a face. 'Right, I need to go and help Alf, then see Tristan, see you later!'

'Oh, aren't they delightful!'

Freya heard the voice trill as she pushed open the café door after her lunch break. She froze. An older lady dressed in pink florals was standing up, leaning over the tables, peering at Freya's paintings. No, not peering, admiring. Freya hung back, intrigued. Angelo was standing next to the woman, nodding along encouragingly.

'Now, I like this one; it's so dreamy!' She clutched Angelo's arm. 'Those beautiful lilac colours. Is it dawn or dusk? I don't know! But I think that's why I like it, because it's all ambiguous. I've been travelling all over Cornwall in search of art – I've got a few bits, but it's just the same old fishing boats over and over, terribly dull. I need something with more oomph.'

Angelo glanced over at the half-open door. Catching Freya's eye, he winked. Freya couldn't help but smile; at least someone appreciated the lack of fishing boats.

'And this one! Oh my. I fancy having that hanging above my telephone table. I could imagine I'm back here while talking to the insurance man.'

At least she didn't want to hang it in the downstairs loo, Freya reasoned, smiling to herself. She imagined the scene playing out as this verbose lady chattered away to her friends.

'Are they for sale? I can't see a price.' The woman peered closer.

'Why don't you ask the artist?' Freya shook her head but Angelo grabbed her wrist and pulled her into the shop.

'Did you paint these?' she asked, casting an eye over Freya, taking in her frayed shorts and the T-shirt with the chocolate stain on it.

'Erm, yes.' Freya tucked her hair behind her ears. Angelo gave her an encouraging look. 'They've all been painted here this summer, right over there on the harbour. I love the way the dawn light hits the sea, how it fills the sky. The different colours. How fleeting it all is. That dawn will never be repeated again.'

'How romantic.' The woman sighed. 'Well, I think they are lovely. Are they for sale?'

'Erm, yes, they can be, if you want any of them.' Freya couldn't believe her luck.

'I want all of them!' the woman announced. 'I love the wispiness of them, like a dreamy mist, the light all sort of oozing together. How much do you want?' She was already fishing in her bag for her purse.

'Two hundred for the lot,' Angelo interceded, probably

knowing that Freya would sell herself short. The woman looked from him to Freya and back again. Freya's heart sank. There was no way anyone would part with two hundred pounds for five rushed watercolours.

'A steal!' she trilled, her face beaming. 'I don't have two hundred on me, but I can write you a cheque.'

Freya nodded, shocked. She didn't know when she'd get to deposit it but she liked the idea of having a spare two hundred pounds. The woman dashed off the cheque, tore it out and presented it to Freya. They shook hands. Angelo was already lifting the paintings off the wall and looking for something to wrap them in. Freya unearthed an empty box and lined them up, a bit of kitchen roll balled up to give them some cushioning.

'Marvellous! Can you carry them to my car please? It's the red one, just parked across the road.' She turned to Freya and passed her a business card. 'Do keep painting and keep me updated. I'd like something really dark and stormy if you get chance.'

Freya pocketed the card. 'Thank you! I had no idea anyone would want to buy my paintings.'

'Why ever not? You'd better paint some more, those walls are looking pretty bare now,' she said as she ushered Angelo outside.

Freya watched as the woman bustled about telling Angelo exactly how she wanted the paintings stowed in her car boot. Angelo watched her get in and waved as she drove off before bounding back into the café.

'Your first sale!' he cried, picking Freya up and swinging her about. 'How does it feel?'

Freya let out a whoop of delight. 'I have no idea! It's not sunk in. I've never sold anything before.' She glanced down at him, suddenly aware that she was in his arms; all sorts of things started to bubble up inside her. What had been a spontaneous move on his part suddenly bloomed into something much more potent. Freya gazed down into his dark eyes, which were swirling with the same happiness that was fizzing through her. Held like this, her hands on his broad shoulders, all it would take was a drop of her head and she could kiss him. The notion of a possible kiss pulled at their mouths and, although Angelo slowly put her down and took a step back, the seed had been sown. He rubbed the back of his neck, something Freya had observed him do when nervous. Nervous because of her? Freya smothered a giggle; the thought emboldened her.

'Well, I'd better get going and I . . . think you should paint some more,' Angelo said, clearly flustered.

Freya shook her head, laughing in disbelief as Angelo left, then she got back to the serious business of café work. Hair up, apron on, high with success, she glided through the afternoon chores with a spring in her step. Painting had suddenly become a possibility rather than a dream.

The excitement of having sold her first painting quickly fizzled out when Freya realized that if she wanted to keep selling paintings, she'd have to refill the wall. The pressure seized her like a fist gripping a brush too tightly. Painting on demand had never sat well with her and she found herself perched on the harbour wall later that afternoon, desperately trying to cobble something together. The results were disappointing and frustrating to say the least, and made her question her ability again. Freya held the sketchbook out and peered at her efforts. Sure, it was passable, but passable was not enough. It took all her strength not to hurl the entire book among the chip shop wrappers in the nearest bin.

Putting the book down Freya sighed, rubbed her neck and tried to put the painting out of her mind. She'd been for a very pleasant paddle in the shallows and her feet were still caked in scratchy sand. The sun drenched the harbour in shimmering golden light, thick as syrup. Even with the stress of having to paint on demand, Freya realized she was happy, deep-in-her-soul content; it dawned on her like the rising sun. So what if the painting she was working on was a bit rubbish? She was living by the sea, paints and art debris strewn around her, two hundred pounds richer than she'd been that morning. All in all she had nothing to grumble about and her only concern was what to do about her growing attraction to Angelo. Even thinking about him squeezed her heart happily. The way he'd scooped her up triumphantly still made her catch her breath.

'How's it going?'

Freya glanced up. There he was hovering at her side, a roll of paper tucked under his arm. She held out her painting for him. 'Not good. I feel like I'm painting on demand. Did you have to sell all my paintings?'

Angelo took the book from her, awkwardly since he was trying not to drop his paper. 'It's not as bad as you think.'

With a groan Freya snatched it back from him. 'That's hardly praise! And you paused before answering.' She put the book back on the harbour wall and started to pack away her equipment. 'I feel like I'm forcing it.'

'Just keep doing what you're doing, coming out morning and night, and you'll get something you're happy with. Trial and error, remember. Plus, there's nothing wrong with a bit of scarcity. That lady will be showing off those paintings to everyone. She'll be boasting about finding a brand-new artist. That's what people like, to think they have something special.'

'True, but what if she sends all her friends down here?'

'She won't,' he replied firmly. 'She won't want them to have whatever thing she thinks makes her special or unique. Which is your paintings,' Angelo reasoned, adding bitterly, 'that's one thing I have learned: art brings out the greed in people.'

Freya noted his wisdom and, seeing a scowl forming across Angelo's brow, decided not to press the matter. 'Thanks for today,' she said, hopping off the wall, 'for selling those paintings. I probably would have let her have them for free.'

'It's because you've been taught not to value your work. Everyone's creative work has value, whether you spent five minutes on it, or five hours. It's still your time you gave up for it. Don't sell yourself short. She was happy, very happy and you did that. I wouldn't be encouraging you if I didn't think it was the right thing to do. Believe me, I've seen all sorts with my students. People want instant results without the work. You need to do the work because you love it, pure and simple.' He shrugged as if it was common sense and caught Freya's eye.

Freya nodded up at him while he looked down at her. Something unspoken hung between them, their colours running together. Even if Freya was warming to the idea, she wasn't sure Angelo was ready. He still moved around the village like a man watching the shadows, ready to leap at any moment.

Chapter Fourteen

Although Angelo had been given free rein for the mural, Freya noticed Tristan couldn't help but flutter about anxiously while Angelo prepared his final sketches, seemingly worried about how the whole project would be received by the villagers. She tried to reassure Tristan it would be a success, which seemed to briefly calm his nerves. Angelo weathered his gentle meddling with a grace Freya admired, especially since she knew Angelo well enough by now to know he was holding back from speaking his mind. Once Tristan had finally approved the sketches and theme of the mural, Angelo asked Lola if he could borrow the café one evening after closing.

'I need a large space to mock up the entire scene and was hoping to push some of the tables together,' he explained.

Always keen to get involved, Lola nodded. 'Sure, help yourself to whatever you need in the kitchen. Can't wait to see how this all turns out!' She grabbed her bag and waltzed out, sending a mock warning glance at Angelo and Freya as she pulled the door shut. 'Just behave; you're working on a piece of religious art.'

As Lola pulled the door shut, sending the bell tinkling in

her wake, her parting shot lingered. It settled on them in a not entirely uncomfortable manner. Freya, ready to work, tucked her hair behind her ears and reminded herself that she was here in her capacity of artistic apprentice and it was not a date. Even though she'd sneakily applied a bit of mascara at the end of her shift and the air crackled with unspoken desire.

Angelo set the first task. 'Can you move all the chairs out of the way, please?'

Freya hurried to it, stacking them in various corners, even depositing some of them in the kitchen, where she noticed Lola had left a couple of scones under a tea towel to keep the artists going. After weeks of serving sweet treats and learning to bake in a passable manner, Freya's teeth were starting to ache at the thought of any more cake. She felt encased in sugar. When she came back out, Angelo was struggling to move the tables by himself.

'Let me help.' She hurried over and grabbed one end of the table. 'You're not proving anything by carrying them all yourself.' She grabbed the other end of the table he was holding and helped scoot it into position. As a nifty two-person team, they grafted in silence until the tables were positioned exactly as Angelo wanted, even if it left little room for them to squeeze around the perimeter.

'Couldn't you have used the floor in the church hall?' she asked, thinking it would have meant a lot less moving stuff about.

'No, it's a bit more private in here. We can lock the door, pull down the blind. If we were in the church hall, Tristan would be twitching about checking what we were doing. We need table height too.'

'I'm sure Lola could keep him entertained.' Freya wiggled her eyebrows.

Angelo laughed. 'I'm sure she could. He's a great guy but I think this village, although welcoming, is still silently judging. I always feel like everyone is waiting to see what I'm going to do, and expecting some sort of satanic ritual rather than this.' He signalled to the sketches.

'It's the dark hair, dark clothes and motorbike that are to blame,' she teased.

Angelo rolled his eyes. 'I guess I fit the stereotype. Despite the occasional small mind, I feel very at peace here, though. Just look at that view!' Angelo wandered over to the window. 'Waking up to that every morning is worth any amount of gossip.'

'I'm sure given time they'd accept you.' Freya's brain was screaming to ask if he was planning to stay here permanently, but she kept her voice light.

'Let's see what they make of this first.' Angelo paused as if to compose himself and admitted, 'I also feel like I need to prove myself to the villagers, so I want this to be good.' He tapped the sketchbook.

'Me too, for Lola and Tristan. They're so keen for this festival to do well, it's rather putting the village committee to shame.' Lola and Tristan had been seen, heads together, chattering away about how to boost the profile of the Fisherman's Fair to gain maximum footfall.

'Sounds like we're on the same page, which is a good start.' Angelo grinned at her. 'So, scaling up a drawing. First we need to carefully tape together these sheets of paper,' he explained. 'It's the only thing London has going for it at the moment – proper studios and the ability to get larger sheets of paper.' He tossed a roll of tape at Freya which she caught expertly. 'Good catch.'

'I was never good when it counted,' she said as she tried to unpick the end, 'like rounders during sports day.'

'Ugh, sports days, what a way to make kids feel shitty about themselves. No prizes for guessing I was not star of the football team. Did you like school?'

Freya stopped to consider this; she'd not thought about school for a long time. 'I guess so, well, as much as the next person. All my mates were there; we had fun.' Freya shrugged. 'I know people say it's the best time of their lives, but really? School? Surely other stuff is better? Or maybe it's the lack of responsibility that makes them think that? I guess completing a geography project is a lot less of a worry than paying your rent.'

Angelo shrugged. 'I think people only like school in hindsight. Other than the kids who peak in secondary school. I was awful at school, your stereotypical bad boy, bunking off, not revising, spending too long sulking in the art rooms. I was such a cliché!' Angelo chuckled. 'The only thing I never did was smoke behind the bike sheds. Never been a smoker. Somehow I scraped the five GCSEs I needed to go to college and then I didn't need to worry about maths or geography or anything else.' He positioned two sheets next to each other, lining them up edge to edge, and signalled to Freya to pass him some tape. 'Now I wonder if I should have concentrated on something else, had a backup, but I guess everyone in their mid-thirties thinks like that.' He gave Freya a self-deprecating smile as he reached for more tape.

'Are you having some sort of reverse midlife crisis?' Freya quipped. 'Instead of buying a motorbike, you're contemplating a quiet life by the sea?'

Angelo shrugged. 'Maybe. How old are you?'

'Twenty-seven.'

Angelo laughed. 'You say it like it's ancient. Try being thirty-seven!'

Freya laughed, and when Angelo didn't seem bothered by the age gap, she chose to completely ignore it herself. Ten years wasn't really all that much in the grand scheme of things and she was pretty sure the attraction was mutual. Freya cosied up to the thought as she watched Angelo concentrate on getting the paper taped neatly together. The silence was companionable and focused; they worked well together.

'Now what?' Freya asked as she stepped back, pleased with how the table was covered in a big sheet of paper, the joins hardly noticeable.

'To scale up a drawing I need to create a grid pattern on this sort of tablecloth sheet and then on the sketch, then you just sort of transfer it over by making a similar grid on the wall. It's how all the old Italian masters did it.'

Freya nodded, and her stomach began to rumble.

Angelo looked at her and laughed. 'Well, I guess it's getting late,' he said.

'I'll see what I can rustle up.' Freya ducked into the kitchen and pulled open the fridge; Lola had told them to help themselves and Freya planned on taking full advantage. She pulled out some cold meats, cheese, salad and found some crusty bread wrapped up on the side. Freya stared at it all, wracking her brain, wanting to impress Angelo with her scant skills.

Angelo stuck his head around the door. 'What are you planning on making?'

Freya surveyed the items before her but didn't feel inspired. 'Don't know. Some sort of salad I guess. It's a bit like an indoor picnic.'

Angelo came so close to her, Freya stopped concentrating. 'Have you got any tomatoes?'

She fetched the tomatoes from the fridge and passed them to Angelo, and then watched as he tested their firmness, even sniffing them. When they met his approval, he nodded. 'Pass me that board, please.'

Freya passed it to him, then took advantage of the situation to stand closer than was necessary in order to watch Angelo deftly chop the tomatoes into tiny chunks, tipping them into a bowl and slugging in a good measure of olive oil. The warmth from his body wrapped around her. He smelled good, the same wild manly scent she'd breathed in when he'd first arrived in Polcarrow. Freya just about stopped herself leaning in for a sniff and instead quipped, 'Those are some chopping skills you have. What are you making?'

'Bruschetta,' he announced. 'Proper decent bruschetta. That's the thing I most miss about Italy, the food. Especially Mum's cooking, so simple but delicious. I can't sneak round for dinner now she's in Italy, like I did when I was a student.' He chopped up an onion so finely that Freya was mesmerized by his skills. He threw it into the bowl and mixed it all up, adding salt, pepper, but he was disappointed that Lola had no garlic.

'She's cooking for the cream tea crowd,' Freya reminded him.

'True. Can you slice the bread for me, please?'

Freya sliced the airy sourdough and then lightly toasted the bread, all as instructed. Angelo heaped the tomatoes on top of the golden slices, drizzled them with more olive oil and pushed a plate across to Freya. He watched as she bit into the bread and smiled with relief as she sighed with foodie happiness.

'Oh, that is amazing!' Freya mumbled through a second bite. 'Much better than whatever I was going to cobble up.'

Angelo seemed a little bashful at her praise. 'It's honestly nothing. If I had known you were this easy to please, I would have made lunch for you ages ago.' His eyes sparkled with all sorts of meaning and, rather than respond, Freya heaped some escaped tomatoes back onto her bread and continued eating.

'So,' Freya said through another mouthful of bruschetta, 'you talk about Italy a lot. How long since you've been?'

'About a year. Mum lives out there on the family farm

in Tuscany, helping my aunt run it. Not sure how much helping she does, though – she's not one to get her hands dirty.' Angelo smiled wistfully. 'I should go back more, but it's hard. Mum's been out there for the past five years, ever since my father died.'

'I'm sorry to hear that. Were you close?'

Angelo shook his head. 'My father and me? No. Not at all. He worked in the city and never supported my artistic ambitions. He blamed Mum for making me soft. She was an opera singer. They were such an odd pairing. I think marrying Mum was the most emotional thing he ever did, and she was also the only one who could put him in his place. I don't have any siblings. Somehow, if they'd been able to have more children, I think things would have been easier. Less pressure on me, at least.' Angelo paused to collect his thoughts. 'When he died, I didn't know what to feel. We hadn't been in a good place for years. He never supported my art, thought I should follow the family into the finance industry, but I don't have a head for numbers. Borelli is her surname, I preferred to use that to my father's Burrington, especially as an artist – the whole Italian package.' Angelo let out a hollow laugh. 'Mum was devastated though. I never thought it would hit her like it did. She sold the house I grew up in and went back to Italy.'

'Oh, Angelo, that's so sad,' Freya said even though it was such a meagre word to use. She reached out and gave his hand a squeeze.

Angelo squeezed back. 'Don't be. I appreciate it, but don't

be. I still don't know if I am sadder for the loss of my father or what his death did to Mum.' He paused and finished eating his bruschetta. 'Come on, let's not get maudlin, there's still a lot of work to do.' He got up and headed into the café.

Freya decided to give him a few minutes to collect himself, so she filled and ran the dishwasher. When she emerged from the kitchen, Angelo was behind the counter whipping up a couple of coffees.

'I can't drink coffee this late!' she protested, already aware that even without the extra caffeine she'd pass a sleepless night thinking about Angelo and what he'd told her.

'Nonsense, we drink it all the time in Italy,' Angelo said over the hiss of the steam.

'But we're in Cornwall!'

'Humour me.' He turned to her, sliding two small cups of foamy, rich coffee across the counter. 'It's just after seven o'clock, we have at least two hours of work left, I've just made you probably the best bruschetta you've ever eaten – that's going by your reaction, by the way, not how I feel about my own cooking skills – and it's sunny out. We're painting a religious mural. At least for this evening can we pretend we're in Italy? Deal?' Angelo raised his coffee cup.

Freya studied him for a few moments, touched that he was trying to make sure she had a lovely evening despite all the work they needed to do. She picked up her cup and gently knocked it against his own. 'Deal.'

Then, without breaking eye contact, Freya took her first sip. 'Wow! How did you learn to do that?'

Angelo's face lit up and he laughed. 'Florence. When this is all over, I'll take you there. You can meet my mum. She'd like you even if she always disapproves of my choices.' Although the plan was spoken lightly, there was an edge to it that made Freya hope it was more than a momentary whim.

Realizing there was no one she'd like to show her Florence more than Angelo, she picked up her cup and chinked it against his. 'I'll hold you to it.'

It took three nights to scale up the drawings, and although Freya was not actively involved in the sketching, she enjoyed hanging around the café watching Angelo, learning from him. He'd found an old bandana to tie his long hair back. Freya had laughed when he'd first put it on. 'You look like a pirate! Maybe you should dress as one for the Fisherman's Fair.' Angelo had seen the funny side of this and made some pirate noises and then pretended to hobble around the café with a wooden leg until Freya couldn't stand for laughing.

The evenings passed companionably. Angelo talked about his time in Italy, and Freya, wondering if that was the last time he'd been truly happy, asked the question.

Angelo paused to think about it. 'What makes you say that?'

'You told me about Italy, the little bars you went to, the villages you visited, the art, the food, the coffee, but you never said anything about art school, or your career.' Her words petered out, afraid he'd slam the door shut on her.

Angelo finished the bit of drawing he was working on

before replying. 'I was in Italy almost twenty years ago. I should have moved on by now, you're right. Maybe I just remember it as something beautiful and golden and pure. Yes, pure, because it was all simple. I had no idea where I was heading; I was just on a gap year drinking a bit too much, flirting with hard-to-crack Italian girls and gorging on everything, food, culture, art. You name it, I tried it. Art school was a bit sterile after that. I think I sort of fancied myself as a bit of a modern-day Renaissance master.' Angelo stepped back and surveyed the scaled-up drawing. 'But art school wasn't all bad. It had its moments and it did give me experiences. And, without sounding crude, money to pursue what I wanted. Or what I thought I wanted.' Angelo stretched out his tired fingers. 'What made you decide to study art?'

Freya shrugged. 'I guess it was because I was good at it. I wasn't very good at anything else, not enough to pursue it at least. I wanted to experience being at uni too, which was fun. I guess I thought I'd be more of an artist if I did post-graduate study at a proper art school. Turns out I was wrong, but I guess it will be an experience to look back on.' Freya shrugged as if it didn't mean anything anymore that she'd spent money and years studying without anything to show for it at the end. 'What about you? Why did you study art?'

Angelo turned to Freya and studied her for a long time, as if contemplating what version of events to tell her. Freya perched on the edge of a spare table, suddenly nervous but unwilling to stop Angelo if he was finally ready to open up.

'Because, like you, it was the only thing I was good at.' Angelo stopped and gave Freya a long, resigned look before continuing. 'What you need to understand about everything I tell you is that I was young. Very young and hungry, in both senses, for fame and for security.' When Freya nodded, he turned back and continued to draw while very slowly pulling out the threads of his life. 'Even before my graduation people were talking about me, about my eye for detail, my skills, but they always spoke about these things coupled with my looks. Dark, Italian, moody, brooding, you name it, like some tortured romantic hero, and it was easy to play into this.

'Like you, I did an undergraduate and I had a place on a postgraduate degree, but I never needed to take it because the dream landed on my lap. I was twenty-two, Freya, twenty-two and, frankly, clueless. All these art critics, patrons, gallery owners came to the degree show, everyone picking like vultures over our art hoping to harness some of our talent for their own gain. That's when I met Thomas Hardgreaves – well, I met his daughter first.' Angelo scoffed and shook his head. 'Vanessa Hardgreaves was the most beautiful girl I'd ever seen. Tall, slim, a mane of bright golden hair, and I was young and stupid and instantly smitten. Her father was extremely influential, and if you had him as a backer, you were essentially made. I never stopped to think about it or what it might mean for my life. Dazzled by Vanessa, I signed that contract and signed away my life. I know it sounds overdramatic, but at the time I didn't realize that whatever Vanessa wanted, she got, and what she wanted was me.'

Freya couldn't help but be taken aback by what he was telling her. She experienced a flicker of jealousy at the thought of beautiful Vanessa. Freya tried to smooth it out, but Angelo seemed to notice.

'She was a nightmare. I'm not asking for your sympathy – the first few years were wonderful, very hedonistic. I was nominated for awards; I sold pieces of work for unthinkable amounts of money; we went on lavish holidays. But I was losing touch with myself. It was addictive to be wanted like that. There were things I wanted to do, projects and styles I wanted to explore, but Thomas wouldn't allow me. I reached thirty and realized not only that I was trapped, but that my desire to make art had all dried up.' Angelo stepped back from the drawing he'd been working on. 'The thing that will always puzzle me is why Vanessa didn't just let me go. Her career as a high-class events organizer had taken off and she derided my desire to go back to my roots and tutor in various art schools. She'd call me a failure. I wanted to settle down, have a family, but she said she couldn't slow down her career. For five years she told me next year, next year and each year passed the same as the last. I was working less; we were spending less time together; she resented me being in the studio, but didn't want me to accompany her anywhere. And still she wouldn't let me go. I was trapped and miserable. She wouldn't let me leave.' Angelo thumped the table in frustration then looked over at Freya. 'She certainly wouldn't understand any of this!' He gestured to the drawings and around the café to the seafront outside.

Freya sank back into the lowering shadows. It was too dark to work properly but she didn't want to ruin the moment by flicking on the light.

'Please don't judge me for what happened next,' Angelo asked in a small, shamed voice. 'I was falling into depression. I was isolated. Everyone thought I had the dream, but I had nothing. I'd lost myself. I did find a way to start sculpting again, though. The feel of the metal beneath my hands was life-giving and I could twist all my hate, disappointment and sorrow into my sculpture. I had no plans of selling it; for the first time in years I was making art just for the sake of making art. But Vanessa got wind of what I was doing. One evening I turned up at my studio to find the sculpture had gone. Vanessa had taken it without permission and, after a few phone calls, I learnt she was planning on auctioning it at the event she was hosting that night.' Angelo turned to her, shame flashing across his face. 'Freya, I saw red. I jumped in a taxi, still in my work clothes, and gatecrashed the event. I hadn't even been invited.'

Angelo took a breath and rubbed his face. In a small, pained voice he said, 'I ruined everything. I fought the security guards; I interrupted the auction – some glossy affair with free-flowing champagne – and climbed onto the stage. With my bare hands, I pulled the sculpture apart. I ruined it, growled at everyone that it was not for sale. Vanessa and I had a blazing row on the stage, and she was forced to give back the money to the bidder who had bought my work. Her father intervened and I think it was only his influence

Jennifer Bibby

that kept my disgrace out of the papers and the police from arresting me.' He dropped his voice. 'I am not proud of how I behaved, Freya. I was a complete monster that night. I left in a blind rage, hurling abuse at everyone. I went back to the apartment and packed a bag. Vanessa tried calling but I couldn't face her. I never wanted to speak to her again. I had no desire to see her. I just packed what I could carry on the back of my bike, left a note telling her I couldn't do this anymore and asked her not to contact me.' Angelo exhaled. 'It was a shitty thing to do but I just needed someone to hear me, see me. A cowardly thing, but what else could I have done? Let them gaslight me further into being their cash cow? There's still so much left to sort out, the house we shared, the contracts. It's such a huge mess.'

Even through the shadows, Freya could sense Angelo's desperation. She could imagine him storming the event, destroying his reputation and future with his bare hands. 'It's okay,' she said softly as she went over to him, laying her hand tentatively on his shoulder, when what she really wanted to do was bundle him into her arms and fuse the broken pieces of him back together. 'It's okay; I don't judge you. It sounds like things were pretty awful. Vanessa sounds like a right cow.'

Angelo let out a small snort of laughter and relaxed into her touch, taking her hand and squeezing her fingers. 'This is why I don't want anyone to know I'm here. I'm not ready for her to find me yet. I'm not ready for that conversation. Or the press. "Bad Boy of the Art World Kicks Off", I can see it

202

now. Anyone would love the scoop, "What became of art's young dream".' He laughed bitterly. 'You're right: Vanessa was a right cow, but it took me years of her manipulation to see that. The kicking and screaming just because she's wasn't getting her way. It was tiresome. Draining. She liked the idea of me as an artist but didn't like the reality of it, the nights spent locked in studios, the paint stains, the solitariness of creating something. But you, Freya, you understand.' His voice was almost a whisper. He pushed her hair off her face, studying her.

'I know how it feels. Well, maybe not all of that, but being trapped with someone who doesn't understand,' Freya assured him, her gaze transfixed by his. 'Matt was the same. He thought doing art was cool and quirky when he met me at university. It was fun and unpredictable, but as soon as he got a proper job and had to wear a suit, a girlfriend who paints pictures and wears tie-dye was slightly less fun. He resented my art but never spoke to me about it. He let it fester, and it destroyed us. Now I'm here.' With you, she thought, and much happier, but the moment was too precarious to say it.

'No, we're both here.' Angelo slowly pulled her closer, his eyes never leaving hers, their lives becoming as entwined as their fingers. He leant his forehead against hers, and for a few moments, there was nothing other than their breathing, their hearts beating in time. 'You and me, Freya, we're not so dissimilar. I'm thankful to have met you. He sounds like an idiot. He clearly didn't deserve you.'

His hand was at the nape of her neck, fingers lightly

tangled in her hair. She thought he'd kiss her. Her lips pricked with the anticipation; her heart thudded with desire, her body leaning into his. And perhaps he'd been planning to, but the moment froze around them and, instead, he pulled her to him, moulding her against the length of his body. Wrapping her own arms tightly around him, Freya had the unnerving sensation that she had come home.

Chapter Fifteen

That moment changed everything for Freya. She could no longer deny that something was growing between her and Angelo, and that it had the potential to blossom into something beautiful. He seemed unperturbed by the age gap and, despite his stories of a flighty youth, Freya felt she could trust him. Yes, he was troubled, but he had been honest about what had caused his issues and it would be clear to anyone that Vanessa was a nasty piece of work. Angelo seemed keen to stay in Cornwall and Freya had no plans to go anywhere else. London felt like it had happened to a completely different person. In Polcarrow, Freya had come back to life. She was loving her summer by the sea and how every day reacquainted her with a part of herself she thought she'd lost. The bright dawns helped her bound out of bed, while the thought of Angelo put a spring in her step and the rest of the village squeezed her tightly as if they never wanted to let her go. Life was playing out in beautiful Technicolor.

As the weather grew hotter, things started to slow down on Alf's boat, and the old fisherman had taken to sitting outside the café first thing in the morning, wearing an ancient

Jennifer Bibby

pair of sunglasses. 'Lola needs to get some of those parasol things,' he told Freya when she brought him his tea. 'This sun is in for the duration.'

'I'll get some water for Scruff,' Freya offered in lieu of a parasol and was giving Scruff a quick scratch behind the ear when Angelo sat down opposite Alf, a small brochure in his hand. 'What's that?' she asked.

Angelo put it on the tabletop; a local estate agent's name was printed in blue at the top.

'Bayview House?' Alf asked, curious, reaching across for the brochure. 'They've really flattered it in those photos!' He chuckled and passed it back to Angelo. 'Polcarrow stolen your heart, son?' he asked with a sneaky glance up at Freya. 'Thinking of moving down here?'

Angelo shrugged, looking uncomfortable with the sudden scrutiny. 'I was curious. Thought I'd take a look around.'

Alf made a face. 'It's been empty for ages. No one local can afford it and it needs too much work, I imagine, for people after a second home. Built in the 1930s by a businessman who liked to come down here on his holidays. They were here every summer, but after he died, the son wasn't so interested. They were an all-right sort, but never contributed to the village, just liked our quaintness I suspect. What I wouldn't give for a nose around there!'

'Do you want to come?' Angelo asked.

Alf shook his head. 'Not enough to hobble up the hill in this heat. What time you going?'

'Ten.'

'Take lots of pictures to show me later. Going at a good price, but I reckon you'll realize why. Be careful. I don't trust that estate agent,' Alf warned. 'Definitely haggle.'

Other customers began to arrive, so Freya left the two men to put the world to rights over breakfast, although Angelo seemed to mostly be nodding along to whatever Alf wished to say. On her way back out with a couple of pots of tea, she slipped a coffee in front of Angelo before heading back to her duties. She was tired from several late nights helping him with the mural, and the summer rush was building, but she was buoyed up with a type of happiness that she only found in being creatively productive.

Lola emerged from the kitchen with a basket full of fresh scones wafting their sweet scent through the café, then popped outside to join Alf and Angelo, fanning herself with a menu. 'It's scorching in there! And I still have cheese scones to make. Gosh, not much cooler out here, mind. Morning, Angelo, how's your art project going?' She made it sound like it was a school project.

Angelo furrowed his brow at her. 'It's going well, but I'm not telling you anything else because I don't trust you not to tell Tristan.'

'Like I'd do any such thing!' Lola protested. 'What have you got there?' She wrestled the slightly crumpled brochure out of his hand and, for once, was rendered speechless.

Angelo pulled it back. 'I'm just taking a look. I'm curious.'

'It'll be all over the village by lunchtime,' Lola warned. 'You sure you want to look at it all by yourself?'

'Alf offered but he doesn't fancy going up the hill in this

heat.' Angelo glanced at the old man, who was sitting back enjoying the sun on his face.

'Always good to get a second opinion,' Lola persisted. 'The amount of rubbish I would've invested in if I'd gone by myself and allowed my whims to carry me away.'

'He's just having a look,' Freya reminded her but she was not at all surprised by what came next.

'Take Freya!' Lola was already untying Freya's apron. 'It's not busy and I could do with a break from the kitchen.'

Freya batted Lola away. 'I can do that myself! Won't this be worse? Won't everyone be talking more if I go? And it's getting busy.'

Lola's face was a picture of innocence. 'It'd be nice if for once I wasn't the centre of all the speculation. I ended up palm-reading for a load of nervous teenage girls I found hanging around last night. They'd come from the next village, been told there was a witch here. A witch! What is this? Medieval times? Now you two go and cause a bit of scandal.' She shooed them off and Alf waved them on their way.

Angelo and Freya made their way through the village in silence, both of them enjoying the sunshine on their bare arms, and the way the village felt a lot jollier, as if it was on a school break. Freya leant into the quiet; with very little traffic the whoosh of the sea wound its way through the cobbled streets and alleys, the occasional seagull the only disturbance. As clichéd as it sounded, it was pure bliss. She glanced across at Angelo who was checking a message on his phone, the brochure stuffed in his pocket. Was he really thinking of buying the house? Or was he, like everyone else, simply curious?

A sleek red car was parked at an antisocial angle outside the property gates, the radio blasting out a hit from the Eighties. Freya didn't need an introduction to guess this was the estate agent. Seeing them approach, the owner of the car flicked off the radio and unfurled himself from the driver's seat. Tall and slightly cadaverous, he had a full beard but a perfectly bald head.

'You must be Angelo.' He stepped forward and seized his hand. 'I'm Nigel. And you are?'

'Freya.' She shook his hand too.

'Excellent!' He looked from one to the other, sizing up the possibility of a sale and quite clearly jumping to the conclusion that they were a couple. 'Bayview has been on the market for quite a while. It's gathered a lot of interest, but sadly no buyers. There have been a few offers, but they fell through for various reasons.' Nigel laughed nervously as he unlocked the door. 'Don't worry, it wasn't because of the house.' He gave the wall a friendly slap. 'But issues with the buyer's lenders or their chains falling through. Now, I'm not going to lie to you, this house needs an awful lot of TLC, but if you fancy a fixer-upper in a beautiful location, then it may well be the house for you.'

Once Freya and Angelo had nodded to confirm they fully understood, Nigel moved aside and allowed them to step over the threshold into a wide hallway with a curved staircase that led up to the first floor. The black and white chequerboard tiles were dusty but light flooded in through the downstairs windows. Freya's eyes widened with astonishment. The house, although its beauty was somewhat faded, had clearly been an absolute stunner in its youth. Freya sniffed, noting the air was stale and unloved. They made their way silently through the hallway, Nigel pushing open the front-room door. An old chandelier hung sadly from the ceiling and the floorboards needed a good sweep, but both Angelo and Freya gasped at the view from the large bay window.

'No wonder it's called Bayview!' Freya whispered, almost putting her nose to the grimy glass. The whole of Polcarrow fell away from them, with houses tumbling down the hills, and the church tower and the sea twinkling seductively.

'It's stunning, isn't it?' Nigel enthused, clearly hoping this was a guaranteed sale. They followed him through to the back of the house where the large kitchen gave way to a dining room and large overgrown garden with a summer-house hiding in the back corner. 'The garden has a lot of potential. I think they used to have garden parties here.'

Angelo raised an eyebrow at Freya, and she hid her smirk behind a hand. Nigel clearly didn't have a clue if garden parties had really taken place there. They wandered around the rest of the house; four decent-sized bedrooms, and a large bathroom complete with an old-fashioned suite and a claw-foot bathtub big enough to swim in. Freya imagined lounging in it for hours with a book, a glass of wine and a box of chocolates. With a hot Italian man by her side, she mused.

'All original features, if you like that sort of vintage thing.'

Nigel went to sit on the edge of the bath, then thought better of it as it was covered in years of dust.

As Angelo was keeping his cards very close to his chest, Freya told Nigel, 'I do, and it's amazingly well preserved. There is so much good natural light in here.' The light was stunning; warm and golden, the sort you would curl up into and feel safe. Freya allowed herself to indulge in a brief fantasy of this as her house, the walls smoothed over and painted a pale cream, the floorboards sanded down and bright rugs and paintings adorning the floors and walls. She coloured in the blank canvas with a life that was only a dream.

After they'd inspected every room, and uncovered some delightful nooks and crannies, the tour of the house was over. Freya and Angelo found themselves outside shaking Nigel's hand.

'Call me if you're interested,' Nigel said, hopefully. 'I don't think it's going anywhere fast. It's been on the market for ages so I'm sure I could negotiate an extremely reasonable price.'

'I'll think about it,' was all Angelo said, poker-faced. They leant against the outside wall and watched Nigel drive off, the notes of Meatloaf's 'Bat Out of Hell' receding around the corner. They exchanged amused looks and stifled giggles. Then silence; blissful silence full of possibilities. Freya forced herself to wipe her mind clean. She couldn't afford to buy the house, so what was the point of dreaming?

'Come on.' Angelo eventually stood up. 'We've both got work to go back to. Nigel definitely thinks he has a sale the way you were mooning over everything,' he grumbled.

Freya sighed and ignored his dark look, not seeing any harm in a little bit of daydreaming. 'Angelo, are you really thinking of buying that house?'

Angelo stopped and stared thoughtfully up at it. 'There's so much I need to think about right now, Freya. I'm just exploring my options. I like the idea of living here, but could I be here forever? I think I could, but I need to be sure. Anyway, as Nigel said, the house isn't going anywhere fast.' Without saying anything else, Angelo set off down the hill, leaving Freya feeling more at sea than if she'd been out on Alf's fishing boat.

'What was it like?' Lola asked as she swapped aprons with Freya upon her return to the café. Angelo had shoved the brochure into his back pocket and announced he was going to see Alf.

'Beautiful – really spacious and full of light. You can see the whole bay from the front window, the village just sort of drops away down the hill. But it's in a state. A proper needs-a-lot-of-work state.' Freya turned to Lola as she scooped her hair up and sighed. 'But it's a real dream property. I'm having to stop myself from mentally decorating it.' Matt hadn't so much as let her bring a cushion through the flat door, let alone have any say in the décor.

Lola pursed her lips thoughtfully. 'I wanted to have a look when I moved down here, but the estate agent said he was fed up of nosey tourists looking around it. Did you take any photos?'

Freya passed her phone across. 'They didn't come out very well, though.'

'It's gorgeous. That staircase! Reckon he's considering buying it?' Lola asked with deliberate lightness in her voice as she passed the phone back.

Freya shrugged. 'I have no idea. He keeps everything close to his chest. I think he was just curious. Stop looking at me like that!'

Lola shrugged. 'Like what?'

'Like you know what's going on. Because I don't!' Freya threw her hands up in the air.

'I don't even need a crystal ball to tell you what's going on. You both like each other, but you're too scared to do anything about it. Plus, you're both ignoring the fact that at some point you're going to have to think seriously about your futures.' Lola paused. 'Honey, you can stay here for as long as you like, for the next ten years if you wish, but I won't let you spend that time just making pots of tea.' Lola gave her a quick kiss on the cheek and whirled into the kitchen to start prepping for the lunch rush.

Staying in Polcarrow, making a life here – Freya considered it and was surprised to find just how happy the idea made her. She gazed wistfully through the café and out towards the sea. Was it really possible? Pushing herself up, she headed into the kitchen, where Lola was busy making up a batch of chicken and bacon sandwich filling.

'Lola, are you sure you're okay with me staying here? I mean, once the summer is over? I like it, but you know I

213

don't know what to do next and I just ... well, it's all too busy at the moment for me to think about it. The painting is going well – I'm really enjoying being able to paint what the hell I want – and I know I can't go back to London, but beyond that ...' She shrugged. 'I can't bear to think about it.'

'Darling! Don't be so maudlin. I wasn't trying to throw you out, you silly goose!' Lola scooped some filling into a soft brown roll, threw a handful of rocket on top and passed it to Freya. 'I love you being here! You, me, Tristan, Angelo – it's brought a vibrancy to the community. We're a little team. Stop thinking about the long-term future. It's big and scary for all of us. Tell me, how's the mural going?'

Grateful that Lola was happy for her to stay, Freya relaxed. 'We've been scaling up the sketches and I think Angelo wants to start on the church wall soon, but he's still got Alf's boat to finish.'

'It's given Alf a new lease of life having Angelo here, having someone interested in his boat. The first time he came to the café he told me that since the fishing had fizzled out, the whole village was dying. My heart went out to him; he's been here all his life, and despite all the changes he's seen he still loves it here.' Lola paused. 'Freya, I don't want this town to die. Neither does Tristan. That's why the Fisherman's Fair needs to be a success.'

Freya nodded, touched by her friend's passion for her new home. 'I'm sure it will be a success.'

'Glad you're feeling positive.' Lola squeezed her hand. 'I feel like I need an ally against Cathy; she's still sour about everything I do.' Lola shook her head. 'She should just get over it. Fancy helping with the bunting making?'

'I'd love to help, but my sewing skills are rather rubbish, and the mural . . . I have no idea how much help Angelo will need, or want.'

Lola seized her moment. 'Have you thought about making a move?'

'What?' Freya almost choked on her sandwich, her face flushed as she remembered the intimate way they'd held each other the previous night. 'It's too soon. I admit there've been a few moments, but not the moment. I need to be absolutely sure.'

Lola hesitated. 'Just don't leave it too long, and I don't want to hear that you're not ready. No one is ever ready for anything.'

The café door's bell jangled, stopping Freya from saying anything else. She slipped out into the café and back to work.

Although Angelo said nothing more about Bayview House, Freya noticed he carried around the brochure folded up like a piece of origami in his back pocket. Sometimes when he thought no one was looking he'd take it out, have a quick surreptitious look at it and then put it away. The whole village was whispering under their breaths about Angelo visiting the house, but Freya didn't think it was her place to warn him how rife rumours could get. Apparently Nigel had been heard spouting that he felt sure the house would sell to the lovely young couple who'd taken a look at it that week. The long, curious looks that were cast from her to Angelo and back again as the villagers jumped to all sorts of conclusions further proved to Freya how embroiled she was in this tall tale.

'Ignore them,' was Lola's advice, which Freya had no option but to take. Lola had grown a thick skin over the years; having always been so obviously different from everyone around her meant that she had constantly courted controversy. She was right: people liked intrigue to liven up their humdrum daily lives. But although Freya didn't mind living with the extra attention, she knew deep down that Angelo would hate it.

Work was due to start on the mural, but in order to keep the rumour mill as quiet as possible, Angelo was working in the church after hours, sneaking in through the back door with instructions for Freya to follow when she'd finished in the café.

'Take this – I foresee a long night.' Lola pushed a picnic basket over the counter to her, filled with a selection of sandwiches, fresh berries, two slices of cake and a bottle of wine. It looked suspiciously romantic.

'We're there to work,' Freya reminded her, pulling out the bottle of wine and putting it on the counter. 'Not seduce each other.'

Lola sighed. 'Really? Such a shame. You're no fun, Freya.' She shoved the wine back into the fridge. 'It'll keep until you're ready.'

Freya rolled her eyes and hoisted the basket over her arms. 'Patience, Lola, patience.'

'You two can hide as much as you like but the village has eyes everywhere. Trust me, there'll be gossip.'

'So best not to feed it with a romantic picnic in the church, then. What are you up to tonight?' Freya deflected.

'Bunting-making with the WI ladies. They're going to teach me some sea shanties!' Lola grinned and gave a little hornpipe dance.

Freya laughed. 'You couldn't write your life!' She waved goodbye to Lola and headed out of the door into the soft evening light. She imagined the songs of the fishermen floating across the tide and a wave of nostalgia broke over her for a time she'd never even known.

She went up to the church and knocked three times on the door. Angelo opened it and tugged her inside before anyone could see.

'This is all a bit secret,' Freya whispered, making a big show of tiptoeing in.

'Why are you whispering? No one's going to hear us through these stone walls. What have you got there?'

'Lola sent some supplies. She said she could foresee a long night.' Freya passed him the basket.

Angelo snorted with amusement. 'I swear that woman is some kind of witch.'

Freya opened her mouth then thought better of it. What could she say? 'Actually, she is a witch and saw your arrival' would sound mad. She followed him into the church where there were several stepladders and buckets of hot, soapy water waiting.

'Ready for some hard graft? We need to give the wall a really good clean,' Angelo explained as he placed the basket on the floor next to the back pews. 'There's no point painting on a dirty wall. Imagine how many decades of grime, fingerprints and dirt there are on these walls.' He threw a sponge at her. 'I hope you're used to hard work, apprentice!'

Freya put the sponge between her knees, gathered up her long hair into a high bun and pulled off her shirt, glad she was wearing just shorts and a vest top underneath. It was cool, however, in the church. Freya found she rather liked the way Angelo's eyes skimmed her curves as he tried and failed not to look at her.

They set to work in silence, Freya quickly slopping water over her feet. 'Do you ever wonder what life was like for all the people who have attended this church throughout the centuries? I do. All those weddings, funerals, boats lost to the sea.' She stepped back and wiped her brow. 'It really puts our moment in time in perspective, doesn't it?'

Angelo nodded in agreement. 'Yes. I hope they like what I have planned – I don't fancy being haunted by an unhappy fisherman.'

They lapsed into silence. The task was a lot harder than Freya had expected. After about ten minutes of cleaning, she was starting to feel it, and Angelo had been right, the water in the buckets was turning a filthy grey. They emptied and refilled the buckets three times until the wall was in the correct state for Angelo to start work on it. He ran his hands lovingly over its surface. Hot and flustered, and not just from cleaning, Freya exhaled and loosened her limbs with a luxurious stretch.

'Perfect. Let's have something to eat while it dries.' He rifled through the basket, pulling out the picnic and spreading it on the pew between them. 'I've never picnicked in a church before.'

Freya accepted a sandwich from him. Soft white bread with chunks of local ham. She wiped away an ooze of honey mustard. 'Neither have I. It's not the usual picnic spot, is it?'

'Peaceful though,' Angelo said through a mouthful of sandwich, eyes focused on the altar. 'Tell me, is everyone talking about us viewing Bayview House?'

Freya nodded. 'Nothing stays secret for long here. Plus, they all think we're a couple now.'

Angelo smiled with amusement. 'There are worse things for them to think. Like me being a Hells Angel, for one.' He turned to her, 'I like the house. I like it here and I like you,' he said frankly, 'but I need some space to figure it all out, you understand? These past few months haven't been easy for me. But I find I am happier here than I ever expected to be. None of this was planned. I expected to be here a few days, drink myself silly for a bit, then move on.' He reached across and took her hand to stroke it, his fingers lingering long enough to hint at more. 'Thank you for saving me from the drink, for always being here, for helping me. I'm not sure I'd finish all this myself.'

'Are you saying you stayed for me?' Freya tried to hide the smile that played on her face. Angelo was still holding her hand. It felt safe, right.

'Maybe. Yes. Partly. There's something magic here.' Angelo focused on his sandwich, flustered in a way Freya found adorable. 'You've all been so good. It feels right to repay your generosity with a bit of art.'

That was good enough, Freya thought, glad the picnic basket was providing a barrier between them while the holy presence of God lingered watchfully in the corners. She didn't want to add committing a sin to the list of Angelo's possible indiscretions. They sat, fingers entwined, eating and watching the evening light twinkle through the stained-glass windows, the light washing like waves on the old stone floor.

Chapter Sixteen

Angelo leant over the counter and read the Fisherman's Fair flyer while he waited for his coffee. Freya had left him in the church just before midnight the night before, but from the shadows under his eyes, she guessed he'd been working until the early hours. The last couple of weeks had been intense. She set his espresso down in front of him and he knocked it back, stifling a yawn.

'I think I need another one.' His voice was gravelly with lack of sleep.

'What time did you work until?' she asked, turning back to the coffee machine.

'Three, I think.' He rubbed his tired face. Freya passed him a second coffee. 'Thanks.' He tipped sugar into the cup and stirred. 'I'll take this one more slowly.' He paused and stared at the flyer before holding it up to Freya. 'Sandcastle building competition?' Angelo asked, turning the flyer towards Freya whose face lit up.

'I know!' Freya exclaimed. 'How exciting is that? I'm thinking of entering.'

'Seriously?' Angelo asked, slightly puzzled. 'Isn't it for kids?'

'Yes, I think it might be.' She pulled an exaggerated sad face. 'It's been years since I made a sandcastle,' Freya enthused. 'Olivia and I would always make one close to the sea so that the water would flow in and fill the little moat. We'd buy those little flags to stick in the top. What? Why are you looking at me as if I'm mad?'

'I'm exhausted and you're babbling on about sandcastles.' Angelo put the flyer down. 'I have a confession.' He paused for dramatic effect. 'I've never built a sandcastle.'

'What? Seriously? You've never built a sandcastle?' Freya stared at him in shock, her own mug paused halfway to her mouth. 'Did you never go on a seaside holiday? You know, naff caravan with a fight over the bunk beds, a clubhouse with dodgy kids' entertainment?'

Angelo shifted uncomfortably and laughed. 'Nope, you're really selling it by the way. I spent my summers in Italy with my cousins, remember?'

Freya shook her head, unimpressed. 'You might have had a belly full of fine art and good pizza, but you have missed out on a true English tradition. We must remedy this!' she announced. 'I can't believe you've never built a sandcastle. That's quite sad.'

Embarrassed, Angelo shook his head. 'Why's it such a big deal? I'm sure my mural painting prowess more than makes up for my lack of sandcastle building.' He finished his coffee. 'Right, see you later, I'm off to help Alf. We're on the home stretch.' Angelo rolled his neck from side to side and massaged out some of the tension as he made his way to the door.

Watching him go, an idea formed in Freya's mind. Angelo's life was all work, work, work at the moment. It was time, she decided, for a little fun. Plus, she hoped this would be the perfect opportunity to push their relationship over the friendship boundary.

Freya was waiting with arms full of buckets and spades when Angelo arrived at closing time, swinging open the café door, bringing with him the smell of varnish and warm wood.

'Surprise!' She held up the collection of lurid castle-shaped buckets.

'What the . . .' Angelo stopped in his tracks. 'What's this?' He picked up a bright yellow bucket and pulled the neon pink spade out for inspection.

'Sandcastle-making kit. And that is definitely your colour. I figured that if I want to win, I need to practise.' Freya shrugged as if it was obvious. She moved over to him and extracted the tools from his hands. 'And I think it's time you did something fun. Also, I can't get over the fact you've never built a sandcastle.'

'But I only have a week until the unveiling. I can't take any time off!' Angelo protested.

Freya made a face. 'Yes, you can, and there's no arguing about it. Two hours at the most. I have a picnic, I have buckets and spades, and I know a beach where hardly anyone goes.'

Angelo raised an eyebrow and stepped closer. 'Is there more to this than just sandcastles by any chance?'

Freya ignored his smoulder. 'I'm trying not to cramp your

bad–boy style. I'm sure you don't want everyone watching you make sandcastles, do you?' She bopped him playfully on the head with a spade. 'I thought we could have a swim. I've not had a chance to be in the sea yet.'

'Now that is truly shocking,' Angelo conceded as he picked up the picnic basket. 'Actually, neither have I. We've been a bit rubbish at this whole summer by the sea thing, haven't we? Let me go and get changed into my trunks.'

'We'll have a race then. See who can be the first one in.' Freya restacked the buckets for easy transportation and tucked the spades under her arms. A towel had been thrown across the top of the picnic basket, which she passed to Angelo when he came back down. Then she ushered him out and locked up. 'Turn left and carry on going. We're going to the other side of the headland.'

The evening air was thick and golden. Freya's heart skipped along with her feet. She was lighter than she'd felt all summer. And Angelo had been correct about one thing: this was about more than just building a contest-winning castle. She was hoping that if she got him alone, got him to drop his guard a bit, things might progress in a more romantic fashion. She knew they both wanted it, but that he was holding back until the mural was finished. Angelo seemed relaxed beside her and she was happy to listen to him talk about Alf's boat. She had no specific plans to seduce him but wanted to try and tempt him over the barrier he seemed to put up between them. Plus, swimming was the only way she could think of to innocently get his top off and hear the story behind the tattoo.

'The boat is pretty much done,' Angelo was saying as they made their way up the steep headland, pausing to catch their breath at the top. 'Wow, what a view!' The whole of Polcarrow Bay was stretched before them, the evening sun glinting off the windows. Angelo's eyes strayed over to Bayview House, but Freya held her tongue.

'I came up here a lot when I first arrived,' she told him. 'Perfect to get away from everyone and do some thinking.' Those slightly grey days seemed a lifetime ago now, and everything that had happened to bring her to Cornwall felt like it had happened to a different person. 'Come on.'

They made their way down the other side of the headland. The steps that had once been hewn into the hillside were eroded despite local efforts to shore them up with planks and a rope for walkers to hold onto.

'This is like an extreme sport!' Angelo chuckled as he gingerly followed Freya down. 'No wonder no one comes here.'

'I think they keep it in a state of disrepair to deter anyone but the hardiest tourists. It keeps it local and special.'

They stepped onto the sand and Angelo let out a whistle of appreciation. The small cove was embraced by high craggy rocks, which created shelter and shade. Freya had timed their visit perfectly; the sun was streaming onto the beach, twinkling invitingly on top of the waves. She kicked off her trainers and sunk her toes into the cool sand with a sigh of relief. Slowly, Freya made her way across the beach, dumping the buckets in a jolly pile. She then took the picnic basket from Angelo and plonked it down beside them. Angelo looked slightly out of place and Freya knew it was now or never. Before she lost her nerve, she tugged off her shorts and pulled her T-shirt over her head. She'd brought a red bikini down to Cornwall with her, but hadn't thought it'd take this long for her to wear it. She giggled when she noticed Angelo was trying not to stare at her too obviously.

'Come on!' She reached across and tugged at his T-shirt. 'I told you it's a race!'

He made to grab her but she was too quick, running down to the sea, splashing into the shallows, the cool water a sudden shock against her ankles. Freya waded in slowly, the water rising up over her calves, the sand shifting and sinking between her toes. Despite her burst of bravado, she wasn't sure she wanted to go all the way in. Closing her eyes she inhaled deeply, centring herself, getting ready for whatever was going to happen next. The anticipation buzzed over her skin, on the back of her tongue. Two more steps forward, away from the safety of the shallows. Then Angelo sploshed in behind her, swirling the water around them. He stopped beside Freya, his arm touching hers. Looking down at her, with a smile spread across his face, he reached for her hand, curling their fingers together.

'You ready?' he asked, eyes glittering.

Freya swallowed and nodded; she felt ready for anything with him by her side. She tightened her grip. 'Yes, I think so.'

'On the count of three. One ... two ... three!' Before Freya knew what was happening, Angelo was running for-ward, pulling her with him. Crashing through the waves, they shrieked with laughter. As the water surged up around her waist, Freya lost her footing but Angelo caught her, pulling her to him, holding her firmly in his strong arms. The moment caught them. Eyes met. Time slowed.

Freya pushed herself forward as Angelo slowly lowered his head and kissed her, the touch of his lips setting her soul alight. Freya kissed him back, slowly to begin with, then deeper, hands, hair and hearts entwined, the tide gentling rolling in around them.

Wrapped in a towel, Freya sat on the picnic blanket next to Angelo, loose of limb from the sea, the kissing and the bottle of wine she'd slipped into the basket that morning. The sun was starting to go down and a chill settled on her skin. She was happy deep in her soul and wished she could preserve the beauty of the evening in all its perfect rosy goldenness.

Around them lay the remnants of the picnic and a few crumbling sandcastles. Angelo hadn't quite bought into the idea of making a complete sandcastle fort; he'd dragged her away, distracting her with kisses and telling her it was a competition for children and she needed to let them win. Angelo had come out fully from behind the cloud he'd been carrying round with him since arriving in Polcarrow and she wondered if this is what he had been like before Vanessa and her father had whittled away the parts of him they'd wanted.

Freya looked over at him; his skin bronze in the sunlight, his hair tangled from the sea. Her eyes were drawn to his back, so she took her chance to ask. 'Your tattoo – how did that come about? I have to say it's pretty . . . impressive.'

Angelo laughed. 'It's a bit unusual, isn't it?'

'A bit?' Freya scooted around to study it better. It was so intricately executed, the details painstakingly repro- duced. She ran her hands tentatively down his back, over the pained face of Jesus and the weeping sorrow of the two Marys. Angelo groaned contentedly at her touch. 'It's beau- tiful, but why?'

Angelo turned around and pulled Freya towards him so she was sitting astride his knees. His hands were on her hips, anchoring her to him. 'I visited this church when I was in Tuscany. There's a fresco by an unknown artist in this tiny little church in an almost forgotten village. Not the village my family is from, mind. The city was suffocating me and I needed to get out, so I got on my bike and drove until I reached this little village. It was baked golden, the shutters all closed up against the sun, and there was a small coffee shop where they treated me suspiciously.'

Freya darted a quick kiss on his chin. 'Seems to be a theme.'

Angelo chuckled, kissing her neck. 'Yes, well. There was this little church and I went in to escape the heat and to think. There was this most outstanding crucifixion painting. I'd never seen anything like it – it floored me. The priest couldn't tell me anything about the work but he had some prints of it and he gave me one. I had it in my studio where I could see it every day. I turned to it when I felt lost, confused, broken. It never let me down. The tattoo seemed like the best way of carrying it with me permanently. Oh God, it hurt, it took days but it was worth it. Vanessa hated it. It freaked her out, she said.' He rolled his eyes. 'She never understood anything. Not like you.' Angelo stroked her cheek.

'And this?' Freya put her hand over the sacred heart symbol that was on his chest. 'When you said you believed, I didn't realize it was quite this much.'

Angelo gave a low laugh and snatched her hands away. 'I don't know if I do, but my mother does and it's hard to avoid it if you're brought up by a Catholic mother. I don't know how much I believe but I respect it. Do you have any hidden tattoos?' He tried to pull the towel away.

'No! None!' Freya yelped. 'My mother would've killed me.'

'Mine would have liked to, but I got away with it because it was religious.' He picked up the bottle of wine and took a swig before passing it to Freya. 'What's your family like?'

'Protective.' Freya shrugged. ''I'm not sure hanging out with a motorbike-riding, paintbrush-wielding bad boy with a tumultuous relationship with his religious faith is how they'd like me to be spending my summer,' she teased.

'I am not a bad boy, Freya,' Angelo growled. 'That's just what the papers used to write.' His eyes darkened and his grip grew tighter. 'Have you been looking me up? If you have, it's all lies.'

Shocked by his change in mood, Freya pulled back. 'What? No! It's just the tattoos, the dark hair, the bike . . . I was joking.'

Angelo rubbed his face with relief and pulled her back in. 'I'm sorry. I've always been pegged as the wild child of the art world. It's not something I enjoy and it's not true. I've spent ten years trying to escape that moniker. I don't care about partying and drinking. I want a quiet life.' His hands clasped her face, his eyes earnest and true as he kissed her. 'I want a quiet life here with you. You are the only person who understands me, the only person I can show my true self to. That's what I like about you, you're not awed by who I once was, you're not afraid to put me in my place, you understand me. You make me feel like the real Angelo Borelli, not the one found in old gossip columns.' He kissed her slowly. 'And what Angelo Borelli wants more than anything is to stay here, forever, with you.'

Freya melted into his kisses, her brain scrambled by his declaration. 'Forever is a very long time, and this is so new.'

'I know enough to know what I want.' He leant back in the sand, pulling her with him until they were snuggled on the blanket, gazing up at the softening sky with night sneaking in around the edges. 'I've never felt peace like this in any place other than in that church looking at that fresco. It's like it strips away all the excesses from my life and I'm just me, in this moment, with nothing else around me. Everything I left behind in London feels like it belongs to a different person. I'm cleansed of all that. I don't ever want to leave here, Freya. If anything, I think I'm asking if you'll stay.' He turned to her, their eyes meeting.

Freya stared back at him; his intentions were shining

seductively in his dark eyes. Did he really mean it? Or was it just the moment? He's run from things before, a cautious voice warned, which Freya silenced. Was jumping into a new relationship so soon after splitting with Matt the right thing? Angelo was looking at her as if she was the answer to everything and all she had was more questions. 'I want to stay, but you know, the practicalities of life. Money, somewhere to live.' Freya sighed and trailed off, not wanting to kill the romantic mood outright.

'We'll find a way,' he reassured her. 'Here, with you, everything feels possible. For a long time, life felt impossible but this summer has proven to me that the simple life exists, and it's the simple life I want.'

Freya smiled at him, drunk on the wine, the moment and the flutterings of love that were stirring in her heart. Angelo's romanticism was slowly colouring her own thoughts a dreamy shade of rose and Freya was easily seduced by the notion of the simple life, because in that moment she realized that, despite her reservations, it was the life she wanted too, if she could be brave enough to grasp it.

Chapter Seventeen

With less than a week until the Fisherman's Fair, the preparation for the event was ramping up, fuelled by a mild panic that nothing would be ready on time. The WI ladies held emergency meetings each morning over cups of tea and slabs of cake, laying their colour-coded lists over the tables and filling the usually calm café with chaotic chatter. Lola kept out of the way, hiding in the kitchen, baking multiple batches of scones, which she then froze. 'I'm not staying up all night baking,' she'd grumbled to Freya, after having her capabilities questioned by Cathy.

Bunting was strung up across the village, giving it a jolly holiday feel, which both cheered up the locals and gave hope that visitors would come. The village buzzed with industry watched over by Alf and Scruff, the only two members of the community who kept up any semblance of calm. Alf sipped his tea on his favourite table outside the café, Scruff dozing at his feet, watching over the proceedings.

'This is mighty exciting,' he told Freya, eyes glinting with joy. 'Takes me right back to when I was a lad. How's Angelo doing with his art project?'

Freya smiled, amused by the way everyone referred to his great artistic feat as an art project. 'Well, I've not seen him for a couple of days because he's been working so hard.' Freya was missing him and the easy companionship they'd found.

'Cheer up, he'll be finished soon and you'll be able to enjoy the festival together. I can tell you're fond of each other. Fills my old heart with hope to see you young ones falling in love.' Alf clasped her hand, his eyes shining happily.

Falling in love? Freya blushed and laughed off Alf's sentiment, but couldn't deny that, yes, she was falling in love with Angelo. Although she planned to keep that knowledge to herself for the time being. Angelo lit up her life, brought an extra bit of sparkle to her mornings and the thought of seeing him helped her glide through her chores and kept a smile on her face when she was dealing with difficult customers.

After their blissful evening on the beach making rose-tinted future plans, Angelo had plunged himself into tunnel-vision work mode. He'd been up with the dawn, bleary-eyed, knocking back double espressos, sneaking quick, rough kisses before darting off to the church. The villagers were starting to whisper and speculate about what Angelo was doing. They were excited to see what he was producing, looking forward to the extra prestige the mural would give the village. More and more people were finding excuses to visit Tristan or had rediscovered a religious persuasion that amused the vicar. Freya was split between helping Angelo and helping Lola. Everyone seemed to need an extra pair of hands, and when she'd visited Angelo with a picnic supper, he'd hardly paused from his work to stuff a pasty in his mouth. To avert curious gazes Angelo had kept the dust sheets over the parts of the painting he wasn't working on. He was happy to see Freya but she knew he didn't really need her there so she offered up her skills to whoever needed them. Be it bunting-making, sign-painting or helping Lola whip up batches of scones.

Some of these tasks were less suited to her skillset, such as baking. Lola watched her pat out the scone dough with a disdainful eye; it was too thin and cracked.

'The WI ladies will hang me if they're not uniform!' Lola exclaimed as she squished Freya's dough together and began to painstakingly roll it back out again and shape the scones to her specifications. 'They need to be eight centimetres and perfectly round!'

'Ugh, you know I'm not one for baking, I'm going to find some signs or something to hang up.' On her way out she grabbed the pile of buckets and spades and donated them to the sandcastle-building competition, having resigned herself to the fact that she would not be taking part. Buoyed up by all the pre-fair excitement and keen for it to be a success, Freya pressed flyers into the hands of everyone who came into the café, going for the hard sale in the hope of tempting visitors. All that was left to do was to wait for Saturday morning to roll round and for the festival to unfurl. Freya couldn't wait to see it all come together.

*

On Friday morning, Angelo came down to the café, deep shadows under his eyes, his whole demeanour wild and unshaven. Freya recognized the jittery, dishevelled look that accompanied the final push towards completion of a project. Outside the sky was overcast so Tristan and Alf were breakfasting at the window table, worrying about the weather. The delicious aroma of toast and Lola's home-made marmalade curled around the café.

'Morning,' Freya said to Angelo. 'The usual?'

Angelo yawned, his voice gravelly with lack of sleep. 'I think I need a triple espresso this morning. Can I have some of that toast?'

'Of course.' Freya rang it through the till and turned her back to make his coffee. 'Ready for tomorrow?'

Angelo tipped sugar into his coffee and gave it a thoughtful stir. 'Yes. But nervous.' He lowered his voice. 'What if no one likes it?' The worried look on his face almost broke Freya's heart.

Freya rubbed his tired face and dropped a quick kiss on his nose. Angelo nuzzled his face into her hand. 'I'm sure they'll all be amazed. Why would anyone not like it?'

'You'd be surprised.' He raised an eyebrow. 'Some people will dislike something just for the sake of being contrarian.' He sipped his coffee and closed his eyes in bliss. 'I tell you what though, I'm looking forward to a good night's sleep.'

'Morning!' Lola bustled out of the kitchen with a plate of thick toast oozing melted butter. 'Alf and Tristan have my special marmalade – I'm sure they won't mind you joining them.'

Angelo went to take the toast from her, but instead Lola carried it over to the table and plonked it down. 'Eat up, and sit down. We all need a rest – busy day ahead for us all. Right, if you all want some free sandwiches come round the back door. If you're lucky I might read your palm too!' she quipped.

Alf chuckled. 'Think I'm a bit old for all that prediction stuff!'

Tristan made a face, his religious tendencies at odds with Lola's psychic predictions. He quickly changed the subject. 'Ready for the unveiling tomorrow?'

Angelo slowly spread marmalade on his toast. 'I think so, just a few finishing touches to add.' He cleared his throat and glanced around the group; 'I'd like to invite you all to a private viewing tonight. Nine o'clock. You've all been so wonderful to me these past few weeks and I can't think of any other way to repay your generosity. And I'd value your opinions so I can brace myself for the village approval.'

Alf gave his shoulder a squeeze. 'I'd be honoured, son. And don't worry about what that lot think. Especially not that Cathy. She doesn't like anything! Not even Lola's cakes! Imagine being her!' He shook his head disapprovingly. 'What a miserable life that would be.'

'We'd all be honoured to come,' Lola said. 'And I stopped worrying about what the village thought long ago. I'm sure your work is wonderful. I'm looking forward to it! We should go to the pub after.'

Tristan clapped in approval. 'I concur! Freya?'

Freya, who had been watching the scene unfold, her own heart bursting with excitement, slipped out from behind the counter. Angelo held out a hand to her and Freya surprised them all by going in for a full-blown hug. Lola, Alf and Tristan all raised their eyebrows and burst into applause.

These wonderful people had become her second family.

'I wouldn't miss it for the world!' she exclaimed, snatching up a piece of Angelo's toast as the sun began to break through the clouds.

At nine o'clock that night, the August sky already lying dark over the bay, Lola and Alf slipped into the church. Freya had headed up early to help Angelo tidy up and Tristan was already there in an official capacity. The staggered arrival was an attempt to ensure that the villagers wouldn't indulge in any more gossip than they already had. Angelo had already hung the dustsheets over the finished mural, so even Freya hadn't seen it in its full glory. She fizzed with excitement and pride as she distracted herself tidying up various paintbrushes and sweeping the floor. She couldn't wait to see the finished piece all in one go, having mostly seen it close up or in expertly rendered sections. Angelo was silent, contemplative and, Freya suspected, a little nervous.

'It'll be fine.' She gave his arm a reassuring rub, 'The villagers are curious but not barbarians. It's not like you've painted loads of nudes on their church wall or done The Last Supper in the style of Picasso.'

Angelo managed a smile and kissed her hand. 'It's not just that. I haven't signed it; I don't want the press crawling all over it. Imagine the scoop. "Former artistic bad boy painting religious murals." If they found me now, I'd never rest.' He stopped as the church door banged shut.

'Why are churches always cold?' Lola shivered, wrapping her yellow cardigan tighter around her and surveying the interior. Angelo had turned on all the lamps so the church was bathed in a soft light. 'So this is where you've been hiding?' She came over and linked her arm through Freya's. 'I think we should just take a moment to be still. Tomorrow is going to be manic. Then, who knows? I can feel it in the air – change is brewing.' She shivered for dramatic effect and gave Freya a reassuring squeeze.

'Not more of that witchy talk?' Tristan emerged from his office, dog collar off. 'Okay. So we're all here, and as much as I don't share Lola's beliefs, I think she's right. Tomorrow is going to be busy, so we need to just enjoy this moment and try to get an early night.'

'I thought we were going to the pub? There's a big glass of white wine with my name on it,' Lola said, practically drooling. 'And we need to toast Angelo!'

Angelo smiled appreciatively. 'While I'd prefer to postpone any celebrations until after the rest of the village have seen the mural, I am in need of a pint or two.'

His request was met with approval. Lola nodded with satisfaction and Scruff whimpered and lay down at Alf's feet. Angelo's eyes glittered with nerves as he surveyed his audience, who were waiting with bated breath. Freya shot him a smile and a thumbs up.

Freya's faith in Angelo sat unsteadily on his shoulders. It had been a long time since anyone had supported him in a project like Freya had, a project that had come from his heart. Angelo stepped over to the wall and paused; this would be the first time he saw the mural in its entirety. He'd been working on sections, concentrating on small bits at a time. As the finality of this moment washed over him, he started to pull away the dustsheets, letting them drop, vanquished, onto the floor.

The big reveal was met with silence and his stomach squeezed in anticipation. Slowly, he dared himself to look at his audience, and relief washed over him to see four pairs of eyes staring in amazement at his mural. Even Scruff sat up and gave it an appreciative bark.

Freya swallowed, the painting was more astounding than she'd imagined, and the emotions it stirred almost choked her. St Peter stood at the prow of his boat, preaching to a group gathered on the shore. Curled around the prow were two mischievous-looking mermaids. Freya couldn't be sure in the dim light but she thought she detected a resemblance to herself in one of them. The entire mural had been executed in blue, yet Angelo's skill had added depth and beauty to its simplicity. It was as intricate as any Renaissance Italian fresco, but fresh and modern. Freya wanted to run her hands over it, feel the work beneath her fingers. She knew she could study it for years without ever fully understanding the depths

Angelo had plunged into to finish it. The work humbled her as much as it moved her. She wiped away a sneaky tear, but any words of appreciation had dried up in her astonishment. Instead, she squeezed Angelo to her, eyes shining and whispered, 'That is one of the most outstanding pieces of work I've ever seen. I hope you're proud of yourself.'

Angelo squeezed her back, trying to shut out the critical voice in his brain that picked up on flaws no one else would see: the eyes slightly too close together on one of the figures, a drape in the fabric that didn't hang as naturally as he'd hoped. Something rushed through him, spreading warmth from his heart into his limbs; a mixture of relief, awe and pride. He choked back tears. It had been a long time since he had made art that moved him so much. 'Yes,' he whispered to her, bestowing a kiss on her forehead, 'I think I am.'

Alf's chuckle broke the seriousness of the moment. 'I like what you've done with St Peter!' His own craggy face had been immortalized in blue paint for the foreseeable future. 'That'll give the gossips something to complain about. And the mermaids!'

'I don't recall approving any mermaids?' Tristan asked, panicked. 'There aren't any mermaids in the Bible.'

Lola swatted his arm. 'Ssh. It's an homage to the seaside, don't you see? It's not just religious but a reflection of the seafaring life, and anyway, you can't have a seaside without mermaids!'

Rightfully chastised, Tristan broke away from Lola and crossed over to Angelo, grabbing his hand to shake it before pulling him into a manly hug. 'I have no idea how to thank you. It's wonderful. It's so much more than I expected or hoped for. I'm sure I'll get used to the mermaids!'

Angelo gave Tristan a slap on the back and released him.

'Are you sure you don't want to sign it?' Tristan asked. 'It's such a shame not to have your name attached to it—'

'I'm sure,' Angelo cut him off. 'I'm here to keep a low profile, and I'd like people to enjoy the mural without my name distracting them.'

Protest swirled in Lola and Tristan's eyes, their mouths briefly opening to voice their objections before closing. The vicar nodded solemnly. 'If that's what you wish.'

'Thank you.' Angelo made his way back towards the painting and started to gather up the dust sheets. 'Let's cover this back up and go to the pub. There's a pint waiting for me.'

Chapter Eighteen

Saturday morning dawned clear and bright with promise. Lola dragged Freya out of bed at the ungodly hour of six o'clock, already annoyingly chirpy despite the two large glasses of white wine she'd consumed in the pub the night before. Freya, limbs aching with weeks of accumulated tiredness, dragged herself into the shower in the hope that hot water would revive her. When she felt slightly more awake, Freya pulled on shorts and a stripy T-shirt and followed Lola down to the café, lured by her friend's promise of breakfast.

'So – you and Angelo?' Lola inquired as they entered the café.

Freya yawned and glanced at her. 'What?'

Lola took her hand and gave it a squeeze. 'That was quite a kiss on the way back from the pub last night. Don't think we didn't notice. And all that hugging and hand-holding.'

'Lola! It's none of your business,' Freya exclaimed. 'Don't you have some cream teas to be prepping rather than quizzing me about my love life?' Seeing that Lola would not be deterred, Freya gave in. 'Okay, it's very new, I didn't think I needed to announce Angelo and me to the world. Not that with the mural we've had time to tell anyone. I don't know

242

why you're acting so surprised; you've been team Freya and Angelo all along.' Freya huffed.

'All right, all right, keep your hair on. I'm just happy for you, that's all,' Lola said as she disappeared into the kitchen.

Freya looked across the harbour where the sun was glittering welcomingly on the sea and, taking a few deep breaths of the salty early-morning air, she could feel the excitement that had been gathering over the last week bouncing in her chest. In a few hours' time she hoped the streets would be bustling with performers and joyful children, and everyone would be full of cream teas and happiness. Freya hugged the excitement to herself; the moment was imbued with the promise of perfection and she tried to ignore any twinges of apprehension that it might flop.

Lola didn't say anything else about Angelo but greeted him warmly when he emerged for breakfast, yawning and looking in need of a good night's sleep.

'I think I'll sleep for about a week after this!' he growled as he passed his cup back to Freya for a second coffee. Then in a lower voice, 'Fancy joining me?'

Freya's heart skipped at the insinuation. 'That's a very tempting offer.' She winked, flushed.

Angelo leant across the counter and stole a quick kiss. 'I'm off to help Alf get the boat out.'

'Don't you want any breakfast? Lola's cooking up a load of bacon.'

Angelo looked torn. 'Stuff some in a couple of buns and I'll take it to Alf. If he doesn't fancy it, I'm sure Scruff will.'

Freya disappeared into the kitchen and came back with two soft white rolls oozing bacon and brown sauce. Angelo grabbed them. 'Better take some flapjack as well. What are you on today?'

'Helping Lola with the cream teas, mainly. I'm expecting to be pretty busy. Chained to the café until the big reveal.' Freya sighed.

'Well, I hope I can steal you away for that. I'm not sure I want to face that alone.' Angelo pulled her to him.

Touched by his flush of anxiety, Freya touched his face and pulled herself up on tiptoes to give him a quick kiss. 'I wouldn't miss it for the world.'

Angelo, his face suddenly solemn, squeezed her tightly, as if he never wanted to let her go. 'I could never have done any of this without you, you know. I don't know how to thank you. You understand, don't you, why I can't go public with this yet? I'd love to put our names on the mural but . . .'

'It's okay, I understand. Honestly, I do.' Their eyes locked, sealing the moment. They shared a kiss full of understanding of the past and promise for the future. 'You'd better get those rolls to Alf before they get cold.'

'Oh, yes.' Angelo let her go and laughed. 'See you later.'

Freya watched him leave, wondering how long it would take to get used to his intense Italian ways. Their hearts felt bound together, but Angelo always seemed like a storm about to blow.

By midday, Polcarrow Bay was filling up with day trippers who'd come for the fair. They meandered happily through the bunting-draped streets, the children sticky with ice cream and the parents weighing up the merits of tucking into a pasty versus a cream tea. Freya was just helping herself to a quick sandwich when the café door swung open and Angelo swept in. Agitated, he grabbed her hand and pulled her into the stairwell that joined the café to the apartment.

'What's up?' Freya managed through a mouthful of chicken and avocado, reaching out to try to soothe him. 'You look like you've seen a ghost.'

He grabbed her hands. 'Not a ghost, Freya, but there's a journalist out there.'

'So? Surely that's good, isn't it . . . ?' Her voice trailed off. No, it clearly wasn't. 'Don't worry about it. Sue probably organized some coverage of the fair.'

'No, Freya, he's been talking to Alf, taking photos, asking about the boat. Alf is in his element, but all the while he kept looking at me as if he knew me. Or if he doesn't know me, he's trying to figure me out.' Angelo paced up and down the small space, like a wild caged beast.

Freya put her hand out to stop him. 'No offence, Angelo, but you've hardly been famous for years. Look at you, all in black, wild hair, you probably look strange next to Alf. Well, not strange, but you're hardly as wholesome as a cream tea, are you?'

Angelo looked blankly at her and shook his head. 'Wholesome as a cream tea? I've seen it before – he was definitely trying to place me. If it gets out that I'm here, then Vanessa will be straight down. I can't have that. The press will come, everything will just implode. I can't face having all this disturbed.'

'Stop it, Angelo, please.' Freya grabbed his hands reassuringly. 'Seriously, stop working yourself up like this.' She peered through the glass partition. 'There's a queue forming, and there's a fair that needs to be run. I very much doubt some local journalist is trying to get the scoop on you. It'll be okay, and whatever happens we'll face it together.' Seeing his face fall, she stepped forward and gave him a quick kiss. 'If you need to hide out, stay here, help me. Looks like I'll need it.'

As a team, they worked together smoothly. Angelo seemed to calm down a little and stopped jumping nervously every time the door opened. The counter was really only meant for one server, and the close confines made Freya's pulse race. She was sure he was taking every opportunity he could to brush past her, run his fingers over the back of her hand or drop a quick, secret kiss on her neck or shoulder. Freya was flustered from more than just the sunshine and couldn't wait to get him alone.

The village throbbed with life. Alf's boat was sitting proudly outside his boathouse, gleaming with brand-new paint. Freya managed to steal away to have a quick look at it during a brief down period and found Alf regaling a small crowd with tales of seafaring derring-do. Scruff was in his element as children gathered around to scratch behind his ears and watch him roll blissfully onto his back. Freya saw no sign of the journalist sniffing about and nor did Alf mention him; he was too busy teaching a group of children how to tie ships knots. Even Freya was fascinated by how deft his gnarly hands were.

Steve, the pub landlord, was strutting around in full pirate regalia, music blasting across the bay from his pub garden. He caught up with Freya on her way back and wiped his brow. 'All right, Freya? How's it going? It's mad out here, mad I tell you. Ask Lola to save me one of those cream teas. I'm off to judge the sandcastle-building competition – reckon I'll need one after!' He waved goodbye and hobbled down the steps to the beach, where a group of children stood around a variety of crumbling sandcastles.

Freya took a moment to survey the village, her heart bubbling with joy as she greeted various villagers and gave directions to lost visitors. She had never felt as much a part of anything as she did today. The sea breeze tickled her skin and she closed her eyes to the sun, allowing its warmth to erase the tiredness that was threatening to seep into her limbs. This is home, she thought with a start. This is where I want to live. She made her way back to the café, and as she stepped through the door, Angelo's eyes met hers and she knew she wanted to stay here with him. They could do Bayview House up; they could paint and travel to Italy. Things might have been moving fast with Angelo, but Freya reasoned it was worth the chance. She slipped behind the counter and pulled him into a quick, tight hug.

'What was that for?' he asked, eyes twinkling.

Freya shrugged. 'I'm just so much happier than I ever expected to be.'

Angelo kissed her forehead. 'Me too. Let's escape all this later. Right now, we have coffees to make.'

The party atmosphere prevailed throughout the afternoon, but Freya noticed that the closer it drew to the unveiling of the mural, the more nervous Angelo got. It started with a few nervous tics: checking the clock, running his hands through his hair. Then he went quiet, the flirting and joking trickling to a stop as he retreated into himself, deep and introspective, as if putting up a protective barrier. Freya hated to see him struggling with his nerves, exacerbated by the phantom journalist. Where appropriate, she gave him reassuring looks and squeezed his hand. When the time came for the unveiling, Freya wasn't surprised to hear him say he wasn't going to come, that he'd man the café.

'I won't hear it!' Lola cut in. 'The café is shutting for a few minutes and we're all going to the unveiling. Afterwards I'm giving you both the rest of the day off. You can stand at the back if you want.' She shrugged and, throwing her apron on the counter, sauntered out of the café door.

Freya turned to Angelo, holding out her hand in encouragement. 'Come on. It'll be fine, really. Also, I didn't see that journalist when I was having a look earlier; they've probably gone.'

Angelo swallowed and nodded, his face pale. Freya gave him a reassuring hug, surprised that after years of exhibitions this artistic rock star was reduced to jelly over the unveiling of a mural in a sleepy seaside village. She found it quite endearing.

'Thanks. I'm sorry; I don't know why I get like this. It got better for a short time, but I was physically sick before my first exhibition.' He gave her a sheepish smile. 'I could do with a stiff drink.'

'That's because you care, and people's reactions matter to you,' Freya told him, wondering if her own blasé approach to showing her work back in university had partially lead to her downfall. She'd once been branded 'overconfident' by one of her undergraduate tutors. She cringed to recall the scathing response to her postgraduate degree show. All in the past, she told herself as she steered Angelo out of the door and locked up. 'And, sorry, but I don't have a hip flask for emergency rations.'

Most revellers were still busy enjoying the outside activities; the beach was full of kids covered in sand and ice cream, parents relaxing in the late afternoon sun, and couples strolling around the shops holding brightly coloured paper bags full of purchases. Angelo clung on to Freya's hand a bit too tightly, but she liked the feeling of being there for him, of their newly forged relationship. The crowd gathered outside the church was not as big as Angelo had feared, but Freya had secretly hoped it would be bursting with people. The mural was stunning and unique and she wanted as many people as possible to witness its unveiling. Tristan opened the church door and the assembled crowd made their way inside.

With her bright red hair, Lola was easily visible down the front chatting away to Sue about the festival. Tristan cast a questioning look at Angelo, who shook his head in response and took half a step back into the shadows.

Freya turned to Angelo with a grin the Cheshire cat would envy and squeezed his hand. 'This is it!' she whispered and did a little jump for joy.

Angelo's smile didn't meet his eyes, he pulled Freya to him, as if holding on to her for dear life. Nervously he scanned the assembled crowd.

When it seemed like no more people would be arriving, Tristan stepped forward. 'Thank you all for coming to the revived Fisherman's Fair. I'm sure you all agree it's been a great success. I'd first like to extend my gratitude and offer a round of applause to the organizers, Sue, Cathy and Jan.' A smattering of applause echoed around the church. 'Along with Lola, owner of the café, a newcomer to Polcarrow like myself, who's jumped into the breach and made sure the festival was a success.' Lola made a good show of pretending to be embarrassed while Cathy shot daggers at her for stealing the limelight.

'Now, without further ado, it gives me great pleasure to unveil a specially commissioned mural carried out by two local artists, who have, sadly, wished to remain anonymous.' Tristan made a pained, sad face before continuing. 'However, do not let the lack of a name detract from the beauty of the work. If anything, I believe the artists intend the audience to enjoy the work, to reflect on its deeper message, without a name distracting from what they were trying to say.'

Tristan reached up and pulled away the dust sheets,

revealing the mural in all its finished glory. The sunlight streaming through the stained-glass windows gave the impression that the painted sea was actually glittering.

Freya gasped at Angelo's skill. When they'd seen the mural the previous evening, the sun had nearly set, and so this little trick had not been in play. Angelo had clearly painstakingly planned the work so that the ripple of sunlight would bring the sea to life. Gasps of awe and a round of applause echoed around the church, and as Tristan stepped away to talk to Lola and Sue, the crowd moved forward.

'I think it's a success,' Freya whispered, her eyes glittering with happiness as she looked up at him. 'How on earth did you do that with the light and the sea? It's mesmerizing.'

'Magic. Well, a painstaking process of planning sounds less romantic.' Angelo let out a sigh of relief. But then he froze. Freya followed his gaze to a man with wild blonde curls and a checked shirt standing at the front. Instead of looking at the painting, he was looking straight back at them. 'I think it's time to go,' Angelo said. 'Don't look back, Freya, just go.'

They slipped out of the church from a back exit. Angelo clearly didn't want to be stopped by anyone, which Freya thought was a shame; she would've lapped up the praise and attention. 'Was that him?' she asked.

Angelo nodded as he almost dragged her at a run to Lola's cottage. 'Yes. The journalist.'

'Wait here.' She pulled him into the alley between the cottages and gave him a long appreciative kiss. Then she ducked into the cottage and grabbed a bottle of Prosecco she'd had

251

chilling especially for that evening. Along with a punnet of strawberries, some crusty bread and local cheese, she stuffed a picnic blanket into a bag and together they escaped across the headland to their hidden beach. They didn't expect to be alone, but thankfully, the bright lights and thrills of the festival had ensured that everyone was on Polcarrow's main beach. The sounds of people enjoying themselves wafted joyously on the breeze. Angelo spread the picnic blanket on the sand and dropped down onto it, starfishing with relief.

'It's done! It's done!' He held his arms out to Freya and pulled her down on top of him for a celebratory kiss. Then, taking her face in his hands, he studied her seriously. 'I would never have been able to do any of this without you. None of it. No, don't be bashful. You've saved me, Freya. You have saved me. Now let's just pray you're right about that journalist.'

Heart racing at the intensity of his gaze and his words, Freya licked her lips, searching for something to say. She had been fragmented, her life in pieces across the country, but with Angelo holding on to her so firmly, she knew she would be able to build herself up again. He was full of grand gestures and big love, and she was blinded by his kindness and glamour. She had never expected to find this level of happiness so soon. Now the mural was finished, she could concentrate on her own work again, which thrilled her. The break had certainly been the tonic she needed to refresh her creativity and the mere thought of painting again excited her. Slowly she bent down and kissed him, his forehead, his eyelids, his nose, jaw, working her way to his lips. The ferocity of her feelings for him shocked her, and although she'd only known him a few months, she couldn't imagine living without him.

Angelo gently pulled back. 'Slow down,' he said. 'We have all night. And anyone might find us here.' He reached for the bottle of Prosecco and popped the cork, the fizz running down his hands. Taking a swig, he then passed it to Freya and, passing the bottle back and forth, they drank, celebrated and dipped into the picnic, weaving together dreams for their future as the sun dipped lower in the sky.

Angelo spoke about Bayview House as if he had put in an offer and was waiting for the keys. He talked about promises for an autumn trip to Italy where they would drink in the wine, art and culture. Freya was giddy with the mere thought of it, pleased that he seemed to be putting the journalist out of his mind. Her imagination was full of images of rooms flooded with bright sunlight, canvases daubed with paint, a sheepdog lolling by the fireplace. Angelo had created for her a future she'd had no idea she wanted, and allowed her to help colour it in. As the night drew in, the setting sun cast them in a pastel pink hue that Freya thought was ridiculously romantic, and they wrapped themselves closer and closer in their own world until the cooling air made Freya shiver.

'Come on, back to mine,' Angelo suggested. Their kisses were fervent as their edges blurred together. He pulled her up, his eyes glittering. Together, they hastily gathered up their picnic, and suddenly everything changed, became more charged.

With feigned casualness, they scrambled up the path and slipped through the lengthening shadows round the back of the café, their steps interspersed with kisses. The sounds of an all-night party drifted from the pub. Angelo deposited their rubbish in the bin and she followed him inside, up the stairs, her heart pounding as she waited for him to unlock the door. As soon as the door was shut, he had her in his arms. His kisses grew more intense, hands made their way under clothes, tangled through hair, and they left a trail of shoes, T-shirts and belts on the way to the bedroom. As Angelo kissed her, Freya gave herself up to complete bliss. They made love by moonlight and slept entwined until the dawn crept into the bedroom and stirred them awake with new hope.

Chapter Nineteen

With the Fisherman's Fair and all its accompanying stress finished, Polcarrow relaxed. The following day was languid and sunny, the villagers slowly emerging from well-deserved lie-ins to discuss the festival. The resounding conclusion was that it had been a success and whispers about how to improve it the following year rustled through the bunting-draped streets. Freya woke wrapped around Angelo, full of a satisfied bliss she didn't wish to stir from. But once their eyes were open they couldn't ignore the clanging sound of Lola below them in the café kitchen. After a quick shower and some hurried kisses, they emerged, tousled and happily sleep-deprived.

'You two.' Lola bustled over to them and bundled them into a hug. 'It warms my heart. Just take care of her, okay?'

'Or what? You'll turn me into a frog?' Angelo teased in a low growl.

'Honestly!' Lola shook her head. 'Now, do you two lovebirds want some bacon sandwiches?'

Freya's stomach grumbled loudly.

'I'll take that as a yes. Help yourself to coffee. I'm not officially open yet but if Alf and Tristan turn up, let them in.'

'You do it,' Freya suggested, pushing Angelo behind the counter. 'You make better coffee than me.' More canoodling than coffee-making took place and when Lola emerged with two bacon sandwiches, she rolled her eyes.

'I'm already thinking about a Christmas bazaar,' she told them as she flipped the sign on the door to open. 'For anyone other than Alf and Tristan, I'm just doing bacon buns today, and takeaway hot drinks.'

A slow stream of villagers ambled down to the café for a late breakfast, which most then took to the beach where the tide had washed away anything that was left of the sandcastles from the competition. Despite his desire to remain anonymous, many locals had seen Angelo working in the church over the previous weeks and came to congratulate him on the mural. Freya enjoyed watching him bashfully receive their praise and deflect their requests for commissions.

'You could have quite a lucrative business here,' Freya pointed out to him.

'I need a rest. Plus, there are other projects I want to focus on. Once I'm established, then I'll start making art again, but only when I'm ready. I didn't expect all this, to be honest. I thought this village was hostile to change.'

'Everyone likes something that makes them unique,' Freya reminded him. 'It'll put Polcarrow on the map.'

Angelo looked uncomfortable at that thought and Freya decided not to say any more. She had no idea how long he expected to keep his identity under wraps; the village was full of gossips. Had it been her, she'd have been proclaiming her success from the rooftops. 'So what are you going to do next?' she asked.

'Spend some well-deserved time with you.' Angelo kissed her. 'And call Nigel, but I think he might be on holiday – Tenerife or something.'

'You're seriously thinking of buying Bayview?'

'Yeah. I loved helping Alf with his boat, getting my hands literally dirty. I can't go back to art just yet, but I need a project.'

Happiness bubbled up in Freya. All those sun-kissed summer dreams they'd had were going to come true.

'Come on, you two, enough,' came a jovial voice, followed by a bark.

Freya and Angelo broke away from each other to make space for Alf. 'Morning,' Freya said. 'Did Scruff enjoy himself yesterday?'

'Yes, but those kids all spoiled him. Bits of pasty, sandwiches, I even think the naughty bugger snaffled some fudge. I don't know what the vet will say, hey?' Alf scratched Scruff behind the ear before turning to Angelo. 'Well done, lad. That painting went down a storm. You both disappeared after the unveiling, but it was the talk of the town. No one knows how you got the light where the sea should be.'

'Skill, Alf – perseverance, planning and skill. There's nothing magical about it,' Angelo said, bursting Alf's bubble.

'Such a shame. Still, might attract the visitors. About time too. We've got everything all these other places offer. Morning, Lola,' he called as she stuck her head out of the kitchen door to ask if he wanted a bacon sandwich. 'Ooh, could you slip a fried egg in it please?'

'For you, Alf, I'd do anything.' She winked.

Freya jumped up to make him his tea and fetch a dog biscuit for Scruff. 'Was the fair as you remember?' she asked from the counter.

'Not at all,' Alf scoffed. 'Not at all. Well, things need to be modernized, and I'm not against modernization – the essence was there, but it was a lot more sedate back in my day. Just a bit of dancing, some ale, none of these sandcastle-building competitions. Scruff enjoyed that, though, even if he did make one boy cry when he sat on his castle.' Alf shook his head in despair, but whether it was over Scruff or the crying child, they couldn't tell.

Lola brought out his breakfast and watched as Alf lifted the top of the bun to check the egg. 'Smashing. I was going to wait for Tristan but I saw him cornered by Cathy, so he'll probably be a while. Something about litter. Since you're all here, I'm going to tell you my news. Guess who's going to be Polcarrow's next star?'

Three faces stared at him slightly blankly and then it registered. 'You, Alf?' Lola asked, clapping her hands together in delight.

'Yes. That journalist, Martin something-or-other from the Gazette, wants to feature me in Cornish Life magazine. Apparently there's not many like me left. He was very impressed with my boat and the restoration of it,' Alf said proudly. 'I said I didn't get it done without any help, mind.'

Freya took Angelo's hand and gave it a reassuring squeeze. He glanced at her and she could tell he was struggling not to let his own fears drown out Alf's happiness. 'Wow, Alf, that's great!'

'He was interested in you, lad,' Alf told Angelo. 'Asked me some questions.'

'What did you tell him?' Angelo's voice was tight. Freya felt him tense up.

'Oh, nothing much. Just that you'd helped me with my boat, that's all. I might be old, but I'm not daft. It's not my place to be spreading gossip. Not after everything you told me.'

Freya glanced up at Angelo; he clearly had the loyalty of his new friends if they were prepared to protect what they knew of his past.

Angelo nodded. 'Thanks, Alf. Has he got all the material he needs?'

'No. I asked him to come back later this week, Thursday I think. I was going to ask Tristan to look him up on the computer, check he's legitimate. I'm not that easily flattered, even though I do deserve my own feature in Cornish Life magazine.'

'That you do, Alf, that you do,' Lola said. 'Isn't this exciting?' She glanced from Freya to Angelo and back, thrilled with Alf's big moment.

'Yes, it's fantastic,' Freya joined in enthusiastically, not wanting any of Angelo's concerns to spoil the moment.

If Alf sensed Angelo's worry, he didn't mention it, just

tucked into his breakfast. 'I'll go and rescue Tristan after this,' he said.

Freya was disappointed to see Angelo retreat back into himself following Alf's announcement. It reminded her of when he'd first arrived; it seemed as if his mind was constantly elsewhere, and nowhere good at that. Her stomach twisted queasily as her new happy life felt suddenly precarious. Tristan had verified that Martin Somersby was a legitimate journalist, who regularly wrote features for *Cornish Life* magazine, but this did not appease Angelo.

'He's still a journalist, Freya,' Angelo pointed out, 'and Alf confirmed he was asking after me. I'm not ready for all this to become common knowledge yet.'

Freya was forced to watch him fret. Angelo had started to pace about like an agitated beast. She watched him until she could bear it no longer. 'Angelo, please stop, you're just making this worse for yourself,' she implored, grabbing his hands and forcing him to a standstill. 'Whatever will be will be.'

Angelo sagged in on himself. 'Truth be told, I need a distraction. Nigel isn't back for another ten days. Scruff only needs walking once a day and even that is more of an amble. I really think Alf needs to stop slipping him the odd bit of scone every now and then.'

Freya smiled. 'Well, you can take that up with him. The rest of us daren't. Hey, how about you do some painting? Borrow my things and have a go.'

'I've not painted like that in years,' Angelo reminded her.

'Just have a go, seriously. I can't bear to see you pacing up and down like this. I don't know what to tell you other than it'll be fine.'

'You don't know that, Freya,' he said darkly. 'I know how these people rip you apart and pick over the remains.'

'Then talk to Alf. He'll understand. I'm sure he'd cancel the interview if he knew what it means for you.'

'I can't do that to him, Freya. He's thrilled at the prospect of being in the magazine, and he's already told half the village. He deserves his moment,' Angelo said, defeated. He took in a deep breath and let it out in an anguished sigh. 'Okay, I'll take your paints and have a go.'

Painting went some way to soothing Angelo's mind. He returned to the café on Monday evening full of amused joy at his efforts. 'The brushes are so tiny.' He laughed and showed her what he'd done. 'I'm not suited to delicate work.'

The harbour scene was a bit wobbly, and Freya giggled at it. 'I like it,' she said. 'It's cute!'

'Cute?' he growled, as he picked her up to carry her up the stairs. 'I've never had my work described as cute before.'

'I'm worried,' he confessed later that evening as they sat in bed eating pasta with calamari, 'that all that mural work was a fluke. What if I've lost my talent? That piece I destroyed in London hadn't been around long enough for me to really look at it. What if it was rubbish?'

'I'm sure it wasn't. Baby steps, remember, little baby steps and you'll find your way back.' She dotted some kisses up his arm, blissfully happy and selfishly not wanting anything to intrude on it. Freya was glowing from the inside out from the sheer joy of being a woman who had fallen on her feet after being so cruelly tipped over. She studied Angelo, messed-up dark hair, his face unshaven due to distraction more than style, and although she knew this was only the start of their journey, she loved him and wished he could see himself the way she did.

However, this bliss did not last long. Over the next couple of days Angelo swung from loving and carefree, full of summer promises, to twitchy and sullen. Freya wondered if they should leave the village when the journalist came, go on a day trip somewhere, but before she could suggest it, Angelo stalked into the café on Wednesday morning and shoved the local paper under her nose. Across two pages was a spread all about the festival, including photos of the crowded beach, a couple of cute kids covered in ice cream – and the mural.

'Wow! Our own feature! This is wonderful,' Freya exclaimed, then, catching Angelo's morose face asked, 'Isn't it?'

'It talks about the stunning mural in the church and how they'd love to uncover the mystery artist.' Angelo stabbed at the paper. 'I am that mystery artist and I don't want to be uncovered.'

Sure enough, in a bubble on the bottom right-hand corner was a request for information about the mystery artist. 'But we all know and respect that. I don't think you have anything to worry about. Everyone here is loyal,' she tried to reassure him.

'They are until money is involved. Imagine how tempting a couple of hundred quid to blow my cover would be for someone? I can't have this happen, Freya, I can't. I came down here for peace, not to end up back in the papers. They'll drag everything up, everything I've sought to distance myself from.' Angelo wrung his hands together, eyes flashing with fear.

He was such a picture of despair that Freya couldn't find the words to argue the point. A dark dread settled over her: what if he hadn't told her the whole truth and simply edited out the bits of his past he didn't like? 'It will all be fine. Honestly, Angelo, it will be. No one will betray you. They wouldn't risk the wrath of Alf and Lola for one. I'm here for you, anyway. If they want to know who the artist is, I'm involved too. We can face it together.'

Angelo stared at her long, hard and bleakly, his voice aggressive with hurt. 'This is not your battle, Freya. With all due respect, I know you're trying to help, but you haven't got a clue. You have no idea what all this could do to me. To us.'

As Angelo stalked off, Freya was crushed by the sense she had failed him.

That night everything felt subdued, waiting like a paused breath. Angelo had distracted himself by making lasagne; the smell curled down the stairs and into the café, calling Freya up. With trepidation, she climbed the stairs, expecting him to be angry, but surely he wouldn't make dinner if he was mad with her? The door was unlocked and she slipped in. Angelo was in the kitchen, prepping a salad, singing along to the radio. She watched him, trying to preserve the moment, sensing that everything would be different after tonight. Freya slipped off her shoes and swallowed back her tears. Overwhelmed by love and fear, she padded through the kitchen and slipped her arms around his waist, pressing her face against his warm back.

'I'm sorry,' she whispered. 'I'm sorry that I don't understand. But I'm here for you. I know you're scared, but we can do this together. I won't let them hurt you again.'

Angelo relaxed against her, unpeeled her arms and moved so that he was cradling her against his chest. 'It's okay.' He kissed her head. 'It's okay. I'm probably overreacting. But it's the nerves, Freya, the nerves about what people might say or dredge up. I can't have anything disturb the peace here.'

Freya glanced up at him, and their eyes caught deeply for a long moment. They kissed slowly as if trying to kiss away all their troubles, hands slowly sneaking under clothes. Angelo murmured that dinner would still be a while as they made their way to the bedroom.

Later, sated with wine and love, the sky dark outside the window, their little haven lit only by a low lamp, Angelo took Freya's face in his hands and kissed her.

'Do you trust me?'

'What? Yes, of course I do.'

His voice was solemn. 'Whatever happens next I need you

to know that I love you. I love you in a way I never expected to love anyone. Freya, trust me, it'll all be fine.'

'What's this about?' Freya's brow furrowed. He made it sound like an ending, not a beginning. 'Angelo, I love you too. What do you mean it'll all be fine? Nothing bad is going to happen with that journalist. I'm here for you, and we can face this together, but I need to know what you mean.'

'Just that I love you,' he whispered as he nuzzled into her neck, his mouth full of kisses rather than words.

Chapter Twenty

A distant rumble roused Freya from her sleep. There had been talk of storms, so she gave it little thought. Instead, she rolled over and went to snuggle up to Angelo. The bed was empty; nothing but crumpled sheets and the scent of him on the pillow.

She stretched out, eyes closed for a few more blissful moments, waiting for him to return with breakfast. It wasn't strictly protocol, but Angelo sometimes snuck down into the café and returned with two expertly made cappuccinos complete with stories of Italy balanced like biscotti on the side. As Freya opened her eyes to another overcast morning, the sun-baked streets of Tuscany seemed even more appealing than usual. A proper holiday, she thought with a sigh, with lazy mornings and other people making her breakfast.

She lay there a little longer, listening to the caw of the gulls and the whoosh of the waves through the open window as Polcarrow slowly welcomed the new day. After ten minutes, Angelo still wasn't back and unease crept coldly over Freya as the previous day's events slowly came back to her. Angelo's agitation about the journalist, his reassurances that everything would be fine. But she realised she couldn't have heard a roll of thunder as the morning was bright. Could it have been the sound of a retreating motorbike? She tried and failed to explain what else could have made such a distinctive growl.

Throwing back the covers, Freya hauled herself out of bed. The silence in the tiny apartment was absolute. Much greater than a pause. There was something horribly vacated about it. She pulled on her shorts and T-shirt and made her way around the apartment, her brain and heart not quite processing what she was seeing. Or not seeing. The apartment was empty of Angelo's things. His boots, which had taken up residence by the door, were gone and his bag was no longer spewing art detritus in the corner. On the table were a couple of spotted bananas, a flyer for the fair and a three-weeks-old paper she had no idea why he'd kept. Freya flicked through it, searching for clues in among the car parking disputes, the reports of aggressive seagulls and adverts for local gardening businesses. Nothing. No note. Panic rose in her chest, squeezing out the air as the world plummeted beneath her. Angelo had left. Left Polcarrow. Snuck out in the night like a thief. Or a coward, she thought as her stomach churned with the realization. That's what he'd done before: hopped on his bike in the early hours and ridden away from his life in London. She tried to rationalize him leaving and removing his belongings, but Freya knew Angelo was a man who ran from his problems rather than facing them.

Her mind flickered over the previous days: the restlessness, the snapping at her, the strange admission of love, the reassurance that everything would be fine. He must have known when they went to bed last night that he wouldn't be here when she woke up.

Freya dropped onto one of the kitchen chairs. Why not tell her he had to go away for a while? Why sneak out after a summer of making plans, interweaving their lives together? Unless he wasn't coming back. No, surely he hadn't spun her a lie. Bayview House was in such a state; surely no one would lie about wanting to take that on . . . unless he was just a misplaced dreamer? Her brain was incapable of figuring it out, of trying to be practical while her heart cracked. There had to be some explanation even if he hadn't left a note.

Robotically, Freya made her way downstairs to the court-yard and sagged against the doorframe. His motorbike was gone. She cursed herself for missing him by minutes. The 'if only's' started to crowd into her head; if she had woken up she might have been able to stop him, talk it through with him. Freya pushed her hands through her hair, baffled. Last night Angelo had seemed fine with the idea of them tackling the journalist together. She'd believed she'd convinced him it would all be okay. Maybe she'd just foolishly assumed?

Freya kicked herself for not pressing him for answers, for not making him discuss whatever was playing on his mind, for allowing herself to be distracted by kisses and red wine. She searched her memory. Angelo had appeared fine; his mood had been lifted. Unless he had been only pretending everything was all right? Or maybe it hadn't been planned? Maybe something had happened while she slept. Freya turned the possibilities over in her mind, convincing herself that something must have happened, and it must have been something serious for him to tell her he loved her and then to leave. She didn't feel in her heart that he could or would have duped her.

She was still standing there, staring into space, trying to figure out what had gone wrong, when Lola arrived wearing a jaunty yellow and purple dress. Lola stopped in her tracks, taking in the absence of the bike and Freya's bare feet.

'He's gone.' The words stuck in Freya's throat. 'H-he's left.'

Lola looked confused. 'Gone where?'

Freya shrugged and the tears pricked. 'I don't know.'

Lola glanced around as if this was a prank and Angelo was hiding somewhere, then, seeing how Freya was trying to keep it together, took two decisive strides across the courtyard and bundled her into a hug. 'Oh hon, don't cry, you don't know for sure that he's left.'

Freya sobbed until she felt a bit sick, then pulled back, red-faced and snotty. 'I've not cried on your dress, have I?' She wiped her eyes with the backs of her hands.

'Oh, don't worry about that. Come on, you need some tea.' Lola ushered Freya inside and flicked the kettle on. 'Did he not leave a note or anything? He might have just popped out to get something?'

'No note. Nothing. But he took all his things. You don't pack up your stuff to nip out to the shop,' Freya pointed out. 'He just got up and left. Like he did before.'

'What do you mean?' Lola got the mugs out and began to make the tea.

'This is what he'd done when he arrived here. He'd just got up, got on his bike and left his London life behind. Including his ex-girlfriend.'

Lola narrowed her eyes as she placed Freya's mug in front of her. 'I never had him pegged as a scoundrel, though he was always troubled. I knew there was something he was fighting internally, but I thought he'd found peace here.' She reached up onto the shelf and brought down the biscuit tin. 'He did seem a bit funny about Alf's interview – was that it?'

'Yes. And the fair being in the paper. He was twitchy about the journalist at the fair, so came to the café to help me and, I guess, hide. He wouldn't say why he was so worried. What on earth could be that bad that he had to leave? I know he was worried someone would call the paper and tell them he'd painted the mural.' Freya rooted around for a custard cream, and having secured a few, sat back on the kitchen stool and looked at Lola. 'Who on earth behaves like this?'

'Someone who has demons they need to tackle,' Lola supplied.

Freya silenced her with a look, not in the mood for mysticism. 'He told me he loved me and that it'd be all okay. Who on earth tells someone they love them and then does a runner? I don't understand. We'd agreed to tackle this together. Whatever "this" is.'

'Ooh! He loves you?' Lola beamed.

Freya narrowed her eyes. 'He's got a funny way of showing it.'

'It's a mystery,' Lola said. 'I like a good mystery.'

'It's not a mystery, Lola. It's my life and the second time in six months a man has decided my future without discussing it with me, and then left me in the lurch. He's gone. He seemed fine yesterday evening after our argument so I didn't press it. I wish I had now.' Freya sunk her head into her hands. 'What is it with me? Am I the problem?'

'No,' Lola replied quickly. 'You had no reason to believe he'd do a dawn flit, did you? Also, don't you dare compare Matt to Angelo. Totally different stories, darling. Matt was just a bit of a knob and Angelo is troubled, we all know that. Angelo will be back, I feel it in my bones. He's not done here and he loves you!'

'Lola, right now that makes it worse, not better!' Freya groaned, glancing up at Lola. 'How on earth do you just leave someone you love without saying goodbye, or telling them why? Surely the whole idea of being a couple is facing life together?'

For once, Lola didn't have an answer. 'And do you love him?' she asked.

Freya knew her answer would determine what happened next. 'Yes, Lola, I do love him. That's why I want to understand what's happened, but I've left it too late, haven't I?'

Seeing Freya's lip begin to wobble, Lola hurried around and pulled her friend close. 'Let it all out, Freya, let it out. He's an idiot if he doesn't come back. But I firmly believe that Angelo is meant for you and what is meant for you won't pass you by. They say the course of true love never did run smooth.' She paused in the middle of rubbing Freya's back.

'Gosh, not sure how well Nigel will take this; he was dead set on Angelo buying Bayview.'

Despite everything, how much it hurt to have that future pulled from under her feet, Freya couldn't help but laugh.

On Lola's insistence, Freya headed back to the cottage for a shower. 'Take your time!' she urged. 'Have a bath. There's no need to rush back. I can handle it. Looks like a slow start this morning.'

It was early enough that no one was about to bat an eyelid at Freya's bare feet; her shoes were still lying on the floor of Angelo's apartment. She let herself into the cottage and headed for the bathroom, barely glancing at her reflection in the mirror. A bath would have been lovely, but she didn't think wallowing in a tub of water would help her feel any better. Not that she really knew how she was feeling. At a guess, hollowed out, processing, shocked and angry.

She scooped her hair up and stood under the shower. Thirty minutes later she headed back to the café, refreshed and dressed.

'Oh I wasn't expecting you back so soon,' Lola said. 'I told you to take your time.'

'And do what? Mope? Worry? No, I'd much rather be back here, thank you.' Freya pulled off her hoodie and tied the floral apron around her waist. Lola gave her a funny look. 'It's fine. I'm fine, well, as fine as I'll ever be.' She flashed a smile that didn't reflect how she felt.

'Okay, if you're sure.' Lola extracted herself from behind

the counter. 'I'll go and make a chocolate cake. Chocolate cake is always a cure for a crisis!'

Freya laughed. 'You should write a book. Lola Cures All Ills, or something.'

'You know, I might just do that.' Her eyes twinkled. 'There's no end to my talents, you know. By the way, I went up to the apartment while you were out and collected all your stuff. I didn't think you'd fancy going up there for a while.'

'Thanks.' Touched, Freya pulled her bag towards her and checked the contents. All her things were there; phone, phone charger, shoes. She swallowed back the finality of it all.

Seeing Freya's face blanch, Lola quickly added, 'I'm sure he'll realize what an idiot he's been and rock up with a massive apology tomorrow.'

Freya cast Lola a long, lingering look, trying to dampen the rising hope. 'I'll give him until the end of the week, benefit of the doubt that he's avoiding the journalist. If he's not back, it's pretty clear he's not coming back. Don't read the cards either – I don't want to know. They're what got me into this mess in the first place. New love, the dark man.' Freya rolled her eyes.

Lola made a sad face, and Freya suspected that she'd be reaching for the tarot deck later that night despite her warning. Not wanting to continue the conversation, Freya pushed her bag under the till and started to rearrange the perfectly neat set-up on the countertop, before turning the radio on to try to lift her mood. Distracted by a Nineties pop classic, she almost didn't hear the door open a few minutes later.

Luckily, Scruff barked to announce his presence, so Freya hurried from behind the counter to fuss him.

Alf was all dressed up in a shirt and tie ready for his meeting with Martin Somersby.

'Look at you, Alf – very smart,' Freya remarked, and the old man did a twirl.

'Thanks. I need to make a good impression. You'll spoil him, lass,' Alf warned as Scruff rolled over onto his back. 'All this fussing doesn't do an old dog any good.'

'You're only jealous,' Freya joked as she stood up. 'What can I get you this morning?'

'What have you got?' He followed her over to the counter and perused the selection. 'Granola bars – oh no, too healthy. I'm feeling a bit naughty today so I'll have a bit of that chocolate brownie. Is that a bourbon biscuit stuck on the top? Well, I never, Lola and her magic baking.'

'Tea?'

'Yes please, a nice strong fisherman's brew. Can't abide that muck our vicar drinks.' Alf made a face and hobbled back over to the window seat, where no doubt Tristan would soon join him.

Freya made Alf an extra strong mug of tea in his favourite blue and white striped mug, which they kept behind the counter especially for him, and, adding a couple of dog biscuits to the tray, carried everything over.

'I don't think Scruff should have any of that brownie,' she said. They both looked at the dog, who put his head back on his paws with a whimper of resignation.

Alf studied the colour of his tea before giving it a thumbs up. 'Lovely. That's perfect.' He had a look around the café. 'Where's your young man this morning? I thought I heard a motorbike when I took Scruff out first thing. He wanted my advice about doing some of the stuff in Bayview.'

Freya sat down and composed herself. 'Alf, he's gone. At least, I think he's gone. He's taken all his stuff.'

'What? Why?' Confusion flashed across Alf's face. He put his mug down.

Freya shook her head and pressed her lips together. 'Alf, he was worried about the journalist, especially after the paper asked for information on who the mystery painter was. You know he had troubles in his past and you must know he was big in the art world. He was worried the journalist would dig up some dirt on him and destroy his peace.'

Alf's face fell. 'Oh, Freya. He never said anything. If he had, I would've cancelled. This is just a bit of vanity for me. I wouldn't have done it, had I known it made him that uncomfortable. That Martin was giving him the eye on Saturday,' Alf mused. 'A bit too interested for my liking.'

'Angelo didn't want to ruin your moment,' Freya said. 'He said you deserved it.' She sniffed. Really, she thought, it was a bit of a selfless act, if misguided.

Alf reached out and squeezed her hand. 'Don't cry, lass. People don't leave without a good reason, not if they love someone. He was troubled, that boy, deeply troubled. I know his past in London wasn't happy. If Angelo loves you, really loves you, then he'll be back, and if he doesn't come back, well, it's his loss! Isn't it, Scruff?' Scruff barked in agreement, which made Freya laugh through her tears. Alf passed her a napkin. 'I don't know what Nigel will think,' he said. 'He was banking on him buying Bayview.'

'What Nigel will think about what?'

Freya glanced up to see Tristan standing above her, a concerned look on his face.

'Angelo's left,' Alf explained. 'Freya here had no idea, no idea. Now that's a rotten thing to do to the woman you love. I was just saying that Nigel was banking on Angelo taking Bayview off his hands.'

Tristan sat down. 'Angelo's left? When?'

'This morning,' Freya said. 'He'd been worried since the fair featured in the paper.'

'No note,' Alf supplied. 'I feel awful – it was all because of this interview. Angelo didn't want anyone raking up his past. It's all my fault.'

'No, it's not, Alf, it's really not,' Freya reassured him; she hated to see him so upset. 'Angelo is just rubbish at tackling his problems.'

Tristan took his time to respond, composing his words carefully. 'Oh, Freya, I am sorry to hear that. I'm surprised too. The last time we spoke he was keen to make a life here, said he couldn't imagine living anywhere else. But he was troubled.'

'If I had a pound for everyone who said that . . .' But deep down Freya knew it was the truth, even if she didn't need to keep hearing it. 'Being troubled doesn't exactly explain or excuse anything though, does it?'

'No, it doesn't, but honestly, I thought we'd come a long way since he first arrived. I managed to coax his demons out and felt confident he'd reached a point where he could put his past behind him. He did keep mumbling about having amends to make,' Tristan mused, 'but I couldn't draw him further on the subject, and then he got into village life and seemed ... well ... settled.' The vicar shrugged.

Lola emerged from the kitchen with a tray of toast and marmalade, before Freya could respond.

'It's a mystery.' Lola set the tray down. 'Angelo's always been a mystery. There's always been something that none of us could put our finger on. It'll all come out, I feel it in my bones.' Lola shivered for dramatic affect.

'Yes, well, while I don't quite share Lola's, erm, mysticism on the subject, the sentiment is right. Things do usually reveal themselves, and there's usually a good reason for bad behaviour,' Tristan said.

'Unless he's just a coward who runs from all his problems,' Freya reminded them. 'He's done it before.'

There was a pause as Alf, Tristan and Lola exchanged glances. Eventually, Lola piped up, her voice full of fake brightness. 'Well, if that's what he is, then is that who you truly want?'

Freya closed her eyes. She was thankful to have such well-meaning friends but was starting to wonder if she had really known Angelo as well as she'd thought.

Chapter Twenty-One

Friday evening rolled around and there was still no sign of Angelo. Freya had slowly slipped into resignation that he probably wasn't going to return, despite Lola branding this a defeatist attitude. She and Angelo had been living in each other's pockets all summer, so they hadn't bothered swapping numbers – there'd been no need to – and now she regretted not having any way of contacting him. Freya wondered if he would even pick up.

The whole village had been buzzing about the feature in the paper, so much so that they hardly noticed Angelo's absence. So much for them cashing in on his fame, Freya thought glumly. All this upset for nothing. Alf's meeting with Martin Somersby had been a success, even if Martin had been a bit too interested in the dark-haired man who'd been helping with the boat. Alf had used all his Cornish charm to deflect away from Angelo, and Martin had left Polcarrow pleased with his article on the old fisherman.

'Even took a photo of me standing next to old Betsey Jane.' Alf had bristled with pride when he had regaled Freya, Lola and Tristan with his story over breakfast. 'I definitely think I have the face of a cover star.'

They'd all revelled in Alf's moment of glory and tactfully nothing more had been said about Angelo. Freya's emotions were all over the place but she tried her best to hide them as she didn't want Alf feeling guilty for the part he'd unknowingly played. She had reassured him, when he'd voiced his concerns, that he wasn't in the slightest bit to blame.

'Come on, we're off to the pub,' Lola announced as they locked up on Friday. 'If any week requires wine, then it's this one.'

Freya linked her arm through Lola's and let out a sigh as they strolled along the harbourside. 'I feel so bad for Alf. He's really blaming himself for what Angelo did, but I can't seem to explain to him that it's not his fault. Alf does deserve his moment, but Angelo didn't have to be so dramatic about it all. In fact, I think he's made it worse by buggering off than if he'd just spoken to Alf about it. My brain is so full of all this. I don't know what to think anymore.' Freya sighed as they reached the pub.

Lola tutted as she pushed open the pub door. 'Bottle of white, please, Steve, and two bags of crisps. Salt and vinegar, and do you have those ham and mustard ones?'

'Sure – you're the only one who likes them.' Steve pulled a bottle of white wine from the fridge and set two large glasses in front of it. He looked at Freya. By now the whole village knew Angelo had gone and rather than sticking their noses in they had remained discreetly supportive and kept all speculation firmly behind closed doors. 'I heard Alf got interviewed for the paper,' he said.

'Not the paper – Cornish Life magazine.' Lola gave Steve a long look to deter him from asking any more questions. With a shrug he took her money and tossed two bags of crisps on the bar. Lola bestowed upon him a smile that had broken many hearts in the past, picked up their wine and snacks, and headed outside. 'Reckon it's too cold?'

Freya shook her head. 'I have my jumper on, plus we might as well make the most of the last warm evenings.'

They took a seat nearest the edge of the garden, pleased to find one with a sea view. Lola cracked open the bottle of wine and poured two glasses before studying the label on the bottle. 'It says Pinot Grigio, but who's to know? Cheers! To chasing off demons.' They chinked their glasses and Lola admitted, 'I am shocked that he's gone. I know you asked me not to read the cards, and I respected your wishes, but I never saw this.'

Freya sipped her wine and thought about this. 'In a way, I'm not. He did the same thing back in London. But there he smashed up his work, had a blazing row with his ex and stormed off. I feel stupid for believing he'd be different down here, that what he did in London was a one-off. Now no one knows where he is.' Her face blanched as a horrible thought occurred to her 'What if something awful has happened to him? He could be in hospital or dead for all we know!'

'He's not dead, Freya.' Lola rolled her eyes.

'I know that, but it's a possibility. And you can't deny he's shown truly cowardly behaviour. That's how he ended up down here, don't forget that. He just jumped on his bike in the middle of the night and headed off. In fact, he didn't even have a destination in mind – no, Lola,' Freya cut in as Lola opened her mouth to speak, 'none of that "destiny brought him here" stuff. And what's he done now? The same thing he did then. I feel like a fool, like I ignored warning signs, but, Lola, there weren't any.' Freya took a deep gulp of wine. 'I can't keep doing this, thinking like you do, all this destiny and in the cards stuff. I'm trying to deal with this as real life and all the big ugly stuff that comes with it. You have no idea how confused and hurt I am right now. I feel like I've been turned inside out and have no idea how to put the pieces back together.'

Freya sniffed and Lola pulled a neatly folded hankie from her bag and passed it to her. 'No bog-standard tissues for you, Lola,' Freya dabbed at her eyes and took a fortifying breath. 'Half the time I want to lie on the ground, cry and never get up. The other half I want to hunt Angelo down and rip him to shreds. I miss him and I love him and I hate him, all at the same time, and my brain can't cope with that. I can't face all this talk about him coming back, because it gets my hopes up. I want him to come back so much; I want to be with him, snuggled up to him, laughing behind the counter, but if he comes back I will never be able to forget him leaving me. How would I ever trust him again?' Freya glanced over towards the sea where twilight was descending lilac and soft on the horizon. 'You have to remember, Lola, artists are incredibly self-involved. That's why I lost Matt, because I was so wrapped up in this crazy idea that my stupid

Jennifer Bibby

attempts at making stupid art were the most important thing in the world.'

'Hold it right there, young lady!' Lola banged her hand on the table, startling a gathering of seagulls who were plotting how to grab their crisps, and making Freya jump. 'How dare you call your art stupid? It's your passion and your blood. It's been the one constant thing in your life. You need to stop thinking that you lost Matt. You didn't lose him – he lost you. Well, you probably lost each other, but that's what your twenties are for: experimenting with life. From where I'm sitting you didn't have much to lose anyway, just some guy who turned into a corporate prick. It's also not your fault your drive and ambition made you put his needs second. You're in your mid-twenties – this is the time to be selfish.'

Lola topped up the wine glasses and sat back. 'And yes, I admit Angelo has shown shitty behaviour, and when he comes back, I'll be having very stern words with him, but in my experience people who behave badly usually have good reason. And, again, it's also nothing to do with you. You cannot fix him. He has to fix himself. I never want you to think you could have done anything different. If you'd woken up and tried to stop him getting on that bike, he might still have left. There's something he's clearly afraid of but until he comes back and tells us we'll never know. Maybe he was scared by how he felt about you? Or how quickly everything was moving?'

Freya, lips pressed together, nodded, taking in everything Lola said.

Lola reached across and took Freya's hands. 'Please never doubt what that man felt for you. He was struck by you that very first moment he came into the café. I saw the way he looked at you every day. For God's sake he wanted to buy Bayview, which every sensible human being knows should probably be condemned. There's no way anyone on this planet would contemplate buying that house unless they wanted to be here for the long haul. Why do you think something so grand is so cheap? You'd probably fall through the floorboards.'

Freya couldn't help but laugh. 'So maybe I should be thankful that I'm not going to break my neck on a rotten staircase.'

'Well, as I'm wont to say, every cloud has a silver lining.' Lola smiled and did a little shimmy.

Freya sipped her wine and let her brain scramble Lola's rant into some sort of coherent life message. 'Lola, I hear everything you're saying, but please don't mention Angelo coming back again. I can't keep on waiting. For how long? A month? Six? A whole year? The whole point of me being down here this summer was to sort myself out and realize I don't need anyone other than myself. I wasn't meant to fall in love with someone like Angelo. In fact, I wasn't meant to fall in love at all! And what if that's all it was? A nice summer fling to help me move on from Matt?'

Lola pulled an 'oh please!' face. 'Do you really believe that?'

'No, but maybe I should. No one knows where Angelo is. None of us thought to take his number. I can't sit here waiting for him. This is the twenty-first century. Women don't wait for slightly shady menfolk like they did back in the nineteenth,' Freya pointed out as she took a swig of wine. 'He's not gone to war or anything noble like that. He's basically just fucked off because he can't face his own problems. And even if he did come back, am I supposed to live my whole life like this? With someone who jumps at every shadow or pointed camera? Maybe this is a blessing in disguise. I have to let him go, Lola. I've been going out of my mind this week. I've hardly slept. I keep thinking of how different it all could have been and if I don't let it go, I'll drive myself mad.'

Freya paused, resigned. 'You know, we discussed everything. Living together in Bayview, going to Italy, the art we'd make. I bought into this whole life he presented to me. He did that to me, Lola; he allowed me to get comfortable in that shared fantasy, and then he just left me. He planned our future and then didn't even have the decency to say goodbye. All of this because he was scared someone might recognize him. He should be dead to me.'

'That's a bit dramatic,' Lola said.

'Maybe, but not more dramatic than how he's behaved,' Freya pointed out. 'He's probably lying in some B&B somewhere trying to pretend all this didn't happen. It's not just me he's hurt. He never said goodbye to Alf or Tristan. You know what, Lola, I've decided that it's stupid men that have caused all my troubles this year. I'm going to try and forget about them and, like I was meant to do all along, concentrate on me. I'm going to go and get more wine and when I'm back

I don't want to talk about Angelo or Matt. It's not my art, or my family, or my girlfriends who've caused me trouble this year, but men, rubbishy men who can't face up to their issues or have an honest conversation. I'm done with it.' Freya stood up. 'I'm off to get more wine. What?'

Lola gave Freya a little round of applause. 'Welcome back, darling. My old feisty Freya, how I've missed you. Only took a bit of heartbreak and a dodgy bottle of Pinot Grigio to bring her out.'

Freya gave Lola a squeeze and said, 'I just hope she's here to stay,' before heading to the bar, her legs already slightly wobbly and her mind nicely numbed.

Freya woke with a cracking head and some regret for insisting on a third bottle of wine, which she had been too drunk to drink more than half a glass of before Lola bundled her home. That half a glass had sent her over the edge. The bottle of wine had its cap screwed back on and was now languishing in the fridge. Freya's stomach heaved at the thought of it. She'd quite happily never drink again.

Awake and unable to get back to sleep, Freya padded into the bathroom and splashed her face with water. Catching her reflection in the mirror, she knew a long hard day was ahead of her. Bed beckoned her back, but she knew it would be worse if she went to sleep for an hour now. Instead, she threw on an assortment of clothes and made her way downstairs, stuffing a bottle of water into her hoodie pocket as she let herself out into the cool purple dawn.

It felt like an age had passed since Freya had last risen with the dawn, her sketchbook and watercolours tucked under her arm. Not that the morning was spectacular enough to be preserved in paint, just a rather grey lilac shadow over the harbour meaning they were in for a cloudy day. That suited Freya fine; she didn't fancy squinting into the sun with a hangover.

Freya shivered as she climbed up the headland, putting some distance between herself and the village. The chilly breeze sliding cold fingers under her clothes, a warning that the seasons were changing. It had been liberating last night to denounce Angelo and reclaim her rights over her own future. However, literally in the cold light of day, Freya crumpled. The bravado had been alcoho-induced. She didn't want to let Angelo go; it was just that she didn't have any other choice. It was like letting go of hope.

Freya didn't know if the wine was to blame, or if the past six months were catching up with her, but she felt raw, stripped back and exposed. Pulling her hood up over her head, she sat down on the bench and closed her eyes, trying to trap the tears, but it was like trying to stop the tide. They flowed, sadness, grief and frustration streaking her cheeks. Erupting into big ugly gulping sobs, she imagined Lola urging her to get it all out and wished she'd thought to bring some tissues. Instead, Freya ended up sniffling into the hem of her grey T-shirt.

Cry it all out, she told herself. Just this one time, let it all out. Below her, the waves crashed against the rocks; to her left was the path to the secret beach. Freya regarded it and briefly thought of picking her way down to the smooth sand, but she was frozen to the spot. What was the point of making this worse than it was? She would not revisit the scene of the crime where Angelo had relayed the life he wanted for them in such seductive detail. Those memories would be strewn like flotsam across the sand, tangled like seaweed washed against the rocks. It was a life, Freya realized, that she'd allowed herself to become swept up in. It was a life of Angelo's creation, not hers. The cosy comfort of it had allowed her to pack up her own hopes and dreams and set them on a shelf. And now she found it almost impossible to separate her own wishes from those Angelo had woven around her.

Have I been foolish for believing him? she wondered bitterly, and tried to convince herself that she hadn't been. Whatever he'd done since, she truly believed Angelo meant everything at the time but she knew she would be stupid to pin her future on Angelo returning. A man who ran away. Yet Freya could not stop the ache in her heart, which made her double over as the sun attempted to rise.

She thought of the beautiful home they had planned to make and the future they were going to fill it with. The art projects they would work on. Her own space, something Freya yearned for, where she could leave her paintings half done and not have to worry about cleaning up for anyone else. At least I still have that art, she reminded herself; it was her constant comfort. It felt ironic that Angelo, having been so instrumental in giving her the boost she needed after Matt, had managed to make her feel just as heartbroken. Lola would say there was a lesson to be learnt, which brought a wry smile to Freya's face. 'Don't tie your future up with men' was clearly what she was being taught. They always had their own agenda. Although the irony wasn't lost on her that Angelo clearly had no idea what he was doing with his life. A lost soul.

Actually, Freya told herself sternly, now was the time to forget about the men in her life, and focus on herself. What she wanted from hers. After three months of making coffees and painting pleasant pictures, it was time to face up to the idea that she needed a plan. People from back home were starting to want answers as to her future plans. Her parents, Lily and Fiona, all dropped hints about how nice it would be when she went back. But Freya knew she didn't want to return. How could she step back into that hectic city life, all elbows and aggression, when she had happily discovered a seaside haven? She needed a solid plan, something watertight, that no one, not even Lily would be able to find holes in.

A few deep breaths of fresh sea air helped Freya think clearly. Could she really stay in Polcarrow long-term? She couldn't see Lola dissuading her. But could she stay here without Angelo but surrounded by the memories they'd made? Freya hesitated, but the thought of packing up and leaving the community who had embraced her in her hour of need made her heart ache. After this summer, would she ever be content to wake under steely landlocked skies, and have to deal with fights for the bathroom in shared housing and time-prescribed commutes? No. That was one thing she was sure of.

Freya fully understood why Lola, after a practically itinerant life, had been drawn to Polcarrow. The place had its own charm and enchantment, and Freya realized that Angelo hadn't been the only thing she had fallen in love with that summer. Freya knew she had to find a way to stay here. Surely she could paint and try to earn money from it; after all, every seaside town needed a local artist. And if that didn't work out, Lola would no doubt have other harebrained schemes to embroil her in over the winter months. The thought was strangely comforting.

Cheered by the prospect of living by the sea long-term, and knowing she needed to discuss this with Lola, Freya stood up and wiped her eyes for what she hoped would be the final time. Standing on the headland, she surveyed the sleepy village laid out below her. The little boats bobbing in the harbour; the church tucked away just off the main street, kept safe from the elements. Freya thought of Alf waking up to find Scruff had snuck into the bedroom again, but secretly not minding at all. Tristan preparing for a day of smiling through the village gripes and the unguarded look of affection on his face whenever Lola appeared with a tray of tea and toast, magic imbuing all of her bakes. There was more than enough room for an artist to set up easel in this town. The notion filled Freya with a warm fuzziness that was all of her own making. She turned towards Bayview House, perched on the top of the hill, and imagined the sunlight flooding the airy rooms filled with the remnants of a life that was never to be. Freya offered the house a sad, resigned smile and slowly, mentally picked her way through those rooms with their stunning original features, through the garden wild with flowers and birdsong, a house that was still waiting for its moment. Freya left the dreams of her life with Angelo at the foot of the stairs and walked through the front door, pulling it shut behind her. She wished that life farewell and rather than the grief she expected to rush through her, she was surprised to find peace nestled in her heart.

By the time Freya arrived at the café, the usual breakfast club was in situ in the window seat. Showered, dressed and ready to face the day, Freya bent down and scooped Scruff into a cuddle.

'You look incredibly perky for someone who had to be almost carried home last night,' Lola remarked.

Freya stood up, much to Scruff's disappointment. 'Ugh, I am never drinking wine again.'

Alf chuckled. 'We heard you had a few.'

'Bottles!' Lola supplied affectionately, and held out the plate of toast to her. Only Tristan's Christian morals stopped him protesting at half his breakfast being given away.

'What were you doing up on the headland this morning, lass? No, don't give me that look. I might be old but my eyesight is perfect. Twenty-twenty, it is. They used to say I could spot fish miles off.'

'I was doing some thinking,' Freya said, squinting slightly as a weak lemony light struggled through the clouds and flickered across the table. 'You've all been so wonderful this summer. You've welcomed me here, cast no judgement and have all been incredibly supportive this past week. I've realized I love Polcarrow and I don't want to leave.'

Alf looked proud as if the magical appeal of the village was all down to him. Lola put the tray down and Tristan grabbed his breakfast as she enveloped Freya in a hug. 'Do you want to stay?'

'Yes, Lola, if you can afford to keep me on over the winter months. I want to start painting properly again.'

'How exciting! Of course I can keep you on. I have loads of plans to get us through the winter. I'm going to do Christmas cakes, I'm planning a bonfire night with Tristan, but don't tell anyone yet, and there's talk of a Christmas festival.' Lola radiated joy at the thought of all these projects she could get stuck into. 'Isn't this going to be fun?'

Tristan and Alf raised their mugs in a toast. Freya grinned giddily back at them; she'd never felt so sure of a decision as she did about this one. 'Just one thing,' she said. 'I know he was your friend and I know you all have your own opinions on what's happened, but I'd prefer it if Angelo remained in the summer. Autumn is a time for shedding and moving on, which is what I intend to do.'

Lola, Alf and Tristan exchanged a look before all nodding their acquiescence to Freya.

Chapter Twenty-Two

Summer sneakily rolled into autumn, bringing with it the most beautiful dawns and dusks Freya had ever seen. They were more dramatic than the soft awakening of a summer day. And the nights were drawing in so quickly, it felt like if you blinked, you'd miss the changeover. September had seen a decrease in tourists following a post-Fisherman's Fair flurry, and Polcarrow started to hunker down.

Freya hauled her art materials out from under her bed, pulled on various mismatched layers and made her way out of the cottage. The morning air was fresh and the salt clung heavily to her skin; she could almost taste it. The sky was as dark as a bruise, but on the horizon a small, pale finger of hope was pushing through. Freya waited, watching as the light grew bolder, the day pushing its way through the folds of night. She mixed the colours – indigo, white, pale yellow – and quickly, almost without looking, splashed them across the thick paper.

It quickly became a morning ritual, an act of defiance, a way of showing she had survived Angelo leaving. It was a strange but beautiful way of ticking off the days. The paintings grew like a series, some dark and moody, others light like a leftover of summer. There was something reassuring about colouring in the grey of her life. Freya dated each and every one and allowed herself to revel in the pride of what she was creating. Finally, after years of having her artistic eye steered in other people's direction, she was doing what she loved most. Just painting, experimenting with light and texture. Pushing herself each day to develop her skills, testing what worked well and discovering what would be consigned to the bin. Painting filled her with joy, which in turn seeped into the cracks that Angelo had left in her heart and began to slowly fill and heal them.

Paintings once more hung like bunting above Freya's bed, a jolly reminder of her perseverance and achievement. It was hard to stop herself looking at them with a critical eye, but mostly she was pleased with what she had created.

One morning, she was coming back from the seafront, irked by the way the light wouldn't transpose and feeling a little defeated – she had taken loads of photos to pore over later in a bid to figure out where she was going wrong – to find Lola standing, open-mouthed, in Freya's bedroom doorway, staring at her paintings.

'What are you doing?' Freya said, instantly defensive and wincing inwardly.

'I . . . brought you this.' Lola held up a mug of tea. 'Freya, these are, well, wow, they are beautiful.'

Freya took the mug of tea, grateful for its warmth after being out in a rather blustery wind. She curled her fingers around it to bring them back to life. I need fingerless gloves, she thought. 'Thanks. It's been therapeutic.' She watched as Lola made her way down the line of paintings, touching some of them gingerly.

'I'm serious, Freya; they're brilliant, so atmospheric. That one, where it's all dark, that's really powerful.'

Freya studied the paintings. 'It's liberating to be painting what I want, after years of having to fit my work into assignment briefs or push boundaries I wasn't comfortable with.'

'You should try that gallery again,' Lola suggested.

Freya shook the thought away as another one dawned on her. 'Maybe we could display them in the café again?' she suggested nervously. 'But properly this time, buy some better frames, mount them properly.' The ideas started to grow in her mind.

Lola bounced up. 'That's a perfect idea! We'll have a mock gallery-opening in the café, invite the locals and show your paintings. Don't shake your head like that, young lady. Why did you spend so long at art school if it wasn't to show off?'

'Because I liked painting. Then art school told me painting wasn't enough. My parents told me art was just a hobby and the careers adviser said there's no money in it.' Freya sighed.

'And yet you persevered. Do you know what that takes, Freya? Courage. I know you don't think you have any but you've needed that courage this year. If you can find enough to move your life from London to Cornwall, you can find enough to let me hold a gallery evening. Come on! Everyone would love it. Alf, Tristan, the WI. I could even invite a couple of gallery owners, your parents. I'll do canapés, crack open some fizz, that sort of thing. The locals will love it! I'll love it! Mini scones, little quiches . . . what?' Lola asked as Freya held her hands up as if to physically stop her getting carried away.

Freya laughed. 'I don't mind displaying them as part of the café, but a whole evening?' She made a face, unconvinced. 'Who would come and look at them?

'Everyone!' Lola said, as if it was a no-brainer. 'Everyone would come. The season is coming to a close. They loved Angelo's painting. Everyone is so proud that that came out of their little village. They'd love this! Honestly, Freya, they would. One night, please, pretty, pretty please with a cherry on top, just for your Auntie Lola. You really do deserve this.'

I do deserve this echoed in Freya's head. Lola was right: it did take a lot of courage to pick herself up and paint again after failing her degree. She knew the villagers would love having their own local artist to boast about. Freya finished her tea and gave in; Lola's enthusiasm once she'd decided to do something was a force to be reckoned with. 'Okay. We'll make a night of it.'

'Excellent!' Lola gave her a squeeze and smacked a quick kiss on her cheek. 'It'll be worth it, honestly.'

Freya shook her head in disbelief. 'When do you plan to hold this extravaganza?'

'How about Friday?' Lola suggested. 'Gives us a week to sort it all out. Get some frames. Yes, Friday at eight p.m is perfect. That'll leave us time to change the café around a bit after closing time.'

'Friday is fine,' Freya confirmed as nervous excitement fizzed in her belly.

Without even pausing for breath, Lola was on it. She procured a number of frames so quickly that Freya was amazed at the contacts Lola seemed to have tucked up her sleeve. She then stuck up posters in the café window, which piqued the interest of the locals. This was quickly followed by menu planning, the whole event snowballing out of Freya's control.

'You can wear this!' Lola announced as she tossed a dreamy blue and white maxi dress at her on Thursday evening. 'Curl your hair, bit of lippy. Just in case …'

'Just in case what?' Freya asked suspiciously as she unfurled the dress. She had to admit that it was gorgeous.

Lola had the grace to look a little guilty. 'I may have tipped off the local press, but I'm sure they'll have bigger events to worry about,' she quickly reassured Freya when she saw her friend's stricken face. Journalists were still a sore point for Freya, although she was determined not to be cowed by them like Angelo was.

'Why are you getting so carried away?' she asked Lola, perching on the side of the sofa. The floor was covered in her paintings, a patchwork of dawn skies. They were trying to figure out which were the best ones to display. Freya had spent the past few days trying to quell the sickly combination of excitement and nerves. What if people just popped along

to humour her? She couldn't face another artistic humilia-
tion. Two heartbreaks was one thing; two creative flops was
quite another.

Lola sat back. 'Because you need to realize that this is your
life. You have done all this.' She gestured at the paintings.
'Not Matt, not Angelo, and not all those art buffs you studied with. I'm hoping that if you let everyone see what you
are capable of, if you see their reaction, you'll realize how
talented you are. I'm really proud of you, how you've turned
your life around these past few months. The villagers are
excited and curious too.'

'Nosey. You always told me they're nosey,' Freya huffed.

Lola chose to ignore this. 'And I have to admit, I think
it'll be good publicity for the café,' she said.

Her words struck Freya. This was about more than just her
artistic whims, but about village life, and more importantly,
Freya realized, a chance to help give back to Lola, who had
a business she needed to sustain. It wasn't just about herself.

Freya draped the dress over the back of the sofa and slid
onto the floor beside Lola, pulling the painting she was
holding out of her hands. 'Not that one. It's just, well, meh.
It's nothing. If I'm going to display my work, we need to
carefully curate about ten or twelve paintings, not shove all
these in everyone's faces. What? Did you think I didn't pay
any attention during my time at art school? Now, I definitely
want to include this one.' She held up one of a smouldering
grey sky, where the dawn light was coming through like a
scattering of pink petals on the sea.

They spent the evening lining up the paintings. Freya had managed to amass over twenty, her largest ever collection of works in a series. Was this a series? Freya wasn't sure. At art school, they'd always been encouraged to produce art in series with themes running through them. Staring down, eyes slightly blurred by wine, all she could see was a brightly coloured tapestry of therapy. She had painted to help mend her broken heart, and it had helped, she realized.

She had been sleeping better now that she had a reason to get up, and instead of spending all her time dwelling on Angelo, she was preoccupied with Lola's makeshift gallery. She'd even taken the plunge and invited her parents down. Now that the season was waning and they had been on their cruise (ghastly, apparently, never again) they had some spare time to visit. Olivia had been quick to offer to drive. Freya realized she had missed them but was nervous in case they tried to convince her to move back home. If the event was a disaster, then they'd probably bundle her in the car quicker than she'd be able to cry for help. There was only one thing for it, Freya reasoned – she had to make sure the night was a success.

Friday rolled round far too quickly for Freya's liking. As soon as the 'closed' sign was flipped, Lola was delegating jobs to Freya and to Tristan, who had been roped in but looked very much as if he was enjoying himself.

'Never thought Polcarrow would become an artists' haven,' he said to Freya as he swept the floor. 'You and

Angelo have certainly put this place on the map. Word has spread about the mural, even if the artist remains anonymous.' Tristan gasped and stopped himself. 'I'm so sorry, I shouldn't have mentioned him. How are you? Or is that making it worse?'

Freya smiled, amused to see the vicar worried about putting his foot in it. 'It's fine. Honestly. I'm fine too; I just want to get this over with.' She dropped her voice to a whisper. 'You know what Lola is like when she gets an idea.'

Tristan grimaced, rolled his eyes and recommenced his sweeping. 'Look, Freya, if you ever want to talk about anything, you know my door is always open.'

'Thanks, I'll remember that.' Freya swallowed the lump in her throat, touched by the vicar's consideration. She hadn't been to the church since the unveiling of the painting. Freya knew she would have to face it at some point, but the wounds were still raw. She had heard tourists discussing it over their lunches but she had never volunteered any extra information.

Lola sent Freya back to the cottage to change and 'do something with her hair'. 'Come back looking like a mermaid or something,' she instructed. 'Tristan and I will finish off here.'

Freya glanced at the paintings. 'I'd really prefer to stay and hang my work.'

'Nonsense. We've discussed it and, anyway, we can shift things about when you're back if we need to. Off you go. Shoo! Shoo!'

Suspecting that Lola really wanted some time alone with

Tristan, Freya headed back to the cottage. The blossoming relationship between the café owner and the priest was the village's worst-kept secret and as she let herself into the cottage she suspected half the villagers would be turning up primarily to get the gossip on the unusual lovebirds. Even though Lola remained tight-lipped about the whole thing.

Freya's phone pinged with a message from Olivia: On our way, got held up in traffic, should be there for the grand unveiling. Hope the chippy is open! Xxx Freya's stomach clenched at the thought of her old life colliding with her new one. She couldn't help but feel that her parents were coming to give her new venture their seal of approval. Or disapproval. Five years at art school and she was technically still just making coffees. It was a lovely gesture of Lola's to host the gallery evening, but as her nerves began to set in, Freya was struggling to believe that it would be a stepping stone in her career. Pushing that thought away, she took a deep breath and exhaled, deciding to enjoy the experience while it lasted.

Dutifully, Freya teased her long hair into waves and applied her make-up, excited despite all her reservations. She never usually wore very much anyway, but Lola had given her a few lessons and Freya could recreate them passably. Her eyes shimmered and looked larger with the soft brown eyeshadow and lashings of mascara, and although she felt as if the deep wine-red lipstick was wearing her, Freya had to admit she was pleased with the finished result. She slipped on some jangly silver jewellery and twirled in front of the mirror. It was selfie and social media worthy, so she snapped a few photos, uploaded them and wrote a short post about her upcoming exhibition.

As she pressed the 'post' button, she felt only slightly guilty that she'd applied a very glossy filter to the entire evening. Fiona and Lily had been invited down, but it had been too short notice for their busy London lives. Freya had been disappointed by this, but had gladly accepted their invitation for her to head to London the following weekend to celebrate Lily's birthday. She hadn't realized until their exchange how much she'd missed the camaraderie of her old friends. Her phone buzzed with good luck wishes from them both, which gave Freya an extra boost of confidence as she made her way out of the cottage.

The setting sun trailed thick orange clouds across the sky, like a banner. Freya locked up the cottage and made her way back to the café. Pushing open the door, she gasped in surprise. Most of the tables had been moved, and on the counter was a delightfully mismatched assortment of glasses for the drinks reception. The paintings were hung in the order Freya had recommended, and she had to admit they looked wonderful; the frames and the lighting really elevated them away from the humble sketches they'd been when clustered in her sketchpad. Hope fluttered in her chest; this could really work. The paintings didn't have names, but Lola had neatly written out cards with the date they'd been painted and stuck them underneath.

'What do you think?' Lola asked as she emerged from the kitchen with a plate of mini sausage rolls.

Speechless, Freya threw up her arms and gushed, 'It's . . . well, it's amazing. Thank you! It's better than I expected!'

'Oi!' Lola gave her a friendly slap on the arm. 'You should never doubt me. I've spent a lot of time doing lots of different things. Okay, I've never run a gallery, but I've been to enough. Now, how much are you going to sell the paintings for?'

'Gosh, I'd not thought of that.' Freya paused as she tried to figure out a rate that would reflect their worth, but not put anyone off making a purchase.

'Well, you must; someone will want one and not just your dad. I guess if you haven't thought of a cost, then you could take expressions of interest. What did Angelo sell those other ones for? He knew what he was going on about,' Lola suggested before grinding to a verbal halt. 'Right, I'm waffling, let me get the rest of this stuff out. We've got about fifteen minutes before the doors open.' Lola stepped back. 'You look wonderful. Keep the lipstick, it suits you better than it does me.'

Freya helped Lola set out the canapés, and then they were left with spare time and neither of them knew what to do. Freya practised the deep breathing and smiling that Lola had taught her, even if it was accompanied by the anxious wringing of her hands. She was rather pleased to notice that Lola was twitching about with tablecloths and constantly smoothing down her skirt while throwing glances at Tristan, who was waiting by the door. Freya smiled to herself; seeing Lola nervous helped to calm her down. Freya poured a bit of Prosecco into two glasses and passed one to her friend as she joined her behind the counter.

'Cheers! You look fine, Lola, stop fussing with your skirt. Anyway, Tristan has seen you in a lot worse.' Freya held up a finger to silence Lola's protests and dropped her voice. 'Plus, he's a vicar so should be less interested in the outer appearance than in what is inside.' Freya paused reflectively and squeezed Lola's hand. 'Actually, I don't think I've ever properly thanked you for everything you have done for me. I know it was a whim when I came down here and it was just meant to buy me time, and I've not always been easy to have about, but I really love it here.' Freya took Lola's hand and gave it a squeeze. 'Whatever happens next, this summer has really changed my life. For the better. Thank you.'

Lola's eyes shone with emotion and she pulled Freya into a hug. 'I've loved having you here. Honestly, it's been a dream. I mean it, you can stay as long as you want. I feel it in my bones, tonight will be a success.'

The door chime jangled and the girls pulled apart. Right on cue, Alf entered, an ancient striped tie clashing against his blue checked shirt. 'Never been to a fancy gallery showing,' he mused. 'Scruff wanted to come but I don't value his artistic opinion much.'

'Oh, Alf, you should've brought him!' Freya rushed over and gave the elderly gentleman a kiss on the cheek. 'If you want any paintings, you can have one for free. But don't tell everyone you're getting special mates' rates.'

Alf tapped the side of his nose and gave her a wink. 'Safe

with me, my love. Ah, Tristan!' He made his way over to the vicar and accepted a glass of fizz. 'Lola been putting you to work in here?'

Tristan laughed off the implication. He and Lola were unsure how to proceed when it came to making their budding relationship official. Freya had heard them whispering over red wine at midnight several times but she didn't think there was anything more going on than mutual affection and attraction. The vicar and the local witch, as Lola jokingly called them: not a likely pairing. Both outsiders who had found their footing on the rather steep slopes of the village. It seemed fitting that they would end up together. Freya was sure the villagers would give them their blessing. Her own heart dipped, and to take her mind off her recent heartbreak and to stop herself wishing Angelo was here, Freya snapped a few photos and uploaded them onto social media. Deciding one glass of fizz should be enough to take the edge off her nerves, she tucked her phone under the counter and took a sip from her glass.

The door swung open and her heart jumped. Olivia rushed towards her. 'This is fantastic! This place is amazing! No wonder you don't want to come home. The sea! It smells divine. There was terrible traffic. I think we should've left earlier, but you never know, do you?'

'Hello, love.' Her dad came and kissed her on the cheek, followed by her mum. He gestured to the walls. 'What's all this about then?' David was a bit at sea when it came to art. He either liked it or didn't like it; didn't see much point in trying to 'understand' it.

Freya distributed glasses of Prosecco. 'Well, they're paintings. I've been getting up early each morning and going down to the harbour and, well, painting. These are all the different dawns. You can see how the light is changing as we leave summer behind. It's so peaceful being out when no one else is. Just me and the sea air. I love it.'

Susan squeezed her hand. 'They're very beautiful. Dreamy. I like these a lot better than what you did in London.'

Freya pocketed the praise. 'Well, in London I wasn't allowed to do what I wanted. Not really. There were specifications and experiments. I've always preferred just to paint.'

Her dad chortled. 'Don't we know it! Remember that rainbow she painted on our newly decorated living room, Susan. Gosh! We left it up as long as possible, but we always knew you had some talent.'

Freya's brow furrowed, not wanting to have this conversation. 'Then why have you always tried to stop me painting?' she asked.

Susan looked a bit sheepish. 'We just didn't think there was any money in pursuing it as a career. I know that's rash coming from me with my love of the eccentric, but I was lucky. It was a different time when I met your dad. You need that bit of security to fall back on. I even had a part-time job when you went to school. Do you have that here?' She glanced up at Lola who was deep in conversation with Alf and Olivia.

'Not now, love,' David said. 'There's plenty of time for Freya to decide what she wants to do. Gap years can be very important.'

'Have you heard from Matt?' Susan said, changing the subject, and David, face in palm, went to fetch more fizz.

'No, and I don't expect to, either,' Freya replied firmly in the hope it'd end that line of questioning.

'It's just . . . He was such a nice, stable lad.'

Freya took a deep breath. 'I've not heard from him. It's over. We weren't happy together. He realized that before I did. Mum, this is my night. I don't want to keep talking about what you want me to do next. I have no idea, honestly, but I love it down here and I'm not ready to leave yet.'

Susan gave her daughter a quick squeeze. 'I know. I'm sorry, but I do worry.'

'Mum, please don't. I'm fine.' Freya's eyes flashed a warning, but as she said the words, she realized that she really was fine; it wasn't just a platitude.

It was pretty easy to call the evening a success. Someone from the local press turned up to take photos and interview Freya. Freya begrudgingly admitted to herself that she had enjoyed the experience, even if she suspected she'd waffled a load of nonsense about her paintings. Five of them sold, including one snapped up by Nigel.

'These yours?' He sipped his wine. 'They're pretty good. I have some commission coming in, finally got Bayview off my hands. Mystery buyer.' He tapped the side of his nose. 'They got it at a steal, though, but at least I don't have to try flogging it anymore. Still got my eyes on that Porsche, even if I don't quite have enough for it yet. I was really counting on the commission from your boyfriend buying it.' He sighed before realizing his mistake. 'Oh, I am sorry. Here you are all heart-broken and I'm worried about my commission.' He regarded his empty glass. 'I've had a bit much; I should probably go.'

'It's fine, really,' she reassured him, taking slight umbrage at the word heartbroken; her heart was merely a bit bruised now. She watched Nigel put his glass down and make his way out. Freya's stomach dipped sickeningly when she thought about what he'd just told her: someone had bought Bayview? Freya shook the thought away. Tonight was not the night to process this news.

Olivia sidled up to her and rather casually dropped in, 'What did he mean about a boyfriend? You never mentioned anyone.'

Freya glanced up at her sister and forced out a laugh. 'He's an estate agent. He's confused me with someone else.'

'Hmm.' Olivia raised an eyebrow indicating that she didn't believe a word, but that she was going to let it rest for now. Instead, she took a step back and studied her sister. 'You know, Frey, this is pretty cool. Your own gallery showing. Okay, it's in a café, but it's amazing Lola did this for you. I can see why you love the place. That old bloke with the clashing tie and shirt – he's brilliant! Whatever Mum says, just do what makes you happy. I've not seen you this happy in a long time. The sea air's clearly done you some good.'

'Thanks.' They had a quick hug and Freya mused about how she'd probably hugged more people this evening than she had her whole life. 'How long are you here for?'

'Until Sunday. Then we have to drive back.' Olivia rolled her eyes.

'You could've got the train.'

'Shockingly expensive last minute. Plus, we're taking turns driving. It has its fun moments.' Olivia grimaced. Their mum was a careful but slow driver and their dad probably the world's worst navigator. 'They don't trust the satnav.'

'Come here for breakfast tomorrow,' Freya suggested, 'and then I'll show you around.'

'Sure you and Lola will be up in time? She's been drinking a secret bottle of wine with that dishy priest.' Olivia waggled her eyebrows suggestively. 'It's all happening here.'

Freya laughed. 'Lola plays hard, but works harder. She'll be dragging me out of bed with the dawn. You'll probably have half the village here tomorrow morning, desperate for a look at you.'

'Like that, is it?' Olivia's eyes sparkled with amusement.

Freya smiled. 'Yes, but I wouldn't have it any other way.'

Chapter Twenty-Three

After hitting the snooze button three times, Freya struggled out of bed. Lola had closed the café at ten p.m. and the party had moved across to the pub. They hadn't rolled in until gone one a.m. and Freya had been too giddy with her success to get straight to sleep. She'd lain in bed trying to ignore the desire to talk to Angelo and tell him all about the evening. She had been doing so well with getting over his departure, but not sharing her finest moment with him brought the sense of loss flooding back. It was all she could do not to get swept up in it. Then, coming out of the shower, she checked herself in the mirror. She might look tired but her eyes were sparkling with something she'd not felt in a long time: a sense of success. And that success was all her own making, nothing to do with Angelo. He hadn't been there hanging her paintings, or calling the local press. She swept all thoughts of him away as she wiped the steam from the mirror.

The mornings were getting darker now. Out of nowhere, it seemed as if the brightness of summer had been swiftly smothered by the encroaching autumn. It was getting harder to know what to wear. Jeans felt constrictive against her legs, which were tanned from a long summer of exposure. She wasn't ready to be bundled up in layers yet. Anyway, by midday she was usually pulling the outer ones off.

Lola was downstairs already, fully made-up and in a yellow dress.

'How do you do it?' Freya said.

'Do what?' Lola cocked an eyebrow as she carefully applied her lipstick with a brush.

'It's seven a.m. We've been out all night. You're fully dressed and made-up. It's not human, Lols, it's not.'

Lola preened. 'Tristan says I'm not a normal woman. Though I'm not entirely sure what he's insinuating. I can't think a vicar has a huge back catalogue to compare me with. You ready?'

They spent the first half an hour hauling the tables back into place and putting the used glasses in the dishwasher. Freya washed the floor while Lola knocked up a couple of batches of scones and a carrot cake. Freya's stomach rumbled and she headed into the kitchen to see what she could plunder.

'Hands off!' Lola admonished. 'You can have breakfast with your family. I'm going to offer them the works. On the house. Full English – or Cornish as Alf would say, pancakes, toast, fruit. Whatever they want. The bread has been delivered; you can have a slice of that if you want.'

They munched on thick crusty slices of fresh sourdough smothered in local butter while sitting on the back step, drinking tea. The morning air was fresh and restorative.

'You know I'm having someone in later to clean Angelo's

apartment, don't you?' Lola said in a gentle voice. 'No one's been in there for weeks. It's too nice an apartment to waste as a shrine to him. I should have told you before, but I didn't know how you'd feel. I wanted to wait until the right moment.'

Freya nodded, unable to speak. It felt final, yet at the same time the right thing to do now that she was turning a new leaf. 'Yeah, I think I'm fine with that. It's all a memory now anyway. I guess it'll be a bit of closure.'

Lola put an arm around her and gave Freya a quick squeeze.

The café looked spick and span by the time Freya's family arrived, with Alf, Scruff and Tristan following close behind. Olivia wouldn't stop fussing Scruff.

'I must get a dog!' she kept exclaiming. 'Look at him! So fluffy! Something small, though, like a floppy spaniel. It must be wonderful coming home to a dog every day, so much more appreciative than a man.'

Susan and David exchanged looks. Olivia had very little desire to settle down. Freya wondered where she'd got all her self-assurance from. Maybe it was being the eldest child. Olivia had always forged her own way while Freya had toddled comfortably along behind her.

Tristan pushed some of the tables together so they could all partake of the breakfast buffet. Lola brought out platters of local bacon, fried, poached and scrambled eggs, and Freya made teas and coffees before they all sat down together. Scruff was in his element, stealing bits of bacon and toast from almost everyone.

'He's loving this.' Alf chuckled. 'Aren't you, boy? Getting a taste for the finer things in life.'

'What are your plans today?' Lola asked Freya.

'I thought we could have a walk along the coast. The scenery is beautiful,' Freya told her parents.

'Can we take Scruff?' Olivia asked, her eyes shining.

Alf stroked his dog under the chin. 'Yes, he could do with a good walk, just don't let him off the lead. He's not figured out yet that the seagulls are the bosses around these parts.'

That settled, Freya helped Lola clear the table. 'You sure you can spare me all day?'

'Of course. I ran this place by myself for a bit before you arrived; plus, it's low season and you've hardly had a day off all summer. Go and convince your parents it's the right thing for you to stay here. Then come back for a cream tea. If nothing else, that should do it.'

The weather was beautiful; sunshine glittered seductively on the sea; there was a light breeze, but it was warm enough not to need coats. Scruff tugged at his lead in a bid for freedom, but Olivia respected Alf's rules and kept him on it. They walked across the headland, Freya's heart jumping at the sight of the path that led down to her and Angelo's little cove. All those dreams washed out to sea now. She didn't take her family down to it. Instead, they carried on to the next bay and stopped at the pub. Once the bags of crisps were opened and the drinks on the table, David proposed a toast.

'To Freya!' They all chinked their glasses together. 'I have to say, I much prefer coming to visit you down here than in

London. Much prettier. And friendlier. I know we've been asking you to make your mind up, but it's your life. If you want to stay here a bit longer, that's great. I was so proud of you last night. My little girl, all grown up, with a blossoming art career. It's done you good coming here.'

'Thanks, Dad.' She squeezed his hand.

Olivia snuck a few crisps to Scruff and studied her sister. 'It suits you being down here. You look so much healthier and happier. There are loads of holiday homes – we could pop down properly for a good long stay!'

'And you're always welcome to come back home, any time,' Susan added and squeezed Freya's hand. Susan opened her mouth and closed it again, before curiosity got the better of her and she asked, 'Who's that young man Lola is with? Is he really a vicar, or is it fancy dress?'

Freya laughed. 'Yes, Tristan really is a vicar. He arrived here not long before Lola did. He'd worked in some tough city parishes and was burned out. They were both outsiders and just sort of, well … they're not actually together yet. I think Tristan is still a bit shocked that he's fallen for Lola and Lola's enjoying the attention. They're being very tight-lipped about whatever is going on, though.'

Susan raised her eyebrows and took a big gulp of her gin and tonic. 'Well, I never thought I'd see Lola settled down in any form.'

'I think we all get tired of moving about,' David mused. 'London isn't for everyone. Stay here, Freya. You're living everyone's dream.'

Yes, she thought as she glanced over the bay where seagulls were fighting over a chip, time now to make her own dreams come true. And that was a thrilling possibility.

Freya waved her parents off with promises to visit at Christmas, warmed by the prospect of a familiar festive get-together. Scruff barked in delight and she didn't have the heart to tell him he wasn't invited. Then she took him onto the beach for one last run-around, hoping it would ensure that he'd curl up quietly to doze in front of Alf's fire that evening.

It was late afternoon now and the wind was getting up; storms had been predicted for the following week. Clipping Scruff's lead on, Freya left the beach and frowned to see a scruffy white van parked like an eyesore outside the closed café. Wondering if it was a camper lost on their way to the campsite, Freya approached cautiously. There had been rumours of rogue tradesmen doing the rounds recently, although Alf had quickly dismissed the reports, saying you couldn't trust the people in the town the rumours had come from. 'All of them are liars!' he'd declared with a thump of his mug on the tabletop to emphasize the point. Still, it didn't hurt to be careful.

Crossing the road, Freya stopped in her tracks, her heart almost leaping out of her chest. Standing by the driver's door, wrapped in a long coat, dark hair blown wild by the sea breeze, was Angelo. Freya shook her head, convinced her mind was playing tricks. Scruff barked happily and bounded forward, throwing himself at his old friend. Angelo bent down to give the dog a fuss, his face so full of joy that it momentarily wiped the past month from Freya's mind. However, when Angelo glanced up hopefully, Freya watched his face fall as he realized he wasn't going to get the same warm welcome from her.

'Freya.' He said her name like an attempt at an apology.

Freya gathered Scruff to her to buy herself time. The way he said her name contained so much longing. Although she had lain awake many times imagining this moment, not once in her wildest dreams had she ever thought it would happen. 'What are you doing here?' she asked so brusquely, Angelo shrunk back.

Freya glared at him as the realization that this reunion was not going to be as smooth as he'd thought broke upon him like a wave.

He reached into his pocket and pulled out a set of keys. 'I thought you would have heard.'

Bayview House. No way, she thought. 'But Nigel told me a mystery buyer bought it.'

'I am the mystery buyer.' Angelo looked pleased with his ingenuity. 'Well, not me, but I instructed my agent to proceed with the sale on my behalf. I didn't trust Nigel not to blab so I asked to remain anonymous.'

'Ah yes, of course, all that sneaking about and never quite revealing the whole truth.' Freya shook her head in disbelief. 'No word, nothing, Angelo. Not a goodbye note or a follow-up text. Nothing. You just rode off into the dawn again and now you expect me to be thrilled that you're back and forget what you actually did. You promised me a life, told me you loved me, and then left. Not just me, you left Alf, Tristan and Lola, all those people who were good and kind to you.'

Surprise flashed across Angelo's face, and he stepped forward. 'Freya, I can explain everything. I know I acted badly and honestly you have no idea how hellish the past few weeks have been for me, but if you listen I will tell you everything.'

Tears sprung in her eyes and she sniffed them back. 'I can't, Angelo. I just can't, not now. It's too much. I made a decision to live my life for me, without you, and now you're back, who knows how long for . . . I just can't right now. I never, ever expected to see you again, you know.' Angelo stepped forward as if to explain. Freya held up her hand to stop him. 'No, save it, I can't hear it, and I need to get Scruff home.' Freya turned to the dog. 'Come on, boy.'

Stunned and shocked, Freya walked right past the turning up to Alf's cottage and found herself outside Lola's instead. She knocked on the door without looking back.

'Freya! What on earth has happened? You look like you've been a ghost.'

'Don't look now, but Angelo is back,' Freya hissed.

Lola, of course, couldn't help but peer out of the doorway, down towards the harbour, where a lonesome dark figure was staring back at her. 'Come in, I'll take Scruff back.' Lola bundled Freya inside. 'Go and sit in the living room. I'll be back in a jiffy.'

Lola grabbed Scruff's lead and, without changing out of her slippers, went to deliver him home. Freya kicked off her trainers and threw herself onto the sofa, pulling one of Lola's ludicrously bright crocheted blankets over her. What on earth had just happened? Well, Angelo had bought Bayview House and come back to move in. Not that it was in any fit state to live in. She didn't think he'd dare ask for his apartment back. Surely he didn't think they'd just welcome him back with open arms? Freya's head hurt, the joyous mood that had had her skipping on clouds after the gallery night evaporated. She closed her eyes, hurt and anger swelling in her stomach along with a little betraying flicker of love that she tried to smother out. She closed her eyes and tried not to think.

Freya was still lying there in the almost dark when Lola returned. Snuggled under her blanket, she listened to the sounds of the kettle boiling, cups being placed on saucers and Lola humming as she reached for the cake tin.

'Flick the lamp on. I'm not having you lying here like a Victorian lady with a fit of the vapours,' Lola chided as she bustled in with a loaded tray. Freya turned on the lamp and Lola put the tray on the small table. 'Tea and cake, that'll fix it.'

Freya stared at her friend as if she'd gone mad. 'Honestly, Lola, I don't think tea and cake is going to make this any better.'

Lola made a face. 'It might not, but you won't know until you try.' She pressed a plate with a large slab of carrot cake into Freya's hands, then poured the tea. 'I always said he'd be back.'

Freya rolled her eyes. 'Don't. Just don't do all that smug psychic stuff.' She braced herself to tell Lola the next bit of news. 'He's bought Bayview. Angelo was Nigel's mystery buyer. He's moved here.'

Lola wiggled her eyebrows. 'For you!'

'No. No. He can't move here for me. That's ridiculous. You're meant to be on my side, cursing his name,' Freya pointed out. 'Anyway, I'd made my mind up. I'm living my life for me. If he wants to camp out in that tip of a house, then he's welcome to. Not a word, Lola, not a single word in all these weeks and he expects me to just forgive and forget?' Freya crumbled up her cake with her fork.

'Are you at least going to talk to him? Find out if he had good reason?'

'There is no good reason. He freaked out about the newspaper and the article before even waiting to see what would happen. Without thinking about me.' Even as she said it, Freya felt her heart waver in its cage. Flashes of the blissful summer came back to her along with the realization that he'd done what he'd promised: he'd bought Bayview to be his home. 'How do I know he won't do it again?'

Lola was silent for such a long time, it made Freya uncomfortable. 'I have something to show you,' she said.

It was the hesitancy in Lola's voice that pricked Freya's interest. She'd never heard her friend sound so unsure before. 'What?'

Lola put her tea down and pulled a sketchbook out from behind the chair. It was black, the cover slightly battered, but Freya's heart lurched at the sight of it. 'The cleaner found it under the bed,' Lola said gently. 'I think you should take a look.'

'Have you had a look?' Freya asked. Lola simply nodded.

Against her better judgement, Freya held out her hand. The book was heavy, and for a moment, Freya sat with it on her lap, not sure if she wanted to see what was inside. With an encouraging nod from Lola, she started to turn the pages. Rough sketches of the sea, of Alf's hands, even one of a sleeping Scruff, snippets of Polcarrow life rendered quickly in smudged pencil by Angelo, his remarkable talent shining through. Despite everything, Freya wondered how he did it; how did he draw so well? Like an old Italian master, she thought with a sad smile. Then, on the next page, gazing back at her was her own likeness, dark hair roughly rendered, but her eyes shining with life. Freya swallowed, uncomfortable. She glanced at Lola.

'There's one of me.'

'There are several of you.'

Freya gingerly turned the pages. There was her behind the counter, a quick sketch of her with Alf, all too intimate for how removed from him she now felt. It was like looking at herself in another life. A life that had been sure and happy. Freya slammed the cover shut and flung the book on the floor. 'It doesn't change anything,' she told Lola sternly, even though she knew it changed everything.

Chapter Twenty-Four

It didn't take long for the news of Angelo's return to circulate. Cathy saw him pull up outside Bayview House and let himself in, and straightaway she picked up the phone to let Sue know. Before long, the news was being passed around the local grapevine. Everyone in Polcarrow tucked themselves into bed that night wondering what was going to happen next and also secretly glad that Bayview had not been bought by a greedy developer seeking to turn it into holiday flats. As much as the village needed its visitors, it didn't want its rustic charm ruined.

The knowledge that Angelo's return had spread like wildfire around the village pleased Freya; Angelo with his reclusive nature wouldn't like being the subject of gossip. Surprisingly, though, the villagers had the good grace not to turn up en masse at the café the following morning, and Freya, who had passed a rather sleepless night turning her dilemma over and over in her head, was thankful for this.

'Did you not sleep, love?' Alf asked gently when he saw her yawning behind the counter.

She gave him a sleepy smile. 'No – too much to think about.'

'Well, you've had an exciting weekend, what with the unveiling of your new paintings. I really like them and I hope I'll see more. You shouldn't be so modest, you know. You have a fair bit of talent there, girl. It's all looking up for you, isn't it? Your family coming all this way and now your young man is back.'

Freya's brow furrowed. 'He's not my young man, Alf. He's not anything to me anymore.'

Alf made a sympathetic face. 'I know he hurt you, and what he did ... well, it wasn't right. You don't just leave people you've bonded with like that. But at my age I've come to realize people only act irrationally if there's a good, serious reason behind it. Scruff was disappointed too – we all were, lass – but I intend to listen to what he has to say and then make up my mind. I know it's none of my business, but I suggest you do the same.'

Freya pursed her lips and said nothing. 'Maybe in due course, Alf, but not yet. What can I get you?'

Alf clearly decided not to push. 'Have you got any of those teacakes?' he asked. 'Toasted with lashings of butter? It's starting to be teacake weather if you ask me.'

Freya watched as Alf shuffled over to the window seat. Tristan arrived just as his friend was sitting down, and requested his usual. With a smile on her face at the normality of the morning, Freya went into the kitchen to make the toast. Lola had popped to the bank in town, so Freya was grateful for the slow start. She placed everything on a tray and carried it over to her favourite regulars, including a dog biscuit for Scruff since she wasn't sure a toasted teacake was the sort of breakfast a dog should be having.

'I see Angelo is back,' Tristan remarked with a quick, anxious glance at Freya.

'She doesn't want to talk about it,' Alf interjected.

'No, I don't want to talk to him,' Freya clarified.

'But why?' Tristan asked. 'You need to give him the opportunity to earn your forgiveness.'

'Yes, exactly. Earn. Not just swan up, dangle the keys to Bayview in front of me and expect to take up where we left off. And I don't have to forgive him, you know.' Freya took a breath; it wasn't fair to vent her anger on Alf and Tristan, who were just trying to be supportive. 'Sorry. It's been a shock, that's all. I'll leave you to your breakfast.'

With a final ruffle of Scruff's fur, Freya retreated into the kitchen and took some deep calming breaths. What she needed was some breakfast. The teacakes smelled divine, so she stuck one under the grill until it turned golden brown. Keeping her ear on the door, she scrolled through her phone until she found the National Rail app. Her trip to London was exactly what she needed to give herself some thinking space. After booking her ticket, Freya texted Lily and Fiona to let them know what time she'd arrive. Lots of excited happy emojis bounced straight back and Freya was warmed by the comfort of uncomplicated old friends, the prospect of Friday night Prosecco and lazy Saturday brunches, and by the chance to try to forget what Angelo returning might mean.

The doorbell jingled so Freya put down her phone and went out into the café. Her heart skipped a beat. Angelo was lingering in the doorway exchanging rather awkward pleasantries with Tristan and Alf, who didn't look as if they were about to invite him to join them. Good, Freya thought uncharitably. He needs to know he can't just swan back in here like nothing has happened.

When he turned towards her, their eyes met, and Freya wasn't sure about anything anymore. He looked miserable. Dark shadows under his eyes, hair wild and unbrushed, but still totally gorgeous. Freya smothered those traitorous thoughts and raised an eyebrow at him. 'Can I help?'

'Double espresso, please.' His request was formal but his eyes tried to latch onto Freya's.

Freya turned her back to make it in a takeaway cup, all the while trying not to listen to Angelo telling the others that there was no heating in the house and that he was hoping the engineer would come out that afternoon. It sounded like he'd spent his first night in Bayview camping out. It couldn't have been much fun, she imagined, cold and lonely ... and ... Stop it. She couldn't be sympathetic towards him just yet.

When she turned around, he was at the counter. Not leaning on it in the friendly way he used to, but looking so unsure of himself it almost broke her resolve. She pushed the plastic lid on and, watching him fumble in his pockets for change, simply said, like a peace offering, 'No charge.'

'Thank you.' Then he lowered his voice. 'We need to talk.'

Freya shook her head, unable to speak with so many

conflicting emotions rising in her chest. 'I can't. You need to give me time.'

Angelo nodded and picked up his coffee. Freya watched as Alf rose to his feet. 'I'll walk with you, son,' he said. 'Take Scruff.'

Angelo gave Scruff a quick fuss, relieved that at least the dog seemed pleased to see him, before taking him by the lead. Freya and Tristan looked on as Angelo and Alf left the café and headed over to the harbour wall. The sunlight was trickling weakly through the clouds.

Tristan raised his eyebrows. 'I'm not sure I'd fancy being told off by Alf.'

Freya smiled as she cleared their table. 'Nor would I.'

They couldn't resist watching as Alf gesticulated to articulate the point he was making and Angelo nodded along, clearly taking in every word. Freya couldn't help but think a bit of justice was being served.

Whatever hard feelings Alf had harboured towards Angelo, they quickly dissipated after that one heart-to-heart. Freya would have loved to know what had been said, but her pride stopped her prying. Angelo had retreated back to Bayview to wait for the heating engineer and Freya had no idea if she was relieved or disappointed not to see him again that day.

However, the next morning, clearly undeterred by whatever Alf had said to him, Angelo pulled up a chair and joined the breakfast club.

'He's making an effort,' Lola said as she passed Freya a plate of toast to take out.

Freya made a non-committal noise and exited the kitchen. She did not linger around their table like she would have done in the past, but quickly retreated behind the counter, slightly annoyed to be the one who had to give way to Angelo. Surely Tristan and Alf should have taken her side? And Angelo should have given her space? But then, maybe she was being too harsh on Angelo, she thought. Perhaps she should listen to him; if his reasons were good enough for Alf, then maybe they could be good enough for her.

The three men were speaking about the renovations to Bayview, which would be painstakingly slow. Angelo had hired a skip to clear out all of the junk left behind and, from where she was standing, Freya thought she detected in his voice a hint of regret for taking on such an ambitious project. One thing was becoming increasingly clear: Angelo acted first and thought later.

The man himself was polite but distant. Only the desperation swirling in his eyes told her he wanted to talk to her. Probably to try to justify his actions, Freya thought grumpily. She wondered why on earth, considering he'd clearly made a permanent return to Polcarrow, she couldn't just give him five minutes to explain his side of the story. She knew she was being stubborn, but his return had scattered her emotions all over the place. Half the time she was wistfully reliving the blissful summer day they'd spent together; the rest of it she was sharpening her tongue over what to say to him.

'I don't understand why I'm like this,' she said to Lola when they made their way into the café on Thursday morning. 'When I see him, I feel everything and it's exhausting. I'm so angry at him, even for coming back. It's ridiculous.'

'No, it's not; it's love, my dear, and being spurned. Personally, I think he's making an effort. He's clearly coming into the café to see you, but Tristan thinks he doesn't dare talk to you. I have to admit, Freya, most of the time I'm expecting you to tip his coffee over him!'

'I'm not that bad, am I?' Freya asked with surprise.

'Uh-huh.' Lola unlocked the door. 'The whole village is desperate to know what's going to happen next. Sue even asked outright if you two are back together. Now, don't get all sulky; you know what they're like. I don't think they've had this much excitement in years. It's like a soap opera for them.'

Lola retreated into the kitchen leaving Freya all out of sorts in the café. As much as she was uncomfortable being the subject of gossip, she knew Angelo would absolutely hate it.

Alf turned up as she was pulling up the blinds, a paper tucked under his arm. He pulled it out and passed it to her. 'Reckon you'll want to have a look at this!'

Freya took it from him and gasped. In the bottom right-hand corner, staring back at her from the front page was one of the photos from the gallery night. She studied herself, all dressed up in the floaty blue dress, hair and make-up done, standing in front of one of her paintings. 'I had no idea it'd be front page news, Alf!'

'Why ever not? The article is on page three.'

Freya opened up the paper then began to read.

'The sleepy village of Polcarrow has become a secret haven for artists. For years Cornwall has inspired painters and writers alike, but until recently Polcarrow has remained off the artistic map. On Friday, the villagers came together to hold a showing of local artist Freya Harris's work. A recent graduate from the London School of Arts, Freya has spent the summer in Cornwall, working in the local café and building a portfolio of impressive paintings. We are sure the dreamy dawn scenes will soon be in high demand.'

There followed the contact details of the café. Freya threw her arms around Alf and gave him a squeeze. 'I'd better show Lola!'

'Show me what?' Lola stuck her head out the kitchen door.

Freya waved the paper in her direction. 'This! I'm on the front page!'

Lola squealed in delight. 'I knew it would work!' She skimmed the words. 'Better get ourselves prepared for a busy day. I'm sure everyone will want to come in and see the local celebrity.'

Freya knew Lola hadn't needed to tap into her psychic ability to predict how busy the café would be. It bustled that morning, mainly with locals popping in, asking for their paper to be signed. There was a lot of chatter about how this could be used to raise Polcarrow's star.

'People like a local artist,' Sue said as she watched Freya sign the paper. 'I really think we could use this to update the village website. It's ancient and mostly about the coastal walk.'

Cathy made a face. She notably hadn't come in brandishing a paper. 'We don't want to be overrun,' she grumbled.

Sue rolled her eyes and tucked her paper back into her tote bag. 'I'm getting lots of ideas for revamping the village. It's nice to have ... erm ... fresh blood to help out. I don't see why we can't become a more metropolitan haven. It's worked for other places.'

Freya watched them sit down and continue with their friendly bickering. She had to admit that she was enjoying her local celebrity status. It was everything she had ever wanted: recognition for her art. She sent a photo of the article to her parents and to Olivia and posted it on her social media pages. Her dad had instantly texted back requesting that she get some copies of the paper so he could show his friends at the golf club. A warm fuzzy feeling of success buzzed in her veins and she was so busy mentally figuring out what to paint next that it was only when someone gently tapped the countertop that Freya glanced up. Her heart leapt to see Angelo standing there, a proud smile on his unshaven face and a copy of the paper on the counter between them.

'It looks like you've been busy since I've been away. I always knew you could do it,' he said sincerely.

'Erm ... thanks.' She wiped her sweaty palms on her apron, convinced that everyone had stopped paying attention to their coffees the minute he'd approached the counter.

Angelo, aware that the volume in the café had dropped, lowered his own voice. 'Freya, this is killing me. It's driving me mad seeing you here and you acting all, well, like you hate me.'

'I don't hate you.' The words were out before she could think. 'But you should have considered my feelings before just leaving.'

'You really think I don't regret that?' he growled angrily. 'God, Freya, how can we resolve this if you won't even look at me, let alone talk to me? I may have acted like a fool, but my feelings have never changed.'

Their eyes met, and neither one of them wanted to be the first to back down. All the feelings they had allowed to grow over the summer were still there, but the beautiful blooms of new love were now tangled with thorns. Freya opened her mouth to speak, then closed it again. She peered around Angelo and, almost comically, everyone went back to their business of morning coffee. Freya couldn't help but smile, but when she turned to Angelo, her eyes were steely, giving nothing away.

'Not now,' she told him. 'We have an audience.' She took a deep breath. 'After we close.'

Angelo, pleased with this small win and knowing he was lucky to receive this grace, nodded his head, picked up his copy of the paper and left. Freya watched him go, her resolve beginning to crumble.

Chapter Twenty-Five

At four o'clock, Freya glanced up and saw Angelo waiting across the road, gazing wistfully out to sea. She resigned herself to the fact that there was no more cleaning or faffing about she could do behind the counter to put this off any longer; the moment had come. Hanging up her apron and pulling her hair out of its messy bun, she quickly checked herself in the mirror; not that how she looked really mattered considering Angelo had seen her in all sorts of ways over the summer. She would have to do as she was, and actually – she pulled herself up straight and proud – that was more than good enough. Stomach turning with the nerves she'd just managed to keep at bay all day, she left the café, locking the door behind her. Angelo turned to see her, his face flooding with joy, and for a split second, Freya forgot that she was angry with him and smiled back. Maybe it was a trick of the changing light, but as she crossed the road, it was like the previous month hadn't happened.

'You're here,' Angelo said in disbelief.

Freya glanced around. 'Come on, let's walk. I don't want everyone to see us together.'

Disappointment flickered in Angelo's eyes, but he didn't object. He followed Freya as she marched towards the edge of the village and took the path up to the headland. They strode in silence, and even when she sat down, Freya said nothing, simply focused on the shifting light out at sea, the bright morning having faded into a dove-grey evening. They sat for a few minutes gazing at the view, each searching for the right words. Freya's heart thumped, but she couldn't tell if it was from the way she'd rushed up the hill or from being so close to Angelo. She took a deep breath and looked at him. His dark eyes were sad and confused. But words failed her, and she looked back out to sea. After all, he was the one who wanted to talk, who owed her an apology.

'Freya, why won't you speak to me?' Angelo eventually asked.

Freya sighed and admitted, 'Because I don't know what to say. You just left, and now that you're back there seems to be some expectation on your part for me to just forgive that.' Her tone was barbed. 'I did not deserve for you to treat me like that.'

Angelo took the shot. Freya watched as he composed himself, clearly determined to remain calm. 'You're right. I acted in a bad way and you did not deserve it. I need to tell you everything. Freya, I don't expect you to forgive me, even though I hope for it, but I'd like you to at least listen, rather than always walking away or shutting me down. I'd like you to try and understand.'

'Well, I'm here, aren't I?' She threw her hands up. 'Go

ahead.' She went back to staring out to sea until she felt Angelo's gaze shift from her. Breathing slowly until she felt calm, Freya knew deep down that despite her hurt, she needed to find a way to understand.

'I am sorry that I hurt you. It was never my intention. I've come to realize that I'm not always very good at considering others or putting them first. I don't need to tell you about my past; you've already heard it. When I arrived here, I had no idea what I wanted. I just needed to get away from London. When I got off my bike, I thought this would be a sleepy village where nothing happened, perfect to lie low in. I didn't bank on meeting the likes of Lola, Tristan, Alf or you. Especially you.' He glanced at Freya before turning back to the view. 'It sounds stupid but that afternoon I arrived and saw you behind the counter, it's like I knew why I'd been led here. Then you told me off for my drinking and, well, no one had ever told me off before. People had always deferred to me, and I'd pretty much got away with everything. Honestly, Freya, you have no idea how normal you made me feel. You were the first person to see me and accept me as a flawed, failed human being.

'I honestly thought I'd never paint again. I was a bit depressed, but getting involved with Alf, the festival and doing that mural showed me something no one else ever has: that art can be done for love and sheer enjoyment. It doesn't have to come from a place of money-making. You were the first person to show me that by simply getting up every morning and painting for the sheer hell of it. You made me see everything I'd lost. You gave me a chance to think about how I'd been living, and while I've been away, I've been doing a lot of soul-searching. I wanted to come back here, because, Freya, it's the one place I've truly felt like I fit in, where I've been accepted for me. Polcarrow is my home, in my heart. I know I have issues, that things are difficult, but this is the only place I feel I can truly heal, and I can't do it without you pulling me up and helping me along. I've bought Bayview and I'm not going anywhere. I want to stay here and paint. I want to get involved in community projects and give something back. I would love nothing more than for you to help me with that. For us to do this together. I missed you every damn second that I was away. It felt like I'd left half of me behind. I missed the life we had planned and I'd do anything to get it back.'

Freya digested his heartfelt plea, allowing the idea of their shared future to nestle in her brain. The rooms of Bayview opened, sepia-tinged and her resolve began to soften. 'I think it's a bit too soon for that, Angelo,' she said softly.

'Yes, of course. Freya, leaving you and Polcarrow was the worst decision of my life. The way I did it was so selfish too. I can't explain it other than to say I was an idiot, and I was scared. When I saw that article in the paper, and with the journalist coming to talk to Alf, it was like all the walls were closing in on me, like I would never, ever be able to escape who I once was. I panicked. Selfishly I saw only me. You have no idea how much of a mistake that was,' he said bitterly.

Jennifer Bibby

Freya turned to him, eyes blazing. 'We could've faced it together. I never cared about the Angelo who sold art for thousands of pounds, the bad boy the press once wrote about. I bet they don't actually give a shit about you any-more. But I did. We could have tackled this together, talked about it, made a plan. This is just your ego. No one else cares, only me. For what it's worth, everyone was too excited by the article to even consider ringing that number. All of this was for nothing. The only person you hurt was me, the one person who would've stood by you, whatever they dug up. But you were too much of a coward to face any of it, the press, me.'

'If I was that much of a coward,' Angelo snapped, 'would I be here now, trying to win you back?'

'Oh, is that what you're trying to do with all these woe-be-me stories? You know, I felt like such a fool that morning when I woke up and you were gone. Then I realized you'd done exactly the same to Vanessa. Neither of us deserved to be treated like that. You can't pretend it's some artistic thing – it's just shitty behaviour. What should I believe now? Is this everything or are there more skeletons waiting to crawl out of your closet? I feel like I don't know you anymore!'

Angelo clasped her hands and knelt down in front of her. 'Freya, just listen to me. How many times do I have to tell you I'm sorry? What do you want me to do? Crawl through the streets begging your forgiveness? I have never known misery in my life like the misery of the past few weeks. Yes, I did a shitty thing, abandoning the woman and the place I love. Don't think I haven't spent all this time beating myself up over that. Yes, I know, I could've turned back, but I needed to know if this was truly my home. I needed to leave here to realize I would never be happy anywhere else. Because I found a happiness here I never expected and didn't think I deserved. Everything came to me so easily when I was younger and when it all collapsed, I doubted myself so much. Not just my artistic ability but who I was as a person. You helped me see who I actually was.'

Running out of steam, he sagged back. 'Freya, I swear to you there are no more secrets; I've told you everything. I was shocked by my own reaction to the journalist; it made me realize I hadn't dealt with my past as much as I thought I had. One of the reasons why I've decided to live here is because Polcarrow makes me stronger, you make me feel stronger.'

Freya shifted but said nothing, there was too much for her overwhelmed brain to process. 'Where did you go?'

'I went to Italy,' he said. 'I went to see my mother. God, I was a mess, and there is nothing you can say to me, Freya, that she hasn't already said. I never imagined I could still be so harshly told off by my mother. She really kicked me while I was down, and I know I deserved it, even though it wasn't easy to hear. We talked about a lot of things that I won't go into now but it helped.' Angelo turned Freya's palms over and studied the lines. 'But she told me that I was the biggest fool she's ever met and she was embarrassed to have me as a son if this is how I treat women. She never liked Vanessa, but she made me realize that I needed to go back to London and talk to her properly. Then she said to me that I needed to come back here and beg for you to forgive me, not even to have me back, just to forgive me, and that I'd be lucky if you'd even look at me after how I'd behaved.' Angelo's eyes met Freya's and he managed a wry smile. 'So, I'm doing only slightly better than she thought.'

Freya couldn't help but allow a flicker of a smile to dance across her lips. Every part of her wanted to reach forward and bundle Angelo into her arms, wanted to wipe the past month clean. Despite how she'd locked up her heart, Freya realized she hadn't thrown away the key. She reached out now and stroked Angelo's hair, pushing some rogue strands away from his face, noticing the dark shadows of sleepless nights under his eyes, the internal struggle he was only starting to deal with. She swallowed.

'Angelo, please, I don't know what to say. It's not that easy. This is a lot to take in. Well done for admitting you have problems you want to work on. I can see it's been a long, hard journey for you and I'm willing to help, but you have to want to do this for yourself, not for me. You still hurt me; admitting your issues doesn't negate that. I don't know how to let go of that and trust you again.'

Angelo nodded as he processed her words. 'Freya, I love you. That's the one truth I have left. I came back here for you. I bought Bayview. I went to London and I tied up all my affairs. I made things right with Thomas Hardgreaves. I'm turning over a new leaf. I faced my fears and did an interview with a journalist I trusted, and you have no idea how scary that was for me, but the story will be coming out in some Sunday supplement in the New Year.'

Freya hid the surprise that flashed through her. Angelo was clearly committed to making an effort to deal with his demons. 'That must've taken a lot.'

'It did, but it worked to tell someone my side of the story, like it helped to tell you.' Angelo continued, 'I sold artworks to raise the money for the sale and my mother passed me some of my inheritance so that I could buy Bayview outright. I'm not going anywhere, Freya. I'm staying here where my heart belongs. You can have all the time you need. I'll wait for you, wait for your answer. I'm not asking for us to get back together, although I pray for it. I just . . . Freya, I just can't go on like this.' Angelo let go of her hands and stood up, eyes shining with emotion.

Freya studied him silhouetted against the sky, a picture of absolute misery. Her stomach churned. It would be so simple to reach for him, to tell him it was all going to be fine. To get back together. But she needed time. 'Angelo, please, I need to think. It's been a tough year for me. You knew I had my heart broken before I came here. One note, that's all it would've taken. One note. Even better, we could have talked about things. I would have listened and I would have supported you, but you just seem to run away from everything. How will I know you won't do that again? Buying Bayview House doesn't just erase that. How do I know you won't run away the next time the going gets tough?'

Angelo looked forlorn. 'The only thing you can do is take

my word that I will never leave you again. When I saw you on the front of that paper, I was so proud of what you had done. I really believe that you have the ability to achieve your artistic dreams. I've been such a fool, Freya, such a fool. I'm standing here asking you to forgive me, when I don't even know if I can forgive myself.'

Freya rolled her eyes. 'Stop being so dramatic and Italian. It's not helping. You made a decision and your decision to leave affected what happened in my life, because then I realized my life isn't about you or Matt or my parents wanting me to go and teach, it's about what I can do. Angelo, I hear everything you've said, but I need to process what you're telling me and what I feel. Right now, I feel everything. Everything I felt for you is still there, but I had to put that away when you left. I just . . . I can't . . . I need time, Angelo. Other people may have influenced my past, but right now, I must be the only one who influences my future.'

Chapter Twenty-Six

'Ugh!' Freya slammed shut the lid of her overnight case and dropped onto the bed beside it. 'I have no flipping idea what to take!' Packing for her hastily planned London trip had, of course, been left to the last minute. Freya had been far too distracted by her conversation with Angelo to start the previous night. And the lack of sleep wasn't helping.

Lola, who had been standing in the doorway for the past ten minutes watching as Freya bundled clothes in and out of the carry-on case and then stuck them into a smaller over-night bag, took a sip of her tea and reminded her, 'You're only going for two nights.'

Freya shot her a look. 'Yes, but they want to go somewhere fancy for cocktails. What on earth do I wear for that? I've never been a swanky cocktail bar kind of girl! And I've spent the summer in a combo of shorts, leggings and hoodies.'

'If it's any consolation, they'll be insanely jealous of your natural tan. Drink your tea, it'll get cold.'

Freya grabbed her mug and flipped the case lid back open.

'What about the dress you wore for the café gallery night?' Lola suggested.

'I thought about that, but isn't it a bit too floaty to be zipping around London in? The Tube's always windy. I've got my good black jeans and a couple of tops. Plus these.' Freya lifted up a pair of heeled ankle boots that Lola had lent her. 'I've not worn heels in months, so if I break my ankle, you'll have to come and fetch me, okay?'

Lola rolled her eyes. 'You won't break your ankle. You'll have fun.' Lola seized the moment to ask, 'What are you going to do about Angelo?' Her question was lightly phrased but dripping with curiosity.

Freya narrowed her eyes at Lola. 'Do we have to do this now? Didn't I tell you enough last night? I was awake almost all night thinking about everything he said.' It didn't help that Lola was making Freya feel like the bad guy for not just telling Angelo they could start again. Freya paused thoughtfully. 'Honestly, Lola, what would you do? I'm actually curious. If this had happened to you and the guy had come back and poured his heart out with all of these reasons and excuses, what would you do?'

Lola sipped her tea and thought carefully about her reply. 'You need to work out if you love him enough to put this behind you,' she said. 'You both came from quite a damaged place and maybe the summer was just a palate cleanser? It's clear Angelo thinks it's more than that, having moved here for good. But what about you? I'd ask myself what I would regret more – never giving him another chance or giving him a chance and risking having my heart broken. Because I'm pretty sure if you said yes to him, he'd be so grateful he'd never put another foot wrong.'

Freya frowned. 'That's a big question for this early in the morning.'

With a shrug Lola peeled herself away from the wall. 'But you'll have plenty of time to consider it on the train. If you want a lift to the station, you have thirty minutes.'

Remembering her journey down, Freya made sure that she was equipped with enough distractions to ensure that she wouldn't spend the five-hour journey going over the Angelo situation again and again inside her head. Armed with a crossword book, a thriller she'd grabbed from Lola's shelf and a trashy magazine, plus a generous picnic whipped up by Lola, Freya took her seat and settled in for the journey. But her brain couldn't settle. She quickly got frustrated with the crosswords because she couldn't get enough correct answers. After attempting about six different crosswords and never getting any further than four clues in, she abandoned the book. The trashy magazine fared better: reading about a woman who married her hamster because she believed he was her reincarnated dead husband distracted her from her own woes for all of ten minutes.

But as the train continued to speed across the country all Freya could think about was Angelo. All she could see was the desperation in his eyes for her to forgive him. But what he had done was unforgivable, wasn't it? The more miles she put between her and Polcarrow, the more she wondered if she was the one being an idiot. He had laid out his reasons and they were all believable and in line with everything he had told her over the summer. He clearly hadn't been thinking straight. But what if this wasn't a one-off? Could she be with and support someone who clearly hadn't dealt with his demons to the extent he believed? Did she even want to get back together with him? The attraction still flared between them, but Freya knew the most peace she had ever found was in the weeks when she had been concentrating solely on her painting, doing something just for herself. She wasn't ready to give that up yet. But Lola's question had been huge: could she live beside him in a small community without being with him? The thought of him giving up and meeting someone else stabbed her, so she was pretty sure the answer was no. Freya closed her eyes to block out the big thoughts. Alf and Tristan had welcomed him back. Was she just being stubborn?

As the train pulled closer to London, Freya decided to put it out of her mind and see what happened when she got back. Angelo, having bought Bayview, clearly wasn't going anywhere. Her heart panged to think how lonely it must be in that wreck of a house, having to fix it up before being able to make it homely. As gestures went, buying it was huge, and secretly she knew the villagers thought he was a bit mad for doing so. But whatever happened next, she knew she had to put herself first. Angelo's return had distracted her from her plans to start touring local galleries to see if they'd take her work; that was what she needed to focus on now. As the train pulled into Paddington, Freya shoved Angelo to the back of her mind and started to gather up her belongings, leaving the crossword book for the next passenger.

The grimy air of London belched around Freya as she exited the station, trying her best not to be pushed along by the rush-hour traffic. Had this once really been her normal? she wondered as she watched commuters cut each other up in their desperation to snatch the last free seat. Had she once been the same, glued to her phone, clutching a takeaway coffee, oblivious to everything around her? Guiltily, she suspected she had. In London, there was no time to stop, no time to take a breath. It was crowded and dirty, the air tinged with smog, and Freya realized how much Cornwall had cleansed her. She squeezed herself onto a bus and made her way to the bar Lily had chosen, praying that they'd have somewhere she could stash her overnight bag. There wasn't time to get to Lily's flat and back before the table booking.

Thankfully, there was a cloakroom for Freya to leave her stuff in and the maître d' showed her over to the table where her friends had already started on the wine, heads together, gossiping furiously, as if they'd closed around the gap Freya had left behind. She gave a small cough to announce her presence. Lily and Fiona instantly dropped their conversation and started squealing as they bounded off their high stools and threw themselves at Freya.

'Seriously, guys, I know you're glad to see me, but I can't breathe!' Freya laughed, tears running down her face. 'Happy birthday, Lily. Your gift's in my bag in the cloakroom.'

Lily batted away her words. 'You might need to get a glass, and ... maybe a bottle?' She pulled the almost empty one out of the ice bucket.

'No worries!' Freya made her way over to the bar. She almost winced at the price of a bottle of Pinot Grigio. While the barman assembled the order, Freya looked around her. The bar was gorgeous, all low golden lighting and big green ferns. The cocktails were chalked on a board behind the bar next to an impressive selection of gin, the bottles glittering like jewels. Freya felt very much like she was on holiday. She paid and made her way back to the table, unscrewing the cap and topping up their glasses.

'Cheers! How's your birthday been?' she asked.

Lily rolled her eyes. 'They made me sit in a chair in the middle of the office and sang happy birthday to me. It was awful. But we had cake and fizz at tea break rather than tea, so not all bad. How's Cornwall been? Ready to move back to the big smoke?'

Freya laughed. 'Straight in with the big questions! Cornwall's been great. It's so beautiful and peaceful. It was a bit of a shock to come back here.'

'I can imagine!' Fiona's eyes were wide. 'Your photos always look amazing on Instagram.'

'Well, Cornwall needs no filter!'

'How's it going with Lola?'

Freya chose to ignore the slightly disapproving tone of Lily's voice. 'Wonderful. I do think she's really settled down this time. The café is a success, her baking is to die for and she has the most adorable little fisherman's cottage. There's an old fisherman called Alf – he's such a darling, so kind, full of all sorts of stories and he has a gorgeous sheepdog called Scruff.'

The two girls nodded along. 'What about surfer dudes?' Fiona asked hopefully.

'I wondered how long it would take you to bring that up!' Freya laughed before explaining, 'We don't get the right sort of waves. It's quite a small bay. We see more ramblers walking the coastal path than surfers. Sorry, Fi.'

Fiona made a face. 'I was just hoping you'd have met someone nice down there after how horrible Matt was. Sometimes I still can't believe you two actually split up; you were our hope that solid relationships existed, but I guess it shows what we know.'

It irked Freya that they'd brought Matt up so quickly. 'Matt's the past,' she said. 'I've hardly thought about him, so can we not talk about him, please?' Although taken aback by Freya's sharp tone, Lily and Fiona both nodded. 'I've just been so busy helping out in the café. They had this summer event called the Fisherman's Fair – it was fantastic. I sold most of my paintings last Friday and got in the local press.'

Fiona squealed. 'That's amazing! I saw it on your Facebook page. You'll be making your millions soon!'

Freya laughed. 'I don't know. I'm not sure I'm that good, but it's a start. When I go back I'm going to scout some galleries, see if they'll display and sell my work. These were just on paper, watercolours, but if I want to go big I need to invest in canvas, oils and so on, so I can try and make bigger paintings that are more bespoke, sell for more. It's still quite new, so yeah. Enough about me, though. What about you two? I was hoping you'd come and visit!'

'It was hard to get time off work,' Fiona said. 'I'm really trying my best – there's a promotion I'm after so I can't drop the ball at all. Although if I don't get it, I'm seriously thinking of taking a career break and going travelling. Everywhere I go I'm being taunted by adverts showing the blue seas of Thailand. Ugh!'

'Well, not to play devil's advocate, but getting away has done me the world of good. There's more to life than London,' Freya gently reminded her.

Fiona smiled. 'That's what's nagging me, but everyone is telling me to work hard for the next couple of years, get in a good secure position, then take a break. I wish I'd taken that gap year straight after uni instead of that graduate scheme.'

Freya gave her a sympathetic look but decided not to say anything else. After all, she was still just making coffees for a living, and just praying her art would give her some extra cash, even if it didn't take her anywhere. 'What about you, Lily? Anything new?'

Lily gave the girls a coy look. 'Well, work is all good, and I'm dating someone . . . Stop it! Stop squealing like that, the pair of you! It's quite new. I met him on Tinder of all places. His name is Tim, he's an accountant. Now I know he doesn't sound fun, but he is, he really is! We have the same drive and ambition. Plus, he's well-read and well-travelled without being a complete smug idiot about any of it.'

'How long has this been going on for?' Freya asked; it sounded like, together, they would be an unstoppable force.

'A month. But he always texts first; he sets up all the dates; he's keen without being pushy. Get this, ladies, he actually asked to meet my friends!' Lily sat back, smiling smugly at her good fortune.

'Do you think he's got any nice friends?' Fiona asked a bit too keenly.

'Fi, it's a bit early for that. Even I've not met them yet, although one of them is having a thirtieth birthday party next weekend, so I'll make sure I do some scouting,' Lily promised.

'You'll have to keep us posted,' Freya said as she topped up their drinks. 'He sounds like a keeper!'

'He does, doesn't he?' Lily smiled smugly before changing the direction of the conversation. 'Have you thought about getting back in touch with Matt while you're here? You just had one massive argument and moved down to Cornwall. You never really talked about anything.'

Fiona shook her head in disbelief, but Freya responded calmly. 'No, Lily, I have no desire to contact Matt. I just said I didn't want to talk about him. I've moved on. You see, I've made some big decisions. I'm going to stay in Cornwall. I won't come back to London; it's just too big and grim and dirty. I've never had an opportunity to promote my art here the way I did last week. It might not be secure and it might not be the same as your five-year plans, but I'm happy down there, like proper happy. You need to come and visit. You'd love it.'

Lily and Fiona exchanged glances. 'Hang on,' Lily said. 'Did you just say you've moved on?'

'So there were surfer dudes!' Fiona exclaimed.

Freya shook her head. She hadn't been planning on telling them about Angelo, but the desire to unburden herself, to get the opinions of her two closest friends, was overwhelming. Also, they were fresh and eager ears. She took a deep breath. 'So, yes, there was ... is ... someone, but it's complicated. His name is Angelo. He used to be a big thing in the art world, years ago. I wasn't overly familiar with him, so I doubt you'd be. He was huge, a rising star and then it all collapsed. Anyway, he arrived in Polcarrow soon after I did, and he decided to stay. We started spending a lot of time together. We were both figuring things out, licking our wounds, and we fell for one another. But then he left. Just got up in the night and left. No note, nothing. That was over a month ago, but last week he came back. He's bought some old house he wants to renovate and he wants me to give him another chance, but I don't know. He just left me, ladies.'

'Did he have a reason to leave?' Lily asked, eyes narrowed suspiciously.

'I guess for him it was a reason. You see, the Fisherman's Fair I mentioned featured on the front of the local paper and a journalist was sniffing about, so he was afraid his past would be dug up, but apparently he's working on his issues and keen to make a fresh start.'

Fiona, who still believed in true love, despite going on loads of awful dates, sighed. 'What's this house like?'

'Honestly? A heap.'

'He's bought a heap of a house and wants to live in some sleepy village? That's got to be true love,' Fiona swooned.

Lily wasn't so easily swayed. 'Yes, it might be true love, but you need to be careful. Set out some rules. Make him work to get you back.'

Fiona made a face. 'Have you got a photo?'

'Um, yes, I think so.' Freya swiped through her phone, through all the stunning, seductive shots of Cornwall, until she came across the only photo she had of her and Angelo together, on the beach celebrating the success of the Fisherman's Fair. She turned her phone round to show them. Fiona's eyes nearly popped out her head.

'He's a hottie. Why are you even asking these questions?'

Lily rolled her eyes. 'This is why you're single, Fi. He might be a hottie, but if he's a complete shit, his face doesn't matter.' Lily turned to Freya and gave her a long hard stare. 'No thinking about this. Just answer yes or no and that will be your answer.' Lily paused before asking, 'Do you love him?'

'Yes.' It was out of Freya's mouth before she could stop it; the undeniable truth that, yes, despite everything, she still loved him.

'Well, there's your answer then. Now we need to work out how to make him work to get you back.' Lily hopped off her stool. 'This calls for more wine.'

The weekend carried on in a whirlwind of Prosecco and avocado-laden brunches, and as wonderful as it had been to see her friends after so long, two days in London was more than enough. Freya craved the tranquillity of Cornwall, the open views of the sea and the gentle rhythm of life.

As she squeezed her friends goodbye on the platform, her happiness to be returning home was tinged with sadness to be saying goodbye to Lily and Fiona. They said farewell with promises to visit on their lips. Freya waved to them from the window as the train pulled out of the station and wound its way down through the country, the scenery popping with autumnal bursts of colour. The journey couldn't pass quickly enough for Freya, and she was sure her agitation was annoying the gentleman sitting opposite her, judging by the looks he kept casting her over the top of his paper.

Freya took a taxi from the station back to Polcarrow Bay, despite Lola offering to pick her up. The light was just starting to lower as they pulled up by the harbour wall. Freya paid her fare and got out. She waited while the driver sped off before climbing over the wall and taking in a deep, cleansing breath. The air was fresh and salty, almost sweet after a weekend in the capital. She kicked off her shoes and, leaving her bag sheltered by the wall, she ran towards the shoreline, the waves breaking invigoratingly cold over her toes. Freya turned around and studied the village; the lights slowly flickered on like embers in the night. She imagined the cosy congregation in the pub, the way the dawn would stain the morning sky. The scent of coffee being prepared and toast being laid before Tristan. Alf and Scruff and Lola with her cherry-red hair. Angelo, and whatever would happen next. Yes – Freya smiled and hugged the thought to herself – she'd been silly to ever doubt that this place was her home.

Chapter Twenty-Seven

Freya's trip to London to see Fiona and Lily had allowed her to finally put her London life to bed. She returned to Polcarrow with a sense of comfort and closure, the polar opposite of how she had felt when she arrived before the summer. Freya reflected proudly on all the things she had achieved since coming to Cornwall: the friendships she had made and the calmness that she was experiencing internally. Life in Polcarrow might never make her money-rich, but it would enrich her life in other more wholesome ways. *Living the seaside dream*, she thought to herself on Monday morning when she opened the café, even if the weather was starting to turn. The forecast that week was scattered with sobering rain showers, but Freya was looking forward to witnessing the changing of the seasons over the bay. All those vibrant apricots, pinks and wispy purples had been the perfect way to get back in tune with her creativity. But now she craved to do something more explorative that would mean something to her, yet remain open to interpretation by others.

The change in the weather interested her. That morning had begun deep and dark, with a bright pink light on the horizon; not the same dreamy pink of June, but a cold vibrant magenta that had flashed through the sky before vanishing. The clouds it left behind were a heavy purple grey, dense with the threat of rain. Freya loved clouds, but they had been considered too ethereal and insubstantial at art school, so her appreciation had been saved for the few moments she'd lain on her back in crowded London parks. Polcarrow had given her daily opportunities to consider the shifting shapes, the way the light flickered across the fluffy surfaces, the dimples of darkness on otherwise pristine white. She had been sketching them for a while and her phone was full of photos of the sky over the bay. Freya decided she would paint a sequence, maybe four larger canvases, and then see if anyone wanted to display them.

Café trade was slow that morning; just Alf and Tristan asking her all about her trip to London. 'I was worried you'd decide to stay there,' Alf told her. 'Not that it matters because it's your life. I went once when I was a lad to see what all the fuss was about.' He made a face and shook his head. 'Not for me, lass, not for me. Too busy, too smoky. How do people live so far from the sea? I went to that River Thames, but what a disappointment.'

Freya gave Alf's hand a squeeze. 'Well, I'm back and I'm planning on staying for as long as Lola will have me.'

'Where is Lola?' Tristan asked. He was halfway through his toast and he never usually made it that far without Lola popping out of the kitchen.

'The delivery didn't arrive. The farm van has broken

down, so she's popped over to collect the eggs and milk, I don't think she'll be long. Don't worry, she's not done a runner,' Freya reassured Tristan before heading back behind the counter. Angelo hadn't arrived. It was gone nine and he was usually here by now. Freya wiped that thought away, pretending that it didn't matter. She pulled out her word puzzle book and settled in for a long morning.

So engrossed in trying to find the final three types of Italian bread in her word search, Freya hardly paid attention to the door opening. It was only when a tall figure was standing over her that she glanced up at the customer, registering a flicker of disappointment that it was not Angelo. Hurriedly, she stashed the book away. 'Good morning,' she said. 'Sit in or takeaway?' She cringed when she noticed that she hadn't yet cleared the table of Alf and Tristan's breakfast things.

'I'm looking for Freya Harris,' the man said. 'Is that you?' He was tall with closely cut white hair, and she guessed he was in his fifties. A neat red and white polka dot pocket square poked jauntily out his jacket pocket.

'It depends who's asking,' she said, trying to sound friendly.

'My name's Daniel Trevena. I own a few galleries – one in St Ives, one in Newquay, and I'm hoping to open one in Penzance next spring. I saw your article in the local paper, and an acquaintance of mine was at the showing and bought one of your paintings. I was impressed! And rather jealous. I like to be the one to find new local talent.' His blue eyes sparkled. 'So I thought I'd come down here and see if I could find you . . . if that is you.'

Freya smiled; she might not have her make-up on, but she didn't think she looked that different from her picture in the paper. 'Yes, it is me, but I'm afraid I sold all my paintings that night, so I don't have anything for you to look at.' Seeing how disappointed Daniel looked, Freya quickly continued. 'But I am planning a new sequence. Something more seasonal for winter,' she blustered, realizing that this could be her big chance. 'I love the way natural light works, you see, and I'm planning to do something with ... erm ... clouds.' She cringed inwardly, knowing how rubbish the idea sounded and reached for her phone to show him the photos of her pieces. Then the bell rang as the café door swung open, and they both glanced around. Angelo was standing there, blue paint on his hands. Not now, Freya thought. Not now.

'Sorry, are you busy?' Angelo glanced from Daniel to Freya.

Daniel gave Angelo a long look, almost as if he recognized him.

'This is Daniel,' Freya said, and flashed him a warning look to tell him this was not a good time for any dramatics. 'He's come from St Ives where he has a gallery. He wants to see some of my work, but it's all sold. I only have these photos on my phone.' Freya turned back to him and flicked through the pictures, pleased to be able to show Angelo she was a success. The title of sold-out artist warmed her heart as she continued to explain her work to Daniel. 'You can see the evolution of the pieces.' Gosh, all those years at art school hadn't been wasted if she could use phrases like that. She dared a glance up at Angelo as Daniel scrolled; amusement danced in his eyes. 'I love working with watercolours. I enjoy the ethereal washes you can create, the way the colours bleed and merge, just like they sometimes do in nature. I'm planning to use oils and acrylics in my next lot of work.'

'You have such a beautiful way of using the colours,' Daniel said as he passed the phone back. 'They're fantastic pieces, unlike anything I've seen down here. It makes a change from the usual fishing boats. There would definitely be a market for this sort of stuff. Are you able to get a few samples together and bring them to me on Sunday? I hope that's not too short notice.'

Panic flashed through Freya, but she said, 'No, of course not.'

'Excellent.' Daniel held out his hand and Freya shook it.

'There's a mural in the church that Freya was involved in this summer,' Angelo pointed out. 'You may wish to have a look. Freya can show you.'

'But Lola isn't here and I can't just close up the café,' Freya reminded him, slightly annoyed that he was jumping on her artistic bandwagon.

'I can mind the café,' Angelo suggested.

Irked but slightly curious at the urgency in his tone, Freya untied her apron and marched out from behind the counter.

'Ah, is this the famous mural I've been hearing about? Someone told me quite a famous artist did it.' Daniel looked between Angelo and Freya suspiciously.

Angelo shrugged. 'I heard that too, but I can't confirm. I know Freya was involved and it's worth having a look at.'

Freya shot Angelo a puzzled look. What on earth was he doing? She passed him her apron and opened the door for Daniel. The air outside was nippy and fresh, and she wished she'd taken the time to put her coat on. As they made their way up to the church, Daniel remarked on all sorts of things about the village, from the boats to the quaint little buildings.

'I had no idea there was any type of art taking place in Polcarrow. Although it shouldn't surprise me – Cornwall is awash with artists – but it's rare to discover something new.' He stopped outside the church and ran his hands over the seashells embedded in the wall. 'How peculiar and extraordinary. This is a real undiscovered gem.'

Freya seized the church door handle and paused. She hadn't been in the church since the great unveiling at the Fisherman's Fair, but she was determined not to show any nerves.

She pushed open the door and regretted slightly that the sunlight wasn't flowing through the blue stained-glass windows to give the painting the at-sea effect Angelo had created.

Daniel walked over to it, too close to start with, checking out the detail before stepping back to admire it. Freya watched him taking in the mural, the beautiful, expressive faces Angelo had painted. It stirred something in her, a mixture of discomfort and pride. The mural was still outstanding, on par with anything in a Renaissance church in an Italian town. Did Angelo know how skilled he was?

Daniel turned around, a look of amazement on his face.

'This is amazing. How have you all kept this so hidden? What part did you do?'

'I helped scale up the drawings, painted some of the sea. To be honest, I was more of an assistant,' she admitted. 'But it was a lot of fun. I finished my master's earlier this year, so I enjoyed the freedom of being down here creating more organically.' She cringed inwardly; she'd never been very good at selling herself artistically. She preferred the paintings to speak for themselves.

'Still a fantastic project to be involved in.' Something caught Daniel's eye and he crouched down, inspecting it. 'Angelo Borelli ... was that ...?' He made a signal in the general direction of the café. 'I'd heard he'd gone a bit AWOL.'

Freya blanched. How did he know? She stepped closer and saw something in fresh blue paint along the bottom edge. Her name and Angelo's were entwined with the date the painting was unveiled. Was this why Angelo had wanted her to bring Daniel here? So that she could see he wasn't hiding anymore?

Daniel was looking at her as if he had struck artistic gold. Freya smiled back at him. 'So now you know!' she said.

'Polcarrow is more interesting than I expected. If you don't mind, I'd like to go back to the café and have a chat with both of you.' Daniel looked very pleased with himself.

Freya's heart sank but she nodded her head. Daniel took out his phone and snapped a few pictures of the mural, muttering away about how outstanding it was. Freya hung back; it was hard to look at the painting as an artwork without remembering the summer she'd spent creating it with Angelo. She longed to know what it was like to view it through fresh, distanced eyes, rather than through her close-up, nose-to-paper perspective. It thrilled her to hear Daniel gabble on about the skill and to know she had been involved in its creation. However, underneath it all, a low anger buzzed through her at the thought that Angelo might steal her moment.

Chapter Twenty-Eight

Freya stepped back from her painting and studied it with a far too critical eye. There was nothing like a little bit of pressure to put a block on creativity. Daniel Trevena may have an eye for spotting talent, she grumbled inwardly to herself, but he didn't understand the first thing about the way the artistic mind worked. As for Angelo, well, that had been her second surprise of the morning. Back in the café over cappuccinos, Daniel had tried to enquire if Angelo was working on any other projects, but Angelo would not take the bait.

'I'm currently on a sabbatical from the art world for an indefinite period of time. I'm renovating a house and that must take priority. If it's local talent you wish to showcase, though, I urge you to take Freya on.'

Expecting him to steal her thunder, Freya's jaw had almost hit the ground. Angelo's endorsement of her work went a long way to convincing Daniel that she was the fresh local talent he was after. As grateful as she was to have Angelo sing her praises, Freya still bristled that she hadn't been given the chance to win Daniel over by herself. It was even more important now that she produced a painting that would impress him. Freya found herself slaving away over a couple of smaller canvases, painting away in her sketchbook every hour God sent, and generally hating what she was producing.

On Thursday morning, three days after Daniel's visit and following another almost sleepless night, she knew she needed to get a second opinion, and that the most valued opinion would be Angelo's, because, despite her determination not to allow her gooey feelings towards him to take hold, he was the only one in the village who knew anything about art.

Freya waited until the breakfast club was in full swing that morning: Angelo, Alf and Tristan with various hot drinks, a paper and piles of toast, putting the world to rights while discussing the renovations taking place at Bayview. Alf had toddled up there with Scruff and was giving Angelo all his well-meant advice.

'New windows is what it needs. I don't think they've been replaced in years. Gets mighty cold up there, I imagine. Especially in the winter months. Up at the top of the hill it's all exposed, you see, not tucked up like these little cottages.'

Angelo, who never seemed to be wearing less than three layers at the moment, rubbed his hands together. 'It's freezing, Alf, even with the new boiler. The bare floors don't help. I might have to invest in some rugs.' He glanced up at Freya and offered a tentative smile, which did something to her insides that she tried to ignore. 'How's it going?' he asked her, eyes flicking to the sketchbook she was clutching.

Freya made a face. 'Not well. I think I've forgotten how to paint. I need a second opinion. What do you think of these?'

She held up her sketchbook and slowly turned the pages, offering up a little bit of information about each painting. 'I wish I'd kept some of the ones from the gallery event. This painting to order thing is horrible.'

Angelo took the book from her and leafed through the sketches, Tristan peering intently at them over his shoulder.

'I think they're lovely,' Tristan said rather blandly. 'I admit that's a rubbish response.'

Freya flopped onto the spare chair and fussed Scruff. 'But I don't want to paint lovely; I want to paint something that makes you feel something.'

'What do you feel when you look at these?' Angelo asked.

Freya groaned. 'Like a failure. Like I can't paint.' She went to snatch the book off him, but he held on tight.

'Tell her they're not rubbish!' Lola said, sticking her head out from behind the kitchen door, a waft of ginger and cinnamon floating out with her. 'Who wants to try my ginger cake? It's fresh out the oven, still warm, perfect for an autumn day.'

Scruff barked his approval and sat up, ready to receive a morsel. Lola came towards them, with a slab of warm ginger cake on a board. 'It's a new recipe.' She began to cut it up into huge chunks. Scruff whined when he noticed he wasn't getting any. Following a visit to the vet, treats were now banned.

Angelo didn't pay much attention to the cake. Instead, he was going back and forth through Freya's sketchbook. 'You need to just choose one scene and paint it well. They all have the start of something in them. This one, with the waves almost coming over the harbour wall, it needs more drama. And this . . . the way the clouds are gathering over the headland, you can almost feel the rain.' He closed the book and passed it back to Freya. 'You have the makings of some very good art there. Don't let the pressure get to you. He's already interested enough. If he doesn't want to show anything, then we'll find somewhere else. You can do this, Freya. I have every faith in you.' Angelo wrapped a piece of cake up in a napkin and put it in his coat pocket. He had recently taken to wearing a long dark grey coat that almost reached his calves. Freya wanted to wrap herself in it, but quickly banished the thought. 'I'll see you all later,' Angelo said. 'I have someone coming to give me a kitchen and bathroom quote.' He pulled a face, gave Scruff a fuss, and gave Freya a wink on his way out, which did not go unnoticed.

'Oooooh!' Lola's eyes lit up. 'The big romance is back on?' She nudged Freya.

'Oh no, no, it's just . . . art,' Freya stuttered, and tried to laugh it off. 'He's still got a lot of patching up to do. What?' Four pairs of eyes, including Scruff, looked back at her with varying degrees of disappointment.

Tristan cleared his throat. 'He's trying really hard, and from what I heard he put that gallery guy onto you.'

'Yes, he's trying really hard, lass, really hard. Coming here every day even though you keep giving him those cold looks.' Scruff barked in agreement with Alf.

'Guys, you are not helping! And that gallery guy came to

363

find me – it had nothing to do with Angelo,' she reminded them. 'I'm trying to stand my ground, make him work for me. I'm still not convinced he isn't going to wake up one day and decide Bayview is way too much and hotfoot it off to God knows where. You all know what state that house is in. It's such a huge project. What if he's regretting it already?'

Lola shook her head sadly. 'Well, don't give him any more reason to regret coming back. We've all been burned by love at some point, but you can't keep holding back like this, or he'll give up. He's not just holding out an olive branch, more like passing you the whole tree.'

'Just keep being friendly to him,' urged Tristan. 'I shouldn't say anything as everything I get told is in strict confidence, but he's struggling, Freya. We've been talking, not just as friends, but as priest and parishioner. If you don't forgive him, then I'm not sure he will ever forgive himself,' Tristan said sadly.

'But he left me,' Freya protested, though, she had to admit, rather pathetically. 'I don't need the guilt trip!'

'Doesn't matter now, love,' Alf reminded her. 'He came back. He's bought that bloody house, he's helping you get on in the art world, he's said he's sorry – what more do you want from him?'

Chastised, Freya glanced around at her friends. 'I want to be able to trust that he won't do it again.'

'Only one thing for that.' Lola squeezed her hand.

'Faith,' supplied Tristan. 'Faith can go a long way.'

*

After two days of blustery autumnal showers, Sunday dawned bright and sunny. Freya took this as a good omen, which was confirmed by Lola, who stuck her head out of the back door and declared it so.

'Sun is shining, that's a positive indication of good fortune.'

'Is that true?' Freya asked.

Lola shrugged. 'Who cares? I say it's true, so it is! How are you feeling?'

Freya made a face. 'Shit-scared, to be honest.' She'd been up most of the night putting the finishing touches to her painting, and even though she knew it wasn't quite her best, she was proud of what she had produced. It had been a challenge to work to a deadline, and despite disliking painting to order, throwing herself into a creative project brought her joy unlike anything else. She might be exhausted and full of trepidation – after all, she really didn't want Daniel to change his mind – but she was happy.

'Well, you look the part, so that's half the job done.'

Freya gave Lola a twirl; she was all dressed up in her skinny jeans and heeled boots, and her hair and make-up was done. The clothes may not have been new but the Freya who wore them was a different person to the one who'd packed them up before her mad dash from London all those months ago.

'Come on, we don't want to keep your fans waiting.' Lola ushered Freya towards the door. She was opening the café early that morning to give Freya a little send-off before they drove over to St Ives. Freya grabbed her portfolio and tottered out after Lola, unused to walking on the uneven pavement in high heels.

Polcarrow glistened in the autumn sunlight, and the sea gently lapped at the shore, diamond sparkles on the edges of the waves. The village was still tucked in Sunday-morning sleepiness, except for the seagulls, who appeared to be having a gang meeting on the harbour wall. Alf, Scruff and Tristan were already waiting outside the café. The vicar was hopping about from foot to foot. 'I'm so worried I'll be late for Sunday service,' he confessed. 'Not that many people turn up, but you never know.'

Lola smiled at him. 'Well, you never know, you might make a churchgoer of me yet.' She unlocked the door and pushed it open for the assembled rabble. 'I'm going to do poached eggs this morning, and I have some of that lovely granary bread left over for toast. See you in a jiffy, my love-lies.' Clearly in a bright mood, Lola blew kisses at them all as she sauntered into the kitchen.

Tristan was wearing an expression that suggested his thoughts weren't totally holy. Alf gave him a look that quickly wiped the smile from his face. Smirking, Freya went behind the counter to make up some big pots of tea. She tried to stop her mind from wandering in the direction of Bayview House and Angelo. She knew Lola had invited him; she hadn't been backward in coming forward about her plans to get them back together. In fact, Lola had been so opinionated on the subject, Freya had been relieved to shut herself in her bedroom painting.

Freya plonked the hefty teapot on the table and went back for the mugs.

'A proper brew.' Alf smiled. 'That's what you want, vicar, none of this Earl Grey nonsense. Let it brew for a good five minutes too. That'll put hairs on your chest!'

Freya gathered up the mugs and, just as she exited from behind the counter, the café door opened and Angelo burst in, clearly flustered. Then he stopped dead in his tracks and gave Freya not only a double-take, but a once-over that sent her pulse racing and conjured up memories of how things had once been. How they could be again, a little voice, which sounded rather a lot like Lola, echoed in her head. Angelo had never seen her all dressed up and she rather liked the effect it was having on him.

'Coffee?' she asked as she placed the mugs down.

'Erm, yes, a double.' He rubbed his tired face and his eyes gave her another involuntary once-over.

A satisfied smile spread across Freya's face as she felt Angelo's eyes on her as she walked back towards the counter in her very tight jeans. She even gave a little wiggle of her bum. When she glanced back, Angelo was looking at her while chatting to Alf about the windows Angelo was hoping to get changed. Freya came back with his coffee. She leant a bit too close to him, teasingly so, before pulling back and telling herself off. It wasn't fair for her to play with him when she was still figuring out what she wanted. Well, she knew what she wanted; she wanted Angelo pure and simple, but she was still grappling with his unpredictable behaviour, which had apparently grown somewhat more predictable if he was planning on buying new windows for Bayview. Get today out of the way, she told herself as she sat down, then decide.

Tristan poured out the tea and Lola emerged with plates of toast and some enviably well-poached eggs. Everyone exclaimed at their runniness; no one else sitting around the table had ever been able to perfect them.

'Magic,' she told them as she sat down. 'A little bit of Lola magic goes a long way.'

Freya stared at her breakfast. 'I think I'm too nervous to eat.'

Scruff stuck his head up. 'I swear he understands us!' Tristan exclaimed.

Alf chuckled and snuck him a crust of toast, dipped in yellow yolk. 'Only when food is involved. When running away on the beach, slightly less so. It's getting a bit harder to walk him, now I'm getting that bit older, so I just throw the ball and he brings it back. Well, most of the time. Sometimes he goes for a swim.'

'Alf, I'd walk him for you,' Angelo said. 'I'd love to get my own dog once the house is all sorted, so I'd consider this my dog-walking apprenticeship.'

'Sounds like a deal, son, but if he gets mucky, you have to bathe him. Too much of an ordeal for me.'

'Deal.' Angelo and Alf shook hands.

'Well, now I have you all gathered here, I have some exciting news,' Alf began, his eyes twinkling. 'You know that Martin – you know he did that interview – well, turns out I'm going to be the cover star of next month's Cornish Life.' Alf reached into his pocket and pulled out a shiny copy. 'He sent me this so I can see what it looks like.' He carefully smoothed the edges and passed the magazine around.

'Oh, Alf, this is amazing!' Lola held up the photograph, which showed Alf and Scruff sitting next to a resplendent *Betsey Jane*. A round of applause sounded around the table.

'All right, all right, not too much fuss.' Alf bashfully batted it all away. 'Martin has been good as gold, not asked anything else about the paintings, even put me in touch with a local radio station. They want to interview me about how the village has changed. Who'd have thought it, hey? Eighty-nine and I'm a local celebrity!'

'It's well deserved, Alf,' Angelo said. 'You'll be able to impart your knowledge to all generations.'

Lola gave him a quick kiss on the cheek. 'People will be queuing up for autographs.'

Alf lapped up the congratulations as Scruff licked his plate clean. 'But let's not detract from the matter at hand – young Freya here.'

'I'd much rather talk about your beckoning fame,' Freya admitted, feeling rather queasy.

Lola dug her in the ribs and raised an eyebrow. Angelo turned to Freya. 'Are you ready for your big day?'

Freya made a face. 'As ready as I'll ever be.' She took a sip of her tea and sat back. 'Thanks for this. If we weren't all together talking about Alf, I'd be a wreck.'

'Can we see the painting?' Tristan asked.

'Sure.' Freya extracted herself from her seat and squeezed past everyone. The canvas had been tucked behind the counter. She lifted it up for them to see. 'I went with the stormy sky idea in the end. I loved doing the clouds.'

The painting was greeted by applause and appreciative remarks. 'What time are you meeting Daniel?' Angelo asked.

'He didn't give a time. The gallery opens at eleven, and he said any time after that. I'm hoping to get it over with first thing,' she confessed as she put the painting down. The canvas was large and heavy. 'I also have my sketchbook and I found some of the less impressive paintings that didn't make it into the exhibition.'

'It's ten fifteen already, so we'd better get a move on.' Lola stood up and then a thought apparently flashed across her face. 'Actually, Angelo, that canvas is quite big. I'm not sure it will fit in my Mini. You have a van, right? Why don't you take Freya?'

Freya went to protest but Angelo got in first. 'It would be an honour and a pleasure. I'll just nip back home and pick it up.' He finished his coffee and stood up. 'See you in five minutes.' Then he was bounding out of the door.

Freya narrowed her eyes at Lola. 'You planned this! All of this!' She didn't know whether to laugh or cry.

Alf and Tristan smirked at each other. Even Scruff wagged his tail.

'Well, you two need all the help you can get. A nice drive down to St Ives, a little look around the town – who knows what might happen?'

'I'll become an artistic success?' Freya suggested.

'I think Lola is hoping for a little more than that,' Tristan gently pointed out. 'I might be a man of the cloth, but even I noticed he couldn't stop looking at you.'

Freya made a face and sat down by the counter, away from her traitorous friends, and fiddled with her phone, writing and then deleting various social media status updates before shoving her phone in her pocket. Five minutes later, the white van pulled up outside the café, and Angelo honked the horn. Freya gathered up her stuff and, to cries of good luck, left the café.

'What happened to your bike?' she asked as she climbed into the van. Angelo had stashed her canvas in the back.

'I sold it,' Angelo said as he put the van in gear. 'I needed this van to get my stuff down here. Sometimes we have to sacrifice things that are important to take a gamble on things we love.' He gave her a lingering look.

Freya froze as she realized he wasn't going to give up waiting for her. 'But you loved that bike.'

Angelo shrugged. 'There are other things I love more.'

With a lump in her throat, and not knowing how to respond, Freya turned to see Lola, Tristan, Alf and Scruff standing outside the café, waving and crying, 'Good luck!' Freya blew kisses and waved as Angelo pulled away, and tried to convince herself that the butterflies in her stomach were art-related, nothing else.

Chapter Twenty-Nine

They made their way along the winding Cornish coast roads in almost companionable silence. *Almost*, because it was tinged with a thousand things left unsaid, at least by Freya. She snuck looks at Angelo as he drove but he kept his eyes firmly on the road and hummed along to the radio. He was clearly done trying to convince Freya of his feelings with mere words. As for Freya's feelings, they were huge; they'd ballooned from a crumpled ball of distrust into something akin to the thrill she got when Angelo had first arrived. She still felt exactly the same: that being in the front seat of the van with him, heading off on an adventure, was exactly where she should be. He'd sold his bike. He'd bought Bayview House. He was here supporting and pushing her ambitions. Why, oh why, could she not let go of a misdemeanour he was determined to put right?

Because I'm scared, Freya admitted to herself. Scared not only that he would leave again, which she was starting to think he wouldn't, but scared of the life that was unfolding in front of her. The life she had always wanted. Artistically she had found more success and recognition in the last six weeks than in the last six years, and part of her wanted to continue achieving this on her own. But she couldn't deny that it had been nice to have Angelo back to talk to about art. She glanced at him again, all wild hair, unshaven face, clothes that looked like they'd been thrown on in a hurry. This time he caught her eye, a smile spreading across his face, his eyes twinkling. He was, she realized, exactly where he had chosen to be. Chosen, she realized, was very different from wanted, it meant he'd weighed up all his options and had chosen her.

'How are you feeling?' he asked.

'Nervous,' Freya admitted, pulse fluttering. She took a few deep calming breaths like Lola had shown her and focused on the sunlight glittering out on the sea. 'I've never been to St Ives before.'

'Neither have I. Have you researched the gallery?'

'Yes, and I wish I hadn't. The art is all at the higher end of the spectrum and shockingly expensive. I'm worried Daniel has made a huge mistake and maybe I'd be better off going somewhere a little less glossy.'

Angelo laughed. 'Freya, stop it. You have every right to be in a glossy gallery. It's a good place to start. You get to choose this, remember. No matter what he offers you, know your worth and stand your ground. But he seemed quite impressed, so you might be lucky.'

'He was more impressed with you.'

'Well, I'm not for sale anymore, so he can keep dreaming. If I return to art I'm going back to sculpture. If Bayview hasn't put me off working with my hands for a lifetime.'

'It's not that bad, is it?' Panic started to set in – that all her suspicions had been correct and maybe he was just a man with a flighty heart.

Angelo made a face. 'Worse than I thought. I loved doing Alf's boat, but this ... this is a whole new ball game. I'm starting to think I've bitten off more than I can chew and should just get the professionals in. Do you think Lola would let me camp out in her apartment again?'

'I was hoping to use it as a studio, but I'm sure it'll be fine.' A little voice inside her urged her to say, 'Stay with me,' but she silenced it. It was all too soon for that, even if, alone in the van, the electricity between them was crackling more than a summer storm. She didn't just want to touch him, she wanted to kiss him. The sooner they got to St Ives, put some space between them, the better. She needed a clear head for her meeting with Daniel.

Angelo indicated to turn into the town and squeezed his van down the narrow streets, nosing his way towards a parking spot. 'I'll give you my number. Call me when you're finished?'

'You're not coming with me?' she asked as she keyed it in and stored it in her phone, a small triumphant smile on her face to have finally gotten his number.

Angelo squeezed her hand. 'No. This is your moment. Good luck.'

They lingered a little too long. Freya wondered if he was going to kiss her, maybe on the forehead, but he didn't. She squeezed his hand back and jumped down from the cab of the van. Angelo went round the back and passed her the canvas. Freya tried to find the words, any words, to thank him, to call a truce, but nothing came other than, 'I'm so nervous.'

'You'll be fine. You'll smash this. Off you go.'

With a nod, Freya turned and made her way along the seafront. It was so much busier than Polcarrow, with its shops and cafés and lifeboat station. Thriving and buzzing even on a Sunday morning. She found the street the gallery was on and tottered up towards it, slightly regretting her choice of shoes, even if Angelo's reaction had been worth it. Freya paused outside, took a deep breath and, before she could chicken out, pushed the door open and stepped inside.

The gallery's glistening white walls were hung with daring, bold, original works. Vibrant abstract colours daubed on canvas, little sculptures like twisted bits of seaweed. Excitement fizzed through her to think her work could be rubbing shoulders with these pieces.

'Ah, Freya!' Daniel came out from the back office, as impeccably dressed as he had been on his visit to Polcarrow. 'So glad you could make it. How was the journey?'

'It was all fine, thank you. Rather glad the rain has stopped.'

'Yes, although these beautiful days will be getting rarer now. Do come round into my office. I'm looking forward to seeing what you've brought, pop it on the easel while I get some drinks. Tea or coffee?'

'Tea, please.' Wielding the canvas, Freya made her way behind the counter and into his small modern office. As instructed, she set the painting on the easel and took a seat.

From this vantage point, she stopped noticing the flaws and saw the painting almost as something from which she was disconnected. It was moody and tempestuous, but there was light shining hopefully on the tips of the waves through a small break in the clouds. She placed her sketchbook on the desk. Pride washed through Freya as she faced her painting knowing she'd done her best.

Daniel returned with two mugs of tea and passed one to her before turning to study the painting. Freya nervously sipped her too-strong tea and tried to slow her racing heart with some discreet deep breathing. She glanced around the office, out of the window, anywhere other than at Daniel while he made a judgement on her painting.

'It's very atmospheric,' he said after a while. 'Moody. I like this bit with the light. It's a very dark painting though. Wouldn't be to everyone's taste.'

Freya's heart sank at this assessment, but she managed to keep her face hopeful. Daniel turned his attention to her sketchbook and the series of dawn paintings she'd tucked in between the pages. These he held up to the light.

'You really have a good eye for colour, for trapping the light in a natural and almost seductive way. I confess I prefer these dawn pictures. I prefer the brightness, but this ...' He turned toward the stormy canvas. 'This is something pretty cool. What are you planning on doing next?'

Freya leant across and turned to the back pages of her book. 'These.' She indicated the sequences of skies she'd been working on. 'I want to do a series depicting the sky, maybe even dawn, midday and dusk. I'm planning on painting seasonally so I can explore the changes as they take place in nature.'

Daniel nodded along, interested, then he turned back to the canvas. 'This is really growing on me. I just want to keep looking at it, studying it. It's really drawing me in.' Taking a step back, he considered the painting thoughtfully. 'I would love to display and sell your work, but first, I would like to hang this in the gallery for a couple of weeks to see what sort of reception it gets, if that's all right with you? I'm pretty sure someone will be chewing my arm off to buy it. You have a lovely eye, Freya, a really natural talent. It will be a pleasure to work with you.' Daniel stood up, signalling the meeting was at an end. A relieved smile spread across her face as they shook hands.

Freya followed him out from the office and back into the gallery, hardly able to believe her luck. Two older ladies were studying the seaweed sculptures, trying to figure them out; Freya didn't think they'd approve if she started to jump up and down with happiness. Daniel took out his phone and tapped in Freya's number. 'I'll be in touch at the end of the week. I'll let you know how the painting goes down, and then we can talk about what would be best for both of us. I have a feeling this could all go very well indeed.'

Trying to smother her excitement, and fear of what reaction her painting would get, Freya said thank you and allowed Daniel to show her out of the gallery. She sneaked a glance back over her shoulder and saw him talking to the two ladies and gesturing towards the back room. Should she stay and spy? No; what if it wasn't to their taste? Freya turned her back on the gallery and closed her eyes. Deep breath, glorious sunshine; now to find Angelo.

The morning had turned unseasonably warm, one final burst before autumn drew the curtains. The seafront of St Ives was buzzing with people taking a Sunday stroll, dogs gambolling happily on the beach, rushing in and out of the sea. Scruff would like that, she thought.

She was about to call Angelo when she saw him coming towards her.

'How did it go?' he asked.

'Fine. Daniel still seems keen, but he's asked for something a bit brighter. He's going to display the painting in the gallery and see what sort of reaction it gets over the next week. I think he was going to show it to two people when I left.' Freya puffed out her cheeks. 'It's done now. There's nothing else I can do.'

'Wait until you tell Lola. She'll send all of Polcarrow down here to have a look.'

Freya smiled. 'I bet she will. She can't help her meddling, but I guess not all of it is bad.' She glanced up at Angelo and there was an awkward pause. Freya tucked her hair behind her ears and changed the subject, 'What did you get up to?' she asked him.

'Not much, scouted out a couple of other galleries, but mostly I paced up and down the seafront getting some funny looks. Turns out Cornwall still isn't quite ready for the man in black. To be honest, I was too nervous for you to concentrate on anything else.' He looked away when he said this, slightly embarrassed.

Freya's heart couldn't help itself; it melted, oozing through the cage she'd locked it in. 'You really are here to stay, aren't you?'

'God, Freya, of course I'm here to stay. I've bought a house, remember? One everyone keeps telling me I'm mad to have bought. Do I need it tattooed on my forehead? I'm staying!'

'I don't think you need any more tattoos just yet.' Freya laughed, realizing she was starting to believe him. After all, he was here with her, sharing one of the most important moments of her life.

'Hey, since it's probably one of the last sunny days we're going to have in a while, do you fancy an ice cream?' Angelo asked. 'There's a place up the street that has all sorts of weird and wonderful flavours.'

Freya smiled at his peace offering. Ice cream may not have been the way she'd planned on celebrating, but it seemed entirely fitting. She followed him across the road to an ice cream parlour; the flavours were all laid out temptingly behind the window. 'What are you going to have?' she asked. 'And you can't choose vanilla.' Freya's eyes darted from clotted cream fudge to strawberries and cream.

'Coffee, probably.'

Freya rolled her eyes. 'Come on, be more adventurous. Let's both have something we'd never normally order.'

Craving something ridiculously sweet, Freya asked for the fudge.

Angelo made a face. 'Fudge? That's not overly exciting.'

'I've never had fudge ice cream before. And it's Cornish clotted cream fudge ice cream,' she pointed out. 'Not just bog-standard fudge.'

Angelo peered at the flavours. 'In that case, I'm going to have banana and chocolate. Before you say anything, I never normally have chocolate ice cream.'

The girl behind the counter heaped scoops onto two waffle cones and Angelo paid. Who would have ever thought that a simple thing like ice cream would signal a truce, Freya mused, as they wandered back towards the seafront, nabbing a free bench so they could eat their cones and admire the view. A seagull hopped off the nearby railings towards them but maintained a respectful distance while keeping a beady eye on their cornets.

'This is bliss.' Freya leant back, allowing the sun to caress her face. 'Thank you for coming with me today, Angelo. I know Lola would have brought me, but actually you're a lot calmer. She probably would have elbowed her way into the gallery.'

'No problem, Freya.' Angelo paused, choosing his words carefully. 'You know I'd do anything for you, right?'

Freya gave a small slow nod. 'I guess it's time we talked.'

'Yes. Or time for you to talk. I've said my piece. It's out there and I don't wish to keep going on about it. I came here, Freya, to start a brand-new life, and I don't want to keep discussing the way I've behaved in the past. I hope I've gone some way to atoning for that these past couple of weeks.'

Freya concentrated on her ice cream, the sweetness a little sickly. 'I feel like such a cow. I was hurt and angry when you left but I held on to that for far too long. I would still be holding on to it now if people like Lola and Alf, and my friends back in London, hadn't tried to make me see sense. I know deep down that you didn't mean it. Even at the time I thought there must have been some reason why you left without saying anything – that you were struggling with stuff.

'So much has happened this year that it was hard to process,' she continued. 'So much has happened and not all of it good. But this is good. Us sitting here eating ice creams is good. Us doing the mural was good. Maybe back in the summer, we weren't quite ready for each other.' Freya shrugged. 'I loved every moment we spent together, and I love you. That's why it cut so deep when you left.' She glanced across at him, although he was listening, his attention was on the harbour. 'Angelo, look at me.' He turned to her. 'I can't do this if I think you're going to leave again. I can't lose you a second time.'

Angelo took her hand. 'Freya, honestly, I am not going anywhere.'

'I know,' Freya said softly. 'I know that now. But I think we need to be careful. If we're going to do this, we need to go back to the beginning and take things slowly.' She paused, studying his face; his dark glittering eyes locked with her own. Unable to smother her love for him any longer, she asked, 'Angelo, can we try to forget what happened and start again, please?'

Relief washed over his face. 'I honestly thought you would never ask.'

Freya smiled, a bright, true smile full of happiness that came from deep down. Being by Angelo's side was exactly where she had chosen to be.

'But if we're making a deal,' Angelo said, 'I think there's only one way to seal it.'

'Okay?' Freya raised an eyebrow, heart racing.

Angelo pulled her to him and kissed her, lightly at first, until she kissed him back, and she found herself wondering whether they'd really be able to take things slowly. As if the seagull suspected this, it squawked a warning, breaking them apart. They laughed, half-melted ice cream dripping onto their hands. Freya smiled up at him, pleased that she had allowed herself to trust again.

'Well, that's a relief,' Angelo said, breaking the tension. 'I really need some help with all that sanding, and frankly, I'm rubbish with soft furnishings. I was hoping you'd take over that part of the project.'

Freya swatted him. 'Was this your plan all along?'

Angelo kissed her forehead. 'Well, if it's going to be our home, don't you think it's only right you have a say?'

'Our home.' Freya swallowed, trying out the words. 'I thought we were taking this slowly?'

'Well, yes, but, as I'm sure you've gathered, the renovation is going to take quite a while, so we have all the time in the world.' Angelo stood up and held out his hand. Freya took it and let him pull her up. 'I think we'd better head home and give everyone the good news.'

Freya smiled up at him before snatching another kiss, then together, hand in hand, they made their way back to Polcarrow, to the town that had brought them together by saving them.

Acknowledgements

Wow! I can't believe I get to do this! Having a novel published has been my dream since I was eleven years old and its mad but wonderful that it's come true. Firstly, thank you, reader, for choosing to pick up *The Cornish Hideaway*. I hope you've enjoyed your trip to Polcarrow and aren't craving scones too much!

Huge thanks to the Romantic Novelists' Association's New Writer Scheme – without the support and feedback from my NWS reader I'm sure this book would've been consigned to the drawer and my lovely cast of characters would not have seen the light of day. Whoever you are, thank you for sending me such detailed and encouraging feedback – I hope I one day find out who you are! I'm so proud to be part of the RNA as it's full of supportive and encouraging people. Thanks to my Surrey buddies, especially Linda, for supporting and celebrating with me, you are a fab bunch!

When I pressed send on my One Day submission in September 2020 I didn't expect to even be asked for the full MS let alone for *The Cornish Hideaway* to travel this far. It has been an absolutely wonderful whirlwind and I've loved every minute of it. Thank you to the Books and the City team especially my literary fairy godmother Sara-Jade Virtue for making my literary dreams come true. I really hope this ball won't end at midnight! Thanks to Alice Rodgers for your wonderful edit of my novel. I truly believe your insights into my characters have made it all the better.

Thanks to all my lovely beta readers whose feedback on various drafts helped shape the story. Alessandra, Loopy, Desiree, Inge and Margaret – I hope you enjoy the finished version. Thanks to all the writing friends I've made via social media who've been cheering me on long before my news was announced, especially Lucy. You've all been fabulous.

Thank you to all my wonderful friends who've been on this journey with me over the years and put up with my constant daydreaming or accompanied me on mad research trip. Shout-outs to Liz, Carla, Helen, Essi, Laura, Sarah and Susan for being fabulous friends, for providing tea, prosecco and adventures. To my pen pals, apologies for falling off the face of the earth this past year – thanks for your support, patience and friendship! To all my University of Bedfordshire colleagues, hopefully by the time this is out we'll all be back on campus for celebrations. Special Thanks to Lesley who has been with me on this writing journey since my undergrad days, you've been a huge support.

Thanks to my family for all their love and support. To my parents Diana (thanks Mum for reading and feeding back on various drafts) and John (and yes, Pops, I will one day write a book with a shark in it!) Chris and Kristina and my niece

Amelia, okay, so you didn't do much to help with this book but it fills my heart with joy that you love books. And Luna, a little Chihuahua with a big personality who has ensured that dogs will always feature in my work.